SHERLOCK HOLMES AND THE GHOUL OF GLASTONBURY

Reports of foul occurrences in Somerset have recalled long-buried, uncharacteristic and emotion-filled memories for the great sleuth and drawn him to confront an evil plaguing the idyllic countryside he knew in his youth and which fostered his unique gifts.

Allan Mitchell

Copyright

Paperback ISBN 978-1-78705-227-7
ePub ISBN 978-1-78705-228-4
PDF ISBN 978-1-78705-229-1

Published in the UK by MX Publishing
335 Princess Park Manor, Royal Drive,
London, N11 3GX
www.mxpublishing.co.uk

Cover design by Brian Belanger

INTRODUCTION

To think of Sherlock Holmes, the man and his times, is to engage with late Victorian and Edwardian London, the centre of a global empire extending beyond all others and the hub of a worldwide financial wheel whose telegraphic spokes were as nerves transmitting signals to stimulate or thwart the flow of capital, the life blood of that and the coming century, to distant enterprises and carry back reports of financial success or failure, reports of life or death for ventures in sterling.

To that London flowed the wealth of much of a world now disappeared, a world reinvented as the old empires fell, some to their knees, some to oblivion, all to the juggernauts of local power struggles and the suicidal effects of world-war. Britain had been the powerhouse, the dynamo producing the force by which the world and the world's view of itself was forced to change forever, though, for a while, Britain was itself a victim of that forced change, a victim of its own success.

To find that London of more than a century ago is generally thought impossible, yet a pilgrim come to walk that maze of streets known to Sherlock Holmes and John Watson can still detect, in essence, a hazy sense of place and time despite the coming of blanket nocturnal street illuminations and the absence of the sights and sounds and smells of the attendant horse. The atmosphere of old London was thick with the smoke and the smells and the shouts which kept the metropolis alive and functioning and a full spectrum of humanity could be found in its streets, a spectrum wider in its extent and more intense in its enterprise than in any other city on the face of the Earth.

That life of London, however and despite the dissipation of the Empire, massively destructive waves of aerial attack and predatory usurpation of economic rank and power, is as strong and as vibrant as ever, in many ways more than ever. While many other great cities of the world exist as splendidly orchestrated showpieces of their inhabitants' cultures and tastes and capabilities, one can feel the sprawling living hotch-potch of London working and breathing as its busy arteries pulse with a throb heard right around the world, a throb not so very different from that of a century past though perhaps louder and somewhat faster, a throb from a heart fully two-thousand years old and determined to beat on.

This is the London which begat and continues to nurture Sherlock Holmes; he is as much a part of that metropolis as it is of him as he battles the forces which threaten any and all of its denizens, from those sitting high in the glittering palace to those walking the lonely lanes of murky Whitechapel. London, though, in many ways, is not Britain and Britain is not London and one must leave the metropolis to discover another Britain, the Britain of the provincial city, the city with its own character, history and heartbeat, the city which may well have vied with London for the seat of government and power, for the abode of King and Parliament, but watched that dream dissolve as so much wealth and power gravitated to London, larger, more diverse and better situated strategically. One may recall York and Sheffield, Bristol and Exeter, Liverpool and Manchester and a hundred more, each important, each with its own historical flavour, each varying through time in its allegiance to the Crown, each unique in its strengths but none quite able to topple London on its rise to its preeminent position.

Yet, between these two Britains exists another, the Britain of the picturesque village and the ripening barley field, of the gurgling rippling brook and the ancient atmospheric battlefield, of the brooding castle and the ruined church and,

from more recent times, the Britain of the redundant canal and the relict railway, all combining to weave the fabric of that land of legends into a mystical cloak beneath which can be found the Britannia of myth, the living soul of a land and its people.

There were times when the great sleuth had to forego London and venture out into one of these other Britains, where inhabitants spoke a little differently, had customs somewhat at variance with those he was used to, had ambitions and expectations inconsistent with those of the metropolis and, more often than not, did not like Londoners coming to interrupt their settled ways of doing things. Such a place, though, found it necessary to call upon the special talents of Sherlock Holmes when confronted with a spate of crimes which the local authorities found impossible to solve and stop. The London man was approached in desperation by a consortium of town dignitaries intent on persuading him to travel westward to help stop the predations of what had been dubbed, in classic hyperbole and unashamed sensationalism by a profit-driven and sensation-seeking press, the Ghoul of Glastonbury.

CONTENTS

SHERLOCK HOLMES
AND THE GHOUL OF GLASTONBURY

"I had seen the boy; and in that boy I had seen the man he would become."

... Aunt Jane

SHERLOCK'S MAPS

MAP 1

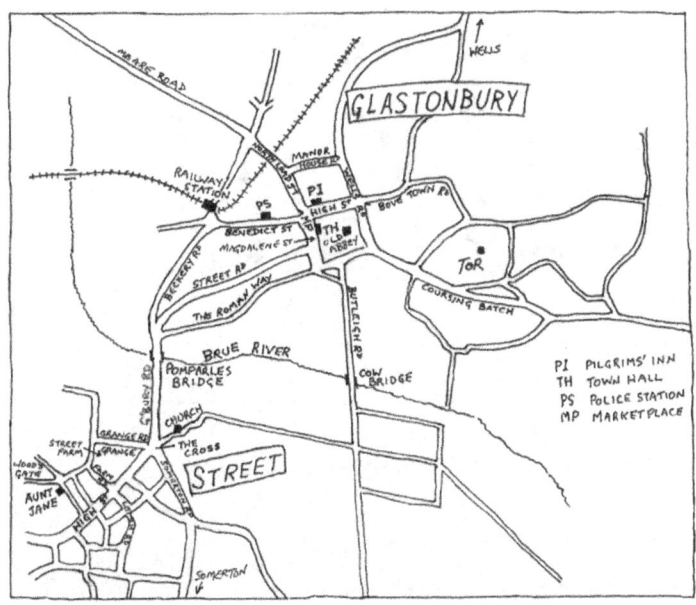

Sherlock's Map of Glastonbury and Street

MAP 2

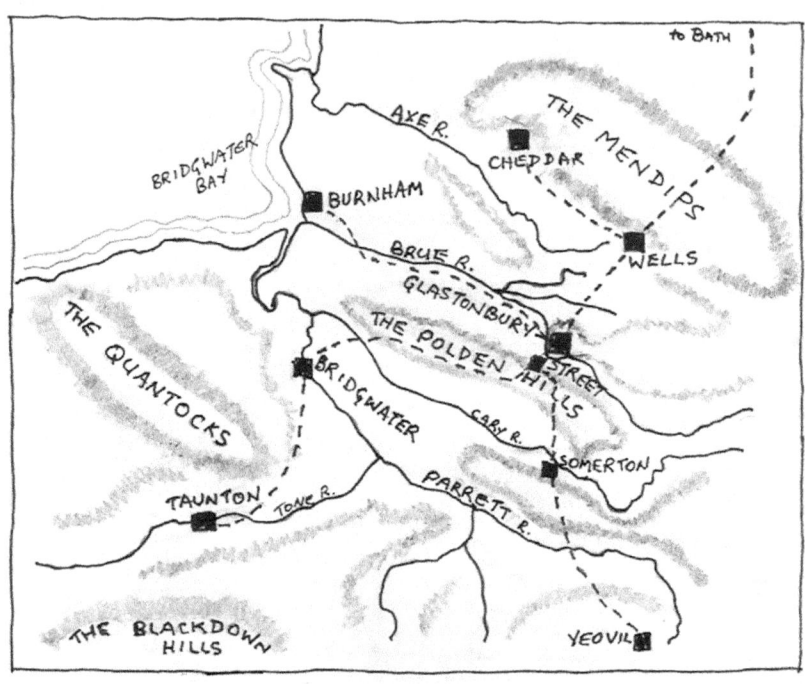

Sherlock's Wider Wanderings in Somerset

SOMERSET UNSETTLED

The Deputation

Sherlock Holmes was, despite his long and close friendship with John Watson, very much the lone wolf seeking out its prey and disdainful of the pack mentality which he observed in so many official investigators. On so many occasions, however, he had been forced to cooperate with or beg the assistance of others who had talents which he did not possess in sufficient quantity. Patience, he felt, was one of the virtues which a detective should possess but not to the extent that it retarded an investigation's progress. There was a time to wait and a time to act, and Holmes felt that the official agents leaned too much to the former while those same agents thought the sleuth's rashness bordered on and often overstepped the bounds of common sense and good judgment. This was a situation which was never to find a wholly satisfactory solution but another situation with a need for both contemplation and action was coming his way. The great sleuth would find his special talents challenged as they rarely had been before as his mind was taken back to where and when those very talents had begun to bud, much later to blossom into the special gifts of a very remarkable man.

To take time after a case to relax both body and mind was essential for the great sleuth, for his body to recover its vigour and for his mind to sort the facts it had gathered into those worthy of being retained for future use and those able to be discarded. It is quite likely that Sherlock Holmes had never actually forgotten a single gathered fact or formulated thought but was able to put up mental walls behind which he could drag and hide the trivia of past cases. In a sense they would be out of mind, but not completely. The situation coming his way, however, would rally the stored-away memories of the sounds and smells and images of a region he had experienced as a boy, one given the freedom to roam the countryside unhindered, and then send those memories crashing through that mental wall while brushing against the long unused emotional parts of his brain as they emerged.

A mingle of muffled voices getting ever nearer should have alerted Sherlock Holmes to the fact that the front door of 221B Baker Street had been breached and that invaders were ascending the stairway to his abode intent upon stealing away his peace, a peace he had found only one hour before in a state of nicotine-fed drowsiness after the successful completion of a difficult and galling case involving blackmail and murder. The great sleuth, however, was oblivious to all and uncharacteristically unaware of the coming disturbance until a tight row of knuckles came into sharp and repeated contact with his door to demand both immediate entry and his full attention.

"What!" shouted a startled Holmes, his now-extinguished pipe falling to the floor and spilling ash all over the rug, "Who is that?"

"Visitors, Mr. Holmes," came the oft-expressed phrase from Mrs. Hudson pushing her way through the crowded space, though her determined Scots brogue did betray a hint of concern, "Gentlemen, surely, but there are lots of them and they're very insistent."

Five men, all well to do, all obviously exasperated, all talking at once, suddenly penetrated Sherlock's inner sanctum showing absolutely no concern for the occupant's privacy nor for the possibility that the man may have been entertaining guests.

"I'm sorry, Mr. Holmes," apologised a flustered Mrs. Hudson, annoyed that these five gentlemen did not offer her tenant the courtesy which came naturally even to the street urchins Holmes referred to as his Baker Street Irregulars, lads she described as filthy and ill-mannered gutter-snipes but who did pay her due deference in their own crude way, "I'm sorry. They just would not wait to be announced. Should I serve some refreshments for them?"

"Thank you Mrs. Hudson." replied her tenant, "These men will start to behave themselves or will find themselves bundled bodily onto Baker Street's hard pavement. As for refreshments, that would be a courteous treat for invited guests or clients who have been bidden to enter, but these men are neither and are not deserving of anything beyond our contempt."

"Gentlemen." he yelled, "A modicum of decorum, if you please, or you may exit the same way you came in. I am not so desperate for company that I couldn't drive each one of you out with my singlestick and Mrs. Hudson has only to blow that police whistle she carries about and several constables will appear in less than a minute and assist in seeing you off."

"Now," he continued with a less expressive tone, "who are you all and just what is it that you want – and just one of you reply, please."

All five men fell silent and four turned to look at one who was pushing himself forward, somewhat pompously Holmes thought. The spokesman introduced himself as Jonathon Bennet, a tall man, bewhiskered save for a shaven chin and an attempted separation of his moustache from his face-widening sideburns, somewhat overweight and with an obvious sense of self-importance and a vocal penetration betraying the nature of a person well used to making flamboyant speeches

9

and giving orders which he expected to be obeyed without question.

"Mr. Holmes," Bennet insisted, "it is imperative that you drop whatever it is you are currently engaged in and return with us to Glastonbury where we have desperate need of your services. We have come to ensure your compliance and will not accept your refusal to accede to our demands."

Sherlock Holmes at this point bent down to retrieve his pipe which he then began to charge with tobacco, that he gathered from the toe of a Persian slipper to the surprise and disdain of his uninvited guests, and prepared it for lighting. Striking a match and holding it up to the pipe's bowl, the great sleuth responded through clenched teeth which held firm the pipe's stem, "Well, let me see ..."

Before continuing, Holmes drew air and flame onto the plug of tobacco and puffed vigorously as ignition took hold. He then removed the pipe from his mouth, held it up in a mocking manner as if to observe that the item was operating correctly, and continued.

"Gentlemen, gentlemen. I am just returned from a most gruelling ordeal at Bath where Lady Ca..., well no matter her name, had misplaced a favourite and very valuable poodle. I'm afraid it took some time to run the poor animal to ground and I must say that I am due for a significant period of rest and recuperation. Poodles, I must say, have a great deal more stamina than they are given credit."

"Poodles!" yelled Bennet, his face growing redder and his whiskers seeming to stick out and make his face seem twice as wide as it actually was, "Poodles. Ridiculous dogs and not worth a moment's worry if they do go missing. No, I must insist that you return with us to Glastonbury and solve a series of most troublesome murders which are keeping visitors from our region."

Holmes remained impassive at Bennet's outburst and retook his seat, all the while puffing away at his pipe and rendering his room barely habitable. He had already, at the mere mention of Glastonbury, made up his mind to take the case but did not care for his clients' manner of approach and was determined to take control and put his tormentors in their places. He took a degree of perverse satisfaction in toying with Bennet's pomposity and reached for a recent newspaper and ran his eye down the columns with an exaggerated motion and made the seemingly disinterested comment of, "Glastonbury, murders; yes, a simple enough little case, one not worth the time it would take for me to travel across the countryside to investigate what a probationary constable ought to be able to solve on a quiet afternoon. It is a pity that those inconsiderate victims have been so troublesome for you but I'm sure your missing visitors will return in due course."

"Now, if you gentlemen will excuse me," he continued, "I have rest to catch up on. Just show yourselves out the way you came in – you know, through that door, noisy, uninvited and unannounced."

Holmes reclined further into his seat resting one leg over its arm and moving his gaze to a random point on the opposite wall as if he were oblivious to anyone else in the room. He then closed his eyes and puffed vigorously away at his pipe causing further clouds of smoke to rise, all the while awaiting the sounds of his rejected clients' outward movement. He was eager to discover if any of the four silent followers would find it within himself to speak without being given leave to do so by his overbearing leader.

Bennet could not contain himself; he marched quickly to the door, opened it and briskly stepped through, calling his silent entourage to follow him and all the while complaining that he had wasted his time on a fool's errand, though he was demonstrably loath to admit that he was the one who had been foolish. Holmes knew, however, from the way in which one of the men had dithered at the doorway, that the matter had not come to an end.

The last of the visitors to reach the door, one Bill Randall -- "A Glastonbury shopkeeper by his look." Holmes mused -- turned towards Holmes and gathered his thoughts before sheepishly offering an apology for the discourteous way he had been interrupted and spoken to.

"I'm sorry, Mr. Holmes," he started, "Mr. Bennet, our mayor does not have a good way about him when he's after something he wants. His manner was unnecessarily offensive but I'm afraid that few of us can stand up to him and risk our standing in our community."

"Oh, again, my apologies," he continued, "I'm William Randall, well … Bill, and I sit on our town's council as an alderman. I hope that all bridges have not been burnt and that you might permit me, at your convenience, to explain our situation and ask you for what advice you may be willing to offer."

"Your apology is accepted, Mr. Randall." replied Holmes, turning and lifting to sit upright in his chair after detecting a note of sincerity in the man's voice and manner, "Could you return at six this evening, alone or perhaps with one other, not that Bennet fellow mind you. At that time my good friend and colleague John Watson will have returned. You may explain all at that time and join us in a light supper, if that would interest you. Meanwhile, I shall acquaint myself with the mishmash of misinformation which passes for factual reporting on the Glastonbury matters in our newspapers."

Randall paused for a moment, looked around to see if he were alone and, observing that the rest of the entourage had exited onto the street, smiled and replied in agreement with, "Yes, indeed, Mr. Holmes. And thank you; you are being far more gracious than could be expected after the manner in which we burst in upon you. So, tonight at six – I'll be here with, perhaps, one other, as you suggested. Thank you again."

That said and agreed to, Randall turned and walked steadily down the stairway to his waiting colleagues, Jonathon Bennet berating him loudly in public for not following on immediately.

"Mr. Bennet," retorted Randall, "it would seem that all your blustering had achieved was to make this country's premier investigator turn away from us. Now, don't start your business with me; after all, at Mr. Holmes' invitation, and after a little mortifying grovelling on my part, I and one other will be meeting and dining with the man and a colleague this evening to discuss matters."

"Well, I don't know if I would care to accommodate the man," insisted Bennet, his reddened face glowing bright through his whiskers.

"That is as well," replied Randall, taking some calm and deliberate pleasure in being ahead of a very difficult man for once, "for your name is definitely not on the invitation list. It would seem that you are persona non grata at 221B Baker Street."

The Lad

Having seen off the invaders from his recently breached citadel, Holmes pondered on the wisdom of having possibly made an enemy of Jonathon Bennet but reasoned that, if many in Glastonbury had been treated with similar contempt, he might have picked up a considerable number of allies. Still, he would have to make efforts to get on the man's good side, if such an unlikely location could be found, for the man was sure to have a fair body of local support to have attained the position which he held.

All this would have to wait, though, and Holmes placed all such conjecture on hold until he could meet with Randall and possibly one other that evening. At that time he would retrieve all matters from his well-stocked and strategically arranged brain attic and discuss them at length with Watson and his guests from Glastonbury and then decide on a course of action. Meanwhile, he would send off various telegrams to colleagues and contacts, including Inspector Lestrade at Scotland Yard, to gather what facts he might on the details of the Glastonbury matters and the state of any official enquiries being made.

Holmes then re-read the newspaper articles but could discover nothing beyond the typical exaggerated and over-zealous reporting of rumour and conjecture as absolute fact. Some details, though, and however distorted they may have been, were of interest and would need looking into for further clarification. He had previously been aware of though not fully acquainted with the details of the deaths reported in Somerset, a region generally regarded as an idyllic location in a peaceful corner of a most visually attractive part of Britain. It was somewhere which actually held fond memories for a man who prided himself on his lack of emotional attachments.

The great sleuth had spent quite some time exploring the secrets of Somerset as a young lad when assigned to the begrudging care of an elderly aunt during school holidays over three consecutive years. He had been left largely to his own devices, however, and had kept to the house as little as possible, a situation which suited both nephew and aunt.

Left orphaned at the ages of seven and fourteen, the two Holmes boys had been shuttled from one set of distant and elderly relatives to another. The family fortune had been settled on Mycroft, seven years Sherlock's senior, and held in trust to be made available upon his reaching his majority. Sherlock's fate and fortune seem to have been afterthoughts though provision had been made for his schooling and progression to university with an allowance to be paid quarterly, this increasing considerably upon reaching adulthood. Mycroft would find himself well-off, though not excessively rich, and, upon graduation, entered into a prearranged career in Whitehall where his intelligence, his gifts of insight and his great capacity for solving problems before they occurred had ensured a meteoric progression.

Mycroft's career had been mapped out for him by parents who had recognised their eldest son's talents, but Sherlock was still a very young boy at the time and, though keenly intelligent, had a nature greatly at variance with that of his brother. The junior Holmes boy seemed listless and unsettled, far more than had been his elder brother at the same age, and he was given to a juvenile adventurism which was lacking in Mycroft and the cause of some consternation for their parents. Death had unfortunately found those parents before a plan could be formulated for their second son, a son who did not fit the standard mold and seemed headed for a future far removed from the respectable role for which the eldest son, the heir, was intended and had been prepared.

The young Sherlock could be precocious but was not one to make friends and had tended to vacate his aunt's cottage after breakfast for yet another adventure, taking a self-prepared packed lunch with him and returning only for his supper and to sleep. The boy's aunt was not unkind but was unused to having company, any company, and was long set in her ways. She had no children of her own, had never married and had made a life into which she alone fitted and in which she had left little room for others. Taking in her young nephew, however, was a family duty and, as long as her arrangements were not greatly interrupted, she was prepared to provide the lad with shelter and sustenance, though her manner was never overly welcoming.

There was, however, beneath his aunt's outward manifestation of indifference, a quiet admiration for a lad who could come and go and use his time exploring her region's mysteries without bothering her in the least. He was as much of a loner as she had become and desired to remain and she, more than anyone, could see that her nephew was destined for something very unusual though, what that was, she could not have imagined. All that she knew had told her that her nephew's future be neither academic nor bureaucratic in nature but something else, something special, something unique. She would not live to discover what that something would be, for before his fourth jaunt to the Somerset Levels and its promise of adventure, word came that she had passed away and that Sherlock would be spending the summer holidays with a few other unwanted boys within the restrictive confines of their boarding school.

Miss Janet Holmes, Aunt Jane to her nephew, had little to bequeath to anyone. Her cottage on the outskirts of Street had been taken on a lifetime lease which, of course, expired the instant that she had, and her possessions were meagre but sufficed for someone content with her own company. In her earlier years she had dabbled with the many varieties of healing herbs of the area, their propagation and their administration, but failed to attract more than a very small following from her neighbours due to her seemingly antisocial nature.

A totally bored adolescent Sherlock Holmes had been moping away his holidays and was surprised when a parcel arrived containing several old herbalist texts and a book full of drawings of plants native to the Somerset region and notations on the efficacy of each, all supplemented by warnings on possible toxicities. There were numerous other books bequeathed to him, some ancient novels which did not interest him in the least, but the package was accompanied by a note written just days before his aunt's death and which stated and advised him simply, "Sherlock, My Dear Boy, these small mementos are all that your ever-admiring aunt has to leave to you. We spoke little together but you brought life and light into my home, but now my days on this Earth are almost done and I must soon repay that debt which we all owe. You will be a man of some substance for I have already seen that in the boy and, if I may offer some little measure of advice, I say to you to always look to the true nature of what you see before you and always be true to the nature within you. Do the things I wished I'd done. Aunt Jane."

Sherlock was unsure how he should act at such a time; his aunt's funeral had been held two weeks before and, though he did feel some sense of loss, he was not unduly upset. He was, though, somewhat surprised at the words his aunt had written, words of warmth, even love, and at the herbalist books she had left him. As a naturally observant lad, he had watched as people collected plants of all types - roots, stems, flowers, fruit, seeds – and had inquired as to their uses, sometimes to hear explanations in depth, sometimes to be told to "be off." He had visited various commercial herbariums and herbalist outlets in the area and befriended the proprietors to a degree, though he could be inclined to wear out his welcome with too many questions. That his aunt had been involved in a subject which fascinated him, though he did fixate somewhat on the poisonous properties of herbs, left him totally surprised.

The lad, now poised ready to become the young man, thought back and wondered if his aunt had actually known about his herbal interests all along but had been satisfied to give him free rein to maintain her solitude while providing for his basic needs. Perhaps she actually liked having someone around, especially an unobtrusive relative, but was too set in her ways to respond appropriately or just didn't know how to express her feelings. Sherlock Holmes may have been a demonstrably unemotional creature all his life but the words of his departed aunt did strike a notable harmonious chord within him.

Those words were to stay with him and would guide him toward a study of chemistry supplemented by an interest in a diverse range of subjects. He began to realise that his uncanny and unconscious ability to observe and deduce that which was not obvious to others could be turned to useful ends. He had learned much from his Somerset visits and wanderings; he had learned that, as with his aunt, people were complex creatures and that one had to look beyond the façade each presented to find the real person within. He had also realised that all living things contained a little evil, just in case it was ever needed. The rose, he knew, would protect itself with thorns and the ever-present and attractive foxglove would draw in the bee to drink its nectar and carry off its pollen but its inner poison would kill anything which tried to eat it.

In fact, it had been on a visit to the herbarium at Glastonbury that he was introduced to and began a lifetime's fascination with poisonous plants, a fascination which readily extended itself to crimes involving poisons and then, in time, to criminality in general. He would like to have revisited the region before beginning his university studies, though with his aunt's demise the opportunities for a lad with limited resources had fallen away. He did, however, retain his interest in the methodologies involved in separating and identifying the active factors of medicinal plants, though he had learned well that the line which separated the medicine from the poison was a fine one indeed. Unfortunately for the young Sherlock, as it seemed to him, school holidays lasted only so long and he all too soon found himself back in the prison-like environment of boarding school.

Sherlock was a bright though difficult student, not so much for being unruly as for being argumentative and given to asking difficult questions and delighting in the schoolmasters' discomfort at not being able to provide suitable answers. He was often bored with his lessons and their subject matter but always achieved commendable results in his examinations, generally to the surprise and feigned dismay of his teachers, all of whom recognised something of great worth residing in the lad, something which they had no way to define let alone to profitably encourage.

University was to prove a positive boon to the developing intellect of Sherlock Holmes. His confidence was to increase enormously, though his affinity with his fellow students would not progress beyond their begrudging acceptance of a brilliant though infuriating fellow student in the institution's august and hallowed halls. Holmes was someone who could, and did, deduce what other students had been up to no matter how hard each tried to conceal it.

His studies did, however, give him access to modern chemical laboratories and the opportunity to develop his analytical skills. He could also interact with a broad range of experts whose work extended into the outer world, including the police forensic experts who would come with specimens to be examined. Holmes, himself, was perceived by a number of those shadowy visitors as being a particularly useful asset due to the depth of his knowledge of poisons and his developing interest in the criminal mind. Also useful was the fact that he could see beyond the specimen and the results of tests performed upon it by combining these with additional and often unnoticed information on the victim and could give a detailed sketch of the probable means by which death had made its mark.

The boy of solitary habits and many interests had indeed become the man. He had become a gatherer of hard facts amid a glut of conjecture and doubt and was now a detective in his own right, an expert investigator to consult when all other conventional lines of investigation had stalled. Sherlock Holmes had become the world's first consulting detective.

There was just no way that Sherlock Holmes could resist a call from the very region which had started him on his way to perfecting his unique set of skills for his chosen life's work. It would be like returning home and seemed a veritable duty.

The Levels

The lyrical ring to the name Somerset began as Saxon settlers followed their warrior bands into a land left disorganised and unprotected by the departure of the Roman legions, though the Cornish Britons effectively contested the intrusion into their greater region for quite some time. Exact details are wanting but the Wessex King Ine seems to have forcefully extended his domain to include the settlement referred to as Somertun, a tun or town whose name holds still-disputed secrets. A century or so later when the great King Alfred rallied his countrymen to see off the Danish Viking invaders, he could speak of the region's people as the Sumortunsæte and summon them as Sumorsæte ealle, Somerset-All. A little over a thousand years beyond this, and after numerous subsequent violent regional disputes, it would be the wont of a young Sherlock Holmes to wander across the landscape and absorb just a little of the atmosphere of a peaceful region born of great turmoil.

As a landscape, the Somerset which led up to the nineteenth century had seemed unchanging on the time scale of a human life, except for the few buildings raised over the years and the slowly altering farm boundaries. The coming of the railway, though, and the encroachment of localised steam power, had accelerated that change and brought permanent alterations as the rails took over the contours of the land, cutting through the ancient estates and blocking many age-old stock routes and carriageways while often demanding new alignments to water courses and drainage ditches. The land, however, had already been tamed significantly for both pasture and plough through the centuries as its seasonal and permanent marshes had been drained away. Tidal surges, however, occasionally teamed up with localised flooding events to flush away many of humanity's long-enduring works together with many of the land's occupants, human and otherwise. When the Great King Alfred had retreated into that same landscape, he had been able to hide in a maze of waterways, small lakes and marshes, all known to the local Saxon occupants but into which the pursuing Danes were loath to enter.

Between the Mendips to the north and the Quantocks to the west lie the Polden Hills, lower features separating the shallow valleys of the Axe and the Brue from the greater system of the Parrett, all draining to the Bristol Channel, except when the waters struck back. Then, as never before, did the region resemble a turbulent sea cut by fearful currents and interspersed with islands. These islands were refuges on which the powerful had constructed their fortifications and places of worship and around the bases of which towns had taken hold to resist the inflow of sea and the inevitable outflow of waters which swept away everything which was within reach and unable resist Nature's indiscriminate fury.

Of course, the young Sherlock Holmes was to learn that there was more to Somerset than its Levels. In fact, Somerset had other Levels, the North Somerset Levels beyond the Mendips, though the ever-wandering and inquisitive lad was never to experience these more distant features. The younger Sherlock was limited to the region reachable by a walk of not much more than two or three hours, though he occasionally talked a neighbour or driver of a passing wagon into a ride to more distant locales. With summer daylight persevering from very early morning until mid-evening, there was no real danger of his getting lost. On his walks, he could stop and search and examine at will and see the district in its fine detail while, atop a wagon, he could day-dream and try to imagine the land as it was so many years and centuries before his own time, before the railways came and before well-formed roads connected communities. In his boyish mind, he could see himself as a participant in those long-forgotten struggles as he listened to the wagon driver relate tale after tale about the "old times" and the "old peoples" and placed these beside what he had learned in the schoolroom. Despite his sometimes annoying ways, Sherlock could be a particularly good listener and, the more he listened, the more Somerset sank into his being. He would push these feelings well into the darkened recesses of his mind, but now in distant London his awakening memories were bringing the feelings back to the fore. Somerset, he was recalling, was indeed a place to ponder and to ponder about.

In the remote past, before the coming of the Celts and the subsequent influx of later peoples and the scourge of modernity, there had been others, others who found the scattered wetlands rich in resources for building materials and food supplies. Significant stands of sizeable timber trees stood high on the surrounding hills and the extensive wetlands were rich with life, fish life, bird life and four-footed game to be hunted. The waters provided more than just sustenance; they enabled the ancient people to build their villages deep in the marshes so that they could be better protected against the predations of nomadic warriors. The land would offer the same to later inhabitants until the region came under the control of much stronger leaders who could muster substantial forces for group defence when the persistence of those nomads proved too much for small isolated villages; then a raider entered at his peril.

By the time the young Sherlock Holmes had trod and ridden along Somerset's laneways and penetrated its remnant wetlands, the old tribal life had long disappeared. A new broader regional identity had been forged within the modern state, a state with an even broader claim to the fealty of the inhabitants, though one which never quite overwhelmed the loyalty of the local people to their place of birth. Sherlock, in a sense, had been in foreign territory but he felt no pangs of disloyalty to an England within a greater Britain. He had only a vague feeling of belonging and certainly no sense of danger from the inhabitants, most of whom had been born to the towns and often daily passed by the region's many natural assets oblivious to the many gifts, and hazards, at foot and at hand. Not only had much of the land been tamed, but in many ways so had many of its people.

Young Sherlock's adventures originally began from his aunt's cottage in Street and generally involved exploring the town for its treasures. As he grew more adventurous, his jaunts centred on Glastonbury and its tor to which he was strongly drawn. Both towns had their own unique points of interest for the energetic youthful explorer and many a shop and tradesman's workshop, though places of toil and weariness to their owners, seemed as magic caves to young eyes intent on taking in all the mysterious goings-on they could see and interpreting them as far as a young lad's imagination was able and dared. Just getting out of Street could be an adventure in itself as there was much to intrigue a young mind keen for novelty but less so for company, unless that company might be someone of interest who was willing to take time to explain the details of his occupation to a lad whose mind was full of questions. That young lad's eye for detail soon enabled him to guess a stranger's occupation with increasing accuracy.

Though Glastonbury held his interest best, the town of Street was his base, the haven to which he always returned and which sustained him and which he grew to know intimately. His aunt had lived in a cottage near Wood's Gate on the town's western extremity, a position requiring him to take any one of three main routes toward the exit to Glastonbury with many possible alternatives being offered should he desire a little variety. High Street cut the town at a diagonal running south-west to north-east and ending at the five-way intersection known just as "The Cross' which gave even more choice to the adventurous traveller.

Sherlock had the option of walking along Farm Lane toward Street Farm and turning right toward High Street or left past the abbey and its grange and then right into Grange Road and on toward the Cross at which point a further decision had to be made. Other options from his starting point offered less in the way of interesting opportunities for asking questions but he did, on several occasions, retrace along High Street and then proceed to the Boot Factory with its busy craftsmen and their noisy machines and skilful antics. The lad had received a privileged upbringing in that he did not want for anything of importance and had no need to work for a living and, so, had little concept of the difficulties of day-to-day life which most of the working people of the town experienced. Fortune may have denied him friends and taken away his parents but it had been very kind to him in other ways.

Glastonbury was only a few miles and an hour's pleasant walk away, more if something of unusual interest took his attention away from his intended and favourite goal. In the latter case, the attractions of Glastonbury might be forsaken for some time, possibly even for that day, as his imperfectly disciplined mind flitted from one novelty to the next. As with his excursions from Street, his home base, Glastonbury had to be traversed before the great tor could be ascended and its intriguing tower reached. The view from the summit was breathtaking and great swathes of countryside could be taken in; he could see Street quite well but, though he fancied that he could pick out his aunt's cottage, the angle of view was too narrow for him to be certain. A pair of field glasses purchased in his second Somerset summer with funds squirrelled away from his allowance gave his observations a great boost in scope and detail despite the piece being of relatively low power and imperfect binocular alignment. The instrument, as limited as it may have been, forced a system of logic into his observations as assumptions which he made about what he could see needed supporting observations to rule them in or out of contention. It was a game he played with visual data gathered at a distance and at a far less than optimum viewing angle; it was a game well-suited to his developing innate talent for critical observation and deductive reasoning.

That same second summer saw the buds of Sherlock's sometimes-macabre interest in poisonous plants burst into bloom as the notion that something attractive and seemingly benign could harbour agents designed to incapacitate and kill. The lad was beginning to realise that life-forms of all types could and would defend themselves and that sometimes their best defence was an all-out chemical attack on anything which came too close or a self-sacrificial "go down fighting" approach to poison the attacker which ate them, in doing so deterring or preventing attacks on other plants of the same type. Sometimes a plant just killed off other plants of different type just so it and its own type could flourish. If this instinct was in the plant, he considered, could it also be in the animal and, if so, in the human? Humans could be violent to each other, that he knew well, but did some humans use poisonous plants as proxies to attack other humans? Once having made that mental connection, the mind of Sherlock Holmes became obsessed with poisons and poisoners and, by extension, the mind of the poisoner and criminal activity in general. His "eureka moment" had opened up a whole new world for a mind never satisfied with what it knew, a mind which now had found the way to a gainful purpose in life for its never-satisfied owner.

Sherlock Holmes now understood crime in its basic manifestation, and he could now start to develop his talents to fight it.

For the remainder of his second Somerset season and for the whole of his third, the fast-growing lad wandered about, seeking out herbalists and asking all manner of questions, sometime highly intelligent types, sometimes inane and impertinent, but always to the improvement of his knowledge and understanding. Crime also interested him but his tendency to ask embarrassing and annoyingly brazen questions of the local constables had him marked as a troublesome pest and an irritating nuisance – his exasperating relationship with the official agencies of law and order had begun. Fortunately for the police at numerous locations in Somerset, though not so for his aunt and himself, Sherlock was never to have a fourth Somerset summer and Glastonbury had to be relegated to memory.

Sherlock's time at Glastonbury was never quite forgotten, but it was displaced by more pressing matters as he matured to the young man and his studies and interests in the criminal mind intensified, ultimately to emerge as a unique collection of skills almost defying belief in their power to enable their owner to observe and deduce what others were blind to and overlooked. His memories of that time at Glastonbury and its surrounds were now churning about in his mind, shaken loose by the first unanticipated visit by the Glastonbury men and now pushing forward as the time approached for a more intriguing and agreeable second.

The Meeting

Watson took great pride in his ancestry, though the details he held did not confidently go back beyond two centuries before uncertainties began creeping in to cloud the overall picture. He knew that his surname meant Son of Wat and that Wat was a common contraction of Walter and that this was purported to have Anglo-Saxon origins. His investigations had ground to a halt, however, on his finding that, while Wealdhere which meant Leader of the Army was indeed the Old English form of Walter, his own version of the appended name, that of Watson, had followed from France in the wake of the Norman Conquest. Still, after eight hundred years, such origins would not unduly concern the average person but the revelation did leave Watson a little perturbed and hesitant to bring the subject up in conversation.

The doctor's immediate ancestry was divided between English and Scottish but he proclaimed himself to be thoroughly British. This, indeed, he was, according to the modern nineteenth century understanding and usage of the term, as well as from his depth of loyalty to both country and crown. Holmes delighted in teasing his serious companion by reminding the arch-patriot that the wearer of the latter headgear was of Continental origin, the Saxe-Coburg-Gotha family having displaced the former Hanoverians from the throne a few generations back. London was cosmopolitan, though, and had been receiving new blood from around the globe for centuries so that the declared facts of a Londoner's ancestry could actually have been ones of convenience or practicality or both. Holmes knew well that suggestions of a journey to Somerset would entice Watson away from the bustle of the metropolis and its millions and that this staunch comrade would imagine himself returning to the heartland of his nation, despite any overt claims to that unique honour being both futile and dangerous.

The Glastonbury deputation had travelled to London as a last resort, its members feeling a little overwhelmed at the city's size and intensity and all given to being somewhat defensive about their rustic origins and accents and apprehensive about being treated like visiting boorish country yokels. Of course, few people they would meet would consider their appearance in the metropolis as anything other than normal, such was the extent of the ebb and flow of visitors from all parts of the country and from so many nations of the Earth. London, itself, had its divides of dialect and manner and, to many of its denizens, the speech of the Glastonbury men would have sounded ultra-English.

Still, William Randall, a man who was master of his own establishment in Glastonbury and more than a match for any who would try to hoodwink him on his home ground, had found himself overcome with doubt on whether he had what it would take to negotiate with such a person as Sherlock Holmes. He did not realise that the great sleuth had earned that accolade by possessing a great aptitude for seeing through people's foibles and facades and disliked the client who would hold back facts for fear of appearing inept and unsophisticated. No, Sherlock Holmes liked straight-talking and had little patience with those who would excessively beat around the bush seemingly unable to flush out the words hiding within. William Randall, for him to be successful in his quest, would need to speak up, describe the predicament which had sent five busy men away from their respective occupations, and then ask for help in whatever manner the London man might consider appropriate. He had only a few hours to choose a companion in his quest and settle on his manner of requesting the advice of a man he had recently referred to as Britain's premier investigator. Fortunately, Jonathon Bennet had abandoned the field and retreated to the comfort of the first railway carriage headed home leaving the matter to his confused, confounded and forsaken followers.

John Watson returned from his excursion and stepped through the front door just as the chimes of five o'clock were fading on 221B's vestibule clock and he hastened upstairs more than ready for his evening meal, quite long overdue as it seemed to him at the time. The good doctor, always partial to and insistent on three good meals each day, had breakfasted early and gone off on numerous errands and had only managed to secure a few minutes' break to feverishly gorge himself on a few less-than-adequate biscuits and gulp down some lukewarm and indifferent coffee – this had to suffice as a midday meal but did not in any way satisfy his yearning for sustenance.

Holmes, though, was not in the least hungry, at least not for food; he had been sitting in his chair vigorously puffing away at his tobacco supply and pondering the newspaper reports, such as they were given the reporters' propensity for sensationalism and embellishment. Watson's appearance woke him out of his smoky stupor and immediately sent him expounding the possibilities of his latest case despite not having been appraised of all the facts by those actually desirous of engaging his services.

"Watson." he trumpeted loudly as his friend and colleague steered his way through the unbreathable length of the room, "Somerset is calling, and I cannot refuse its invitation. Are you keen for a jaunt into our glorious countryside?"

The Doctor waved the smoke from in front of his face only to have it replaced by a further billowing mass of blue emanating from the funnel-like bowl of Holmes' pipe and replied, "Well, if it gets me out of this air that you insist upon fouling with those old ropes you've been burning, the answer has to be 'yes'."

Before continuing, Watson walked to the window and pushed it open as far as it would go, hoping that the outside air would rush in to displace the reeking wafting mass which Holmes had produced.

"Smoking like that will do you a mischief someday, Holmes." he warned his friend, "I declare that you could challenge a straining railway locomotive and beat it for smoke. I like a pipe myself but there is a limit, you know, and this is way past it. Anyway, what's this about Somerset?"

"All in good time, Watson." Holmes replied, "But first we shall have to await two visitors who have news of unsettling developments in that idyllic region of our country; murders, no less, at least that's what the press is insisting upon. I am hopeful of receiving some official account of the matters from our friends down at Scotland Yard, that is if they can be bothered to exert themselves for a promising case of multiple homicide."

"Sometimes your lack of regard for your fellow man is deplorable, Holmes." replied the doctor, "A little compassion for the victims would not go astray, you know."

"No, it would not, my friend," challenged the sleuth, "but neither would it help catch the perpetrators. Rather, it would quite likely hinder our investigations."

"I am expecting two members of a delegation," he continued, "a delegation reduced down from five on my insistence and arrived from the fair town of Glastonbury, no less, one of our country's more resplendent jewels. I spent some time in the region as a lad and remember traipsing over the fields to visit its many intriguing features."

Holmes had rarely alluded to anything from his past and this small revelation came as a surprise to Watson, partly because of its rarity but more for the emotion he felt he had detected in his friend's voice at the mention of Glastonbury. Perhaps his friend had not been able to completely wall up his feelings for the region in that brain-attic he kept so well organised and swept free of any distracting sentiment after all. Such thoughts, though, were interrupted by Holmes informing his

31

colleague that the visitors were expected at six and that a light supper would follow, though Watson did betray his degree of hunger by asking, "How light?"

At this point, Holmes had extinguished his pipe and the in-rush of fresh air through the window had cleared the room of residual smoke considerably. He did not respond to Watson's question fully knowing that Mrs. Hudson's notion of providing supper for visitors would be akin to the biblical account of the loaves and fishes, though the constituents of the forthcoming meal might vary significantly from those specified in the Scriptures. Watson simply sauntered off to clean away the build-up of grime from a busy day of moving about through various parts of the city and returned clean and refreshed and changed into attire offering far more in the way of domestic comfort though still respectable enough for receiving visitors.

Watson sat and listened to Holmes' account of what had ensued a few hours before when the five Glastonbury men burst in, Jonathon Bennet at their head with his bellicose demands of priority over all of Holmes' arrangements and an insistence on immediate assistance. The doctor could only agree with his friend's course of action and became eager to find out how the reduced delegation of two would fare now that they had seen that Holmes would not be browbeaten into action but was prepared, if all the proprieties were observed, to listen to reasoned argument and then make a considered decision.

The two men sat reading newspapers while patiently awaiting the arrival of their visitors. Neither man knew quite what to expect of the meeting and what might eventuate from it; perhaps a new adventure to add to Watson's popular literary record but surely, at least, a welcome diversion for Holmes even though he had only just finished with the previous one. They heard the clock chime six and looked up, folded their newspapers and deposited them on the arms of their comfortable chairs, then stood knowing that the two Glastonbury men would be right on time, or would not come at all.

The jingle of the doorbell informed them that the former of the two possibilities was in play and they remained standing awaiting the knock on their own door and Mrs. Hudson's declaration of , "Two visitors, Mr. Holmes, Dr. Watson. They are expected."

At the sound of the expected announcement, Holmes retreated to the far end of the room and stood seemingly aloof by his desk while examining a document picked up at random as if to declare his supremacy to all who entered. Taking his cue, Watson waited a few seconds and then proceeded to open the door and then greet the two men whom he then bade come in, all the while maintaining an air of practiced formal detachment and superiority. It was a procedure developed and agreed upon so that, firstly, they could take command of the situation and, secondly, the visiting client could be put at ease in an atmosphere of complete confidence and professional competence.

"Ah, Mr. Randall." Holmes announced, looking up while redepositing his document of feigned importance to the desktop, "And a colleague."

"Yes. Good evening, Mr. Holmes." responded the Glastonbury visitor, "And this is my friend and colleague Mr. Brian Jamison who has agreed to support me in this quest we are on. I trust that we are not putting you to too great an inconvenience after the unpleasant events of this afternoon."

"Not at all, Mr. Randall; all that is behind us and forgotten," replied Holmes, "And good evening to you, Mr. Jamison. Now, may I present my good friend and professional colleague Dr. Watson who has my complete confidence and in front of whom you may discuss all matters you might entrust to me."

Cordial greetings were then made all around and the four men sat facing each other, the visitors from Glastonbury being directed to the two easy chairs, as befitting their status as guests, while Watson pulled up a chair from the table and Holmes retrieved another from beside his desk. Mrs. Hudson had been instructed to wait for thirty minutes before serving the meal as this would give ample time for the visitors to describe the situation facing the general Somerset district in broad terms. Specific details could be dealt with during and especially after they had all dined and had a chance to appraise themselves of each other's characters. Randall started things off upon receiving a visual prompt from Sherlock Holmes.

"Well, Mr. Holmes, Dr, Watson," he began, "our region has many fine features to attract the tourist and the pilgrim, numerous fine old monuments and pleasant rural drives as well as many sacred places and shrines visited by people of faith. With the railways extending their ranges, it's now gotten to be that our livelihoods in the towns, in so many ways, have become significantly dependent on the pounds, shillings and pence those incomers bring with them. It's not just a case of extra money in the coffers of the rich and powerful, gentlemen, as many ordinary families rely heavily, if not entirely, upon the work generated in providing for the needs of our seasonal visitors. Some will find work on the farms at one time of year and at other times those same people will be found behind shop counters or mounted on the drivers' seats of carriages and at other such occupations."

Holmes interrupted at this point with, "Yes, Mr. Randall, we are somewhat familiar with that aspect of the situation but I would like to move onto the matter of these deaths."

Before Holmes could continue, a premature knock on the door followed by the call of "Supper, gentlemen" announced the early arrival of the evening meal. Watson jumped up and opened the door with great anticipation, eager for his overdue intake of sustenance, then smiled with delight as he saw that Mrs. Hudson had supplanted the light supper with what many would consider a sumptuous feast.

The Troubles

Settling into his long overdue meal, Watson was lost for a few minutes as his nutrient-deprived brain focused on replenishing the day's missing morsels and did not notice Holmes eating very little. The sleuth explained to his guests that the effort involved in digesting food took much away from his deductive mental processes and that he would abstain from all but his immediate needs. He also insisted that his guests eat as much as they might and that Mrs. Hudson was the sort of woman who took umbrage at people leaving good food uneaten. This message was not lost on the Glastonbury men and never on the doctor, all of whom ate heartily and came back for seconds – compared with the hotel fare offered to the two men which the visitors had left behind that evening, Mrs. Hudson's offering was in no way likely to disappoint.

Mrs. Hudson reappeared after some time to clear away the plates and cutlery and to deliver a large pot of steaming hot coffee and Holmes reached for his cigar case. Smoking a cigar after a meal somehow seemed more satisfying, Watson said more refined, than lighting up an old pipe and imitating the

Edinburgh Express, so much so that the pipe was reserved for times when intense concentration was required and the impact of its emanations on the senses of others would be minimal. The two visitors thanked their hostess profusely and accepted both her coffee and Holmes' cigars, again taking to the easy chairs on their host's invitation. Watson stayed put at the table and cleared away sufficient space for his notebook in which he would record, with as much detail as he could, the accounts of the troubling events in Glastonbury and beyond as the newspapers had been suggesting. Holmes retired to his battered old divan and reclined back giving his surprised guests the impression that he was about to take a short nap after his meal. Watson saw the puzzled look on the two men's faces and quickly offered an explanation.

"Mr. Holmes," he said with just the hint of a smile upon his face, "likes to recline back and close his eyes when listening to his clients' problems. It helps him to shut out all distracting influences and focus on the words spoken and the emphasis given to them. He can then ponder the meaning behind them and begin to form a critical picture of the troubling matters brought before him. He may seem asleep, but I assure you that he hears every word you might utter and, strangely, many a word that you don't but ought to have. To keep a secret from Sherlock Holmes is both futile and wasteful of time, both the client's and his."

"Well," responded Randall, quickly looking at Jamison, his colleague and co-delegate, "Exactly where should I begin? There have been so many strange occurrences in our region over the past few months, some have been unexpected deaths while others have involved otherwise healthy people being taken ill and then recovering only after a considerable period of convalescence. At first, no one took a great deal of notice unless the victim was a relative or friend, but the numbers kept mounting and it was only with the benefit of hindsight that it was considered that something untoward was happening."

"Go on," said Holmes stretched out on his back, his head raised, his eyes remaining shut and each outstretched finger of either hand making deliberate contact with its opposite number.

"If I may break in here," interjected Jamison, "I might add that the situation has not been limited to Glastonbury. Colleagues in other nearby locations have reported similar trends, though there does seem to be a concentration around our fair town."

"And how many affected people are we talking about?" demanded Watson. "Have the district medical officers been active in reporting the numbers and assessing the situation?"

"The medical officer, and there aren't many for the district, has commented on the deaths," answered Randall, "but the numbers are within the bounds dictated by some chart put out by some medical board. It's just that there has been a jump in the number of cases and a change in the age and health of those affected."

"Oh, yes," he continued, "There have been four cases of accidental poisoning which resulted in death but my colleagues, even Mr. Bennet, have reason to suspect that these and several other deaths put down to natural cases may have been the result of foul play. There had been eight known cases of non-fatal suspected poisoning. We had discussed this at a council meeting but the press got hold of it and blew it into a case of a rampant murderer being at large and that many cases had gone undetected and unreported."

"And have you reason to believe that such is not the case?" asked Holmes.

"Well, at first I had not, I freely acknowledge," admitted Randall. "But I am not a medical man. It was only when we started getting queries from medical types throughout the country whose patients had reported troubling symptoms after returning from a pilgrimage or holiday, especially the former."

"Now that the national, and some international, newspapers have run with the story and sensationalised it," added Jamison, "the number of visitors to our region has fallen away precipitously. The situation is bad for business, as we have said, but it is tragic for the victims and troubling for those who may be targeted in the future – that could be any one or all of us."

Holmes thought about the statements for a long and silent minute before sitting up and asking, "Are you telling me that the weight of evidence falls on the targets of these poisonings being pilgrims to religious sites? If so, I would need to know about any special devotional gatherings or public disputes over exclusive usage by one group against one or several others."

"That information is not difficult to collect, Mr. Holmes," explained Randall, "but it is difficult to believe that religious types could be that horrid to each other."

"Given my experience with the criminal mind and having witnessed what one person can do to another," insisted Holmes, "such things are not surprising at all. Look to our own recent history and the horrific battles fought over opinions about just whom God favours best."

"These poisons," asked Watson, his inquisitive medical mind taking charge of the questioning at this point, "is it known if they were from a vegetative source or had the symptoms pointed to the application of some mineral agent? Sometimes a virulent infectious agent, perhaps a bacterium of some sort, has caused the illnesses and deaths. Such agents may cause widely disparate symptoms to show up in different subjects and at varying stages of the infection."

"That is part of the problem, doctor," replied Randall, "No one can actually say with any certainty that there have been deliberate poisonings; murders, in fact. There is a lot of loose conjecture being given too much lip-service, and this is finding its way to the newspapers which are only too eager to support the worst of all possibilities as that approach increases circulation and boosts revenues; theirs but not ours, if I may put it in hard commercial terms."

"It's not that I'm completely hard-hearted for the victims," he added, "for, that, I am not. It's just that the demise of small local enterprises does no one any good, except for those who might be in a position to take some commercial advantage from such failings. No, there'd be many a family in the district struggling to make ends meet if that were to happen."

Jamison had held back for most of the conversation, deferring to his colleague's lead, but he jumped in at this point to add his assurance on that same point. He also pointed out, "We don't actually know that anything of a criminal nature has occurred; it's just that people have died who ought not have, given their levels of health and vitality. We have little more to go on than very strong suspicions of murder."

"A strong suspicion is a good place to start," declared Holmes, "in order to rate that suspicion as being even stronger in contention or to rule it out as being extremely unlikely, though I would always keep it in the back of my mind in case what seem to be absolute facts turn out to have shaky foundations."

"What I would like from you, gentlemen, or from your colleagues," Holmes continued, "is a list of known victims, a list of suspicious cases, together with their addresses and the names of their attending physicians; I would also like to view any police and coroner's reports."

"Does this mean that you are interested in helping us, Mr. Holmes?" asked a very hopeful Randall, his colleague looking on keenly and nodding in agreement with the question posed.

"Indeed it does, Mr. Randall. I'm sure that I, and perhaps Dr. Watson, would be able to find a little time to engage in some investigational work," replied the sleuth who then added the wry comment through a sly smile, "That is unless any more poodles get loose in Bath."

Randall looked around at Jamison and gave a smile displaying some significant relief at the knowledge that someone was at last coming to help out and that Jonathon Bennet would be up against someone whom he neither impressed nor could intimidate. He returned his gaze to Sherlock Holmes and gave a quiet though distinct "Thank you" before rising and saying to his colleague that they should now leave and let the two London men be about their preparations. Jamison also rose and thanked his hosts, both for the meal and for their agreeing to come to the aid of a region facing something or someone of a quite diabolical nature, all despite the fact that John Watson had given no indication of his desire or preparedness to do anything.

That Sherlock Holmes admired and respected John Watson was a fact without the least shadow of doubt but the sleuth did have an infuriating way of presuming his friend's unerring compliance with whatever he might decide by way of a course of action. Watson, thankfully for the successful operation of their partnership, was possessed of a great deal of patience and understood his friend more than any other could and appreciated that Holmes' apparent lack of consideration was merely the effect of his total obsession with the case at hand. There would come, the doctor knew, the time that he would be included in his colleague's thought processes but that would be after all of the major decisions had been made, though there had been times when he had dug his heels in and refused to be dragged into the mêlée without any consultation.

In this instance, however, Watson was of one mind with his often overzealous colleague and looked forward to the challenge ahead, despite the uncertainty of any crime having actually being committed. He had echoed Sherlock's assurance to the two visitors, now clients, and bade them a positive farewell and escorted them to the front door while Holmes began to fill his pipe intending to retreat into an easy chair and his thoughts.

The doctor returned just as the first wisps of pipe smoke began rising and was about to make a derogatory comment on what he called his friend's obsession with breathing in the smoke of a smouldering noxious weed, despite the fact that he himself indulged, albeit at much less an intensity, when Sherlock spoke.

"What say you, Watson?" asked the greatly intrigued sleuth of his medical friend, "You said you were keen for a trip to the country, so, are you also up for a little adventure with a hint of danger attached? With my nose for criminality and intimate knowledge of poisons and your medical training and eye for symptoms, I'd say we've the makings of a very exciting time ahead of us; and we may just forestall the untimely deaths of a good many Somerset residents and visitors."

"Of course I'm up for it, Holmes." replied the doctor, "It's just that I still can't get used to your level of joyous excitement when it comes to people committing cold blooded murder. If it helps stop a fiend and saves a life, though, how could I possibly refuse?"

***

GLASTONBURY GATHERINGS

The Pilgrims

Late nineteenth-century Britain, a composite imperial nation-state built upon an ancient spiritual landscape, had, in its rush to modernity, largely forgotten or at least overlooked its many locations of mystical significance. The established churches maintained an orthodoxy, which focused spiritually beyond the Earth, and powerfully expansive industrial powers crashed through all in their paths and over all objections raised.

The monasteries had been dissolved and largely destroyed three centuries earlier and the governance of the old church became displaced as a new reformed church was instigated. Two centuries later and very large numbers of people found themselves removed from their ancient homes by clearances and forced into the cities and to slave-like work in the factories, this resulting in the old local myths, told and retold generation after generation, losing their vital connection with place and mostly dying away. Deserted hamlets and estate-linked villages dissolved back into the soil which had supported them and often contributed their usable stone for walls raised to keep sheep in and the former inhabitants out. A people's spirit and the spirits of their ancestral lives, however, refused to die out completely and held out in pockets, ready to rise again when the time was right and the people were ready.

In so many locations, the newer churches, many now quite ancient themselves, had been built over features of ancient spiritual significance and had, in part, managed to retain a sense of the ancient mystical presence for those who had adopted, and adapted to, the new rites. Those rites, though at odds with many past spiritual beliefs, had little effect on the practices of herbal healing. The folklore concerning natural remedies gained from the plants and fungi growing in profusion in the forests and fields and along the hedgerows was remembered and passed along from generation to generation and offered the only real relief from disease before the facts leading to an understanding of how the human body actually worked started to accumulate. The old remedies and the new, however, all worked against the fatalist advice of those who refused to consider any other cause for a sufferer's ill-health than God's retribution upon the sinful and the unworthy.

Young Sherlock would have observed how many townsfolk and almost all city dwellers increasingly looked to medicines prepared by the apothecaries but also how, as one entered further into the rural districts, recourse to the herbalist was increasingly to be found. Even in London, however, a knowing grandmother or aunt might well disregard the doctor's prescription and head for one of the great many public parks or grassed paddocks kept for the ever-present horse and pick a selection of plants whose healing properties had been learned in and were remembered from her childhood. More than a few had risked the physician's wrath by offering a remedy other than that offered for sale as a pill or tincture bottled and bearing an official stamp. In its origins, the burgeoning metropolis was, to be sure, a rural area encroached upon bit by bit, encircled and overwhelmed and built over leaving only small islands of green in a landscape dominated by dull browns and dirty black. To recover from an illness in the nineteenth century was very much the result of a highly variable combination of faith, folklore, science and good luck.

A pilgrim could be one thing or many, but always a seeker of something missing in life -- peace, contentment, meaning, health. The corporeal and the spiritual were not separate manifestations of existence, even for the non-religious who nonetheless often found peace and contentment within the old buildings which seemed to offer something, perhaps just an indistinct feeling, but something lost from or not offered by the life being led. An increased level of personal freedom and accessible rail transport to most parts of the country had opened up the prospects for those who could afford and would make the effort to travel further than even their most recent ancestors could have dreamed. The trade in herbal remedies was alive and well and thriving when Sherlock started his appreciation of plants and their properties and he became aware of their potential to kill as well as to heal. He had a schoolboy's fascination with poisons and observed how some purchases involved sufficient material to poison an entire village if used inappropriately but which seemingly troubled no one. Though every town had its outlets for medicinal plants, both intact and as infusions, Glastonbury seemed significantly oversupplied with them, a reflection of the number of pilgrims who travelled there to heal both body and spirit.

Glastonbury, ancient Glestingaburg, never a city, never to lead, was nonetheless destined to become more famous than many of its sister settlements as it gathered the faithful about its holy places and pilgrimages were made from all parts of the country and all corners of the Earth. The high Glastonbury Tor looking down on and commanding the surrounding countryside had drawn in the ancient eyes of the stone age folk and continued on to impress the numerous successive waves of newcomers who discovered the advantages of its height and strategic importance of its position, the magic of its conical form and the sanctity of its mystical setting. There were, however, less obvious points of pilgrimage throughout and around the town and the young Sherlock Holmes, increasingly intrigued by the motives and actions of people of all types, was not slow in seeking them out.

Most would find their ways by train, the fastest, easiest, safest, most comfortable and, with all things being considered, the most economical way to travel, all arriving at the Glastonbury Railway Station, later expanded in size and name to accommodate and service the town of Street. Earlier pilgrims had made their ways on foot or by coach and some on horseback; others had floated in on canal barges; but the railways, magnificently and malevolently intrusive as their arrival had been, changed everything, especially in the numbers and in the makeup of the visitors. The far-more affluent pleasure-seeking tourist had appeared and was prepared to pay more than the typical pilgrim could afford. Pilgrim and tourist alike, though, would gather to hear the legends, many wildly exaggerated and wholly contrived in the distant past by fund-seeking abbots keen to draw the pilgrims and their contributions away from other sites and toward their own.

Joseph of Arimathea, it was said, and with total conviction on the part of narrator, had come by boat to the island of Glastonbury with a goblet containing blood shed by the crucified Jesus and, upon arrival, had inserted his staff into the soil only to see it sprout leaves and then flower as the Holy Thorn. The goblet, the Holy Grail, remains unseen, locked away in secrecy but venerated as the most holy relic of Christendom. King Arthur of the Britons and his Queen Guinevere knew the district well and came to offer up their prayers at the very same holy places the present-day pilgrims attended and at which they hoped to receive a blessing and possibly a cure. Places of pilgrimage with such sacred and notable credentials must surely rate a contribution of substantial proportion to show the worthiness of the supplicant.

For those seeking their country's mythical past, guides would take them to the site of a marshy depression which once held a wide watery expanse along the course of the River Brue. It was a feature sacred to the Lady of the Lake with whom Sir Bedivere had entrusted Arthur's sword Excalibur after the King fell at Camlann, reputedly killed by Mordred who also succumbed to injuries suffered in the same battle. A wily guide could, at the right time of year, assemble his clientele of tourists or pilgrims, or both, before dawn to witness Glastonbury Tor topped by the great and remnant Tower of St. Michael's Church appear suspended above the countryside at sunrise. The rare climatic conditions would produce a Fata Morgana, a phenomenon personified as the Morgan le Fay. Here the Iron Age met the Celts who mingled together with the Saxons and the Normans in a great miscellany of Britain. Any showman. prophet or spiritual guide who could not hold a crowd in Glastonbury and point to a miracle of Nature or God or of humanity's insatiable industry was one unworthy of bearing any such appellation.

All these things, and a great many more, were witnessed by an open-mouthed, juvenile-turning-adolescent Sherlock Holmes, a lad immersed in a region which opened his mind to the complexity of human nature. That nature was sometimes beneficent, sometimes predatory, sometimes generous, sometimes evil, but always incredibly interesting if he stayed emotionally detached and ever observant. His latent skills were beginning to bloom; the detective was on his way.

Lately, though, and despite offering so much to so many seekers of solace and succour, Glastonbury had fallen foul of the Angel of Death, so claimed a notable contributor to the region's newspapers, one who had noticed a jump in deaths concerning rumoured poisonings. Visitor numbers had fallen dramatically as the news was picked up and relayed on by journalists eager for easy and sensational news, news which found its way to the major London and international newspapers. This was news, certainly, but not good news, not for Glastonbury, not for Somerset; an entire service industry had grown around the visitors and sensationalised rumours of some deathly angel lurking at every turn had slowed the inflow of money to the region to below the level of its outflow. Businesses were not resupplying, employers were not taking on seasonal staff, families were beginning to feel the financial pinch and the smell of commercial stagnation was in the air.

Despite the reports of deaths by poison, the local and regional police forces could find no clear evidence of wrongdoing. No factual reason could be found to continue the investigations and the local civil authorities could not convince the official agencies to act further. In such an environment, there was only one recourse and that was to initiate investigations of a private nature and, so, five members of the Glastonbury Council, all local businessmen, met to formulate a plan of action. Pompous and bombastic the group's leader, Jonathon Bennet, may have been, but he did get things done and was not a man to antagonise, not in what he considered his own domain. The group's determinations would be simple, they would be whatever Bennet said they were and the remaining four men were there to agree and utter "Aye!" when Bennet called for the vote to be taken on his 'suggestion'.

As members of the Town Council serving the Glastonbury Municipal Borough, the elected councillors had chosen the aldermen and mayor since the modernisation of 1835. As the borough had previously been under the supervisory control of the lord of the manor, though, the current mayor, Jonathon

Bennet, had assumed that all deference previously due to that lord was now due to his own office and, therefore, to himself. He liked the authority, he liked the robes, he liked the accolades and, despite his overblown self-image, he was a man of some significant capability. One thing the man did not like, however, was being told "No!". Bennet had called and now opened the extraordinary meeting, dispensed with inconvenient formalities and got right to the point.

"Gentlemen," he started, "I have given this dreadful matter some significant consideration and can only suggest that you all agree with me in a decision to summon a private investigative agent from London, a man called Sherlock Holmes who would, no doubt, consider himself honoured by our decision. Now, I am certain that there will be no dissension, so I will consider the matter approved by unanimous vote and begin to make arrangements."

No dissention was evident and so the vote was recorded and arrangements had indeed begun forthwith.

It had been Glastonbury's turn to seek help, to plead to be purged of an evil which seemed intent on spreading death through a population seeking only life, its improvement and its extension. In response, and after some little unpleasantness, two London men, one medically trained and sworn to administer to the afflicted and the other armed and determined to combat criminality with his special gifts of insight and observation had heard that call and were preparing to embark together on a journey, not as pilgrims but as deliverers of a town and region from an evil afflicting both.

The Journey

"Trains wait for no one," yelled Watson, looking out from 221B's upper window and seeing the approach of a Hansom, one summoned to take them to Paddington Station. He also observed his friend's messy state of unpreparedness. Sherlock Holmes could be the worst of companions when possessed by the excitement of a case; chaos seemed always to follow in his wake as discarded clues were scattered about like autumn leaves. At least, though, he would at all times maintain a valise packed and ready with the basic necessities he would need for travel at a moment's notice. A razor, he needed, and a few toiletries, a change of clothes for his personal needs, a wad of bank notes, a note book, a selection of maps, his Bradshaw train timetable, a box containing pencils, stamped envelopes and telegram blanks and assorted loose change, and his specially prepared portable chemical laboratory. Grab that, his hat and coat and he was ready whenever called but was oblivious to the state of disorder he created for everyone else.

"We'll be late," the doctor continued, "and we'll have to wait for hours if you don't bundle all of that paraphernalia into a bag and get yourself downstairs. You can go over all of that clutter when we're on the train."

Watson threw an extra canvas carry bag to the great sleuth and, grabbing both his bulging valise and that of his friend, proceeded down the stairs and out into Baker Street to claim the cab as it came to a halt. Holmes looked up and saw that his friend had departed the room and hurriedly gathered in the great spread of notebooks and documents and assorted papers and thrust them into the canvas receptacle recently provided. The rush to get going to Paddington was a little unnecessary but Watson well knew his friend when he became fixated on a subject, any subject, and was keen to proceed with a good margin of time in hand.

Holmes and Watson had discussed the possibilities presented by the newspaper reports and delivered by the deputation of two from Glastonbury the previous evening, despite scant evidence of any actual wrong-doing existing amongst a mass of conjecture and highly suggestive anomalies. The decision to proceed to the district had been a foregone conclusion after the town of Glastonbury had been mentioned, but Holmes was ever-wary of making premature assumptions. His interest had been captured and the prospect of a difficult case to challenge his cerebral capabilities had whetted his appetite but the sleuth needed to gather in what information he had at hand, despite its age and the fact that it had been dispersed throughout an extensive mass of files, both orderly and chaotic. He had barely begun before Watson shouted out the order to desist and get downstairs.

"I'm coming," yelled Holmes, frantically trying to maintain some order in the documents he had spent some significant time sorting, "But where on Earth is that valise of mine. I declare, Watson, if Mrs. Hudson has cleaned up again, I will not be responsible for my actions."

"Leave Mrs. Hudson alone, Holmes," came the reply from the bottom of the stairs. "Your valise is sitting next to mine in the cab and you should be there as well, sitting next to me. Now, get down here immediately, or it's me who won't be responsible for his actions."

"Yes, yes," said the sleuth, "but don't fuss so; I need my resources and Glastonbury isn't going anywhere."

"Well, nor are we," replied a flustered Watson, determined that his friend would not find an excuse to delve deeper into those tattered files he kept in his ancient battered tin chest and cause them to wait impatiently on train-departed railway stations, "So come, Now!"

Holmes managed to cram all of his selected files into the extra bag and then proceeded down the stairs and out to meet his impatiently waiting colleague. Both men clambered into the hansom with Watson giving the yell of, "Paddington, Driver, if you please. We've a train to catch."

The ride to Paddington from Baker Street was not a long one and the cab arrived with far more than ample time to spare and Holmes commented that it would have been possible for them to have walked and still been on time. Watson, however, wanted his friend's obsession curtailed until they could at least determine the basic facts and could speak with the official authorities in Glastonbury or, perhaps, down at police headquarters at Taunton. They still had no real feel for the case beyond the fact that something serious had caused five Glastonbury men to take time from their busy lives to seek out Sherlock Holmes in distant London. These were practical men who did not waste effort on trivialities and both Holmes and Watson detected a sense of lingering fear amid their obvious concerns about falling trade and diminishing revenues.

"We've time for a light meal, Holmes," announced Watson as he paid the cabbie and grabbed both valises as well as Holmes' bag of files before both made way through the station entrance to the ticket office. "The meals are bearable but filling and will keep us going for some time. We've a change of trains to make on the way, and we can refill ourselves at that point. The reason I pushed for the train at this particular time is that it is unlikely to be full and we would probably have a compartment to ourselves; you ought to be able to go through your files to your heart's content."

"Very commendable, Watson." replied Holmes while purchasing two tickets for Glastonbury, "but we do have more than thirty minutes to wait."

"All the more time to take over a meal, in that case, Holmes," countered Watson, "I am a medical man and very conscious of the need to take my time and eat sensibly to enable my digestive processes to proceed with neither speed nor stress. You may well eat like a sparrow gobbling down what it finds, but sparrows only need to rush in case of hawks while you don't."

"Agreed," conceded Holmes, accepting defeat for the sake of relief from one of Watson's unyielding medical lectures for which he rarely had a satisfactory counter argument.

The meal was uninspiring but filling and, upon its completion, the two men picked up their luggage and moved off to the platform where they had observed their train preparing to depart. There was still ten minutes until departure, time which would be filled with idle banter and recollections of past cases and discussions of how there might be definite parallels between this situation and others which they had overcome. First, they had to occupy a compartment and hopefully claim it and keep it as theirs for the duration of the journey.

Holmes began to occupy himself with his bag of assorted files and was almost too absorbed in their content to notice the shrill steam whistle announcing the engineer's intent to depress the throttle and send live steam charging into the primary cylinder to power the piston and pump movement into the locomotive. It took the jolt of his carriage to alert the sleuth to the fact that the adventure had begun but the interruption was only momentary. Watson, meanwhile, had his nose pressed to the window, or so it would seem to any passer-by, for train travel to the doctor was something to be enjoyed for its own sake. The passing parade of the countryside practically mesmerised the man and took him deep within his memories to a place of great and restful contentment. Suburb after suburb went steadily by until living green began to replace the extended dreariness of grey and smoky brown, until the great metropolis was left far behind and a different Britain came into view. Watson's silent form rocked gently with the movement of the carriage as the very reason for the journey became lost among a multitude of pleasantries, the man's contented state continuing on until his peace was abruptly shattered by one of Holmes' ever insightful but unanticipated announcements.

"Belladonna, Watson," announced Holmes with a suddenness which caused Watson to jump and catch his forehead on the window frame. "It has been a great friend to the murderer over the years, and I cannot begin to guess how many waiting nooses have gone unused and guilty necks gone unstretched for want of a competent diagnosis. 'Beautiful Lady' it may well mean but those petals hide the black heart of a conniving witch."

"And not just Belladonna," he continued, "think about Monkshood and the rest of the armoury which nature has provided for those who kill in stealth. If every cannon and musket and rifled gun were to be collected together, the potency of their totality would pale into insignificance up against the combined might of nature's weaponry. I tell you, Watson, nature has it in for us or else she would not have so many ways to kill a human being."

"That's a bit morbid, Holmes," replied the doctor, "even for you. Just remember, though, that Isaiah tells us about turning swords into ploughshares and spears into pruning hooks and what you see as a deadly weapon might well be transformed to a wondrous medicine to be used for the benefit of mankind, not its destruction. I don't know about Monkshood, but I have seen preparations of Belladonna save several lives when used judiciously."

"Undoubtedly, Watson," conceded Holmes, "but my business concerns the darker side of human nature, the evil in men's hearts and the wickedness done by the malefactor. You are the healer, the best of us all and the seeker after life and light, but I am the one who seeks out evil and Lestrade is the one who delivers it to face justice, the best medicine of all for those who choose the ways of darkness and death."

Watson shook his head in mock frustration and returned to his window while Holmes went back to his files, both in silence, both knowing that the one would never come completely around to the other's point of view. Each man respected the other's capabilities, but each could become infuriated by the inflexibility both could show if given enough provocation. The journey had only begun and Watson knew that his friend would not leave him alone. Holmes was too excited about the case and would not be able to long contain his enthusiasm but the doctor was determined to savour each moment he would have to himself and his thoughts and would give a barely-responsive and non-committal grunt to each of Holmes' further interruptions. Holmes, though, would not even notice Watson's lack of reaction but would continue on completely absorbed in his own contemplations and ponderings.

Both men were engrossed but the subject of Watson's interest would give way as Holmes' words kept repeating themselves in his mind and infuriatingly insisted on his full attention. He wasn't actually conscious of his mind's ultimate diversion away from green fields to the perils of some of the deadly plants growing at their perimeters but his medical training made him more than aware of the stark reality behind the words which his friend had uttered so earnestly.

The military man had seen the effects of tinctures of the opium poppy on soldier and civilian alike during his ill-fated and abruptly curtailed service in India and Afghanistan. The visions of wasted figures and wasted lives sometimes come to to mind to haunt him, but he also saw the beneficial effects on wounded men whose pain was relieved by that very same agent. He, himself, had experienced the relief given to his wounded shoulder and remembered the overwhelming anticipation of further treatments during his recovery. He had emerged from his ordeal with a better understanding of the drug's potential for imposing its addictive and very destructive nature on its often too willing victims but also knew that there were plants far deadlier than the poppy in nature's arsenal.

As journeys generally do, however, this one was progressing and the two men, after several scheduled stops at rural stations to pick up and deposit further passengers, freight and mail, found themselves preparing to depart from one service and transfer to a second for the final and much slower leg to Glastonbury. A quick but unrushed meal was to be had before the procedure of securing a compartment would be repeated, though their exclusive occupancy of a compartment might not be guaranteed.

The Revelation

Holmes had been reading through numerous old files he had compiled and had taken aside one of his Aunt Jane's old herbalist texts, a book replete with notations and comments on trial preparations made and their efficacies when used on herself and, in some few cases, on others. Aware of the perils presented by various of the herbs she had collected and trialled, Aunt Jane had also drawn attention to dangerous plants of the region and of the ways employed to identify the symptoms of poisoning and suggested ways of alleviating a victim's suffering and avoiding fatal consequences. How accurate his aunt's information actually was he could not know with any certainty. He felt, though, that a wealth of observational data was in his hands and that this might point the way to local usage and perhaps to the folklore which might guide some local person intent on doing harm without drawing undue attention from official sources. There was one notation within the book's pages which particularly drew his eye, this being, in a way, a message from beyond the grave as he read two handwritten sentences to himself from his aunt which said: "Sherlock, if you ever come across these lines, you will no doubt be investigating poisonings in Somerset. Be aware that several people have succumbed to this particular plant and that no one had ever suspected murder. Aunt Jane." Also inserted below this, apparently later and during her final days, was a second message, a rider to the first, "Would that you had been a few years older and might have better appreciated your latent gifts in our times together. Stay vigilant when next you visit these parts as I feel that you will be stepping in the path of danger. Perhaps we may discuss this in another and better world in which time has little meaning. Do right, My Boy, and may God bless you. J.H."

Watson had wondered at his friend's continued silence. It was so uncharacteristic of the man when he had someone at whom to express his surprise and indignation, his disdain and utter frustration, or any other response which might convey his undisguised outrage at someone else's perceived folly or apparent incompetence. Appreciative of the silence as he may have been, the doctor had to ask what was so absorbing of his friend's interest.

"You're very quiet, my friend." said the doctor, more in the manner of posing a question than of making a statement. "Is there something of particular interest you have come upon?"

"Well, yes, I suppose that you might say that," replied the sleuth in a far more pensive manner than was usual for him, "although it may have little or nothing to do with recent events in Glastonbury. Let us wait until we have changed trains and I have had more time to think on the matter."

This was stated as the train began slowing for the end of their journey's first leg and the moment was lost as the two London men stood and reached for their valises, hats and coats. Holmes thrust all of his files and extras back into his canvas carry bag, though he did retain a book of immediate and compelling interest and thrust that into the wider side pocket of his coat. Both men exited their compartment and entered into the queue of passengers now waiting in the passageway, all ready to exit at the train's termination. A jolt in reverse of that experienced upon commencement was experienced and the standing passengers felt themselves seemingly propelled forward as the momentum of their still-moving bodies carried them onward when the slowing train braked suddenly and came to a stop. Just as suddenly, the carriage's outer door was flung open and the outrush of passengers took Holmes and Watson along in an ebb-tide of human urgency and deposited them like two pieces of driftwood on a platform rapidly clearing itself of a rush of unreasoning impatience.

"In a hurry, aren't they Holmes?" was all that Watson could say, quite understating the situation. "Though I suppose that train timetables make them that way. I'm sure that in a future age such things will be overcome and the travelling public will be more relaxed."

"It may come to be," responded Holmes, "but the mind of the human being can always think and work its way into difficulty any time two or more needs have to be accommodated at the same time. It is the nature of the beast, my friend, and a beast's nature is rarely seen to change. Now, as it is your nature to eat at least three times during each day, we had better be finding a source of nourishment before the hungry beast within John Watson comes forth and bares its fangs."

"Yes, yes." agreed the doctor. "It would be as well, for I fancy that I can hear some definite growls of discontent coming from deep within this anxious and long-deprived body of mine."

On checking the situation regarding expected times of arrival and departure for the train taking them on the next part of their journey, and confirming that the time to wait was ample for an unrushed sitting, the pair found its way to the kiosk and partook of a meal surprisingly superior to that had at Paddington. Watson delighted in the experience and even Holmes had to admit that it was of a rare quality for the railways. Time, though, had moved along and a distant whistle, all too soon for Watson, announced the approach of their steaming conveyance and of the need to prepare for boarding.

The pair stood watching as the train slowed to a halt in a noisy cloud of steam and smoke and then stood back as several terminating passengers emerged. They then boarded and walked along the passageway looking for a compartment free of occupants and, upon finding the same, entered and took possession. Their luggage stacked on the racks, both settled into their seats, two of them in a compartment made for six but were disappointed when a party of three followed along and bundled themselves noisily in. The disappointment was short-lived, however, as a fourth man called to the others to join him further up in an empty compartment where they would be better able to stretch out and relax. Luck seemed to be with the doctor and sleuth, and they both breathed sighs of relief when the train eventually started to move.

"Now, Holmes," began Watson, "you had started telling me about something which was playing on your mind. Perhaps now would be a good time as we now have this compartment to ourselves and a good stretch of travelling time ahead of us. I would presume that it would have some connection with the Glastonbury situation."

"Well, yes, and then no," was the sleuth's enigmatic reply. "Hopefully no but probably yes, though, if yes, then Belladonna could well be involved."

Watson gave his friend a most quizzical look as if to ask, "What on Earth are you saying, Holmes?" Holmes then telling of his find in his aunt's book and how it seemed to have anticipated their visit to Glastonbury by several decades. He also gave Watson a short rendition of his times in and around Glastonbury as a lad and of his aunt's interests, unknown at the time, which seemed to have strong parallels with those of his own.

"That is decidedly bizarre, Holmes," announced a startled Watson. "I have heard of second sight and premonitions but this does seem to hold evidence of both phenomena. Perhaps, though, your aunt was of a sort to observe what others could only see, or could not see. The lady may well have possessed some of those attributes which you have honed to a sharp edge to cut through the extraneous matter to get at the truth. Your brother Mycroft possesses them to a great degree so why should your aunt not have done likewise? Perhaps she knew you far better than you could have begun to appreciate at the time."

"I am beginning to come around to that position, my friend," admitted Holmes, "for Aunt Jane's letter to me, one penned just before her death, seems in hindsight to suggest that very thing. She may have been possessed of such powers of observation but it might also be a fact that those very powers possessed by a lady living alone in a superstitious rural area and also preparing herbal remedies could well have attracted the stigma of the witch. This may have caused her to withdraw from the world at large and lie low. It would explain much of her unusual behaviour."

"She would have known of your elder brother's powers, surely, Holmes," proposed Watson, "and, if so, would have recognised the same in you as well as your greater curiosity and ability to make connections where few would suspect any existed. She may well have allowed you the freedom to find your own path knowing that you would, in time, learn far more than she could and outdo your brother in whatever direction those special gifts would take you.

"Well, she did seem to suspect that you would return to face some danger in the region, and that the danger would involve poisonous plants. Very insightful of her, I must say. Are you certain that your family didn't make some pact with the ancient spirits of the land long centuries ago?"

"Were I suspicious man, Watson," said the sleuth, "one also given to believing in superstitious nonsense, I might well believe that could be so, but I do believe that you have seen more than me in this instance and have guided me to seeing my aunt in a completely different light. I had thumbed my way through her books and notes at various times but now I see that I must redouble my efforts and read them with the openness of mind with which I discuss matters and listen to my very insightful though incredibly lazy elder brother. There is obviously much to be discovered. I must extend my most profound thanks to you, my friend; you are indeed the beacon guiding me to safe haven and away from hidden reefs and unseen perils against which I am so often in danger of dashing myself."

Holmes went silent, even forgetting his pipe and its powers to take his mind to places it ordinarily could not travel, and drew the book from his coat pocket and his aunt's other texts and notes from his carry bag. He would use his time and the stimulating motion of the train to go over all such ancient documents for what he had overlooked or had never suspected existed. He did not have to look far or long to find that his aunt was far more remarkable a woman than he had ever anticipated.

Within almost every book, his Aunt Jane had left notations addressed to him, obviously for a time long after she had passed from this Earth and when Sherlock's powers had grown and matured. She had written to the man that would be and not the boy she knew, and there was an underlying message of sinister goings-on which would require the efforts of a person of special insight to uncover and overcome. She had anticipated the phenomenon of Sherlock Holmes.

Holmes read on, unable to take his eyes from the books' contents, printed text and hand-written notes alike. That he could become obsessed was well known to his friends and colleagues but this was different, truly personal and beyond anything in the great sleuth's experience. Sherlock's Aunt Jane was speaking, certainly from the pages and from decades distant, but the message had been sent directly to him to be read at a time he would be heading back to Somerset to face some sort of danger. If only he could ask her of the full meaning of her words – there was certainly a message, also a warning, and also something which seemed to contain and express her appreciation for what he was about to do, whatever that was. "Mysterious" did not satisfactorily describe the situation and the closest he could get to the true emotion he was feeling would be to call it "spooky," though he would not admit this to Watson; he could barely admit it to himself.

"When we get to Glastonbury and meet with our clients, Watson," Holmes suddenly announced, "we should say nothing of my Aunt Jane, nor of her messages which she left for me in her books. The substance of our investigations cannot depend solely on our clients' inputs but must involve many others whose trust, as yet, may not always be totally relied upon."

"Of one thing I am now certain, though, my friend," he further insisted, "and that is that the troubles we are about to encounter and investigate involve Somerset and not just Glastonbury and may have been going on for some considerable time."

The Passengers

Watson could no longer peer out the window and lose himself amid the fields and forests of the countryside but was intrigued to a great degree, not only by the nature of the messages left by Sherlock's Aunt Jane, but by his friend's reaction to them. He did not respond verbally to Holmes' statements but merely nodded to acknowledge that he understood his friend's concern. On being offered one of the books, the first to be inspected by Holmes, Watson accepted it and proceeded to turn its pages and tried to gather in the extra notations made so long ago, some general comments, some messages to Sherlock.

The two men had become engrossed in the subject matter when their mental labours were disturbed by a rapping on the compartment door. Holmes and Watson looked up to see the source of the interruption and recognised it as the fourth man who had called his three compatriots to join him further along the carriage. The man, it seemed, had located an empty compartment and the two investigators would, as hoped, have exclusive occupancy for the rest of their journey to Glastonbury.

"Can we be of assistance?" asked Watson, standing to slide the compartment door open and then staring directly at the interrupter, "I don't believe we have met but I do believe that your three travelling companions were also ours for a very short while."

"That is most definitely the case, Dr. Watson," the man replied to the astonishment of both the medical man and the sleuth, "but I did recognise your famous colleague and presumed that you might appreciate your privacy, hence my action to have my colleagues withdraw and leave this compartment to yourself and Mr. Holmes. It is Dr. Watson to whom I am speaking, I presume?"

"Yes, that is the case," replied a non-committal Watson, "but you do have the advantage of me, sir, of both of us."

"Yes … indeed; forgive me," the man replied, fumbling for and then proffering his business card. "I am Adam Renshaw, of Glastonbury, as are my travelling companions. We had been aware that our illustrious and somewhat insistent mayor had intended to pay your good selves a visit with a view to engaging your services but were unsure if he had yet done so, nor if he had been or would be successful in his quest."

"We four," he continued, "had been discussing the probability of success on the part of the mayor and would like to offer what assistance we may, if indeed you have come to investigate certain unpleasant matters, though we would not presume to tell you your business. You have my card and, if you'll permit, I'll now hand you those of my three friends and leave you in peace."

"Thank you, indeed, Mr. Renshaw," responded Holmes as Watson looked toward him for an indication of whether to accept or not, "We shall be pleased to accept your cards and may well have need of some input from any or all of you in the near future. Thank you, again."

"Very well," replied Renshaw as Watson took his friends' three cards from his hand, "Thank you, gentlemen; I shall now leave you in peace and will not disturb or contact you further unless or until you decide it is time to contact us, any one of us. It might be as well, though, not to mention this discussion with the mayor – he does have a strange notion of priority in all matters and his ire is easily provoked."

Holmes remained seated and simply nodded slightly and smiled knowingly as Renshaw withdrew. He then did likewise to Watson who had resumed his seat and was looking at the business cards of Adam Renshaw, Horace Portland, Harold Fraser and Wilson Pettigrew.

"Had Renshaw truly come to offer his and his friends' assistance," pondered Holmes aloud to his friend, "or merely to keep up in a game from which they had been excluded?"

"It's impossible to say definitely one way or the other at this point," replied Watson, "but I can say two things with almost total certainty, one being that any hope for secrecy has been dashed, and the other is that we shall definitely see all four men again in the very near future."

"Indeed!" was all Holmes needed to say as his friend's assessment was entirely correct, but he did add that, "It would be to no avail to get more from Renshaw and those three other men at this point; whatever their motives, we might well alert any wrongdoers to too many details of our investigations before we are in a position to prepare our strategy. I suspect, Watson, that our visit to Somerset may take a little longer than anticipated; it is starting to show the signs of a very complex and difficult case. Aren't you glad we took up the challenge?"

Watson showed a wry smile and gave a non-committal sardonic "Hrmff" to his friend and then resumed his reading of the notes left long ago by yet another infuriatingly enigmatic member of the Holmes family.

Sherlock, however, did not resume that activity; he was determined to think about Renshaw's intrusion and how the man had offered to be of help but had offered no information whatsoever about the case. Renshaw had merely mentioned "unpleasantness" and the mayor's mission and may have known little more beyond that. He had made no mention of murder or of falling visitor numbers and subsequent profits but was keen to separate his friends from Watson and himself and perhaps had come back to merely ingratiate himself with two famous London investigators without his travelling companions' knowledge. Saying little or nothing at this point, he considered, would be the best way forward. Still, he did have their names and would make discreet investigations at an appropriate time.

Renshaw had returned to his friends and confirmed the fact that Sherlock Holmes and Dr. Watson were indeed on the train and seemed headed toward Glastonbury, perhaps at the mayor's invitation, but perhaps not. The sleuth had given little away except for the vague hint of a possible need for information at some later time. "Was the great and famous Sherlock Holmes being cagey or was he just being polite to avoid causing a stranger any embarrassment?" – Renshaw thought this but could not say for certain which was the case and he was becoming less and less certain that he had learned anything in his brief talk with the two London men beyond confirming their identities. Was there something, though, which one or more of his companions was thinking but was loath to express out loud?

Renshaw was a factor of unknown significance but was one prepared to take action, it would seem to Holmes, to find or create a place for himself in whatever was going on. There was no reason to doubt his identity, however, as the man would be unlikely to carry false business cards on the unlikely prospect of meeting someone famous who may be in need of being hoodwinked. Nor would there be any reason to doubt the identities of his three travelling companions and for much the same reason – it would be too great a risk as someone with Holmes' renowned capabilities would surely see through such an ill-considered ruse. Motives were an altogether different matter but the first place to start would be with the business cards which, if taken at face value, might provide some clue and a diversion for the mind of Holmes.

Adam Renshaw's card stated that he was in the furniture business, "new and second-hand" his card proclaimed. This suggested nothing beyond his being a businessman whose activities would take him into many homes throughout the district, for the provision of estimates and quotations, for the removal of items of furniture and for the delivery of those items to his premises and on to those of his customers. His capabilities in moving bulky items of varying sizes, values and degrees of fragility suggested someone of considerable capability and trust. It was also possible that his employees and their friends might be the types to take advantage of a situation, although there was no actual way that a business card might suggest any such proclivity.

Putting Renshaw's card aside, Watson then drew out that of Wilson Pettigrew and saw that he was described as a "purveyor of second-hand goods" and someone who would "pay well for quality items". This was suggestive of a receiver of stolen goods to the suspicious mind of Sherlock Holmes, though the claims could also be a quite accurate description of the business dealings of a fair and honest man. If the employees of Renshaw had a keen eye for valuable item in other people's homes, it could be considered, then Pettigrew could provide an outlet for anything which strayed from its proper location, though any organised criminal gang would likely remove the stolen items to London where their anonymity would be virtually guaranteed.

"Nothing there to stir the matter beneath my detective's hat, Watson," declared Holmes who, despite his suspicious nature, would not actually have expected someone to have "Master Thief" printed on a batch of business cards. Still, trifles were always worth examining and who knows what a vain man might declare to those he was trying to impress.

The next card did incite a little more interest from the sleuth as Horace Portland had declared himself to be an "Herbalist," one charged with "maintaining the health of Somerset." This card did raise one of the great sleuth's eyebrows, though only for a few seconds.

Harold Fraser's card was simplicity itself, simply stating the man's name, declaring him to be an apothecary and the address at which his services might be procured. That address, however, was noted as being the same as that of Horace Portland, the two men's respective businesses being suggestive of having customers opposed to the other's products.

"An herbalist and an apothecary occupying the same premises," stated Watson, "What would you make of that, Holmes? It would go counter to my expectations."

"Not necessarily, Watson." replied Holmes remembering just to where it was they were travelling, "The modern and the traditional often stand side by side in our rural areas and the term 'herbal' does not necessarily lie on the medicinal side of a commercial venture, though I do suspect that it does in this case. We could have a purveyor of culinary herbs. We just won't know until we look; but, look, we must and without making a fuss about it.

"When we do meet with our Glastonbury clients, though," he added, "we should say nothing of our encounter with Renshaw or the matter of his three friends. We should also keep mum on the matter of my earlier association with the region, though I did give myself away a little in our early discussions. These are cards we shall keep close to our vests and should not be revealed until the time comes for them to be played, if that time comes at all. Now, we've time for a pipe and a little contemplation."

The train rumbled on making a stop here and another there, but the two men had retreated into their minds to mull over what they knew and what they might know but which would require clarification. All that they did have was made up of a few tentative suggestions which might turn out to be facts but which might just as likely end up revealed as highly prejudicial statements made by someone with a grudge. It was no time for decisions, not even time for making assumptions; the data was just not there.

The pipes eventually exhausted themselves of tobacco and Holmes thought it best to refill his and continue his contemplations. Watson, however, was tired of thinking about things Holmes had told him he should not, and so he returned to his window and continued taking in the pleasant vista presented. Watson was never so content as when propped up against a window in a train moving steadily through the green countryside of his native land, and he felt at home, regardless of the battles which had been waged over its occupation by successive invaders.

The time would arrive soon enough when he and his friend would make their way to find William Randall and then arrange another meeting at which they expected to hear factual detail and not just fearful supposition.

The Arrival

Holmes did charge his pipe with a second plug of tobacco but was distracted before he had time to ignite it. He had chanced to look out of the window and something, a vision, went through his mind, a vision from his past but one seemingly occurring in the present. Sherlock Holmes did have an unusual mind stacked with the most bizarre facts obtainable but these were arranged in an extremely orderly manner; this was something new, even though it concerned matters far into Sherlock's past, something he had not sought out systematically by delving into the mental files held in his brain-attic and it took him completely by surprise. It was as though a section of his memory had been walled-up to keep it away from his consciousness and had never actually been discarded; now something had breached that wall and the long-separated files came jumping out to the dismay of a very disconcerted detective.

"Something amiss with that pipe of yours, Holmes?" asked a confused Watson, "Or have you had some sort of premonition about the outcome of our upcoming investigations? That match you lit will soon burn your fingers."

"No, no, nothing of that sort." replied the sleuth shaking hard on the match and extinguishing its flame, "But something has sent my mind racing about into long-disused portions of my memory and has dislodged a great mass of material I can't actually remember putting there, even though every image coming before my eyes seems somehow familiar and not at all threatening. I expect that I will soon have things under control."

Holmes looked and sounded puzzled as he added, "It happened just as we came out from that last cutting onto this section overlooking this narrow valley we seem to be passing. I must admit that the view toward that distant steeple beyond that raised clump of trees slightly to left of centre now seems very familiar, something I had originally seen on my first journey to Somerset all those years ago in my early youth.

Strange emotions are welling up from within me, Watson, and I don't care for the sensation at all."

"Welcome back to the human race, my friend." responded Watson, "Now strike another match and light that pipe of yours before you start blubbering in public and completely destroy the image of Sherlock Holmes."

The journey still had some time to go and Holmes decided that the smoke from his pipe might just deter his unfettered memories from cluttering up his thoughts. Watson returned to his window and quite different thoughts while his puzzled friend prepared and lit his pipeful of tobacco then sat back and vigorously puffed away as if he were smoking out some vermin which had invaded the attic, as indeed such could be said to have been the case. Crossings were crossed and underpasses were passed under as the train rumbled on and both men, now oblivious to each other's thoughts, withdrew once more to places distant and quite different.

The visions generated from his unruly memories began to fade as Sherlock Holmes regained the mental upper hand and once more took control over his extraordinarily ordered and disciplined mind. But those visions, as annoying as they had been, had served to remind the sleuth of the emotional hold which the district held over its denizens. He had remembered many facts but had forgotten and ultimately repressed all passions which he felt were unnecessary for the investigator, any investigator, but especially himself. It would, he thought to himself, be advisable to remember those pleasant and connective emotions; after all, each one was as much a fact, at least a factor, as was greed or fear or hate in the criminals he ordinarily dealt with.

A shout of "Next stop, Glastonbury!" broke through the barriers Holmes and Watson had erected and the two men were brought back to the reality of the case and the need to keep their wits about them. They were about to stand on strange ground in a situation which seemed to get stranger by the hour. Both men donned coats and hats and picked up the bare necessities which made up their luggage, though Holmes did have his extra bag of assorted materials.

"Let us wait for a moment," suggested Holmes, holding onto his friend's arm as it started to pull on the compartment door. "We should let those four Glastonbury men whose cards we hold step off and away before we do likewise. It would be as well to keep our distance until we learn a great deal more. We shall certainly be speaking to them in due course but it will be individually and at a time and place of our choosing, and certainly not in the public eye."

"A wise move, I would think," agreed Watson, "Our discussion with that Renshaw fellow was just a little too convenient for my liking, and more than a bit unsettling. Ah, there they go now."

Watson indicated to Holmes that he had seen Renshaw and his three travelling companions walk past their compartment window without looking in and that they all seemed involved in some sort of convoluted discussions with much pointing of fingers and a great many hand gestures. He had no way of telling if any of those discussions involved himself and Holmes but the mood of the four men seemed, to someone looking in, decidedly unfriendly. The two London men made their way to the outer carriage door and waited until all four Glastonbury men had exited the platform before stepping off the train; and none too soon, it appeared, for no sooner had they alighted than, with a sudden lurch and loud whistle, the train was off and on its way.

"Glastonbury!" Holmes exclaimed, as if he had reached a long sought after goal or found a hidden treasure trove following a drawn out search or arduous campaign throughout which he had often despaired of his eventual success, "And not so far to Street, where we might be headed were my aunt still living and desirous of two visitors."

"First things first, though," he continued as he and Watson passed beyond the platform to the exit and surrendered their tickets, "and we must be off in search of our accommodations. We can then begin to acquaint ourselves with Glastonbury and its strange goings-on."

"We appear to be out on the edge of town, Holmes," announced Watson, looking around at the surrounding fields with few substantial building located close by.

Holmes smiled at his friend, saying, "Well, we can take a carriage if you insist or we could stretch our legs and walk. The town proper is but a short distance to the east, and I believe that I can still find the way. North and west get us nowhere in a hurry, south takes us on to Street, so a good detective should be able to get along by a process of elimination, wouldn't you say."

Watson noticed his friend's flippancy and wondered if those visions Sherlock experienced on the train had boosted his sense of humour, as silly as his process of elimination had been. The doctor also considered that Holmes may have been more excited than he, as a friend, had previously noticed or that the sleuth himself would admit. Watson may have considered himself to be in his country's heartland but, to the rarely emotional great sleuth, it was possible that his arrival in Glastonbury was like coming home.

"What say you, Watson?" asked Holmes as they stepped along down the road from the station and then turned east at a brisk walk. "Should we try our luck at the Pilgrims' Inn for a few nights' shelter? The name does have a good ring to it and it is of a considerable age and is right at the start of the High Street, though it does prefer to answer to the name of the George Hotel of late. And it's very close to the town hall. You never know, a man such as yourself might have the opportunity to commune with the ghosts of pilgrims past, to misquote Mr. Dickens and hope he doesn't mind. I made something of a nuisance of myself there on numerous occasions as a young lad, but I'm sure that time would have seen me off the manager's bad books."

"Good Lord," thought Watson to himself. "There must have been something unusual in that tobacco he's been smoking. The man is positively bubbly, so buoyant that he'd float away in the Brue if he were to fall in with a barrow-load of bricks in his pockets. I must check the brand he's using and buy him some more."

"Well," replied Watson, aloud, "I've been on the wrong side of so many who have you listed in their bad books that one more won't hurt. I suppose we are a couple of pilgrims so, why not?"

"Why not, indeed?" came back from Holmes who would have taken little notice of any objection Watson might actually have made.

Onward the two men stepped and before too long they could see the beginnings of the old town, the abbey grounds and the distant tower of St. Michael's atop the tor coming into view, and then the Pilgrims' Inn. All was new to Watson and renewed for Holmes as each turn brought visual cues which summoned memories from a time distant by decades when the detective had not yet emerged but the inquisitiveness necessary for his development was well advanced.

Procuring two rooms was not a difficult task given the paucity of visitors to the famous but recently maligned town, one beleaguered by rumour and avoided by significant numbers of pilgrims who had put off their visits or had sought other sites for spiritual enlightenment. The two London men, their accommodations readily sorted, deposited their luggage and proceeded out to acquaint and reacquaint themselves with Glastonbury, a town and an atmosphere very different from the haunts of London.

The two strolled southward down Magdalene Street past the town hall, somewhere they would have to visit to seek out Jonathon Bennet, the mayor, but not yet, and then entered the abbey grounds to acquaint themselves with buildings now old but comparatively new when measured against the region's antiquity. They had spent a considerable time waiting for and travelling upon trains and were both enjoying the exercise. The junction of the road from Street, well-trodden by the youthful Sherlock Holmes, was passed and that of the old Roman Road which intrigued him so much was soon encountered.

"To the west," announced Holmes as though he had taken on the task of tour guide, "we are taken along the main road which veers southward to Street over the Pomparles Bridge, the Bridge of Perils as many would call it. Sacred ground, Watson; for nearby lived the Lady of the Lake and somewhere thereabouts is where she deposited King Arthur's sword Excalibur for safe keeping in case he should ever come back looking for it. Step over that bridge, Watson, and you leave the mystical Isle of Avalon. Even I can feel the goose-bumps forming."

"Directly to the south," he continued, "runs the Butleigh Road which would take us over the Brue and then through the south moor. To the east we approach the great tor, the pinnacle topped by the remnant tower of the ruined St. Michael's Church. We might investigate all of these when our work here is done and Glastonbury is purged. Take it all in, Watson, for one might say that we have come upon the beating heart and living soul of ancient Britain."

***

UNEASY QUESTIONS

The Sergeant

Watson could scarcely believe his ears; here was the famously unemotional Sherlock Holmes waxing lyrical and sprouting what he could only describe as poetry. "Perhaps, though," he thought, "Sherlock is merely repeating a sentiment he had heard expressed in the days of his youth. But, no matter; I can only hope that these emotions bubbling to the surface will not prove detrimental to his great powers of observation and deduction."

Watson knew that, apart from Somerset being in a place significant in the history of his country, he and Holmes had entered into the territory of others, some of whom might and probably would resent their interference in local matters, no matter how famous the names of Sherlock Holmes and Dr. Watson or how high the office of the one who had summoned them. Both he and Holmes were reasonably certain of Randall's motives while Bennet, the mayor, seemed to be acting out of a sense of fear for loss of prestige, and perhaps from monetary considerations. Renshaw and the other men on the train were suspect and everyone else constituted a series of unknown factors. The police would have to be notified of their presence and the appropriate medical officers would have to be contacted. Many of the significant sights of spiritual significance may have to be visited, but there would be no sense of pleasure or pilgrimage in doing so until the case had been brought to a successful and satisfactory conclusion.

Having seen a small but significant part of the town, the two London men found their way to the police station, a location well-known to the precocious budding detective for the number of times he had come to suggest his own line of enquiry for a number of minor crimes committed in the locality. At times he was treated with some degree of patience, while quickly shown the door at others, especially when he was being particularly insistent. For Holmes' and Watson's purposes, it was now considered necessary to make contact out of professional courtesy as well as a degree of self-interest. The likelihood was that they would have need of police cooperation and assistance at times, and perhaps access to police resources and files, though convincing the local police that a crime had been committed might prove difficult. It would be necessary not to be seen as a threat but, given the reputation of the London pair, and the possible disposition of the local constabulary, that might be unavoidable.

Glastonbury's constabulary was not large; a sergeant and several constables was considered adequate for a town of its size, though extra personnel could be called upon from other locations should they be required. Detectives operating out of Taunton occasionally made use of the local facilities but most crime in the immediate district was of a quite petty nature and local police work was largely administrative and clerical. Complex investigations such as Holmes was envisaging would be beyond the capabilities and resources of the local personnel.

Sergeant Holloway was on duty behind his desk, a location he preferred and rarely left. He much preferred people to come to him with their troubles so that he could despatch a constable to sort things out leaving him to fill out the innumerable succession of reports in precise and minute detail. If the sergeant ever paid a visit, however, the parties involved knew they were in for real trouble, and a constable's discretion might not be forthcoming; if a law had been broken, retribution would be exacted, though leniency might be shown if circumstances warranted it. Holloway did not play favourites, though; everyone was as guilty as he could find them to be if he were forced to leave his desk. He was not an overly popular man but popularity was never high on his agenda; three stripes and the crown on his arm gave him wide powers, and recalcitrant petty criminals were not tolerated and could expect no exemption from his official fury should the good order of Glastonbury remain disturbed. Holmes and Watson entered into Holloway's domain and immediately sensed the man's disdain, though both were actually unsure if that wasn't just the image projected by a man of active and practiced authority.

"Good afternoon, Sergeant," began Holmes. "My name is Sherlock Holmes and this gentleman with me is my professional colleague. Dr. John Watson. We have been engaged by your borough council to look into certain matters which have been causing Glastonbury some significant embarrassment which has, of late, resulted in a reduction in its desirability as a prime destination for visitors."

"You mean that the mayor's income has been affected, don't you?" responded the sergeant in a rather reproachful manner, "Yes, I had been told to expect both of you gentlemen and informed that I ought to cooperate fully. Well, that's not quite how things work around here. You are quite within your rights to ask questions around the town but I do not want to hear of any disturbance to our orderly existence; the law is the law and will be applied as much to yourselves as it would be to anyone, even our councillors. I have had two sitting in our cells after a very heated exchange of views erupted into physical contact and each had to pay a fine before being released."

"If there is something of an official nature which you need," he continued, "I will certainly accommodate you, but with all the proprieties observed. If it is general advice which you seek, then ask what you will and I shall tell you what I may. Now, where are you gentlemen staying, should I have need to contact you."

"We are at the Pilgrim," replied Holmes. "We have made contact with no one at this point, not officially, but we did encounter a man by the name of Renshaw on our journey here; he seemed to know some details of our visit."

"Well, yes, he would." commented the sergeant, with the hint of a snarl on his face. "He's a sly one and has eyes and ears everywhere, though he always keeps just on the right side of the law, at least when I'm looking. Perhaps we ought to discuss a few of the town's idiosyncrasies, its two-legged ones in particular, before your investigations get too far along. I suppose you'll be meeting with our mayor in due course?"

"I have already made Mr. Bennet's acquaintance," replied Holmes, "though I must say that our meeting was not altogether amicable. I basically threw the whole delegation out on the street for not observing the basic tenets of civilised behaviour, though Mr. Randall was apologetic and we subsequently had quite a profitable discussion. The proprieties regarding a client require us to make contact with the mayor before we start our investigations, but our official deference to yourself and your legal authority takes precedence over that of the borough council."

The sergeant relaxed his stern countenance as a broad grin formed across his face and he stated, "I do wish I had been there to witness that, Mr. Holmes. Mr. Bennet is quite a capable man and not such a bad sort but he does like the trappings of his office more than its true function and can get overbearing. I'm glad Mr. Randall spoke up; he is a good type as well but a little short on what it takes to stand up to the likes of Bennet, or perhaps not if what you tell me is true. We should talk again, Mr. Holmes, Dr. Watson, and quite soon."

"We shall do that, indeed." replied Holmes, "Thank you, sergeant, and good afternoon."

"Good afternoon gentlemen." responded the sergeant, "And thank you for the courtesy you have shown by notifying me of your presence and intended activities. Glastonbury is different in many ways, so steady as you go."

"A tough man, that sergeant," commented Watson as the two men stepped out and away from the police station, "but I'd say he plays a good straight bat. Wouldn't you say, Holmes?"

"That is also my assessment, Watson," agreed Holmes. "The sergeant has given us something, just to see our response, and he will come forth with a great deal more if we maintain his trust and show the respect due to his uniform and an understanding of his position. In Holloway and Randall, I believe we have two firm foundation stones on which to start building our case, if indeed we have one to build."

Holmes and Watson walked slowly back toward the Pilgrims' Inn undecided as to whether they ought to contact Randall first or Bennet. There had good reason to take the first option as they did make their arrangements with him, but the second option, that of contacting Bennet would be officially more appropriate though vastly less desirable. If they first contacted Randall just to notify him of their arrival and of their intentions, Holmes reasoned, his part in the arrangements could be acknowledged and the appropriate protocols with regard to Bennet's status and presumed dignity could be observed and perhaps the man might be placated.

Randall's establishment was a good walk from where they were standing but, as the evening meal call was some time off, they could get even more exercise and would be able to retire that evening quite prepared for the next day's activities.

"What actually does this Randall fellow do, Holmes?" inquired Watson, hoping that Holmes had asked the question of the fellow at their first meeting, "He is some sort of shopkeeper, if my memory serves me well, but what sits up on his shelves I don't ever recall knowing."

"Nor do I," admitted Holmes, "Very remiss of me, I must say. I will excuse my inexcusable lapse by blaming everything on the excitement of the unpleasantness with Bennet, though that truly amounts to no excuse at all. There were no tell-tale signs of an active trade to be read from his person or his clothing save for a few ink blotches on the thumb, forefinger and middle finger of his right hand indicating a more than average amount of writing in his occupation. Beyond that, and the fact that his status as an alderman indicates a successful businessman, I could tell nothing."

"Well, I have his address in my note book," insisted Watson, "so if we get a move on and you guide us along with that intimate knowledge of Glastonbury's geographical arrangements you have in that cranium of yours, we shall soon redress our lack of information concerning the man and let him know of our plans with regards to Bennet."

Quickly turning around and cutting through the practically deserted grounds of the abbey, the pair made way and was soon standing outside the premises of Randall & Jamison, Solicitors.

"Well," said Holmes, his triumph mixed with just a little mortification, "I was correct about the writing."

The two men entered, spoke to the clerk and asked to be announced to William Randall and that they were expected on a quite urgent matter. Less than a minute later, the senior partner emerged pulling on his coat and expressing his thanks for the arrival of the man he had described as the nation's "premier investigator" in his town, one so distant from London.

Holmes began by giving Randall an account of his necessary courtesy visit to Sergeant Holloway and of the man's willingness to proffer assistance where he could.

"Sergeant Holloway," repeated Randall. "Yes, a hard man but a true one and exceedingly fair with it. There've been more than a few tearaway types now grown to men in this town who have felt the sharp edge of his tongue and the sudden jolt of his boot and would publicly thank him for both. He's dragged more than one fool into court and then spoken up on his behalf and seen the fellow walk out with a fine and a warning rather than be dragged off to spend a year or more at Her Majesty's pleasure, learning some criminal trade. He'll give anyone a chance, but only one, mind you."

"He did strike us as that sort," commented Holmes. "But, as for Jonathon Bennet, we do believe that the wiser course of action would be to approach him first and officially receive our commission to investigate matters from him. Would you not agree, and would you be there in your official capacity at ten o'clock?"

Randall was silent for a few seconds before replying in the affirmative to both questions. "Yes. Mr. Holmes. I do see the reasoning behind your strategy. The mayor is a man who likes his protocols. So, it's tomorrow at ten o'clock at the Town Hall, then."

"Well, that's agreed." said Holmes, "Thank you Mr. Randall, and good evening."

The Mayor

"A solicitor, Holmes," chuckled Watson as they made way back to their accommodations, "And we thought Randall sold apples or trinkets or some such thing."

"Yes, and Jamison as well," acknowledged the sleuth. "At least now part of our picture is beginning to form, though we have made just a few brushstrokes on a work which will likely require hundreds, perhaps thousands, before it is complete. Now, here we are back at the Pilgrims' Inn, our place of rest and repose, but I do believe I am hearing the definite sounds of hungry diners being summoned to the table."

That said, Watson hurried inside and made his preparations for dining while Holmes, happy to have taken some small action on this first day of the campaign, joined his friend in the evening meal and, when completed, they both retired to their respective rooms to sleep off the events of a busy and somewhat eventful day.

Time was not pressing as Holmes and Watson met for breakfast after the gong had summoned what guests there were at the Pilgrims' Inn from their beds. Their meeting was not timed to occur until ten o'clock and they were only presuming that Mayor Bennet would be there as no actual arrangements had been made. Still, given what they had been told of the man, the probability was in favour of their assumption being correct. As the case had yet to officially begin, Holmes ate relatively well while Watson relished the opportunity to eat as much as he was able and readied himself for an extended sitting.

"I must admit to being a trifle impatient, Watson," remarked Holmes as his friend had risen to make an energetic foray to the buffet table in order to replace the bacon rashers which kept disappearing from his plate. "I am keen to get about gathering hard facts to replace this wild conjecture milling about in the front of my brain. I need to get some semblance of order in those cranial files of mine, as you so colourfully describe my orderly mind in those over-embellished stories of yours."

"You must learn to be patient, my friend," replied Watson returning with a plate bearing what Holmes would regard as three days' rations for a hungry man. "We have to wait for the mayor and cannot go off investigating without his official say-so. We have made contact with Sergeant Holloway and Mr. Randall and that is all that we could have hoped to accomplish by way of showing professional courtesy and establishing trust between them and us. So far, the trip has been a success. Now, eat something -- letting good food go to waste is a crime and don't forget that you are the nation's premier crime fighter."

Holmes did eat a little but the thoughts in his mind overcame any sense of hunger or desire for the satisfying taste of food. His body had been long conditioned to expect little in the way of nourishment when his mind told it that it had to run on its reserves, reserves occasionally bolstered by the odd slice of toast when they had run too low to provide for the brain which that body served. Plates and cups and cutlery were all cleared away by an ever-efficient staff leaving the two men seated at a bare table which seemed almost embarrassed and eagerly looking forward to being dressed in preparation for the midday meal. The three-quarter hour chimes on the hotel clock told the pair that it was time to be off; they had ample time to reach the town hall and wanted to be there on the stroke of ten to meet, placate and begin to work with what had been, to that point at least, a most difficult client. A little tact might well allow the man to save face and put him in a frame of mind to see his first encounter with the great sleuth as nothing more than a misunderstanding, a minor setback in an otherwise promising arrangement. Holmes could be quite tactful if he wanted to be but, sometimes, the man took perverse satisfaction in denying it to those who annoyed him.

Five minutes before the hour of ten showed on the town hall clock as Holmes and Watson mounted the steps and entered, there to find William Randall and Brian Jamison, both impatiently awaiting their arrival. The London pair was to find its intention to approach the mayor had been announced by the two solicitors, aldermen both, and that the mayor's disposition was both calm and favourable. As the town hall clock's bell rang out the hour, the four men knocked and entered the mayoral chambers, there to see Jonathon Bennet approaching with his right arm extended in greeting, though Holmes and Watson could not say for certain whether the gesture was genuine or contrived.

"Welcome, gentlemen. Please do come in and be seated," came from the lips of a man who had only two days before snapped orders at the very man he was now graciously, or so it seemed, welcoming and offering the courtesy of his office.

"Thank you, indeed, Mayor Bennet," replied Sherlock Holmes, taking the mayor's hand but refraining from mocking the man as "Your Worship" as he was tempted to do. "We have asked Messrs. Randall and Jamison to be so kind as to arrange a formal introduction between us so that we may recommence our discussions on a somewhat more amicable basis than previously when we were both obviously greatly fatigued and considerably stressed."

"Yes, yes. Indeed. Mr. Holmes, Dr. Watson," replied Bennet, greatly relieved that he did not have to defend his actions at Baker Street. "Please let us take that introduction as done and take some refreshment before we start our discussions. I must thank you both for coming so quickly to hear of our troubles and also to help if you so decide."

Jonathon Bennet took the handle of a small bell sitting on his desk and summoned the tea-lady who appeared seconds later pushing a wheeled tray containing a pot each of hot tea and coffee, a small jug of milk, a bowl of sugar cubes, five saucered cups and matching plates accompanied by serviettes, spoons and cake forks, all complimented by an assortment of small cakes and pastries, the finest Glastonbury could produce. Despite still being in the first stages of digesting his breakfast, Watson watched eagerly as the tea-lady served each of them in turn. The doctor accepted the mayoral offering with some delight while Holmes would take only a cup of black coffee and declined the solid fare with the explanation that he ate very little while on a case in order to maintain his concentration.

With their refreshments taken, the two aldermen and the London investigators waited for the mayor to speak first, deferring to the practicalities of the situation and the dignity of his office if not actually to the man himself. Jonathon Bennet had been secretly worried about meeting Sherlock Holmes again after their first meeting ended in an ignominious retreat following the detective's refusal to be bullied into action but now he sensed the chance to restart their association on more amicable grounds and with him at least appearing to be in charge. Appearances were all-important to Bennet though, as Holmes had suspected and been advised, there was real ability behind the bluster and belligerence.

"Mr. Holmes, Dr. Watson," the mayor recommenced, "as Mr. Randall has explained in brief, there have been unfortunate commercial repercussions of outrageous newspaper reports of unexplained deaths in our region, in Glastonbury in particular and at sites throughout Somerset generally. I, myself, find it difficult to believe that there have been any deliberate murders but there have been some incidences of death by poisoning, involving some of the wild herbs which grow in great profusion in our district. To put it quite bluntly, we, that is the borough council, would like to enlist your services in dispelling these rumours so that we can put a stop to the stories."

Sherlock gave a quick glance in Randall's direction and could see consternation on the man's face. It was clear from the man's facial expression and from their previous discussion at Baker Street that the solicitor wanted significantly more than a repudiation of the rumours to force a retraction of the reports. Randall wanted the murders proven and the murderer or murderers brought to justice so that the visiting public could be reassured of its safety.

"Mr. Bennet," responded Holmes, "I am in the business of uncovering truth and have no interest in achieving prearranged outcomes of a commercial nature. I shall agree to investigate the matters to which you have alluded but my investigations will go where the truth leads them and, when uncovered, those truths will emerge for all to see. If accidental death is indicated, I shall state that clearly; if, however, murder is indicated, I shall hunt down the murderer and see whoever that may be before a court which may then assign whatever penalty is prescribed. The truth in the latter case will not be pleasant but it will be the truth and the reputation of Glastonbury can then start to be rebuilt on solid ground and not upon some quagmire of lingering doubt about the matter."

"So," continued the sleuth after a pause of a few seconds' duration, "are we in agreement? Before answering, please appreciate the fact that I have no interest in embarrassing Glastonbury's citizens or damaging its reputation further, just the eradication of any agent of evil or wrongdoing which may be plaguing the town and region. It has been my experience that removing the cause of a problem has far greater advantages that covering up the immediate signs of trouble. My good colleague here, Dr. Watson, will tell you that a patient will want to be rid of the symptoms of a disease but he, as the investigating physician, has to get to the root cause and attack the agent of disease for the sufferer's long-term good."

"You put the situation and your position quite well, Mr. Holmes." acknowledged the mayor. "I can take executive action on this matter without recourse to further meetings of council, so I shall respond in the affirmative and engage your services forthwith, and those of Dr. Watson, of course."

"I would expect, of course, and as the public purse will be opening for these investigations," he continued, "that you would report any progress you make to myself and, perhaps, the other aldermen. This would be the right and proper way to proceed when dispensing the community's funds though I shall leave the timing of such reports to your own discretion."

"I see no reason not to do so." responded Holmes, "Though I may need to make use of any specific knowledge that you may have on the matter, whether factual, suspected or even presumptory. At this early stage I shall be gathering data, facts which will enable me to fully appreciate the situation."

"In fact," the sleuth continued, "I was hopeful of obtaining a significant amount of information in close detail this morning. I had assumed that for such widespread suspicion to be aroused there must somewhere exist a tabulated body of facts concerning the victims, their identities, their modes of death, their times and places of death and just who it was who made the discoveries, who signed the death certificates and if any critical examination was performed on the deceased. A temporary jump in the numbers of poisonings would not have attracted such attention – there must be a great deal more, either known or unknown at this time. Facts, gentlemen, give me the facts, all that you have and let nothing stand undisclosed."

"Agreed." said the mayor, "Mr. Randall, could you show Mr. Holmes that document."

William Randall reached into his inner coat pocket and drew out a document consisting of several sheets of paper folded lengthways and containing, as far as he could ascertain, the names and other details of the known victims, those identified as having died in circumstances which could be labelled very suspicious but for which the police could find no apparent motive.

The Document

Randall had, unbeknown to Holmes, approached Bennet and the pair had vigorous discussions on how they, as senior members of a council invested in caring for the district's interests, should proceed. The alderman would have preferred to have continued without the mayor's involvement but knew well that to do so would further alienate a difficult man who felt that he had been slighted, as indeed he had been for good reasons. The mayor, to give him due and to recognise the continued long-term success in his position, was pragmatic and knew when he should push and when he should bend. Randall had been able to persuade the dignitary that his own best interests, as well as those of Glastonbury and beyond, were centred on the commitment of Sherlock Holmes and, so, was convinced to submit to a significant degree of backward arching to get matters underway.

"I might have given this document to you last evening, Mr. Holmes," admitted Randall, "but I thought it best to go over its content and make any amendments I could so that it could be formally submitted on mayoral authority."

Holmes, seeing the desire of Randall to keep the mayor involved at the executive level but effectively excluded from all practical matters during the investigation, received the document and thanked both the mayor and the alderman and asked that his assurances of his own and Watson's undivided attention be passed on to the rest of the Council members. He then asked if William Randall and perhaps Brian Jamison would agree to being attached to the investigation team as the men had considerable local knowledge and seemed willing to assist. As well, the sleuth added, the two solicitors would be able to represent the mayor and the general council in their offices and capacities as aldermen and, in doing so, would lend official local authority which the London pair lacked.

The document consisted of three folded foolscap sheets pinned together at the top left corner, the first sheet containing the names and addresses of victims who had succumbed to poisonings officially declared to be accidental, all victims having otherwise been quite healthy and vigorous. The second sheet contained a similar listing but of eight persons who had recovered after falling ill and having shown the symptoms of various types of poisoning, while the third sheet listed the names of pilgrims who had visited the district and returned home and become ill, their names being compiled from enquires received by various medical practitioners around the country. In some cases, the names of the attending physicians were added while such information was missing for others. In none of the cases was the actual cause of death listed, nor were any of the symptoms pointing to suspicions of poison being involved.

"A good list, as far as it goes," observed Holmes, "but we'll need a great deal more information before we can hope to get the attention of the official agencies."

"We have more, Mr. Holmes," Randall responded, "but it is in a somewhat messy state and needs sorting and compiling. This is underway but the full detailed listings are as yet incomplete. There is much we don't know beyond the fact that quite a few had become ill, some had died and many more are extremely concerned that some poisoner is loose and killing at random. We are keen to find out the true facts of the matter and put people's minds at rest, as well, of course, of preventing any more poisonings, accidental or deliberate."

"If we do nothing," he continued, "we who sit on this council stand condemned for inaction. However, if we announce that we have engaged the famous Sherlock Holmes to investigate matters then we admit the existence of a murderer and also alert that murderer to the prospect of his being caught and risk his going to ground to avoid capture."

"It is a quandary, I admit," declared Holmes, "but Dr Watson and I had already been spotted even before we set foot in Glastonbury."

Holmes then proceeded to relate their strange encounter on the in-bound train with Adam Renshaw, a fact which seemed to irk the mayor and the alderman considerably. They both knew Renshaw and distrusted the man, though not to the extent of suspecting him of murder, and knew that the presence of Holmes and Watson would now be common knowledge well beyond the bounds of Glastonbury and that the newspapers were bound to demand some official comment.

"It is of little consequence." declared Holmes. "The news of our arrival was bound to get out and the talkative nature of this Renshaw will have pre-empted matters by little more than a day. On balance, it may well work in our favour as people can often be made to feel a part of the investigation if we ask for their help in local matters, matters of which we have little knowledge. Many may hold information of an entirely incidental nature, seemingly innocuous and benign information which, when looked at as a whole, may actually point us toward something of great significance unsuspected to date. Our presence, gentlemen, despite warning any murderer to beware, may just induce hesitant people to talk."

Two letters of contract were drawn up for Holmes and Watson declaring them to be investigative agents working for the borough council in the matters of the untimely and unexplained deaths. The letters gave the pair official sanction to question the officials and employees of the council but had little legality beyond that, nor outside the borough. Both London men were quite at liberty to ask questions of anyone anywhere but were conscious of the need to keep the local population on-side and the unconvinced police involved, informed and cooperative, certainly not antagonised and unhelpfully obstructive. The letters completed, they were signed and sealed and then delivered so that investigations could formally proceed. The mayor thanked both Holmes and Watson and asked that Randall and Jamison give the two men every guidance and assistance in the matters. Then, having bowed politely to indicate that formalities were at an end, he proceeded to open the doors to his office as if declaring that time was wasting and that they should all be about their appointed tasks.

All four men took their respective leaves of the mayor and proceeded outward as a group to make a plan of action, the first detail of which would involve going over Randall's document and making a list of vital facts to be confirmed or determined for each of the victims. It seemed as though Sherlock Holmes was embarked on gathering statistics but he explained that the case was complex and that all so-called known facts were to be treated as suspect and that a second document, when prepared, would contain only data whose veracity would stand up to minute scrutiny in any court of law. Sherlock Holmes, so often at odds with pedantic types like Inspector Lestrade, knew enough to admit that sometimes Scotland Yard's insistence on exact detail was correct when others higher in authority had to be convinced.

Selecting a venue for the discussions was relatively easy as the Pilgrims' Inn had a large dining area, barely used of late, one which would double as a convenient meeting room relatively free from prying eyes and ears. Watson made the observation that it was primarily a dining room and, as the hour for lunch was approaching, it might be convenient to meet there in approximately one hour's time for a meal which could be followed by an in-depth analysis of known facts and an assessment of all matters and persons involved.

Sherlock Holmes, though, could not see the need for an intake of even more food, his brain having been stimulated by the prospect of a challenging case probably involving murder but certainly featuring a number of unexplained deaths. He could only shake his head at this obsession people had for excessive sustenance which only acted to dull the senses. Still, a lunchtime gathering followed by a post-lunch meeting would be part of a process which would put facts before him in a systematic manner, facts which would need to be challenged and checked before their verification could be achieved. This would occur at noon at the earliest, but Watson declared his preference for returning to the Pilgrims' Inn to await Randall's arrival while Holmes decided to walk about his old haunts and rediscover the Glastonbury of his youth. This short diversion would enable him to ponder on several possibilities which had started to form into a preliminary hypothesis, one he would keep to himself until he was certain that no other rational possibilities were likely.

Watson heard the town hall clock strike eleven as he entered the Pilgrims' Inn and before retreating to his room advised the inn's staff of his intention to take lunch there with Holmes and two others. There he would lay on his bed and mull over what had just occurred and try to recall from his experiences the symptoms of poisoning from plants common to the countryside, though his actual first-hand experience was not overly high for the native herbal varieties. He had seen numerous cases of poisoning by strychnine and misuse of opiates, certainly derived from plants but glaringly obvious in their actions. Many cases involved personally prescribed medicinal usage which had been taken too far, sometimes accidentally, sometimes deliberately by suicidal individuals and sometimes homicidally by unscrupulous relatives bent on accelerating the inheritance process. Much of the misusage of herbal extracts was difficult to diagnose, often due to the subtlety of the action but more usually to the similarity between symptoms and the ability of tell-tale symptoms of poisoning to be masked by those from other less lethal agents added to draw suspicion away from deliberate murder. Where such confusion was to be encountered, however, he well knew that there were few medical types who could match the breadth and depth of the knowledge displayed in that field by Sherlock Holmes, an amazing fact about his close companion and investigative colleague which he discovered in the first weeks of their dual incumbency at 221B Baker Street.

By the time twelve o'clock sounded, Holmes had returned and Watson had arisen though neither man had progressed far into his musings. Preparations for lunch were progressing at the Pilgrim, and the two solicitors arrived to find Holmes and Watson seated at a table for four which would not suit their post-lunch purposes; the London pair had arranged for another large table to be made available for their deliberations. The two Glastonbury solicitors joined their colleagues and signalled to the waitress that they were ready to place their orders. General discussions followed with Holmes explaining how he had spent three summers in the district as a young lad and how he had explored so many nooks and crannies, specifically in Street and especially in Glastonbury. Learning that Holmes had resided with his Aunt Jane who was a secretive herbalist and that her young nephew had developed interests in that direction long before he had subsequently become an expert in poisons and general criminality further encouraged both Randall and Jamison to feel that they had real prospects for settling their problems.

Lunch was soon finished and both pairs of men were feeling a great deal more at ease with each other when Holmes, who had eaten practically nothing, suggested that they adjourn to the larger table where they could spread out and make notes of the known facts and suggested ways of approaching the people involved. Notepaper, pencils, pens and ink had been provided by the host and, as the four men took their seats, Randall drew the document from his coat pocket and handed it to Sherlock Holmes.

"These four people who have died will provide us with our starting point," began Sherlock. "We shall have to question the medical officers who signed the death certificates for the victims without causing alarm or professional resistance. Explaining that we need their help in an investigation intended to confirm their findings in order to negate rumours of murder should get around any resistance and Dr. Watson's professional standing will be of enormous help in gaining their trust. Inconsistent or anomalous findings concerning a victim's death will be our cue to look further, with or without the cooperation of that attending medical officer. If a pattern of such findings emerges, we shall have proven murder and can start to track down the murderer or murderers. If not, we can issue a statement to that effect but we cannot be certain that the rumours will not still persist."

"Now, Mr. Randall," he continued, "who is first on that list of yours?"

The Lists

William Randall, a country solicitor used to handling wills and probate and land title transfers and such, felt just a little apprehensive now that the long sought after and quite likely dangerous investigation into multiple murders was about to begin. Still, this is what he knew had to happen so he steeled himself, picked up the list, took a deep breath and slowly expelled it before reading off the first name.

"Rupert Wilkins, once a bootmaker; found dead by his housekeeper on the nineteenth of January last." he stated. "I do remember reading of his death as I had, up until he retired just a few years back, made use of his services, as had Jamison here. His shop was conveniently located close to our own premises and his work was of a high standard. I cannot envisage the man as having had any enemies. He was quite a likeable sort; not a young man but quite hale and vigorous."

"No further information, then? Nothing on the circumstances of his death?" queried Holmes.

"Nothing listed," replied Randall, "but I do recall mention of his being found slumped over his table after a meal. It was presumed to have been his heart by those gossips we find out after such an event."

Watson had begun a list of his own, starting with the deceased's name, his occupation and a presumed age of over sixty, that "to be confirmed" or "tbc" in the doctor's shorthand, and that his death may have been associated with consumption of food, though a heart condition may have contributed, that also "tbc." A space for the man's address was left blank and would have to be determined as would be the attending medical officer.

Randall waited until Watson had finished and read off the second name. "Phyllis Staunton, Mrs.; a widow; lived by herself in a cottage off the Bove Town Road. Age, not known for certain but put down as fifty-plus. We handled her will, you see, and we do have a few details. Dr. Fredericks was the attending physician and he put her death down to a fever contracted after exposure in a severe cold snap we had in January, or something of the like in medical jargon. She was healthy and active one day and dead the next"

A smile came over Watson's face at Randall's casual rendering of a professional medical colleague's official cause of death and recorded "fever" followed by "tbc" on his list. Both deaths had involved mature persons with no stated medical conditions known to explain their sudden deaths. This was not a pattern, not yet, but Holmes was listening keenly.

The third death to be listed was that of a younger woman, a Miss Beryl Armitage, aged twenty-eight who lived on the Street Road, and who had succumbed to a convulsion put down to an insect bite, though the death had occurred on a quite cold sixth of February when insects were notable by their absence and despite no bite being apparent on her person. The symptoms had seemed to suggest it, and there were no signs of foul play and a post-mortem examination had not been performed.

"That, in itself, is suggestive." broke in Holmes, "A woman in presumably good health dies in convulsions from a non-existent insect bite and no one is suspicious. This sounds to me like two cases of incompetence, one of diagnosis and one of procedural rigour. Do we know the name of the attending medical officer?"

"No," came from Randall. "We can, of course, find out and the death certificate will be registered and filed in the town hall, as will those for anyone who has died in the borough. The medical report may be there or may have been forwarded to Taunton, I can't say which."

Watson recorded the details once more with three "tbc" and two "tbd" notations added, plus "Taunton" with a question mark. The doctor then added, "I must say that I agree with Holmes. Insect bite, spider bite; either may be correct but to declare it so without physical confirmation falls well below the public's expectations of the medical profession. I would have opted for a post-mortem examination myself; convulsions certainly could suggest a case of poisoning, accidental or deliberate by some agent, human or insect. We owe it to the deceased lady to find out which."

"Quite so!" came from Holmes who had begun to withdraw mentally into his thought processes but who shook himself and stated, "A definite case which needs our minute attention, I would say. Now who is the fourth on that list?"

"Another Staunton," replied Randall, "John, aged forty; a distant cousin to the third victim and also to the husband of the second, though how close I can't say. There are quite a few Stauntons scattered hereabouts and they go back many generations. Found dead after eating a meal and retiring feeling queasy."

"I don't have an exact address," he added, "nor do I have the name of the attending physician. Do you wish to go through the other lists, those who survived? I have the names and most addresses of the local people but little more; fortunately for them, they didn't succumb to whatever ailed them but we are left with the opportunity to question each one directly, of course. For those from beyond our district we have their doctor's names and good descriptions of symptoms which developed after their visits."

Watson recorded all on his own list as Randall read off the names of victims who had succumbed and of those who had survived. All survivors from the district would have to be questioned and the relatives and associates of those who had died would be contacted for whatever information they might provide. The attending physicians would hold vital clues to the modes of death and the official records might also offer some guidance as to cause beyond that officially stated. There was much to do and learn over the course of the next few days but the kernel of an idea was forming in the mind of Sherlock Holmes, one requiring much mental food for thought before it might develop into a full working hypothesis.

In essence, Watson's list was not so different from that of Randall but was organised more systematically with columns holding up headings and with various notations made to indicate a definitely known fact, something requiring confirmation or something simply missing and needful of further investigation. The process was somewhat messy and awkward as some information did not settle neatly into the layout of the new document and long-hand notes had to be appended but, when finished, the investigators could prepare yet more lists, two in number, each specifying a series of tasks to be achieved by pairs of the four investigators according to their knowledge and talents. The game was not yet afoot but was definitely getting readied to begin in earnest.

John Watson, M.D., to give the man his professional letters, Dr. Watson to the world at large, was given the task of approaching the local medical practitioners in order to expand what little knowledge was held in his lists and as he could approach such people with significant professional standing. His letter of contract and the support of Alderman Brian Jamison would give him substantial authority though he also knew that, when enquiring about matters concerning a patient's medical matters, he must proceed as if walking barefoot over ground strewn with scorpions where the slightest false step could be perilous in the extreme. Before proceeding to make yet another list, however, that of all medical practitioners in the immediate district, Watson and Jamison would return to the town hall to peruse the records of recent deaths to fill in what gaps they could.

This left Holmes and Randall to acquire a full set of addresses for the surviving victims, though they thought it best to check in with Sergeant Holloway to appraise him of the outcome of their meeting with the mayor. The victims who had succumbed were more problematical in that relatives and neighbours would have to be contacted and these would be able to provide second-hand information at best, hearsay with little legal application but certainly something of the victims' histories in the days and weeks before their deaths might be obtained. Hard facts and highly coloured vague opinions would be the result and would have to be considered and sorted afterwards. The nature of criminal investigation, Randall and Jamison were about to discover, was not quite as exciting as John Watson's literary accounts but involved the sorting of fact after dubious fact until something resembling a clue made itself apparent. Lestrade and his official colleagues knew the process well and, though Sherlock Holmes was generally able to reject any case which offered excessive boredom, the sleuth had a personal interest in these matters and he had given his word, not just to the mayor but, by extension, to Glastonbury and to all of Somerset. He was determined to deliver security for the living and justice for the dead and, as the four men rose from the table to be about their respective tasks, the investigation had begun and the game was now most definitely afoot.

The town hall was close by and held all such detail in its substantial files and very little time was wasted in acquiring the information with the help of the file clerk, the junior official being ever so enthusiastic to help out in the investigations of the famous Sherlock Holmes, a name which generally opened doors but which had been known to cause a few to be rapidly shut in his all-knowing face. A quick walk to Benedict Street saw Sergeant Holloway seated behind the high desk beside the lower bench which partitioned the public and official spaces of the police station and along from a small door leading off the latter space to an area rarely seen by the general public and best avoided by those of mischievous habits. The sergeant stood and saluted his two visitors knowing that they would have come on official business and with official sanction.

"Good afternoon, gentlemen. Mr. Holmes, Mr. Randall," he stated with simple formality. "I had been expecting a visit from the mayor's investigative team. My many eyes and ears keep me informed of all goings-on in town and beyond. Please, how may I be of help?"

It was obvious to Holmes and probably to Randall that the sergeant was well-informed but was also over-keen to learn of the precise nature of the investigation. As the official "keeper of the peace," Holloway was as eager to find out facts as were his two visitors and did not like being kept in the dark in "his town" as he invariably referred to Glastonbury. This was a fact well appreciated by Holmes and, as the sergeant's reputation was rock-solid, the sleuth had no desire to keep anything from him unless its divulgence was likely to compromise some aspect of the unfolding case. Holloway was to be told of the intention to approach the victims, their relatives and neighbours and the attending medical officers, a list of the names having been prepared for him with an unspoken expectation of strict confidentiality, a confidentiality whose need was well recognised and appreciated by the wily policeman.

After paying their respects and having made their intentions known, Holmes and Randall took their leave of Holloway and proceeded to the former occupational locale of the first victim to enquire of its former occupant and to start gathering information of all pertinent matters and from persons who may have something to add. The information, Holmes well knew, would be a hotchpotch of half-truths, assumptions, guesswork and outright lies. The life of the investigator could at times be trying in the extreme but an experienced ear coupled with an eye sensitive to the visual clues unconsciously provided by the questionee could readily sort out the reliability of all responses. The former premises of Rupert Wilkins, now occupied and run by his eldest son Francis, was the first site to be entered in the investigation and William Randall was keen to watch the great sleuth in action. On that very first afternoon, the pair intended to find out as much as they could of the four victims who had succumbed, though that would be a very optimistic goal; still, Holmes was a seasoned investigator and sunset was quite a long way off on that long summer's day in Somerset.

The Search

Randall had often used the services of the first victim recorded on the list, one Rupert Wilkins who had a boot-making establishment on the High Street, one taken over on his death by his son, Francis. As Holmes and the solicitor retraced their steps and walked past the Pilgrims' Inn, the sleuth made mention of his youthful experiences in the town, and William Randall was surprised that this paragon of investigation whose very name was synonymous with London's crowded streets had spent so much time in and had such intimate knowledge of his home town and his local district. Holmes had previously made some mention of an association with Somerset, but Randall found that the famous sleuth could point out details of Glastonbury which were quite unknown to and never suspected by this native son born and bred and living within its bounds. Holmes had passed this shop many times as a lad but had paid it little mind as all of its operations were conducted out of public sight; his entry to Wilkins' Boot and Shoe Repairs was a first for him but was something Randall had done on a semi-regular basis. The solicitor called out for the proprietor, introduced the great Sherlock Holmes and related the reasons for their visit.

"Dad!" exclaimed Francis Wilkins in a tone of some annoyance. "Dad was as strong as an ox and I don't care what that quack Fredericks says. Dad was done in by someone: I don't know who did it but the man never had a sick day in his life."

"So, Dr. Fredericks was your father's doctor?" queried Holmes.

"Not really," replied Wilkins. "Dad wouldn't go near him, or any doctor for that matter. Didn't believe in them. Doc Fredericks, if he really is a doctor, came along the next day and signed the death certificate; didn't even give Dad so much as a decent look over, just said it was heart failure and went on his way."

"There wasn't much we could do," he continued. "Dad was dead and that was that, so we organised for a funeral. That happened three days later but you'll never convince me he wasn't done in by somebody; I just can't prove it and Sergeant Holloway says that he's got no cause to call for an investigation. After a few others died unexpectedly, I spoke to the mayor; he's a pompous sod but he did say he'd look into the matter especially as the newspapers got wind of something and embarrassed him in his little kingdom."

Holmes thought about these comments before asking, somewhat provocatively, "Is there anything about your father's business dealings or other matters which might point to someone profiting from his death in some way?

"I ask this question, Mr. Wilkins," Holmes continued, "not out of any particular conviction but to determine if there might be some commonality among various local deaths which would point to a particular line of investigation."

"I can't think of anyone who would wish Dad ill," replied Wilkins, "but I am absolutely convinced that his death was unnatural and that someone is responsible. I don't say certain murder but, if not, someone had done something to put his life in real danger. What I will do is go over his papers and contact you if I can find anything out of place. Doc Fredericks, well, his listed 'cause of death' was utter rubbish."

Holmes thanked Wilkins and suggested that he communicate any new information or pertinent discoveries to Randall's office which was quite nearby, then turned to leave and move on to find the former home of the next listed victim. Their walk along the Bove Town Road, which extended from the eastern end of High Street, was pleasant on that warm summer's afternoon, and Holmes could feel the spirit of Glastonbury soaking into his being much as it had done all those years before when he roamed the same streets in search of mental diversion and boyish adventure. The house in which Phyllis Staunton had breathed her last was not far beyond the feature Holmes knew as Mount Avalon and with which he had made the mental connection of place with myth as the legends came alive in his young mind. Phyllis had lived in the house with a younger married sister, Marie, six years her junior, who responded to a knock on her door to see two gentlemanly types standing back at a polite distance, hats in hands.

"Yes, gentlemen," she said somewhat sheepishly. "Can I help you in some way?"

"You may well be able to do so, Madam," came Randall's formal but courteous reply. "I am Alderman Randall and this gentleman with me is the famous London investigator Sherlock Holmes. Mr. Holmes has been engaged by the borough council to look into a number of unexplained deaths in our region, your unfortunate sister being among that number. May we come in?"

"Mr. Holmes. Yes," she responded, "I have heard of you, and read of your exploits. Mr. Randall, I do recognise you. Please, come in, both of you. You will take tea, of course; I was about to prepare some myself. Oh, I am Mrs. Graham, as you may know."

The two men handed over their hats which Mrs. Graham then placed on the small vestibule table after which her unexpected but welcome visitors were directed into a comfortably appointed sitting room.

"My sister and I would sit in this very room and take tea at this hour," explained their hostess, "but now it's a sad and lonely place without her. I am grateful for some company; there is a great need for life to be brought back into this house."

"I did not know your sister, Mrs. Graham," said the alderman, "but please accept our sincere condolences for your sad loss. And, Mr. Graham, is he at home?"

"Thank you, Mr. Randall, and no," she replied. "Mr. Graham travels a good deal on business. He is a representative for the Street Footwear Company and is often away during the week. But what is this about my poor sister? Has something been found out? She did not die from any cold fever; she had not been out of doors for days. Why would the doctor say such things?"

"That is precisely the question which we shall be putting to him, Mrs. Graham," broke in Holmes. "If there is one thing I do not like, it is an unexplained or unexplainable anomaly in a series of facts, and the man's actions fall into that category. My medical associate, Dr. John Watson, the author of those rather fancifully embellished tales of which you spoke, will possibly want details of a more medical nature sometime later, but we would firstly like to hear what you have to say on the matter of your sister's death if it is not too painful for you. You are obviously unsatisfied with the doctor's assessment."

"That, I most certainly am." replied Mrs Graham, totally unsatisfied with the medical assessment of her elder sister's death. "My sister would never have ventured out on such a cold and bleak day. She took great care of her health and had a great many natural remedies against winter's ills, remedies which she prepared herself and which had served her well over a good and healthy life cut suddenly short by something unnatural. People used to come to her for a healing potion."

"Unnatural, you say?" queried Holmes. "By that, do you mean that you suspect foul play, a deliberate act to see your sister dead?"

"That is what I do say, Mr. Holmes," came the reply. "Though who would wish such a thing upon my good sister who had done no one any harm in her life and would tend to any of God's creatures if need arose, I could not say."

"And the doctor who attended, who might that have been?" enquired Holmes, already anticipating the answer.

"Why, that was Dr. Fredericks." replied Mrs. Graham, "I really don't care for him much, always so grumpy at having to attend to the sick. He's just too impatient and says the first thing that comes into his head and will hear nothing to the contrary from those actually suffering.

"But just be late paying one of his bills," she added, "and he'll have someone around banging on your door to collect. He's attentive enough then."

The conversation continued for some fifteen minutes more with Mrs. Graham describing the various potions her sister once prepared, mostly soothing remedies to allow comfortable sleep rather than effecting cures, but Holmes thought to pose one more question before leaving.

"Would Mr. Rupert Wilkins, the late bootmaker up on the High Street have come to your sister for a remedy?

On receiving an answer in the affirmative, Holmes gave a simple "Hmmm" and then, with Randall, rose, gave thanks for their teas and then took leave of an appreciative and newly encouraged Mrs. Graham.

"There are more questions to be asked of both Mr. Wilkins and Mrs. Graham," Holmes declared to Randall as the pair made its way back to the High Street, "but we need to gather more facts before we can show whatever hand we hold in this strange game. This is how investigations proceed; one question here and another there until a coherent picture starts to form to guide the investigator to the decisive facts which fill in the gaps on the canvas. It does not pay to say too much and show just how much one doesn't know, or to push a witness beyond the point where recollection becomes coloured by the imagination. What the unstressed witness provides voluntarily can tell us a great deal, whether it be factually correct or incorrect in its nature. Patterns and anomalies are my stock in trade, Randall, and questions are the tools of my trade, and every problem demands the use of the correct tool."

"Our next port of call is down along the Street Road, if you can spare the time," continued Holmes to Randall as they stepped back at pace along Bove Town Road. "One Beryl Armitage who reportedly died of an insect bite mid-winter. I need to find someone who can tell us of her demise, but I fear that I'm taking you away from your work."

"Our clerks are quite capable of handling most of the enquiries," replied Randall, "and will record any matters needing my own or Brain Jamison's personal attention. I think that my time is better utilised attending to these inquiries, so on to Street Road, my friend.

"Your particular profession would be a boon to the likes of Wilkins," Randall continued. "You know; wearing out all of that shoe leather on all of these jaunts you go about on."

"Yes, legwork is a considerable feature of my work," replied the sleuth, "and no sooner does one foot grip a piece of the ground than the other races ahead to find a place to set itself down. Good leather and a spread of hobnails does wonders, though one needs a good pair of rubber soles to go creeping about in silence."

"No doubt," agreed Randall. "But I don't think they'll be needed to reach Miss Armitage's former residence. I'm actually enjoying the walk; I get so little outside exercise in my profession so let the leather wear a little faster."

The house in which Beryl Armitage had breathed her last was a boarding establishment owned and conducted by Mrs. Waldron, according to official records, a rather starchy and very abrupt woman, attributes no doubt acquired by necessity when dealing with tenants sometimes evasive and often tardy with their rents. Holmes and Randall stepped up to the front door and rapped three times with the elaborate door-knocker.

"I'm coming," came a threatening bellow from within. "Don't bash the door down."

Mrs. Waldron was a sight; she was not overly tall but her overall size and scowling countenance caused each man to take an involuntary step backwards before she continued her welcome with a "Yes? Why are you here and what is it you want? If it's lodgings, we're full; if it's money, you'll get none here."

"It is a matter of unpaid rent which brings us to your door, madam," said Holmes, trying to get the landlady's attention and presuming that she would have had more than one case of tenants leaving with rents in arrears. "That and the circumstances which may have led to some financial distress on your part."

Somewhat confused, the landlady could only manage an indecisive "What?"

"We are here as investigators in the unfortunate case of Beryl Armitage, your late tenant," insisted Holmes, "and our investigations to this point tell us that we are looking into an instance of deliberate murder on your premises. What the Taunton detectives did not want to countenance, Inspector Lestrade and others at Scotland Yard are keen to hear about before descending in force. I am Sherlock Holmes, a consulting detective engaged by your borough council, and this is Mr. Randall, a council alderman assigned to provide official support. We are hopeful that you might tell us what you know of these events and also if there are any monies outstanding."

The mention of "monies outstanding" registered strongly with the landlady who enthusiastically launched into an account of having been left in the lurch by various "misbegotten degenerates" who had taken unfair advantage of her good nature and generosity.

"Well," she then announced after having taken the time to draw breath, "I suppose you ought to come in and I'll tell you what I can."

***

EVASIVE ANSWERS

The Victims

Watson and Jamison had been off seeking out details of the town's medical practitioners as well as its reputed herbal healers, neither one of the two groups showing the slightest inclination to give the other its due in regards of efficacy but neither able to dislodge the other from its followers. To some, a doctor's word was gospel and a scribbled prescription in abbreviated and cryptic Latin was a symbol of some significant status, a certificate to be held up and discussed with the faithful who had gathered dutifully in the doctor's waiting room to be called and informed of the latest socially acceptable ailment shared by others and requiring a pill or tincture whose effects would provide bounteous opportunities for detailed discussion. Many of the herbal healer's followers were just as adamant about the need to return to nature and that the earth provided remedies sufficient to keep the population healthy. To them, doctors were intruders who refused to acknowledge that the spirit of the Earth was something real and these stethoscope-wielding imposters were only there to make money from other people's suffering. John Watson M.D. appreciated well that he would have to be careful when identifying himself to some of the herbalists while he might also incur the wrath of the local medical profession by seeming to question their diagnoses.

While Watson and Brian Jamison were trying to track down the medical reports and make appointments with unhelpful medical officers, Holmes and Randall were about to meet resistance and evasion from a group of former co-tenants of one of the deceased. A wily Mrs. Waldron had taken the opportunity offered by Holmes to vent her considerable spleen about unfinancial tenants, the sleuth hoping that this would make her conducive to giving out information on the state of Beryl Armitage's health and her activities just prior to her death. Holmes began by asking if Miss Armitage's rent was unpaid and, if so, for what period.

"They all owe me money," replied the landlady, "the whole lot of them. It's always 'next week' or 'I haven't been paid yet' but they always seem to have enough to go out carousing on a Saturday night. Beryl Armitage, though, did owe a fortnight's rent, but she always paid up, I'll give her that much; never failed. A seamstress of some description, she was, and got paid when her boss felt like it, as I hear it. Very quiet and not given to the antics of some of the rubbish I have had under this roof."

"As for her health," Mrs. Waldron continued as she began to relax after getting her main gripes off her chest, "she seemed alright to me, not so much as a cough as I recall, and she went mid-winter."

"Insect bites and fevers?" Holmes stated in a quizzical manner, "The death certificate was rather matter-of-fact about that. Does that sound correct?"

"Insect bites mid-winter!" the landlady exploded, "That doctor's an idiot or just plain lazy, or both. Miss Armitage did have a fever when she was carried off, but you'd be more likely to find a hundred pound note in the street than a living insect in all that frost and snow hereabouts."

"The young lady was in work, then; and in fair health or better?" asked Holmes, "And where and for whom did she work?"

"Yes she was, and for Gilbert Prescott; he does dresses and waistcoats and all sorts up off the Magdalene Road," she replied, "There's a group of them does piecework for the blighter; and a blighter he is, always late with what he owes his girls but ready to throw one out of work if she dares to complain. He's never short of a shilling himself, though. Doesn't go without, does he, that man?"

"Sounds a most disreputable type," declared Holmes. "Perhaps Mr. Randall here ought to look into such matters, though I'd say that this Prescott would keep just within the letter of the ;aw; he sounds that type."

"That is unfortunately likely to be true, Mr. Holmes," agreed Randall, "but we do have some powers to investigate the use and condition of premises used for manufacturing. Just as unfortunate, perhaps even more so, is that there are some in my profession who would take the man's money and twist the statutes around the victim's throat until he choked, or she in this case. It's money that talks loudest in our courts of law, make no mistake about that. There's nothing that will better clarify a legal position than arguments in sterling."

Mrs. Waldron did not respond; she knew all too well whose side the law would be on. To her, the law extended no further than the constable and bailiff, the former for matters of violence within her premises, the latter for evicting tenants over-tardy with their rents, though she did get more effective results by retaining a couple of very persuasive toughs. When she did speak, it was to ask what her two visitors actually wanted.

"Well, Mrs. Waldron," responded Holmes, "no doubt you have heard or read of the newspaper reports of poisonings in and around Glastonbury, and we are here to determine if there is any truth behind the headlines. What light could one such as yourself shine on these dark rumours? Do you or would any of your tenants know of anyone who might have had a grudge against Miss Armitage?"

"Well, I can't and I don't," declared the landlady with mock indignation. "But one or two of my other tenants may. She was pals with Misses Judkins and Rodgers; they work for that Prescott pig too. They're not here now and won't be back until evening, after work you see."

"They'd know more about the death of their friend than that Doctor Fredericks," she continued. "They were there when it happened; that Fredericks turned up as they were taking the poor girl's body away. He didn't even look at her; just asked the two other girls questions and filled in the certificate."

"Who brought up the matter of insect bites?" asked Holmes.

Mrs. Waldron thought for a few seconds then responded with, "One of the girls, it was Judkins I think, mentioned a small red mark on the side of poor Beryl's neck. I wasn't there so I don't know for certain; but the doctor couldn't wait to get back to his warm rooms and count his blood money for attending and determining the cause of death."

Holmes looked at Randall, then stood and told a surprisingly sympathetic and somewhat saddened Mrs. Waldron that they would return that evening to gather some first-hand observations from the two young women. Randall told her that he would do what he could to see that Prescott paid up what was owed in Miss Armitage's unpaid wages so that her outstanding rent could be finalised, and look into the matter of his withholding other moneys which he may owe.

The two men, sleuth and solicitor, began back toward High Street, both pondering on the nature of Dr. Fredericks and whether he might be complicit in the deaths or just lazy and

117

incompetent and, perhaps, corrupt. This was not the time to make such decisions, and both knew that much information would have to be collected before that time came. Watson would have to be involved and any questions put to Fredericks would have to be carefully considered beforehand.

Long summer days provided ample daylight for the men to continue, and Holmes thought that he would check in for messages at the Pilgrims' Inn and suggested that Randall do likewise at his premises. They agreed to meet in thirty minutes at the town hall and proceed to visit the home of John Staunton before returning to Waldron's Lodging House. The day would be a very productive one if both upcoming visits yielded as much as the first two and which the third promised.

Back at the Pilgrims' Inn Holmes found a message from Watson telling him that he and Jamison were off to interview a Dr. Gresham out on the Wells Road, the first of four medical men who practiced locally. Randall had found a similar note from Jamison and several others from his clerk on various matters requiring his attention. The solicitor wrote a few comments on each, gave numerous verbal instructions and then proceeded on toward the town hall.

"It's off to Manor House Road for us then, Mr. Holmes." he announced on his arrival. "Unless, of course, Dr. Watson had found something to divert us away from our plan."

"No. Nothing like that from Watson," Holmes replied, "just a note about the movements of himself and Jamison. We can be on our way to find what we can about events leading up to the demise of John Staunton. We'll say nothing about this Dr. Fredericks character; we'll just let the matter of the recording of cause of death come up in conversation and see what those close to the deceased might volunteer. His attending three out of our four suspicious deaths is highly suggestive but may well be explained by his being the only man available at the time; we just cannot say at the moment. We have a lot more facts to collect before we can begin to come up with a preliminary hypothesis, and I left Watson word not to talk to Fredericks until we can compare notes."

It seemed to Randall that they were doing a great deal more walking than asking questions and made comment of his impressions to Holmes, the sleuth replying that, "Walking is necessary to get from place to place, obviously, but it also affords us the time to mull over things in our minds. Many things we hear will not register as being connected at first, or even as significant, that is until the mind has had time to rearrange its new furniture. It is far too easy to take a notion as absolutely factual and act prematurely. Some of my official colleagues tend toward this erroneous behaviour and someone always pays a price, sometimes the detective in embarrassment but more often the innocent man accused and convicted and serving an undeserved sentence, or worse."

"I must admit," added Randall, "that I do step out of the office when things get too complicated, just to clear my mind, you know. So, then, let us walk on."

The pair stopped outside a house in Manor House Road and Holmes tugged on the bell-pull. It took only a few seconds for a lady to respond and brusquely ask her visitors of their business.

Holmes spoke up after the lady had given a short and quizzical "Yes?" with "I am Sherlock Holmes and this gentleman is Alderman William Randall, and we are looking into the untimely deaths of several persons in the district. Am I correct in assuming that I am addressing Mrs. Staunton?"

"Yes you are," replied Mrs. Staunton. "You would be here about my John, would you not?"

"Sadly, yes," responded Holmes. "Would you permit us to ask a few questions about the night on which you lost your husband? Our goal is to determine if anything unusual had occurred up until that time so that we may offer justice for those who have died and, of course, for their families. We also aim to prevent any more such losses."

Mrs. Staunton, her eyes watering a little, bade the two men enter and showed them into a sitting room where they accepted her offer of tea, not so much because they desired the brew but to allow the lady her act of generosity with this time-honoured ritual. After Holmes and Randall had waited several minutes, Mrs. Staunton appeared with the implements and ingredients of hospitality and began the process of pouring with the offering of cream or lemon and sugar to suit the taste of her guests. As she took her seat, Holmes was about to speak up and as gently as possible begin with his questions; before he could utter a word, however, the hostess spoke up rather bluntly.

"My husband did not die a natural death, gentlemen; I fear he may have been murdered!"

"I wanted to put that very question to you, Mrs. Staunton," responded Holmes, "though I did think to approach the matter a little more gently."

"I'm beyond the gentle stage, Mr. Holmes," the lady declared, "and, though it may not be a Christian thing to say, I would like to see someone mount the scaffold for what has been done."

"It may indeed come to that if our investigations prove a case of murder," Holmes agreed without committing himself to a preconceived conclusion. "But first we have to establish the facts of the matters; too much wild conjecture has been made by some unscrupulous journalists around the country and we must proceed in a steady scientific manner so that any wrongdoers can be brought to trial and convicted on evidence, not rumour."

"Your husband," he continued, "was he in good health up until his death?"

"Generally good," came the reply, "but he did have some digestive disorder in the months prior. He had visited the doctor who had prescribed some concoction but this had little positive effect and made things worse by giving John headaches. Mr. Fraser, the apothecary had made up the preparation but John thought to try a herbal preparation from Mr. Portland who shared the premises. He did get significant relief but the doctor was none too pleased; anyone would think that he owned his patients."

"And that doctor's name?" asked Holmes, clearly anticipating the answer.

Mrs. Staunton looked at both her guests in turn and said, "It was Dr. Fredericks. My husband liked him, but I think that he's well beyond retirement age; he just doesn't have what it takes to tend to the sick anymore, if he ever did."

"Fredericks," Holmes echoed while looking around knowingly at Randall, who simply nodded in acknowledgement.

The Lodgers

Mrs. Staunton, once wife, now widow of John Staunton, went on to tell Holmes and Randall how her husband had eaten his usual meal and followed this with an infusion of mixed herbs provided by Horace Portland, something which had given his indigestion considerable relief over the previous month. The mixture, prepared by Harold Fraser with whom Portland shared premises in a very unusual arrangement, had been a simple mixture of sodium bicarbonate and citric acid with peppermint oil added for taste. It had worked after a fashion and given immediate relief but masked the condition without actually removing it, and the relief was short-lived. Rather than neutralise the agent of digestive discomfort, Portland's herbal mixture actually encouraged the digestive system to activate correctly and generally avoid any problem.

On the night of his death, John Staunton had not, she continued, gotten the usual relief but had expelled the contents of his stomach and taken to his bed a little later when his system had settled. An hour after doing so, her husband had cried out in pain and complained of severe stomach cramps. The doctor was sent for but arrived too late, complaining and commenting nastily and quite unnecessarily that if her husband had followed his instructions, the dead man would still be alive.

"And the doctor's stated cause of death?" asked Holmes.

"Natural causes," was the reply, one edged with both anger and grief.

"There was nothing natural about it, Mr. Holmes," she continued, "it may not have been deliberate, I suppose, but my husband was definitely poisoned."

"Do you still have the mixture provided by this Portland?" asked Holmes.

"No." came the reply, "It was on our kitchen table when Dr. Fredericks arrived and not there after he had left, though others had been in the house at the time; you know, neighbours come in to help. I didn't notice it at the time but I have searched everywhere and asked the neighbours if they saw it. One said she saw the doctor pick it up and examine it but could not say if he put it back. It was a distressing time, as you would appreciate."

Holmes looked at Randall and then back to his hostess and stated, "Our investigations have been moved along considerably by what you have told us, Mrs. Staunton, and several matters have been brought closer together. I would like to halt our talks at this point as we are keen to speak with others who have suffered in similar ways to yourself. We will certainly have need to speak with you further but, should anything more come to mind on the matters we have discussed, may I ask that you get a note to .Mr Randall's premises in the High Street. Mr. Randall's partner and fellow alderman, Brian Jamison, is also a part of the investigation and may be trusted implicitly."

Mrs. Staunton agreed to both proposals and saw her two guests to the door, saddened somewhat but relieved that someone had at last taken her misgivings seriously.

It was now approaching home time from work for Beryl Armitage's former fellow lodgers, and the two investigators hurried off back to Mrs. Waldron's Street Road premises to await their arrival. They did not want to give their landlady time to advise the lodgers of the investigation and possibly colour their responses to questions. The pair was directed into the same common sitting room they had occupied earlier and left alone. Ten minutes had gone by when they were joined by another tenant, later identified as one Harold Walters, someone who seemed over-eager to cut short any investigation of Miss Armitage's life, or death.

"Beryl was a really nice girl, Mr. Holmes," he declared while looking directly at the sleuth without any mutual introductions having been made, "but she died and you shouldn't come around here digging up dirt about her. Just go away and let her rest in peace. You're not wanted here."

The man was clearly agitated but Holmes could not discern whether he was acting from some unrequited affection for or actual involvement with the deceased or even at the instigation of some third party. Holmes wanted to engage the man in calm conversation but any opportunity to do so was ended when the man suddenly stormed out yelling, "You're just a couple of parasites. Go away and don't come back or you'll both regret it."

"What on Earth ...," began a startled William Randall, his utterance curtailed as two young women entered asking who it was that wanted to know of their unfortunate deceased friend.

"You would be Misses Judkins and Rodgers," Holmes responded, "and I am Sherlock Holmes, a consulting detective working with Alderman Randall here on behalf of the borough council in the matter of a number of unexplained deaths of local people, your late friend, Miss Beryl Armitage, included."

The two young women went quite pale, both recognising the name of the great sleuth and simultaneously realising that the matter had suddenly become quite serious and would now be investigated fully by agencies well beyond Glastonbury.

"I must tell you," Holmes continued, "that the matters have been referred to Scotland Yard whose official detectives are awaiting my preliminary report before taking charge. I do not overstate the situation when I say that they now have very strong suspicions, as do I, that murder has been committed and will take a very dim view of any and all who fail to come forth with whatever information they may have."

If it were at all possible, the two young women seemed to go an extra shade paler than they were already after hearing Holmes' declaration, one designed to vigorously shake a hesitant tree free of any fruit reluctant to be picked. There was information to be had at Mrs. Waldron's lodging house and Sherlock Holmes was determined to have it divulged.

After all were seated, Holmes reassured the lodgers that he had come to determine the facts of the matters of local deaths put down to causes clearly erroneous, misreported at least. He went on to tell them that he was very unsatisfied with the official report and wanted to hear what either or both had to say on their friend's illness and death, and of the red mark on her neck which Dr. Fredericks had put down to an insect bite.

"I don't know what made the mark on Beryl's neck," remarked the younger of the two, a Miss Violet Judkins, "but it wasn't there when she fell sick. I should know, as I helped her undress and get into bed and sponged her head, neck and shoulders with water to keep her cool; she was burning up with some sort of fever. Marge, here, went off and sent for the doctor but Beryl was throwing her arms around and may well have scratched herself. I just don't know, I was helping a friend not looking for marks on her neck."

Marjorie Rodgers had been quiet up until this point whereupon she took over from her friend and announced, with some annoyance, that, "There were no insects or spiders or other crawling nasties in our room, Mr. Holmes, we keep it spotless and scrub it out regularly. Mrs. Waldron insists on it and inspects things all the time. She can be hard on us at times but she does run a clean house. You don't think that we had anything to do with Beryl's death, do you?"

Holmes smiled a little, looked at both lodgers and replied reassuringly, "At this point, we know very little for absolute certain and all of the people we must meet with are unknown quantities in a perplexing investigation. I have found nothing so far which would suggest that either of you is implicated but our inquiries must be thorough and recorded in detail so that the official agencies can act with complete confidence on them when they become involved."

"By the way," he continued, "Mr. Randall and myself were treated to a fiery exhibition by some gentleman whom we would assume to be another lodger. He seemed very upset at our presence and was quite abrupt in his manner of speaking."

"Oh!" remarked Miss Rodgers, "That would have been Harry, Harry Walters. He was very keen on Beryl, and her death was very hard on him. There was no understanding between them as far as I know, and Beryl never said if there was, but they did sit about and talk a great deal and often walked into town together. I'm afraid he hasn't gotten over her loss, though for that matter, neither have we."

"And what of the other lodgers?" asked Holmes, eager to keep this witness talking. "Would they have had much contact with Miss Armitage?"

"Well," restarted Rodgers, "there are only two others at present. Normally there'd be a full house but all these horrid rumours have kept visitors away. We often had the same people coming year after year on their pilgrimages, though I have only seen three years here myself. Mrs. Waldron keeps the best rooms for them, of course, as they pay a great deal more for short stays. Some might stay a week or two, others might be here for three months. It's a dreary old house without all that liveliness they bring, I must say."

"And the two lodgers you spoke of, regulars I presume," probed Holmes. "What can you tell me about them?"

"Oh, yes. Mr. Pritchard and Mrs. Farrington," came the reply. "Both are elderly and living on pensions, I believe; very quiet, both of them, but very nice with it. We often chat on Sunday afternoons as they both retire early, often well before we get home from work. Mrs. Farrington is in the small room next to us, ours being large enough for a triple and both in the main part of the house. Mr. Pritchard is in the wing, as we call it, the rooms extending to the rear and housing Mrs. Waldron's gentlemen lodgers. Mrs. Waldron keeps the two sections well apart except for dining when we all mess in together."

Holmes nodded and took a deep breath before returning to inquire further on the younger, more vehemently expressive male lodger, "Now, back to Mr. Walters. What can you tell me about him? His work; his background, his interests? Is there anything which you can offer?"

"He joined us in the latter part of last year," she responded, her nervousness on speaking to such a famous detective having dissipated significantly, "and I believe that he is employed as a day labourer for Mr. Renshaw, the furniture fellow, and has done some work for Mr. Pettigrew who has some sort of arrangement with Mr. Renshaw. More than that I don't know though his accent suggests he comes from up north. I only know that much because of the chats we all have at the dinner table. He can seem a little abrupt but he has always been polite to myself and Violet; it's just that his manner of speech tends to the precise matter-of-fact, his upbringing I suppose. I think he and Beryl might have made some announcement if things had not been cut so terribly short as they were; they'd have made a nice couple."

"Hmmm!" exclaimed Holmes looking at Randall and raising both eyebrows/ "Renshaw and Pettigrew. We must speak to them at some point; preferably quite soon."

Holmes could see that there was little more to be had by further questioning Misses Judkins and Rodgers. He had obtained important information about the alleged insect bite and his misgivings about Dr. Fredericks had compounded to the point where the man must be confronted about his inept diagnoses regarding the causes of death of all four suspected victims of foul play. The man was clearly unfit to continue but whether his actions were caused by deliberation or by incompetence Holmes still could not say. He must involve Watson in making such an assessment, though what backing the Glastonbury man might be able to muster to his defence and to what extent he was involved in wrongdoing were both unknown and to act precipitously could be dangerous in the extreme for interfering outsiders.

The Doctors

The long day was showing definite signs of coming to a close and the dining room at the Pilgrims' Inn beckoned, though the two Glastonbury solicitors had returned to their High Street premises before heading to their homes for the evening. Holmes was eager to hear what Watson and Jamison had learned from any of the doctors they had been able to contact, though he knew that information could be difficult to pry from professional men keen never to disclose their patients' confidential medical details. Still, as regards information, a snippet here and a snippet there would add to the mass of data accumulating from various sources, and the theme of the whole enigmatic mosaic would slowly reveal itself as its regathered tiles were painstakingly assessed and put into their proper positions, placed into a pending pile for further sorting, or discarded outright. There were still a great many tiles to collect, a great many empty positions to be filled, though it had been a good day for Holmes, and he was keen to find if it would get a great deal better.

Holmes and Watson were tired from the day's exertions; they, particularly Holmes, had traipsed back and forth across Glastonbury asking questions of people who were generally unconvinced that the deaths of their friends or relatives had been adequately dealt with or explained. Watson had spent much time sitting in and pacing the floors of doctors' waiting rooms with Jamison, only to find a reluctance to criticize a diagnosis made by one of their number. A quick removal to their rooms to refresh themselves was followed by a return to the hotel's dining room where their appetites could be appeased and they could discuss the day's discoveries.

What diners were to be found at the Pilgrims' Inn had already come and gone as the London men took their seats and their dinners were served. Even Holmes had to admit that his body needed recharging after its physical exertions, almost as much as his mind needed to re-sort its many new notions scattered throughout. As the meals were consumed, eyelids were beginning to droop but Holmes insisted that Watson should tell all before sleep found them both, and memories became hazy and indistinct as the dream world pulled them apart and confused them. Watson, though, was a little concerned at the prospect of having little of actual substance to report but took another sip of coffee before taking out his now somewhat annotated list of Glastonbury medical practitioners.

"We, that's Jamison and myself," he started, "have spent much of our day in waiting rooms just …, well, waiting. We first called on Dr. Gresham, but he was out seeing to a patient so we went off looking for Dr. Prendergast up on Manor House Road. He was in but had patients waiting and, try as we might, we could not persuade his nurse that our needs were more urgent than those of others; a good guard dog she would make, I must say, as no one would dare try to get past her."

Holmes smiled a little at his friend's comments, remembering the times he had tried to get past Watson's receptionist, shared as she was, at his own premises.

"Well," Watson continued, "after getting a good ear chewing, we gave our cards to be forwarded to the doctor and took our seats, quite impatient for our names to be called. This did not take all that long as the matters which Prendergast's patients brought him were of a minor nature, either that or he was over-quick with his diagnoses and keen to be rid of them after collecting his fee."

"Sorry, my friend," broke in Holmes, "but did you get any impression that he was the type to show disinterest in his patients?"

"Not really, it was just an initial impression, a wild thought on my part as a medical doctor myself," replied Watson, "but I will have more to say on that matter later. Now, we were eventually summoned to the surgery and both felt like we ought to bow down before this demi-god, sitting up resplendent in his inner-sanctum behind his highly ornate desk filled to overflowing with all sorts of showy medical knick-knacks. We were surrounded by highly impressive wall charts and all manner of apparatus, mostly outdated but still useful. Jamison and I both got the initial impression that patients may have been a necessary but highly inconvenient aspect of his existence."

"You say 'we'," interrupted Holmes once more. "Does this infer that Mr. Jamison was of the same mind in criticising the doctor, someone he may have had dealings with and who may well hold a significant social position in Glastonbury?"

"Jamison said that he had never met Dr. Prendergast," explained Watson, "at least not to his knowledge. You see, Prendergast is old blood in the town, from his mother's side at least, while Jamison and Randall are newcomers, only a meagre three Glastonbury generations to boast of, and social lines are still drawn hard across such barriers in some circles. I have colleagues in Harley Street who have fewer pretensions to glory and nobility. Still, Prendergast did seem keen to know what we were actually hopeful of discovering and had received communications from outside physicians seeking local advice for patients who had spent time in Glastonbury only to fall sick on returning home. He told us of five instances."

"Five!" echoed Holmes, "And did all patients recover?"

"That, he could not tell me," admitted Watson, well knowing that a single death outside of Somerset and suggestive of poisoning would likely get Scotland Yard involved. "But he did agree to follow up the matters with his distant colleagues. Jamison suggested sending each a message by telegraph and request an urgent reply; Prendergast said he would comply."

"Did he have anything to say of his local colleagues, Fredericks for example; especially Fredericks?" asked

Holmes, hopeful that Watson or Jamison hadn't mentioned his name in their discussions.

"Fredericks." mused Watson. "His name was spoken but not by myself or by Jamison. We enquired about Dr. Prendergast's knowledge of the causes of death for the four victims and he simply commented that Fredericks did have his limitations, but he, as a professional colleague, could not be expected to be critical, though he, Prendergast that is, might have looked further into the matters if he had been involved."

"So," commented Holmes, "you have made some headway, then. We shall just have to wait until the doctor's telegrams are answered before we can expect more from those quarters. Did the man strike you as competent, perhaps interested in his patients, or dismissive of their trivial ailments; trivial to him, of course. And, did you get to see Gresham?"

"Yes to seeing Gresham," Watson assured his friend, "but, as for Prendergast, the man did seem competent, perhaps just a little carried away with appearances. I'd say that one's standing in the community is of an overriding concern in these parts, though no more so than in many other places, and the doctor does seem to be a collector of medical curiosities. Some of the surgical implements he has on show look positively medieval and he took a little time to explain his interest, historical as that was. He could, if we don't alienate him, prove to be a valuable ally in our endeavours."

"Yes, yes!" commented Holmes, eager to hear more. "Though we ought not entrust too much to the man at this point; we don't know where his allegiances lie. But, please, go on."

"Well, there's not much of any great substance to report," admitted Watson. "We did finally get to see Dr. Baxter, but not before attempting to see Gresham who also practices on

Wells Road, quite nearby to Baxter. We had to wait, of course, but not for a long. Baxter, it seems, is a newcomer to the area and has not actually been made all that welcome by his colleagues, even though he did buy his practice from a retiring doctor, a man called Harrison. Baxter is the new boy and keen to treat the sick for what ails them, and he is a little like a medical Sherlock Holmes in that he examines his patients for clues in their manners of living and employment, not just in what those patients tell him. He believes in treating and healing the patient not just removing a symptom; quite a change from his predecessor, I believe."

"And a change for the better, I would say," declared Holmes.

"Yes, but old habits, Holmes," responded Watson, "they are the most resistant of all."

"In any case," he continued, "Baxter had little to offer us by way of information as he only took over his practice around five weeks ago, well after the troubles started, and he has had no contact with anyone suffering from the symptoms of poisoning. We then made our way back to see Gresham, hoping that he had returned which, in fact, he had. After a short wait we were ushered into his surgery and could not help but notice the complete opposite in the accumulation of medical clutter from that of Prendergast. The desk top featured a very plain pen and inkwell setting, a blotting board, a notebook and a neat pile of loose prescription forms, and the walls were bare save for his medical diplomas. He was no help at all."

"And from where did the good doctor graduate?" asked Holmes of a weary Watson who sheepishly had to admit that he hadn't actually noticed that detail.

"Well, as the man was of no help, it is probably of little actual consequence," conceded Holmes who then insisted that Watson continue with his report.

Watson yawned, obviously tired and keen to retire to his bed, but looked back at the notes he had made on his list and continued with his account of his conversation with Dr. Baxter.

"Dr. Baxter seems a most competent fellow," he declared, as if to make some distinction between that man and, perhaps, Prendergast, "and he was fully prepared to comply with our requests for information except that he had little to do any complying about. He had treated a few patients for symptoms which could have been the result of poisoning but which could just as readily have stemmed from some pestilent biological agent common at that time of year in these parts. He, too, had received requests from outside colleagues seeking guidance for patients who had returned sick from a visit to Glastonbury and its surrounds, two in number. Like Prendergast, he agreed to contact those colleagues seeking details of their patients' progress but suggested we contact Harrison in Bath."

"And that about covers our day's exertions, mine and Jamison's," concluded Watson, "and I'm now off to bed. I'll leave you to sort out that brain-attic of yours. Mine is full and jumbled and I'll sort it out in the morning, or I'll just shut the door on it and ignore it."

"You should do that Watson," agreed the sleuth, "I need a little more time to reflect on this day's revelations and I've some questions to get ready for our intriguing Dr. Fredericks. A pipe should suffice for what limited information I have, though I do feel that our agent of death lies outside of the medical profession despite, or perhaps because of, someone's apparent incompetence."

Holmes retreated into the inner recesses of his own tobacco-enhanced mental world where numerous scenarios could be visually brought into being and tested. Some would be discarded, others retained until further facts supported their continuation or had them relegated to the oblivion to which so many others had been cast. At this stage, no glaringly significant clues had become apparent but some inconsistencies in the descriptions of Doctors Fredericks and Prendergast would merit further investigation, as would the relationships between and common acquaintances of the victims, deceased and otherwise. There was also Harrison to consider. Lamps were extinguished one by one throughout the Pilgrims' Inn, and Holmes found himself in virtual darkness save for the faint vestibule nightlight and the feeble filtered glow from the streetlamps dimly illuminating Glastonbury's High Street and entering the dining room window. There were many more facts to ponder, many more people to interview, but a busy day had come to a close and all of Glastonbury had entered into slumber, a state now calling the great sleuth so that mind and body could be rested for the next day's exertions.

Morning found Holmes and Watson breakfasting and desirous of being off on the attack together. Randall and Jamison had each expressed the need to attend to a number of urgent matters for insistent clients but with the promise that they would both be available in the afternoon should they be required. The two solicitors had discovered that the excitement of the detective's existence was something experienced only after an enormous amount of walking, tedium and disappointment, three attributes whose quotas had not yet been in any way exhausted in the current case. With their fasts suitably broken, Holmes and Watson both took a second cup of coffee before rising from the table and proceeding out onto Glastonbury's ancient and well-trodden

High Street from which they would make their way to the premises of Dr. Fredericks.

Anticipation was mixed with more than a little trepidation at what might be gleaned from a visit with the intriguing doctor as they stood at his threshold. With the man's response quite probably holding the key to the mystery, though, Holmes and Watson entered into his premises, showed their letters of contract from the borough council and insisted on an interview.

"Send them in," came from an adjacent room and the two men, the sleuth and the doctor, entered intent on getting express answers to their determined questions.

The Warning

Dr. Fredericks was an unknown quantity to the two investigators who, nevertheless, had each formed an image of the man, and an unflattering one at that. Before them and effusively welcoming them both to his premises was a man of substantial physical structure, not overweight and portly but large and athletically built despite his obvious seniority.

"Welcome to Glastonbury, gentlemen," he offered with apparent sincerity. "The word is about that you are looking for suspects hiding somewhere in our fair town."

"What on Earth ....?" Watson thought to himself as Holmes stepped forward and gripped the Glastonbury man's hand saying, "Thank you, Dr. Fredericks. The borough council has asked us to step in to help sort out the rumours of death lurking in the shadows of Glastonbury. I am Sherlock Holmes and this is my professional colleague, Dr. John Watson, also a member of your own august profession."

"And a writer of some repute," added Fredericks by way of a reply. "I trust, also, that Dr. Watson has not exaggerated your capabilities in his literary offerings and that we can expect great and rapid revelations."

"Any success I have enjoyed, doctor," countered the sleuth, "has been hard-won by taking whatever steps had been required, steps as elongated as necessary and as many as necessary. I am not given to making premature declarations of either guilt or innocence and will be certain of my facts before I speak or act."

"Admirable! Admirable!" exclaimed Fredericks while retaking his seat and slapping his desk-top with the flat of his hand to emphasise the sentiment., "Now, we here, all three of us, are busy men, so if you have questions to ask of me then let us be about it."

"The case of Beryl Armitage, a young lady who died last winter, is of some concern," began Holmes. "We have been given accounts of the bite on the victim's neck having been made by her own actions; it seems that her arms were flailing about towards the end and the marks were not there when she was sponged down by her friend."

"Yes, yes," was the doctor's reply, to which he quickly added, "But Somerset is not London and Glastonbury is but a small part of Somerset and here we look after our own, no matter who that may be. The unfortunate young woman, as you have discerned, was not affected by the bite of any insect but had actually succumbed to the effects of some insidious narcotic agent and listing the cause of death in the manner I did was by way of easing the distress upon her family and friends, distress which would naturally follow from the loss of someone so young."

"So, the mis-stated cause was by way of a kindness, then?" asked Watson who was both shocked and surprised that a medical officer attending a suspicious death should be so cavalier about the contents of official reports. As Watson saw it, all deaths of youthful persons were to be regretted but the pain felt by family would be immeasurably worse if it emerged that officialdom had failed in its duty to the deceased, the family and the Public at large.

"Yes, yes. You could put it that way," agreed Fredericks, obviously a little uncomfortable at the prospect of having to account for his actions.

"And the narcotic agent," added Watson, "that is without doubt?"

"Yes, yes." repeated Fredericks, "A classic case; very disappointing and what a waste of human life, but people will not be told."

"There were three other deaths brought to our attention," continued Holmes, jumping in to keep the doctor under some pressure and talking without having time to think, "all attended by yourself, and whose recorded manners of death seem to be somewhat at variance with accounts of those present, witnesses if you will. The deaths were those of Phyllis Staunton, John Staunton and Rupert Wilkins; all toward the end of last winter and all attended by yourself. This, of course, is of some concern to an outside investigator, I'm sure you would appreciate. Could you give us your accounts of the matters? My first report, I must advise you, is given to the borough council but I am also legally bound to keep the local police informed as well as a Scotland Yard inspector who has insisted on receiving any news on the matters."

Dr. Fredericks pulled out a desk drawer, reached in and extracted four slim files and spread them out on his desk-top. Holmes and Watson both bent forward to read the file titles and both noted that they bore the names of all four victims they had just mentioned and made enquiries of during the previous day. It would have been some incredible coincidence that those four files and no others would have been lying there, and Watson did not need the insight of Sherlock Holmes to see the significance - Fredericks had been advised of their movements or had anticipated those four deaths being investigated and had, either way, taken steps to prepare himself for interrogation.

"Yes … Staunton … Phyllis," he started with deliberate slowness. "A case of fever brought on by exposure; very unfortunate as the woman was in fair health. She should not have been out on a day such as the one before her death; should have known better."

Holmes nudged Watson, signalling that they should let Fredericks continue. He had already admitted to falsifying a medical report but had tried to make his actions appear to be those of a benefactor, not someone derelict in his duty.

"Rupert Wilkins, a heart attack," Fredericks continued. "Nothing of any account there, nothing to raise any suspicion; the man did have an on-going medical condition and was getting on a bit. And John Staunton; he died from complications brought on by using quack medicines instead of what I had prescribed. His condition had been a chronic one and was taking some time to settle, but the man, at the probable instigation of others, went searching for some magic witches' brew for a quick cure. Well, quick it was but it was no cure. Very unfortunate, very distressing for his wife."

"So," said Holmes, entering a few notes into a small book he carried with him, "you would stand by your diagnoses in the latter cases, though the first, that of Armitage, you did amend for the reasons you gave?"

"Yes I would," retorted Fredericks, "and I'll challenge anyone to say different. The case of Armitage was exceptional and I took action befitting someone of true sympathy for others, no matter the strict legalities; there was no harm done as the circumstances were not suspicious."

"Now, gentlemen," he added in bringing matters to a conclusion, "I have patients to attend to and my time is precious. So, if you would not mind, I must ask you to excuse me as I have some distance to cover this morning; a rural patient, you know."

At this point, Holmes insisted on a continuation at a later time, but Fredericks became quite irate and told the London pair that further questions would be an unnecessary slight upon his character and good name.

"I have been frank and honest with you, gentlemen," he demanded, "but any further instances of my assessments being questioned, and I'll have a writ served on you both for slander and harassment, Do I make myself clear?"

"As clear as day," replied Sherlock Holmes with a knowing smile, the sleuth now certain that Dr. Fredericks had something to hide. The man was mentally alert and his medical knowledge did seem sound, at least to Sherlock's level of comprehension, though Watson might offer some professional comment when they had left the premises. What the doctor's motives might have been in making those misdiagnoses, Holmes could not say, but Fredericks would not be written off any list of 'interested parties' to a series of 'suspicious deaths', though he could not, with the evidence held at that time, be declared a suspect.

Holmes and Watson found themselves outside and walking back toward the High Street in short time, the sleuth satisfied that headway had been made. The doctor, the old campaigner that was Watson, was visibly shaking his head in disbelief at what he had heard.

"Well," said Watson with just a note of perverse satisfaction, "you certainly rattled that cage and got the bird singing, Holmes. I believe that he's now trying to remember what he said and if it was too much."

"Indeed I did," agreed Holmes, "but we have yet to determine just what breed of bird he is and what makes him sing. He did not seem in any way confused about events, nor did he give me the impression of being incompetent. In your capacity as a medical man, what did you make of him?"

"I'd say that he knew exactly what he was doing," replied Watson, "though I do think that he might get away with his explanation about the erroneous cause of death recorded for Beryl Armitage."

"He's nervous, though," Watson continued. "That outburst at the end ... well, it was tantamount to a confession of wrongdoing of some sort. He does not like being pressured and that may be his undoing. Interesting days ahead, I'd say, Holmes; very interesting."

"Yes, most definitely," again agreed Holmes. "though I'd say that Dr. Frederick's patients may run a poor second to some as yet unidentified other parties when making their demands on his time and attention. He'll be off talking to his confederates at his earliest opportunity; I do wish we had a few Baker Street Irregulars here to act as extra eyes and ears but we must make do with what we have."

"I'm yet to be completely convinced of deliberate homicide," Holmes explained, "but I am absolutely certain that matters have been covered up for reasons unknown but which tend to the extremely suspicious. The game, Watson; it gains momentum!"

"And what of our railway companions?" Watson mused. "Should we not be seeking out connections between Fredericks, perhaps, and that Renshaw fellow, or some of his cronies? There is something to uncover here though I must admit that I'm still not fully certain of just what treasure we're digging for."

"At least I think we might say we're on the right island and have found traces of the trail left by those pirates who buried it," Holmes declared with some definite sense of self-satisfaction. "We'll know what we're looking for when we find it. We have no pirate's map to guide us so we'll just have to do lots of digging and watch for tell-tale signs."

"Signs of what?" Watson demanded in mock exasperation.

"Signs of tales told, my friend," replied Holmes knowing full well that Watson understood that their quest was always going to take them into the unknown. "And we are in the right place to encounter great tellers of tales, standing here as we do on high and holy ground, on this Isle of Avalon. There is someone I would like to seek out, someone who may have shuffled off this mortal coil, as the Bard would put it, or someone still here in Glastonbury but retired from active duty."

"And who might that be?" enquired Watson.

"A policeman, Watson," said Holmes with an air of anticipation in his voice, "A policeman whom I encountered many years ago and who showed great patience with a young lad left abandoned but prone to ask far too many questions and make too many ill-informed and impertinent suggestions. It is a Sergeant Bridges of whom I speak, one who manned the desk now supporting the form of Sergeant Holloway, though how many sergeants have come and gone in between times I cannot say; it can't have been too many. Where I might find him, I can't say; if he's left the district, my search will be futile; if he's still hereabouts, perhaps there's some record of him at the town hall."

"But wouldn't Holloway be likely to have such information?" suggested Watson. "He is sure to have had contact with this Bridges in the course of his duties, long arm of the law and all that."

"Quite likely," Holmes agreed. "But we don't want Holloway knowing all of our plans. If we can locate this man perhaps we can come upon him via a contrived accident, and I can recognise him, just in passing, you know; or perhaps I'll just step up and knock on his door."

The Hint

It seemed to Watson that their investigative nets were being cast over ever so much wider ranges rather than being pulled closer and closer to shore with their catches. This new line of enquiry was likely to add at least half a day more to their quest, a quest yet to make contact with known persons of interest. Now here they were set to embark on a search to find a quite obscure source of dubious information, one which might well end with them both staring at a tombstone in the grounds of the cemetery and having nothing to show for the extra time spent. Watson, though, knew his friend well and, as a result, knew it would be futile to try to divert him away from this course of action. He went along with his friend's plan and bit his lip; after all, Holmes had so often picked a vital clue from a great clutter of facts and conjecture which others had examined and from which they had failed to discern a single useful piece of evidence.

The town hall clerk was again very helpful and informed the London pair that ex-Sergeant Bridges was still living in Glastonbury, supplying his address and directions of how to get there, unnecessary as it emerged as Holmes knew the area well. The walk down to and along Coursing Batch and beyond the looming Glastonbury Tor with St. Michael's Tower looking down upon all who would pass by was a little lengthy but cabs were not so numerous in Glastonbury as in London and exercise was a commodity in grand abundance for those wishing to get anywhere. As with his earlier walk along the Bove Town Road, Sherlock felt emotion welling up inside him, a feeling not unwelcome for the average human being but, average, Sherlock Holmes was not, and he struggled to keep his feelings in check.

Control was soon re-established and the mind of Holmes could once more focus on the job at hand, that of locating Bridges, not such an onerous task as the young Sherlock had walked this path and beyond on many occasions. The house of the now quite elderly ex-Sergeant Bridges was soon located but was showing little sign of life and Holmes decided on a quick foray back to the tor and a history lesson for Watson.

Glastonbury Tor had been the dominant feature of an ancient landscape when the first adventurous humans came to reclaim the land so many eons ago. It was still dominant for those who approached in the modernity of the nineteenth century, even more so with the remnant Tower of St. Michael's Church standing sentinel at its summit as if laying claim to its ancient form, as indeed it had until its ruin in the centuries preceding. Somehow, with that ruin, the tower had become an integral part of the ancient tor itself, a fundamental feature of its legend and mystique, though it was merely the most obvious of many, most of which went unnoticed by all but the most dedicated pilgrim, and some others.

The pair arrived at the base of the tor with Holmes excitedly expounding its height above the surrounding Levels and its estimated volume in cubic yards and how the Church of Saint Michael had been destroyed and demolished, all except for the mighty shell of its massive tower, and how an older wooden church had succumbed to earthquake in the thirteenth century before being rebuilt in stone and how evidence of much older structures had been found giving support in some circles to the Welsh legend of the Fairy King living underground and being in league with the Devil which is why the church was dedicated to St. Michael in the first place. Holmes drew breath only to start again but, it seems, he was talking to himself or, perhaps, the Fairy King of his youthful imaginings. His friend had become lost in the details.

Watson had paid very little heed to what Holmes had been saying, except for the fact of St. Michael's Tower being a shell and something about fairies living underground. The doctor could see that Holmes was drawn to the place in a way he had never witnessed of his friend in all their years of collaboration. It was a bit too much for Watson, the lesson and the effect on the teacher and he suggested going back to Bridges' to see if the ex-policeman had emerged.

History lesson definitely over, such as it was, the pair ambled thoughtfully back to the home of ex-Sergeant Bridges where definite signs of activity could be seen through the open curtains. Holmes smiled a little as he walked through the gate and marched up to the front door, a door which opened before the sleuth had time to raise his hand to knock.

"Well, as I live and breathe," declared the ex-sergeant while displaying the broadest of smiles, "if it isn't Sherlock Holmes. And here's me in my socks and unable to see him off with the toe of my size tens. He'd better come in, then, and his friend; that'd be Dr. John Watson, if I'm not mistaken."

"Mistaken, you most certainly are not," countered Holmes reaching out to grip the welcoming outstretched hand of someone whose form he'd not laid eyes on in decades. "You are correct on both counts, Sergeant Bridges, and those eyes have lost little of that sharpness for which they were renowned; nor that mind, for that matter."

"Yes, yes," agreed Bridges, "but perhaps their edges aren't quite so keen as they had been. I keep myself busy, you know; I might not wear the stripes any longer but I'll be on duty until the day I die."

"You may well outlast us all," offered Holmes who then turned and summoned Watson forward saying, "And may I introduce my good friend and colleague Dr. John Watson, though it seems his fame has preceded him. Those stories of his have spread his name far and wide and have ruined many an elaborate introduction on my part.

"Now, you know who we are, obviously," continued Holmes, "but do you also know why we're here? Everyone else in Glastonbury seems to."

"Well, welcome back to rural England and its ways, Sherlock," declared Bridges. "And a most sincere welcome to you Dr, Watson; your fame indeed goes ahead of you as this young troublemaker with you so rightly suggests."

Watson could not restrain a broad grin at the words of mock disdain used by someone who had known Holmes in his youth and who obviously held the memory with some affection. He would be keen to hear any and all accounts of his intriguing colleague in his formative years though he knew this would be discouraged for reasons of expediency and, perhaps, some little embarrassment.

The hospitality of the house was not forgotten as Bridges excused himself and left his guests in order to place a filled kettle on his kitchen stove and then throw a few more off-cuts into its firebox before stoking the flames back into life.

"Tea will be up in no time," he yelled to his guests, "just find a chair and plonk yourselves down; no need for ceremony. After all, Sherlock Holmes is practically family, you know; the prodigal returned, you might say. A slice of cake each won't do either of you any harm either, I'd offer."

Watson smiled as he took his seat in anticipation of a most welcome refreshment while Holmes excused himself and joined his old mentor in the kitchen.

"It's very good of you to offer those kind words, Sergeant Bridges," said an uncharacteristically sheepish Sherlock Holmes. "I do feel a sense of coming home after a long period of exile and your home has a feel of welcome about it, though this is the first time I've ever set foot over its threshold. But I've come chasing death, I'm afraid, or at least some of its despicable agents."

"You're not the only perceptive person in the room, Sherlock," laughed Bridges. "I do know why you're here and what you've been about. And let's be done with that Sergeant Bridges business; my name is George and you're old enough and experienced enough to call me that. Now, make yourself useful and cut three pieces of that cake on the board, and don't be ungenerous with the thickness. Water's bubbling hot so let's be about our tea and cake and we'll go over a few matters while we all indulge ourselves and you two rest your legs."

As the three sat sipping tea and consuming cake, Holmes related his version of his youthful visits to the police station to ask all manner of questions on procedures and police work, questions -- "How do handcuffs work?" "Is gaol the same as prison?" "Can a policeman arrest the Queen?" "Why are British sheriffs different from American ones?" "Can you get hanged for accidentally poisoning someone?" -- and a hundred others just as inane and just as annoying to a busy sergeant who, nonetheless, did his best to accommodate the interest of an obviously intelligent lad who had lost both parents and was under the care of an elderly aunt.

George Bridges remembered things a little differently and described how a young lad often came and sat in the police station reading lists of regulations from wall charts and studied the pictures of wanted felons, all the while making suggestions of how the police could do their jobs a great deal better if only they would think ahead as he would if he were doing the job. He laughed as he told Watson of the times he had to chase young Sherlock off the premises after his constant chatter drove everyone mad and how he once threatened to lock him up in the cells so he could find out first-hand how it felt.

Holmes smiled with genuine pleasure at all the reminiscing, then he put down his cup and leaned back as his face took on a rather serious expression.

"That, of course," he said, "was then, but now I have come to annoy a completely different set of people -- those complicit in these deaths and in diverting the attention of the authorities away from their true causes."

"Precisely!" was the determined response given by Bridges, obviously expecting more to follow from Holmes.

Holmes then proceeded to tell Bridges of the events of the previous few days, from the visit of Bennet to Baker Street, through the encounter with Renshaw on the train and on to the strange interview with Fredericks that morning. An hour went by with numerous teacup refills being required and occasional input coming from Watson when he felt that Holmes had not been as thorough as he could have been or when medical information had been required. He told of his official meeting with Bennet at the town hall and of his courtesy visit to Sergeant Holloway.

"You've made a good start," commented Bridges, "but I'd be very wary of Renshaw and Fredericks – not the most trustworthy of fellows, I'm afraid. Holloway is a good man but is no detective, and I'd make sure I kept Bennet moderately well-informed and on side."

"Thank you for the advice," said Holmes who then added, "This afternoon we are to meet with either or both of Randall and Jamison, solicitors and aldermen whom the mayor has attached to the investigation by way of being advisors and bearers of official rank and standing. They have been useful in opening a few hesitant doors for us."

"Yes, they would have been," agreed Bridges, "but, again, they are somewhat bureaucratic in their outlook and are certainly not suited to real detective work. In some cases, their presence might well compromise a line of questioning for those unwilling to let the borough council in on the close details of their businesses."

"But, enough," he declared, calling a halt to the serious side of the conversation. "Have you felt yourself settling back into your old haunts in the short time you've been back; into the feel of the place?"

"The atmosphere of Glastonbury on this ancient isle, and indeed that of Somerset, is out there," Holmes declared. "I feel it all about me but it's been hard to fully recapture what I recall feeling all those years ago as a young lad."

"I know that the memories of one's youth are coloured by the passage of time and later events," he continued, "but I know there is something way down deep in my mind which is desperately trying to work itself free. It's the tor; perhaps I should climb it once again and contemplate its ancient mass and all it surveys."

"But Sherlock," countered Bridges with an all-knowing and somewhat mischievous wink, "you don't really think that our tor standing so high above the surrounding lands as it does is simply a naturally occurring solid mound of dirt and rock, do you? Just what do you think might be found beneath, on the inside? Something to think about, my lad, something indeed for that brain of yours to contemplate and work out."

***

AVALON CALLING

The Game

It had begun many centuries before, this regal association with the legendary Arthur, perhaps once a king but certainly one become real when the land of the Britons became Britannia Royal and her many histories merged into her hazily-known but long-related lore. That the man may well have had some basis in fact is rarely disputed, though the details of his birth and life and death are less matters of historical reality than they are notions of belief and legendary belonging which permit, even demand, a focus for a heroic but time-distant beginning of national identity. The personification of Britannia provides the nurturing maternal spirit from which all of Britain's children have sprung while the virile vitality of Arthur is there ever-ready to once again pick up Excalibur, the sword of retribution, and bring it down on all who would threaten his islands. His is a composite spirit which infuses all born on Britannia's shores, and the Glastonbury Tor sitting high over the Isle of Avalon beckons all who would seek a renewal of spirit, both personal and national.

Like so many legends, those of Arthur, Camelot and Excalibur are greatly intriguing, even to those would refute the realities of person, place and article; they are all things of legend and enrich the lives of both storyteller and listener by providing the allure of a realm of adventure and excitement lying above and beyond the mundane lives to which most people are physically bound. To those for whom Somerset provides such a realm, Arthur is there, ever watchful but always just out of sight as the wafting mists of dawning and evening twilight merge the images of the surroundings, and the hard edges our minds need to define our everyday worlds disappear.

Arthur, son of Uther, took up arms under the banner of Pendragon, the Dragon's Head, at a time of great turmoil in his homeland. In the times which he knew, the Huns had pushed the Gothic tribes of central Europe westward and had struck south toward Rome itself. Massed tribes of Franks and Alemanni had surged across the Rhine into Gaul while large numbers of Angles, Saxons and Jutes were leaving their homes on the northern European shores to seek new lands across the sea in a Britannia freed of Roman rule as the legions were withdrawn to defend the shrinking Empire. Some were welcomed as deliverers, others opposed by the native Britons whose armed truce with Rome was replaced by open warfare with the new invader. The resistance by the Britons, as ferocious and heroic as it could be, was to prove no match for the relentless juggernaut of victorious land-hungry warriors moving just ahead of the farmer-settler, except in the territory to the extreme west and north where they could hold their own and retain some measure of their old ways. The newcomers were to assimilate into their new homeland but could never subdue that native spirit although, in their turn, their descendants would find they would have to defend themselves against future invasions as the centuries went by. As the roaming bards began to expound and expand the legends of past heroes in the taverns and marketplaces in towns and villages by the hundreds and thousands, the name of the king called Arthur became synonymous with all things gallant and noble and was invoked any time the Britannia which had become Britain found itself in peril.

The youthful Sherlock Holmes had heard the legends, had listened as the townsfolk of Glastonbury related the tales of Arthur and his knights to the visitor ever-keen to be enthralled in this place of myth and magic; he saw Glastonbury as a place apart, a place from which he was to be torn away but to which, deep down, he was always drawn back.

Sherlock Holmes, once the inquisitive lad but now grown and recalled to that place of legend as the seasoned detective, was remembering how he had sensed the presence of something beyond mere storytelling, something beyond officialdom and something beyond his youthful mind to understand at the time. It seemed to him that he was remembering how certain people never spoke of Arthur and the legends when he was about and seemed to change the subject if he ever raised the matter. Others, he fancied, were all too keen to label the legends as fairy tales but were also ready to relate one or other version with some degree of belonging and pride. The mind of the great sleuth was delving deep into its long-filed and disorganised stores of memory and retrieving them as facts, hazy and disjointed for the moment but starting to resolve and come together bit by bit like the tiles of that imagined mosaic which he knew would slowly reform into a coherent picture of his past.

"What is it that I can't remember?" he asked of himself repeatedly. "There was something which someone referred to which struck a chord in my mind. It was a name or a title or description of some sort, something which I know ought to be familiar but which is as yet out of the grasp of my conscious mind, something which caused others to go quiet when it was uttered in my presence so many years ago."

"What was it, Holmes?" he demanded of himself. "Think, man, think!"

But, think, he could not, at least not intensely enough to jog loose those memories so deeply embedded and never required until now. Perhaps it would come to him as his investigations proceeded; perhaps a name or a face, a sight or sound or smell would trigger that long dormant section of his mind holding the key to that memory he so earnestly sought.

The London pair was to spend a good hour with George Bridges, an hour in which Watson would gain a great deal of insight into the mind of that man he had come to call friend but who had remained a largely undecipherable enigma. Holmes, in his turn, would find that he was starting to rediscover the person he had been before the responsibilities of adulthood had overwhelmed his childhood memories and drawn him into a world requiring his special talents. It would take someone of the like of the former sergeant of police to break through Sherlock's disciplined reserve and the pair was coming away not greatly more informed but ever so much more prepared for their quest.

Above all things, however, the two London men had to keep reminding themselves that they were in Glastonbury on serious business, the business of finding a murderer and the reason that people had to die to protect or enrich the life of another. Not one of the victims was exceptionally well-off and some were quite stretched financially, it would seem, so someone's personal enrichment as a motive seemed improbable. This left self-preservation as the likely contender, unless the victims could be shown to possess otherwise unknown assets.

"But, preservation?" Holmes would continually muse to himself. "Preservation from what?"

The visit with Bridges did not provide the venue or atmosphere for such a question to be uttered aloud; it would have to wait until Holmes could concentrate his thoughts and bring together what he had recently learned with what he was beginning to remember. Laughter from Bridges and its vibrant echoes from Watson made any such process impossible and Holmes had to bide his time and wait for the right moment when silence and pipe tobacco could combine to enhance his thought processes.

So far, the pair had encountered a bombastic mayor, an accommodating sergeant of police, a doctor who had threatened to have the law on them, victims' relatives who insisted that murder had been committed, an old friend who dangled an intriguing secret in front of them, a furniture dealer who seemed suspicious in the extreme and nothing at all to suggest that any of these facts were connected. To Watson, it seemed that they had entered a labyrinth from which they might never emerge; to Holmes, it was food for a hungry mind, one starved of what it craved and kept it functioning at its maximum, the only rate which Sherlock Holmes considered worthwhile.

George Bridges seemed unwilling to discuss some matters too deeply with Holmes and Watson but did offer sound advice on the characters of numerous persons of interest, including any brushes they might have had with the law and what some may well have gotten away with for want of actual witnesses or hard evidence. He seemed more interested in pointing their investigations in various pertinent directions so that they could formulate plans to discover and assess the matters themselves without his direct input. If this were a deliberate ploy on his part, neither Holmes nor Watson could think why he might wish to distance himself in such a way.

Time had passed with subtle hints being given by Bridges in between much good-natured banter on the antics of the younger Sherlock. Added to this were a good many questions on the sleuth's time after leaving Glastonbury and the beginnings of his career as a consulting detective and subsequent fame, the latter by courtesy of the well-inked pen and literary gifts of John Watson. Much more would have been covered had a small clock in the hallway not chimed noon and reminded the visitors that they had appointments to keep, appointments to discuss pressing matters of the moment and not reminisce about days long passed.

Holmes made the first move and explained that he and Watson were to meet with the two aldermen. Bridges responded understandingly and rose to clear away teacups and plates. Holmes and Watson also rose from their seats and started to move toward the front door followed less energetically by Bridges who nonetheless had appreciatively anticipated their need to be off on their quest by gathering their hats from the stand and graciously offering each to its owner. He opened his front door to allow the two men to leave, enthusiastically shaking their hands and bidding them to return when their schedules allowed.

To Watson he expressed his appreciation that the lad he had tolerated and often encouraged so long ago had found a productive endeavour to utilize those special latent gifts which he obviously had possessed, and also a friend who saw the flawed genius within the man and stood by him through all adversity.

To Holmes, he spoke almost as a son, one who might have returned from afar to restore some lost family honour or fortune after being away for so long. He repeated the words of appreciation which he had given to Watson and then added, as the two men walked through his front gate and onto the street, "Remember that tor, Sherlock. Keep it in mind at all times, and those matters subterranean."

The parting words of ex-Sergeant Bridges were nothing if they were not enigmatic and Holmes simply stared at his old mentor for a few moments before forming a smile which could have been construed by an outsider to be anything ranging from all-knowing, through amused, and all the way on to being totally perplexed. Watson, as long as he had known his friend and for all of the dangers they had faced together, could not say which.

A parting nod by the Sleuth followed by a somewhat questioning "Indeed?" signalled that something extra had passed between the consulting detective and the retired though still active ex-policeman, and it seemed to Watson that there was even more mystery to this mysterious case than he had ever considered likely. Things were not as they seemed and were becoming extraordinarily puzzling, even for a place such as Glastonbury; but Sherlock Holmes, he knew, was never one to be drawn to the mundane and commonplace where crime was concerned. If the game was indeed afoot, then Watson, never one to shy away from trouble where his friend especially was concerned, could only hope to keep up as best he could with its ever changing rules and players.

The Question

"What on Earth did Bridges mean by all that?" asked an intrigued but confused Watson on getting out of earshot of the ex-sergeant of police. "All that stuff about the tor and what's underneath?"

"Bridges was pointing us toward something he was not supposed to disclose," replied Holmes, "a secret he has been sworn to keep and never divulge, and it has something to do with something under the tor, perhaps some chamber or tunnel or artefact beneath St. Michael's Tower or the site of the old church. I do believe, Watson, that we've just been served with a silent challenge."

Holmes thought a little more on the words of Bridges and then reverted to matters which had fascinated his juvenile self, teasing Watson somewhat with, "The tales told about that tor and portals to other worlds may have some substance to them, some connection with actual people and events long forgotten except in the slowly evolving mystical lore which goes with such intriguing locations. Remember King Arthur and his knights and Queen Guinevere and the Lady of the Lake. Well, who's to say that the events attributed to such indistinct personages did not occur but have been embellished by the storyteller over the centuries? Why, I know of someone who does that very thing in this day and age; a medical man who might have passed for the magical Merlin of legend had he lived all those years ago."

"What say you, Watson?" Holmes continued, together with a laugh and a slap of his hand on his friend's shoulder. "Perhaps we are aspects of the ancient Arthur and Merlin returned to do battle against some enemy in modern times. In future ages our actions might find themselves embellished a bit and added to the legends. All we need to do now is find Excalibur ... and a good storyteller."

"Yes Holmes," countered Watson in mock rebuke, "the swordsman and the author; they both use sharp implements but, though the match seems very one-sided, you ought to remember the adage that the pen is mightier than the sword."

"Touché, Watson," conceded Holmes, "a definite point to you. Perhaps we ought to declare a truce before you draw that pen of yours in true defiance."

The truce declared, Holmes and Watson stepped up the pace back to and along the length of High Street to the Pilgrims' Inn where Randall and Jamison would be waiting, along with their lunches, though Holmes would be far too intrigued to do very much in the way of eating; even Watson was beginning to feel the excitement.

The pair entered into the darkness of the inn's vestibule and took a moment to allow their eyes to adjust before checking with the desk clerk for messages. A telegram had been delivered for Holmes that morning and the sleuth took no time in destroying the envelope to get at its contents.

"Holmes," it read, "eagerly anticipating report. Keen for country air. Lestrade."

"It's from Scotland Yard," Holmes told his friend. "Lestrade wants a trip to the countryside. Crime must be having a few days off in London or the man's trying to dodge one of his less amenable superiors; I'd put my money on the latter."

"I've heard nothing from Taunton headquarters, though," he added, "nothing to suggest interest or otherwise in the goings-on in Glastonbury. They were sent a telegram informing them of my visit; perhaps they didn't appreciate the significance."

"Of your visit or of events in Glastonbury?" asked Watson, feigning disrespect.

"That will depend on how you describe it in your stories, Watson," countered the sleuth who then gave the doctor little opportunity for a return quip by declaring that, "Now, Randall and Jamison are sure to be waiting, my friend, and I'm sure that you will require sustenance yourself."

Thus thwarted, Watson pointed a moving finger toward the dining room and followed right behind as it made its way toward the solicitors, both hungry and both a little impatient and very keen to hear of the morning's encounter with Fredericks.

Neither one of the two solicitors was surprised to hear of Dr. Fredericks changeable nature, one minute affable, the next argumentative and threatening. It was his way, disagreeable to say the least but the man seemed protected from all criticism by those holding high office and with whom he associated.

"He and Mayor Bennet are quite thick together;" offered Randall. "Lodge members both, as are so many in the town, but there's more. They each seem under the influence of something or someone else but it's hard to put a finger on what or who. Many decisions which have been made by Bennet seem irreconcilable with Freemasonry's tenets and they have been well beyond explanations of brotherly bonding or the municipal needs of Glastonbury. There's something much deeper but of a definite local character behind some of their actions. You've seen the man in action, Mr. Holmes, and you know what a bombast he can be; both men can become quite irrational and belligerent if provoked."

"Well, we did provoke him," insisted Watson, "but only to the extent of telling him that we may need to speak with him further on his medical assessments. He objected strenuously to this despite having admitted to falsifying Beryl Armitage's cause of death. Though he claimed to have had good reason for what he did, such action was both unprofessional and illegal. He could be struck off for such an offence and possibly face criminal charges, particularly if the young lady's death proved to be a case of murder."

"What was his reason?" enquired Randall. "I would have thought that he would have refused to alter anything, unless he'd been told to."

"He said it was to protect her family and friends from the truth." broke in Holmes. "And that truth, as he claimed, was that the young lady died from the effects of ingestion of narcotic substances. I am of the opinion that he has now falsified the cause of death twice, once to the coroner and once to Watson and myself unless, of course, someone deliberately administered a narcotic or some other substance which caused her death. Either way, it would surely constitute a serious criminal offence.

"We shall need to examine the reports from beyond the region." continued Holmes. "We need to have full details from all who fell sick during or after their visits to Glastonbury, their symptoms and what they feel may have caused them. I doubt that we shall get a straight answer from the local men."

"But what of Lestrade, Holmes?" Watson queried. "Should you not send off something by way of a report? I mean, you did alert the man to our involvement and he does deserve the courtesy of a response at least. Anyway, we may be in need of his services as the Taunton detectives seem fully disinterested in the case."

"Lestrade! Ah, yes." replied Holmes. "It's been very remiss of me to have overlooked that small undertaking I'd made to him. I shall attend to that immediately and inform him by telegram to look for it in the post."

That said, Holmes excused himself from his colleagues, returning a few minutes later with paper, pencil and stamped envelope and started to write profusely after retaking his seat. Ten minutes, three pages of scribbled notes and two re-sharpened pencil leads later and the report was ready, rich with detail though with a paucity of informed deduction. Holmes would not commit himself to premature theories before he had collected sufficient data. Lestrade, very much the British bulldog and by virtue of his long-standing professional relationship with Holmes, would be able to sense a juicy case of murder into which he might sink his eager canines and would come running, teeth bared, at full stretch.

"Perhaps," Holmes expressed to the impatient three sitting there with him as he prepared his report, "I ought to post this in Street and not in Glastonbury. Who knows with whom the postmaster might be in league, and I think it would be wise to keep this report away from any prying hands and eyes. There is nothing to be gained by not taking extra precautions in these matters and, perhaps, much to be lost."

"Well," offered Randall, "As it happens, I have reason to be off to Street this very afternoon on a matter which I had decided to postpone in favour of assisting yourself and Dr. Watson. It's just a matter of delivering some documents for signing but I will need a witness. If you or Dr. Watson or both would care to accompany me, I can see to the needs of my client and you can post that letter of yours out of sight of prying Glastonbury eyes."

Seeing that the suggestion seemed acceptable, Randall continued with, "Perhaps Jamison here might prefer to return to our rooms and attend to a few pressing legal matters and we can collect him on our return and continue our exertions."

"An excellent arrangement." Holmes eagerly replied. "Perhaps, though, we ought to make use of a dog cart or trap to save both time and shoe leather. There would be several operating commercially in the town, no doubt."

"Well, definitely," replied the solicitor. "I was not actually intending to walk there."

The course of action agreed, the four rose from the table, Randall setting off to locate suitable transportation and Jamison heading back to work while Holmes and Watson rushed off to the telegraph office to inform Lestrade of a report about to be sent his way.

Fifteen minutes saw Holmes and Watson back at the Pilgrims' Inn awaiting the return of Randall with a trap. The two men found they had little time to wait as they heard the clip-clop and wheel roll of the approaching conveyance coming up Magdalene Street bearing the driver plus Randall and his hastily collected files and ready to collect two more passengers before heading off toward Street at a steady pace. The ride back along Magdalene Street was pleasant enough as was that enjoyed along Street Road whose more southerly end steepened down toward the approaches to the Pomparles Bridge over the River Brue. From the higher ground they could catch glimpses of the old Roman Road along which, Holmes took the opportunity to tell Watson, King Arthur himself might have ridden to do battle with the encroaching Saxons, perhaps including one or two of Watson's ancestors.

"We are not getting back into that discussion, Holmes," retorted the Doctor with the hint of a smile. "After this amount of time has passed, I think I may call myself truly British. You might pick on Lestrade when he arrives; I believe his name is French in origin, from l'Stradt, which does sound a little German and basically means 'of the street' but undoubtedly had a deeper meaning."

"That basic meaning may well suffice to tease the good inspector," laughed Holmes. "We may well bring the matter up if he gets too officious for us."

"So, basically," observed Randall, "you detectives play games with each other, serious ones I would gather, but games of wit."

"That we do," replied Holmes. "Such seemingly silly activities keep the senses honed. There's nothing which can do that so well, short of finding oneself in extreme danger; then you'll find out just how keen the senses can get."

The banter was kept up for a short while as the causeway was approached and the Pomparles Bridge came into view and, beyond it, the rise toward Street which, for a while, had been young Sherlock's home away from the home lost all those years ago.

"Pomparles Bridge," observed Watson. "A strange name. No doubt the surname of some local dignitary or ancient land owner."

"Not at all," returned Holmes, keen to involve his friend in a little of the knowledge he had picked up in his youth. "It's garbled Latin. Once it was Pont Perles, the Bridge of Perils, so called, it is said, for the dangerous flow of the unrestrained Brue in flood. The current bridge is a great improvement on the old rickety structures it replaced, I'm told, though it still looks a little perilous and could do with some attention. Somewhere hereabouts, the Lady of the Lake took possession of Excalibur and hid it for safekeeping. Perhaps, Watson, you might mount a search for the ancient weapon; it must be somewhere, though it's bound to be a little rusty."

"You're the sword wielder, Holmes," came the reply, "and I'm just the pen pusher. Didn't we just have this conversation?"

The Cottage

With Pomparles Bridge crossed, Street Road changed its name to Glastonbury Road, though the locals were increasingly dropping the "bury" suffix and resorting to Glaston, a name deriving from an imperfectly known source, perhaps a person, perhaps a people, perhaps a reference to the broad shining waters it once looked over. Street, though very close to its northerly neighbour, was not Glastonbury and did not generate the same sense of place even though its credentials were age-old and impressive. Perhaps it was the distant tor topped with St. Michael's Tower which drew attention from the more southern of the two towns connected and yet separated by the causeway over the Brue; perhaps Street simply seemed less isolated.

Street, standing on the eastern edge of the Polden Hills, Sherlock was remembering, had been registered in the Doomsday Book as Strate because of the strata or paved road which led to Glastonbury. A Celtic Saint named Kea had once lived and worshipped there, and his holy domicile had given its name to the village of Lantakay which altered to Lega before becoming Leigh which, though still existing in name and form, was then absorbed as Street expanded its boundaries in more recent times. The sleuth's continuous commentary had both Randall and Watson spellbound and their driver shaking his head at the depth of the man's knowledge.

"I wonder," Holmes mused to his companions upon ceasing his historical homily, "if we might have time to drive past my Aunt Jane's old house up near Wood's Gate. It's not far off High Street and I would like to see it; it might even jog a few recalcitrant memories loose. We can then veer right and continue back to follow Grange Road to the Cross and then return to Glastonbury. I walked these streets so many times as a lad and I can still see their twists and turns in my mind."

No objection was made and Watson even teased with mischievous but good-natured comments about "seeing where it all began" and "Street has a lot to answer for" but Holmes was too engrossed in the place to notice, let alone to respond.

Wilfred Road, the address of Randall's client, loomed closer as the trap dawdled along High Street, and Holmes could barely contain himself causing the solicitor to suggest, "If you would like to jump off here, Mr. Holmes, you can explore to your heart's content, post your letter and we can pick you up near Wood's Gate after I have sorted out my client's documentation and Dr. Watson has witnessed the signatures. We should be little more than thirty minutes at our task and a single witness is all that is required. Our horse could do with the rest, as well."

No further enticement to abandon the conveyance and take to the street on foot was needed and the horse did not have to break its gait before Holmes had jumped clear and landed with the announcement of, "I'll see you in thirty minutes." He was then off, letter in hand, away to reacquire and absorb the atmosphere of Street just as he had done in Glastonbury.

Memories – feelings, sights, sounds, smells – came flooding back in such profusion that Holmes was overwhelmed, less with facts than with sensations he had forgotten ever experiencing. For the second time in two days Holmes became an emotional being wrestling hard to steer a wayward mind gone out of control back onto its charted course; Holmes did not like being the random thinker, his was a disciplined mind and it would toe the line and behave. Still, a little enjoyment would not hurt a bit, he convinced himself, and then proceeded along streets not traversed by him in decades until he could retrace his youthful steps to his Aunt Jane's old house, only it was no longer there.

The house was gone, the gardens were gone, and everything looked different. A quite unfamiliar emotion came over the highly disciplined great sleuth and he felt tears welling up in his eyes, something he could never remember having experienced before. A quick wipe with a handkerchief and a rapid succession of in and out deep breaths calmed the unwanted feelings and allowed Holmes to retake control of himself. Such a weakness would not be permitted to assert its supremacy as it did with so many of his associates who did not come up to his standard of mental discipline and whom he judged as having failed to reach their potential in rational thinking and deductive reasoning.

His companions would see none of this, nor would they be permitted the smallest glimpse of human fallibility surfacing ever so temporarily in the man. The others were ensconced with an elderly gentleman and Watson was standing by trying hard not to eavesdrop on another's personal business and waiting only to witness the signatures of client and solicitor and attest to their authenticities. The matters were tedious and the process long-winded but, when done, the pair mounted their waiting conveyance, its horse having been well rested and now goaded toward Wood's Gate and Holmes.

Watson's and Randall's interest in Street was quite unlike that of Holmes who had known it as a base from which boyhood adventures had started while, for Watson, it was yet another rural town of moderate interest. Randall saw it merely as a disjointed extension of Glastonbury housing numerous paying clients and a confusion of ancient land titles. Their faces, on seeing Holmes standing mute and looking at a piece of ground cleared of centuries of history to make way for something new, lost all vestiges of anticipation and they could only commiserate with their colleague in his disappointment.

"Time and tide, gentlemen," he declared, "they wait for no man, as goes the old adage, and the old must make way for the new. I have made my pilgrimage to the site where my most favoured boyhood dreams began and the house, should it have remained standing, might have seemed a structure minus a soul without Aunt Jane. Now, it's back to Glastonbury and back to work, the only thing to clear a mind of unhelpful distractions."

Watson could sense a hint of bravado in the words of his friend and knew that Holmes had indeed been touched by Street as much as he had been by Glastonbury, though in a somewhat different way. Holmes knew it too but would never admit it. He also knew that the memory he had been seeking had been dislodged and was making its way falteringly to the surface. As memories go it would be quite small but the sleuth in him was impatient to come to grips with it so that he could place yet another key tile in the forming mosaic of multiple murder and go forward unemotionally with his investigations.

The ride back to Glastonbury took them along Farm Road and then around the old abbey and its grange, Watson expressing surprise that Street had once housed its own abbey, being so close to northerly neighbour.

"There is more to Street than meets the eye, my friend," admonished Holmes. "It's just that it gets overlooked by not possessing Glastonbury's salient geographical features and the legends which have been so strongly associated with them. Glastonbury stands alone, like a sentinel, but Street is the hinge to which is attached the Polden Hills whose lengthened heights form a northern gate for the lands and townships to the south."

"Well," stuttered Randall, "I've never heard Street described in such glorious terms. I must admit that I shall never again look at the place in quite the same way now that you have elevated it so far above the mundane town I had been seeing all these years with these closed eyes of mine. The hills and the lands beyond do have their own character, and a very attractive character it is when described in such terms. Perhaps, Dr. Watson, as Mr. Holmes would say, I have seen but I have not observed."

"Yes," was Watson's short but amused reply. "Holmes is always saying that, especially when he is one up in our mutual deductions. Still, the countryside of Somerset is glorious and history just oozes from its ancient settlements, as does murder in recent times."

"Quite!" was Randall's reply, one echoed by Holmes and extended with, "We should be focussing on method and motive and leave sightseeing until the guilty party is behind bars."

"It'd be a sad world if one couldn't take what time was available to see the beauty around us," countered Watson who then anticipated the coming refutation by Holmes by adding, "We have come to do a job of work, nasty in its character, and must steel our minds to that purpose, but while we ride back to our respective tasks it would do no harm to remember just what we are trying to save from the evil which has beset it."

The trap's driver had remained virtually silent throughout the journey, such as it had been, but was moved to speak, having heard and noted the nature of his passengers' conversations, something he normally would have had little interest in and would have deliberately shown none. Albert Rutledge was a man of few words when business depended on his discretion but was as prone to listen to and spread gossip as the next man when amongst his convivial like-minded fellows. He had information, of a sort, and was uncertain if and to whom it ought to be offered but, on hearing Holmes describe his native region in such flowery terms, he had decided that the time and opportunity had come.

"Pardon me, gents," started the driver, "I don't generally interrupt my passengers' conversation but I couldn't help overhearing what you've been saying about those folks who died, those four who the mayor is so concerned about. It may not be anything but I do know something which may be of interest."

"Indeed," a suddenly interested Holmes responded, "and what might that something be?"

"Well, I drive folks all about these parts," the driver continued, "and people say all manner of things forgetting that I have a pair of ears too, though I don't generally take much notice of what's being said. It's not my business to know their business but sometimes it's hard not to hear some things."

"Go on," Holmes encouraged the man.

"It was last year," the driver began, "I'd say around November, well before Christmas anyway, that I had to pick them all up on a single day in my little dog cart, in two trips mind you, and carry them over here to Street and deposit them near to the old Manor House we passed on the way here. I took them all back in this trap when they were finished and they seemed a little quiet as I recall it, troubled you might say. I don't know what had gone on but it did seem to unsettle them."

"Point is," he continued, "these four are connected in some way, or they were on that day. I just thought I should say something, to yourself Mr. Holmes, and the other two gentlemen, seeing who you are and what you do."

"And we are immensely grateful to you for doing so," remarked Holmes, all thoughts of his Aunt's missing home now falling rapidly away. "You have indeed given us valuable information, though where that will ultimately lead us is yet to be determined. It would be very useful if you could help us out with the date on which this occurred, if you keep records of such things. But, thank you, Mr. Rutledge, thank you very much indeed."

Rutledge nodded at the sleuth and said he did keep records, not elaborate ones, but sufficient to be able to determine the date required. Randall also expressed his appreciation for Rutledge speaking up as he did and suggested that he could leave any such information, and anything else he might recall, in written form at either the Pilgrims' Inn for Holmes and Watson or at his law offices for himself and Jamison who would pass it on.

That settled and agreed to, the return journey continued with neither the driver nor any of his passengers uttering a single word until they arrived back at the door of the Pilgrims' Inn.

The Dealer

The trip over the Brue to Street and back was not in any way lengthy but it had been surprisingly profitable. A connection of an unknown nature between all four fatal victims had been established and, though it would be necessary to have it confirmed and determine what it was that connected them, it was a clue of a type Sherlock Holmes insisted always existed but might never be found except for chance. One's chances,

171

he knew, were improved by exerting oneself in the field and asking questions of and accepting input from even the mostly unlikely witness. In this case, chance had definitely brought investigator and witness together, and Holmes would not be the one to ignore it and refuse the opportunity it brought to him. It was likely that Rutledge knew more, though he might not realise it, or might remember extra details about that day in November; the man would have to be contacted again soon as his memory was bound to have stirred itself into action.

"Interesting, that Rutledge fellow's tale," declared Watson as the trap went off carrying the solicitor back to his office. "He said a lot and, yet, not all that much of truly practical use."

"It was of great importance, though," replied Holmes, "but I agree that it does not take our investigations much further ahead. That will not happen until we can establish just why it was that the four were at that Manor House, if that's where they were going. We must also determine who else may have attended that meeting, or whatever it was that drew them there. We do progress, though, Watson; we do progress."

"Randall has returned to his office," observed Watson, "and I presume that his client's documents have need of further processing and probable recording but we ought to be off putting questions to Renshaw and those others from the train. We still have ample time to do more this afternoon, so should we include the solicitors or not?"

"Perhaps we should not," was Holmes' considered reply. "You've been sitting down while being pulled around by a horse since lunchtime, so you ought to be up for a good brisk walk to Renshaw's establishment if for no other reason than to get the blood flowing through your veins. We won't need Randall's or Jamison's presence to authenticate our visit, Renshaw approached us and we shall merely be returning the courtesy and responding to his invitation. When we've finished there, we can revisit Mrs. Staunton, also Mrs. Graham if time permits."

"Lead on," was Watson's simple and rapid response, and Holmes pointed in the general direction of North Load Street and Adam Renshaw's "House of Furniture."

What specifically to ask Renshaw was not easy to decide but Holmes considered that he ought to approach the man and ask for his opinion on Fredericks and observe the man's response. He would then try to draw out what the man might know by telling him that he and Watson had sensed that he was someone who would know things about Glastonbury which others would not be privy to. He might just loosen his tongue if treated as though he presented a critical information source in their investigation. If the man held ideas of self-importance, he might divulge far more than he might otherwise have done; if he had acted for reasons devious and deceptive, he would likely be hesitant and cagey with his answers.

On arrival at Renshaw's furniture establishment, more of a rambling warehouse than the grand house its name boasted, the pair found the proprietor barking orders at three men unloading a wagon stacked high with what seemed to be furniture from several households. One of those three men, Holmes noticed, was Harry Walters, once close friend to and now vigorous defender of the memory of Beryl Armitage.

"Mr. Holmes, Dr. Watson," the furniture dealer exclaimed, changing the tone of his voice considerably, "I had been wondering if you'd see your way to paying me a visit."

"Yes, indeed, Mr. Renshaw." replied Holmes as though addressing someone of vital importance which, of course, the furniture dealer might well have been. "We certainly owed you a courtesy call at the very least after you had offered us the courtesy of the train compartment and the interest you expressed in the matters to which you referred."

Both Holmes and Watson would swear that they saw the man's chest bulge several inches and his head swell at least one hat size on being shown such deference by two famous visitors. Renshaw then looked at his three employees as if to inform them that he was far too important to continue dealing with the likes of such underlings and bade the two London men to join him in his office, a space seemingly as jumbled as had been the furniture wagon out front.

Finding a chair in the furniture dealer's jumbled office was not at all difficult; Holmes counted at least twelve though the more comfortable looking of those were closest to the man's desk which was overflowing with all manner of bulky and tattered documents. Just how Renshaw's business operated with the smallest modicum of efficiency was impossible for Holmes and Watson to say but Holmes considered the likelihood that the clutter might well hide documentation of a host of questionable dealings which the dealer alone would be able to locate if required.

"Gentlemen, welcome," Renshaw declared with an enthusiasm which seemed over-contrived to his visitors. "I seem to work in chaos, as you can see, but there is order beneath all this mess before you, a mess which reflects well the nature of my livelihood. I have four main categories of merchandise here. The best I take down to London and get a faster sale and better price than I could dream of in Glastonbury; next best I place in my showrooms and offer for sale locally. Below that is a grade which I keep in my warehouse for people to pick through, though I do auction much of it off for what I can get, just to get some shillings flowing in and to clear a bit of space for the next delivery; the rest I generally get my lads to break up and burn, though sometimes they take it home to use or sell or burn for firewood but I generally turn a blind eye to that as they're good lads and work hard, though I do have to push them along at times."

"As for documentation?" he added, "It's hard to keep up with it and when I do it doesn't make an iota of difference. I just file it by month every so often in case the police need to check on stolen items brought in for a quick sale. My business is mostly cash mixed in with the odd inconvenient cheque if I can trust the buyer. The lads get fair wages and I give them a bonus when business is extra good; my horses get the best oats and my men get good money and that's just good business, not generosity."

"Some would rebuke you for that sort of good business, I imagine," observed Holmes, "yet they would not have employees satisfied with their lots. It would be quite the opposite, in fact, they would have men who would do only what they had to, and as little of that as possible."

"That's about the way of it, Mr. Holmes; we pay for what we get and we get what we pay for," agreed Renshaw, "Now, what is it that I might help you and Dr. Watson with?"

"We took it, from the way in which you spoke to us in the train compartment," replied Holmes, "that there was more you might wish to share with us about these unpleasant matters. There are a few matters which you may well be able to help shed some light upon but perhaps you might begin with what you know."

"I was, in part, interested to determine if our mayor had actually sent for outside help," the furniture dealer freely acknowledged, "and it was a chance to meet the famous

Sherlock Holmes and, of course, Dr. Watson. I had recognised you both from your pictures in the newspapers and when my colleagues went blundering into your compartment … well, I took the opportunity to speak to you and to drag those three noisy bumblers away so that you could have a bit of peace."

"That was actually very much appreciated," Holmes admitted, though he was still unsure if Renshaw was being genuine; the fellow had not volunteered any real information so far.

"But," Holmes continued, "I sense that you have something you wish to tell us, something you feel we ought to know."

"There is something," said a seemingly hesitant Renshaw, "though it may actually be nothing. You see, murder in a town which relies on outsiders coming to spend their shillings and pence and, indeed, their pounds and guineas, is very bad for business. I have little direct dealings with the pilgrims but if people don't work, they can't buy furniture. Many will sell off a bit to bring in a little cash which, of course, is all I can offer them. Without customers for my goods, I find that I end up with a full warehouse and an empty purse."

Holmes looked at the man as if to insist that he stop evading the matter and get to the point. Renshaw, sensing Holmes' growing impatience, continued with, "It's one of my lads, you see, a fellow called Harry Walters; he was keen on the Armitage girl, Beryl, the one who died earlier in the year. The lad was very cut up when she died and, if he was annoyed when that Doc Fredericks quack passed it off as an insect bite, he was absolutely furious when he heard he had told others that Beryl died from some narcotic agent. He was useless to me for weeks after, but I kept his wages up. As I said, I look after my people, especially good workers like Harry. A terrible shame, really, the whole thing, but that Fredericks is hiding something, mark my words Mr. Holmes."

Holmes looked at Watson as if to say, "We may have been wrong about Renshaw," before asking, "And the other victims, do you know anything of the circumstances of their deaths? Have people generally been satisfied with the official causes of death, or not?"

"Only general gossip, I'm afraid, Mr. Holmes," he replied, "but that Fredericks is someone to avoid if you get sick, I believe. Don't know myself, I don't get sick, but if I did I'd go to that new fellow, Baxter's his name; people have spoken well of him though he's quite new to the district."

Before Holmes could ask more, the furniture dealer said that he would have to cut their conversation short as there had been a lot of new stock coming his way, purchases from people whose income had been interrupted by the drop in pilgrim numbers spending money.

Holmes and Watson rose, thanked Renshaw for his time and information and proceeded to see themselves out but Holmes heard his name being whispered by Harry Walters on leaving the building.

"Mr. Holmes," said Harry, his voice lowered to almost inaudible, "I regret my earlier outburst toward you; Marge and Violet told me what you were about, and why. It's just that I still can't believe she's gone. And that Fredericks pig ... well, no insect bite ever took Beryl from us; and I've heard he's said worse about her. It's all wrong ... Beryl was a clean-living girl and we were happy, both in work and putting a little aside each payday for, well, later."

"I have no reason to think otherwise, Mr. Walters," declared Holmes, "and don't concern yourself about your words to me; you had suffered a great loss. I wasn't sure about you at first, but now I realise that it was a combination of grief and frustration talking; a natural response, very natural indeed."

"Perhaps," Holmes added as he started to move away, "we can speak further, at your accommodations."

Harry Walters looked about to make certain his employer wasn't watching then nodded at Holmes' suggestion before whispering "Thanks!" and turning away to continue transferring the furniture wagon's contents into the warehouse, his two workmates signalling for him to get back to work before Renshaw discovered him loafing. Holmes might still have been uncertain of the furniture dealer's involvement in the unexplained deaths, but he was, for the good money he offered his employees, a taskmaster who insisted that every penny of those wages be earned.

Holmes was now uncertain if he had actually been wrong about Renshaw or if the man had been told about their encounter with Fredericks and, presuming that the London detective would have been told about the ridiculous insect bite diagnosis and would have personally witnessed the man's erratic behaviour, there would be nothing to lose by appearing to dislike him as well. Watson was even more confused. Before visiting either Mrs. Staunton or Mrs. Graham, they decided to check for messages at the Pilgrims' Inn.

On their return, they approached the reception desk from behind which the inn's manager advised Holmes that two messages had been delivered for him during his absence and retrieved both from his room's mail box on the wall. Holmes took both from the manager's hand and inspected them, noting that one was a plain sealed envelope bearing only his name while the second had been addressed to both himself and Watson. Thanking the manager, Holmes took both into the vestibule and summoned Watson before opening them. One was from Doctor Prendergast and the other from Albert Rutledge, or Bert as he signed himself.

The Secret

Messages from unexpected sources were not uncommon occurrences in London where Holmes had an extensive network of informants keen to provide reliable information knowing that the unofficial consulting detective always showed his appreciation in kind or in cash. Many of the contacts had been clients for whom Holmes had acted without charge and had gotten them out of messes which were not of their own making but for which, some of them, could have had ended at the gallows after the official detectives had ceased investigations upon apprehending a suitable suspect. Here in Glastonbury, Holmes had no such network, just one old contact and a host of people whose reliability ranged from questionable to good but never to absolute. Still, there was little to do but listen and try to ascertain the degree to which he might trust strangers from this close-knit town with its intriguing history and many secrets.

Two responses from two people of different backgrounds but unknown loyalties had now been received, and all he could hope for was some clue, even the merest hint, to the motives behind the deaths, the murders as he was almost certain they had been. He would take in the information provided and then, by virtue of his enhanced intuitive powers, examine each assertion looking for either consistency or anomaly. The investigation's foundations were solid enough, he thought, but had they been placed upon a solid bedrock?

The letter from Dr. Prendergast, that addressed to both Holmes and Watson, was very much to the point, opening with a distinctly curt "Sirs" and finishing abruptly with "Prendergast" and containing the names, town of domicile, doctors' names and reported symptoms and little more beyond the fact that one of the five patients, a man named Keith from Bristol, had succumbed. The summary seemed a grudging effort on the part of the compiler even though he had readily agreed to the task but the doctor's idiosyncrasies were unknown to Holmes and Watson and it may well merely have been typical of his communications.

"Five who had returned home from Glastonbury showing symptoms of poisoning," commented Watson, remembering the details of his visit and trying without much success to read further details as Holmes waved the letter about while making wild gesticulations, "and one of that number dying from the effects of some poisonous substance ingested in some manner, presumably. We need to look at this letter, Holmes, so we ought to adjourn to somewhere stable where that arm of yours can stop moving; the dining room should be vacant so we'll go there."

Once again, as he had often done in so many small ways, Holmes had treated Watson as a secondary element in the investigative process and, once again, Watson had to bring the great sleuth into line and insist on being involved. After all, this was data of a medical nature and, despite Holmes' knowledge of all manner of poisons and insight into the criminal mind, it was Watson who held the medical qualifications and he who ought to have priority when perusing any communications from a brother medical man.

Holmes, oblivious to his unintentional slight on his long-suffering colleague, agreed to the need for the details to be looked at objectively and on a stable platform and followed Watson to a corner table out of sight of prying eyes, few as those would actually be in the under-occupied Pilgrims' Inn in such trying times for Glastonbury. Watson sat, directed Holmes to take the seat beside him, took his earlier lists from his coat pocket and prepared to record any extra detail the letter provided. Holmes could do little but comply as Watson, rare as such occurrences were, was defiantly insistent on taking charge of all medical data.

"Now, Holmes," instructed Watson, "push that list a little closer to me so I can read it; that Prendergast's writing is a bit of a challenge at a distance and such an oblique angle."

Holmes complied with just the hint of a smile as he realised that his unintended insensitivity had caused his colleague to become impatient with him and just a little officious in his manner. Watson found the list deposited directly in front of him with Holmes taking his turn to look in from the sidelines. The deceased man's details were fourth on the list but Watson was drawn to these before those of the first three, an action which seemed respectful in his view but not really necessary in that of Holmes. Such was the difference between the two men but the determination each possessed to extract all possible data from the document was as one.

"This man, Keith, from Bristol," Watson began, "according to a Dr. McInnis had reported symptoms of dizziness and stomach upsets including severe cramps some days before his death and that all symptoms had started within days of returning from a holiday."

"Presumably that would have been taken in Glastonbury," broke in Holmes, the likelihood being agreed to by Watson with, "That would be a fair presumption but the cause of death is listed as accidental as the man stumbled in the street and was fatally struck by a passing wagon. It doesn't say any more than that, but the man's stumble and his dizziness could well be linked"

"Yes, I do agree," said Holmes, qualifying the statement with, "but we would need more than the mere mention of a stumble to declare it a fact. Go on, what of the others? Had they also reported such symptoms?"

Watson returned his gaze to the name of first patient listed then ran his eye down quickly through the others searching for tell-tale symptoms and finding that all had reported something of the like, though not all had experienced episodes of extreme dizziness, and then replied with, "Well, yes, in general, though it's hard to make definite sweeping statements with the information such as it is, summarised by a second party and second-hand at best. The last on the list, a Major Hemmingway, a Bath man, also reported an irritating rash coinciding with his initial symptoms. Maybe that occurred before he left Glastonbury but that is mere speculation."

Watson paused, returning his attention to the first-listed patient, one who survived, and continued, "Number one is a gentleman by name of Forester and also from Bristol, though we're not told if the same doctor was involved. It just says 'severe abdominal pains and dizziness' and that's all; no details of any prescribed treatments but no mention of death, therefore his recovery is assumed."

"Yes, most definitely," offered Holmes in response. "Not near enough for a conclusive deduction but we can start to form a preliminary hypothesis or two which we can test against future data received. Good, Watson, good; we do progress."

Watson took the words of Holmes as a good omen and continued with Prendergast's list saying, "Number two, doesn't say man or woman, had dizziness and abdominal problems. Name of Brunton, comes from Sea Mills and was attended by a Dr. Davies. I don't know where Sea Mills actually is but that's all for this patient."

"You don't know of Sea Mills? Well, nor do I, Watson," Holmes admitted before adding, "but we'll find that out easily enough. Now what of that patient number three?"

"Again," started Watson, "Male or female not specified but by name of Milton and reporting dizziness and stomach pains. Attended by this Dr. Davies so presumably from that mystery place called Sea Mills."

"Number four we know." stated Holmes, "And what of the fifth on the list? What does Prendergast say about him or her?"

"That's Hemmingway, the Major; remember Holmes." reminded Watson to his friend who smiled at his momentary lapse. "Stomach cramps and that rash and attended by a Dr. Simpson. That's all we have."

"Well, it all suggests a definite pattern and perhaps a geographical grouping of victims, depending on where Sea Mills actually is," reassured Holmes. "Someone in Glastonbury has been very careless or was trying to incapacitate visitors, perhaps terminally, perhaps not, but the result is at least five deaths. But surely Prendergast could have told us all this from the queries sent by the other doctors; I wonder if he sent away for more information at all?"

Watson had pondered exactly the same thing and said as much and was about to say more but, before he could continue, the pair's discussions were interrupted by the manager bearing yet another message.

"A telegram for Mr. Holmes." the manager announced while handing the item to the curious sleuth. "Just arrived, it has. The boy is standing by in case of a reply."

Holmes rapidly tore open the envelope and quickly scanned its contents, it read, "Arriving for holiday tomorrow. Hope there's room at the inn? G. L."

Holmes, so often at odds with Lestrade about their often-conflicting methodologies, was pleased to have the Scotland Yard man's trained and experienced eyes and ears on the job in Glastonbury, eyes and ears on which he knew he could rely implicitly. He looked toward Watson, smiled, winked, folded the telegram and placed it in his inner coat pocket before returning his gaze to the waiting manager.

"No, no reply," snapped Holmes reaching into his trouser pocket to retrieve a sixpence for the boy before rising to ask the manager, "Oh, by the way; you wouldn't know of a place called Sea Mills, would you? Neither Watson nor I know of the place. Would it be nearby?"

"Sea Mills," repeated the manager, "That's a little place to the north and east of Bristol, more or less a suburb of the place these days. Quite a pleasant little location and we have had a few visitors from the place over the years, though none at the moment, more's the pity."

Holmes thanked the manager, then turned to Watson mentioning the telegram and saying, "It's from G. L.; that's Lestrade and he'll be here tomorrow. Doesn't say what time though or if he has any news for us."

"What of the other letter, Holmes?" asked Watson practically ignoring the message from Lestrade and pointing at the almost overlooked second envelope, "More of the same, perhaps?"

Holmes had opened both envelopes received earlier and had concentrated on the one containing most information, helpful as it turned out but still leaving questions to be asked. He seemed to have forgotten the existence of the second but picked it up saying, "It's from Rutledge, our driver," before reading its short message which stated, "Mr. Holmes, that trip to Street was on November the seventeenth and that Miss `Armitage was accompanied by Harry Walters. I know him well, we both being involved in moving things around. There was some sort of a historical meeting they attended, something to do about King Arthur and the Romans or Saxons or some such lot. Hope this is of help, Bert Rutledge."

Holmes read out the message, all the while trying to remember something he had heard over in Street years before and then it dawned on him. He remembered the phrase, simple enough as it turned out, a group of words he heard uttered all that time ago but which were never repeated, not in his presence at least. He remembered that he had walked in on a group discussing seemingly serious matters in hushed tones and that all present had looked his way and gone silent when one of their number had made reference to the "Knights of the Circle."

"The Knights of the Circle, Watson," Holmes declared with some satisfaction, "that's what I've been trying to remember. I could never tell if they were real, or if people were talking about the Knights of the Round Table. You know, Sir Lancelot and the rest, though if they were ever real is something to get you into a very long argument around here. There was something else though, my friend, something mysterious and I think that it has much to do with that strange hint I received from George Bridges"

***

STANDARD BEARERS

The Group

Here, indeed, was something for Holmes to ponder and something extra to keep in mind when he and Watson would approach Mrs. Staunton and Mrs. Graham, though actual mention of the Knights of the Circle would be avoided lest it deter them from freely responding to certain questions. If these "Knights," should they prove to exist, had been active in some seriously semi-political way then John Staunton may have met his death for something he had known or done, or was about to do. As well, Mrs. Graham had lost a sister well-versed in the traditional uses of herbs in the region and had been helpful to at least one of the other victims. It would be of interest, thought Holmes, to determine why either of the two had been involved in that meeting in Street in the previous November, for whatever reason that meeting had actually been called.

Dr. Prendergast had been relatively quick in providing the promised responses from other doctors concerning patients seeking medical attention upon their returns from Glastonbury and Holmes, with Watson's full agreement, suspected that the man had merely compiled the information he had without communicating with his distant colleagues. It would be futile, they realised, to extract more from the man at this point but would await the responses from the other doctors who had undertaken to seek further information.

"Was this man being evasive?" thought Holmes, "Or was he unwilling to get further involved in some matter which involved some degree of personal danger?"

Holmes knew that the question was impossible to answer with any degree of confidence but also considered the possibility that Prendergast was somehow implicated in the deaths or, if not, in the protection of other parties who were. Too many gaps were still showing in Holmes' mental mosaic and the man had a positive abhorrence of missing pieces.

Still, the day's efforts had so far brought forth solid clues and Holmes could count as facts that the victims did indeed have at least one connection between them and that some sort of a society existed in Glastonbury and that society had, and wanted to keep. its secrets. Holmes' greatest difficulty at that point was his inability to definitely prove murder to the satisfaction of the local and regional police forces; Scotland Yard, though, might prove more amenable to his possession of very strong suspicions. Satisfied with events so far but dissatisfied with the level of progress, Holmes jumped to his feet calling for Watson to do likewise so that they could be about the business of detection.

"Come Watson," he yelled, "we must be off. Mrs. Staunton and Mrs. Graham may well be able to help us place some good solid foundation stones for the case which we're constructing. We can't risk it falling down about our ears in front of Lestrade when he appears; we would never hear the end of it."

"No indeed," responded Watson, "though if we lay any more metaphorical foundation stones we'll be able to build a case to rival the heights of Glastonbury Tor, including St. Michael's Tower on top."

"Well," replied the sleuth, "perhaps we might be able to start work on the main structure after talking with the two ladies this afternoon. We still need a great deal more data if we're to impress Lestrade, someone who's more likely to trip over all those stones strewn about and complain than to do something constructive with them."

"A tad unfair, Holmes," rebuked Watson. "Lestrade has his methods and you have yours and they complement each other far more often than not."

"Yes, yes; that is true." agreed Holmes. "But the man is insufferably slow at times with all those legal restraints of his. Let's hope that his visit here will be much more than a symbolic show of force."

John Staunton had succumbed to a flare-up of a digestive disorder which had troubled him for some time. The flare-up happening some weeks after abandoning Dr. Frederick's prescription of a simple antacid mixture which was proving unsatisfactory in favour of a herbal preparation which the herbalist Horace Portland had prepared, the latter preparation giving considerable relief up until the night on which he died. Dr. Fredericks was unsympathetic to the deceased but was seen to handle the herbal product which subsequently disappeared. This behaviour on the part of the doctor was suspicious but Holmes was eager to determine if Mr. Staunton had known or made contact with any of the other victims, victims who had succumbed or had survived.

Phyllis Staunton was a distant cousin to John and was, according to her sister, reportedly free of illness but had succumbed rapidly. She had been an amateur herbalist but a great many people made use of her knowledge and a few insisted on using her preparations exclusively.

Holmes and Watson, having made important amendments to their knowledge in the few days they had been on the case, stepped out from the Pilgrims' Inn headed for the Bove Town Road and the abode of Mrs. Graham. On arrival, Holmes knocked and was a little surprised when Mr. Graham opened the door.

"Ah!" said Holmes, trying hard not to betray his expectations of seeing Mrs. Graham, "It is fortuitous to find you in. I am Sherlock Holmes and have been engaged to look into a number of unsatisfactorily explained deaths, including that of your unfortunate sister-in-law. This gentleman with me is Dr. John Watson who has been likewise engaged."

"Yes. I do know who you are, Mr. Holmes," replied Graham, "But I don't want people coming around giving my wife false hopes and making her go through all that grief again. Our mayor is only interested in his income, that independent of his office."

"We have no interest other than proving or disproving murder," Holmes assured him. "But, if murder is even indicated, there will be further questions I'm afraid. None of us would like to see more victims."

"Today's questions, however," he continued, "do not directly concern the deaths, merely the associations the victims may have formed. May we come in?"

"Well ... yes, of course," consented Graham. "But mind you go easy on Mrs. Graham with those questions of yours. If she becomes distressed, I assure you that I will bring matters to an end."

Holmes nodded his assent and, with Watson following, entered the Graham household to see Mrs. Graham standing anxiously in the hallway. She had obviously discussed the prior visit of Holmes and Randall and expressed her hopes that her sister's demise would no longer be treated as her own fault as Dr. Fredericks had all but declared.

"Mr. Holmes, and this must be Dr. Watson," she started, "please come into the sitting room. I was hoping you would return and now you have. I'm afraid that Mr. Graham is concerned that revisiting my sister's death would prove upsetting. Well, all I can say is let me be upset; I will get over it, especially if the truth finally emerges. Now, may I offer you some refreshments?"

"Thank you, indeed, but no to the refreshments. There is much more to do this afternoon and our visit will be brief and hopefully will cause you no distress," Holmes reassured her. "We understand that your sister may have gone to Street with a group last November. If you know this to be true, could you enlighten Dr. Watson and myself on the reason why?"

"Oh, that'd be the Glastonbury Archaeological Society, the local branch. Nothing officially to do with the Somerset Society, in fact they seem to argue much of the time." replied the lady. "They often went off looking at all manner of ancient structures and artefacts on irregular Sundays. As I recall, she had come in all excited about something, she wouldn't say what, but it did have something to do with some foundations of some old Roman ruins over near Street. You don't think that her interest had something to do with her death, do you Mr. Holmes? It was something she greatly enjoyed."

"That is indeed interesting, Mrs Graham," Holmes replied, "As for the other, we are not yet in a position to make any definite statements but things are progressing, I assure you."

Holmes and Watson, not having accepted their hosts' invitation to sit and take a refreshment, excused themselves while making for the door and explaining that they had similar questions to put to other similarly affected people. The Grahams, after Mr. Graham's initial concern, expressed their appreciation for the continued interest shown by the London pair and invited their return should any other matters arise.

Holmes was quiet for the first minute as the pair stepped briskly away from the Grahams' house but he suddenly spoke up.

"I feel a preliminary hypothesis forming, my friend,' he declared with a definite hint of excitement in his voice. "Very preliminary but definite with it. Let us be off to see Mrs. Staunton and ask of her husband John's historical interests and if she has any knowledge of the Street visit or of any on-going problems between the different societies."

Watson knew better than to push Holmes to share his thoughts at this point. Experience had taught him to wait until his friend was ready to speak his mind, exasperating as the waiting could be. The doctor could sense that Holmes was fixating on the Street visit by the archaeological group and the fact that Mrs. Graham had made mention of the local Glastonbury and regional Somerset archaeological societies arguing about something, perhaps a discovery of some sort, perhaps priority in all matters of historical significance. Sherlock Holmes, Watson knew, would have sensed something which he had not, perhaps something involving his earlier days as a lad in the region. All that Watson could manage was a compliant, "Of course, Holmes. Lead on."

The silence continued until the home of Mrs. Staunton came in sight whereupon Holmes declared to his companion, "Now, let us just see if we can get a few more of those foundation stones set in place, Watson. We have made good progress and we ought now to be able to accelerate the pace."

Mrs. Staunton was pleased to see Sherlock Holmes return; she had been encouraged by his first visit with William Randall and she had read of the sleuth's London exploits. So, his being accompanied on this visit by his chronicler Dr. Watson was especially welcome for she knew that, together, the pair had solved the most infuriatingly complex of crimes and had come to Glastonbury determined to repeat that success. That her husband, John, had succumbed in the way he did was made worse by Dr. Fredericks' inference that the man would still be alive if he had not abandoned his own prescribed treatment in favour of another, especially that which he would refer to as some witch's brew. Holmes needed more information to fill in a few more glaringly empty spaces and, on the pair being invited in to sit and take tea, started gently to question the lady.

"Mrs. Staunton, we have been making some headway with the matters Mr. Randall and I recently discussed with you but would hope that you might shed a little more light on a few matters."

Mrs. Staunton nodded to the sleuth and replied that, "You may ask what you will, Mr. Holmes; I shall be pleased to tell you whatever I am able."

"Thank you, indeed," Holmes responded and then continued with, "There are two principal matters I wish to have clarified, one is the source of your husband's herbal remedy and the second is that of his involvement with historical investigations of the region, specifically in Street late last year."

Pausing for a moment and placing her teacup back onto her sitting room table, Mrs. Staunton told the London pair that her husband had gotten the originally prescribed preparation from the apothecary Harold Fraser and happened to mention to Horace Portland, both men sharing the same premises while operating separate businesses, that Dr. Frederick's prescription was not delivering lasting relief. The herbalist had then provided him with a sample herbal infusion mixture for him to try.

"That herbal infusion each night gave a great deal more lasting relief than did that stuff of Fredericks," insisted Mrs. Staunton, "and the headaches virtually disappeared. John stopped taking the doctor's prescribed mixture unless his upsets were severe, which they progressively ceased to be. He had just gotten a new batch of infusion mixture from Mr. Portland and took some after our evening meal on the night he died."

"You're a medical man, Dr. Watson," she suddenly declared. "Do my husband's symptoms suggest something other than an upset stomach, something worse that Dr. Fredericks didn't see or even look for?"

"Well," replied a hesitant Watson, "I did not examine your husband but with what you have told us I would have suspected a stomach ulcer, though I must stress that would only be one of several possibilities to be confirmed or refuted by on-going medical tests. Did Frederick not take the matter further?"

"No he did not," was the angered reply. "My husband trusted that man and paid a high price for placing his life in incompetent hands. Dr. Fredericks told him the condition would go away of its own accord in due time and wrote him out a prescription and sent us his bill."

"A case of incompetence bordering on the criminal, I would say," broke in Holmes, "and perhaps a great deal more. But I must press you for what you can tell me of the other matter, that of the historical investigations."

"John did so love going off to see all those old ruins," she replied, a note of calm despair obvious in her voice, "though I rarely accompanied him. I wish now that I had but I possessed little interest in such things. He would go off with that group of his and come home with all manner of tales about what he had seen; he would sometimes bring back some rusty piece of something and tell me that it was a Roman something or other, or Saxon or much later and then clean it up so that it could be placed on display in that museum of theirs. Whatever they had been after late last year had them all excited but no one would speak of it, at least not when I was about."

"And might you know where they had gone to get so excited?" Holmes asked expectantly.

"Well, yes; I think so." replied Mrs. Staunton, "John made some mention of going over to Street to do a little digging. Whatever it was, it had motivated him so much more than usual. Does this have anything to do with his death, or that of those other people?"

"Perhaps, Mrs. Staunton." Holmes replied. "But I would ask you not to discuss these matters with anyone except Dr. Watson and myself for the moment. Things are definitely falling into place and the truth will soon emerge for all to see."

The Inspector

Mrs. Staunton was pleased with the fact that matters were progressing and thanked Holmes and Watson for their involvement. She was in the process of seeing her visitors to the front door when she remembered something, something annoying at the time but trivial in its substance.

"Oh. I had forgotten," she suddenly announced. "There had been a burglary at the Somerset group's little museum here in Glastonbury and another at their one in Somerton earlier in the year. John said that the damage to the windows was a nuisance but that nothing had been taken in either case and that it seemed as though the thieves had been looking for something in particular but found nothing to their liking. All really valuable items are kept in a strong safe and brought out only for display but no attempt had been made to open or even remove the safe in either town. I can't imagine the rival Glastonbury people being involved. There have been arguments over access to historical sites now and then but nothing like that. It must have been children or someone after something specific for a collector, perhaps."

"Perhaps," came from Holmes, echoing Mrs. Staunton's final word as the pair stepped out into the street, "But it does give us the basis for yet another clue."

"Interesting, that burglary which wasn't," commented Watson as the pair made its way back toward the Pilgrims' Inn in anticipation of the first call for dinner. "Especially so as another occurred in Somerton and all at a time when the Glastonbury archaeological people had been excited about something they had found, something special. It could have been as Mrs. Staunton suggested, the act of a collector or collector's agent, but I'd not be so quick to dismiss the possibility of Glastonbury people being involved and that there might be some connection with all the deaths, or at least some of them."

"We could wait for Lestrade's arrival," Holmes continued, "or we could make a quick diversion to see Sergeant Holloway now, before dinner. He's sure to be there behind his desk and we can ask him about the museum break-ins."

Watson, as keen as he was to sit down for his evening meal, agreed that such a visit would be useful and that Lestrade's courtesy visit would provide yet another reason to put questions to the sergeant, though it would be in front of a senior colleague removed from the constraints and complications of local politics.

The sergeant was, as ever, happy to respond to the pair's questions as long as the proper formalities and courtesies were observed. Keen to comply and keep the policeman on-side, Holmes told the man as much as he dared without revealing his key suspicions and brought up the matter of the inconsequential burglaries in a manner which suggested that only the uniformed officers would actually know what was going on.

"Yes, a matter of some annoyance, Mr. Holmes," announced Holloway while reaching for the records of the still-open case, "especially as we were unable to find any motive for the break-in, nor could our colleagues in Somerton. Nothing was taken, nothing that anyone could determine, and no damage was done except for that to the windows through which the offenders gained access."

"Was there no one of suspicion, no one new to town?" queried Holmes, hoping to encourage the sergeant to speculate on possibilities which had been entertained. "Could it have been a local person looking for something in particular?"

"Perhaps, Mr. Holmes, perhaps," agreed the sergeant hesitatingly. "But as little damage was done and nothing had been taken, the Taunton detectives were not interested in coming over, and we had other things on our plates to get on with. As for someone being new to town, that describes Glastonbury's natural state; there are always people coming and going, though somewhat fewer after the newspapers got loose with their stories of some ghoul going about committing multiple murders."

"I see," said Holmes, numerous possibilities going around in his ever-inquisitive mind. "But the case is still open, not filed away?"

"Still open," declared the sergeant. "And it will stay that way until we are satisfied that it was an isolated case of wanton damage or a robbery gone wrong."

"But it wasn't isolated," insisted Holmes. "Exactly the same thing happened in Somerton ant more or less the same time."

"Indeed it did, Mr. Holmes." the sergeant declared in agreement. "Indeed it did; and would that we had more people to chase down the offenders. If there is one thing I don't like, it is a crime gone unsolved in my town."

"Quite," commented Holmes, noting well the use of "my town." "And I must notify you that a colleague will be joining us tomorrow, a colleague ...."

Before Holmes could finish, Sergeant Holloway broke in with, "Yes, Inspector Lestrade; he'll be on the nine-fifteen train from London in the morning. We know all about it, as does everyone in Glastonbury, no doubt. Please be sure to inform him that Glastonbury is not London."

All Holmes could manage was a "We most certainly shall," before both he and Watson began to laugh almost uncontrollably at the futility of trying to keep a secret in Glastonbury.

Their duty done in respect of reporting to Sergeant Holloway, the pair walked at a leisurely pace back to the Pilgrims' Inn to partake of an unrushed dinner after which they could mull over the day's revelations and place them beside those facts and notions already encountered. There were still many details to be determined, many tiles to be placed into that mosaic which Holmes was trying to reconstruct, but the case would be a great deal more advanced when Lestrade arrived than would ever have been possible without the benefit of Holmes' youthful experiences in the district. Lestrade was not critical to their investigations but would prove a valuable ally by bringing the authority and reputation of Scotland Yard to bear.

The two men eventually sat down to their meals, Holmes taking no time to finish the meagre portion he had chosen while Watson took his time over his, it being considerably more substantial than that of his friend. Having finished eating and with daylight still hanging bright over the countryside, Watson stood and, with medical authority, suggested a constitutional stroll to aid digestion and enable a good night's sleep free from indigestion. Holmes' response, though positive, was predictable and focused on such exertions being necessary only for people who overindulged in their intakes of food.

The walk, as such walks would naturally be, was a pleasant meandering exploration of the nooks and crannies of the old abbey site with its ruins and purported resting place of Arthur and Guinevere, an important though disputed place of pilgrimage for those who sought contact with the mythical past of Britain. Holmes had passed it by many times in his youth and was somewhat immune to its mystical significance but Watson truly felt that he had come to a place where he could sense the echoes of the birth of his native land. There seemed a sense of real purpose in his visit, a purpose beyond that of catching a modern-day murderer.

An hour went by before the pair began its way back to the inn, there to relax with a nip of whiskey and a contemplative pipe before heading up the stairs to a hopefully deep and restful sleep. Lestrade would be coming in the morning and Watson felt that some sort of conveyance should be sought to pick the man up from the station for a quick ride back to the inn just in case he hadn't had time to take breakfast along his journey. This left Watson in something of a quandary as he would have to decide to have breakfast before leaving to meet the train or to wait until he and Holmes had returned with Lestrade. The safest course of action would be the first option as Holmes and Lestrade might decide to go straight to the police station to meet with Holloway and then proceed to seek out the witnesses. Watson did not get to make a decision that night for, when he retired, he went straight into a deep sleep almost as soon as his head hit the pillow.

Morning came soon enough and Watson made the strategic decision to descend the stairs to the dining room but found Holmes already sitting there sipping coffee and chewing away at some unidentified morsel waiting for him to appear.

"There you are, Watson," came from the sleuth. "I thought you might be going to sleep till noon and I hadn't the heart to disturb that chandelier-rattling slumber you were enjoying. We have some significant time for you to enjoy one of your sumptuous breakfasts before Rutledge calls for us at nine to take us to the station."

Watson looked at the clock and noted that he had something over an hour in which to enjoy his breakfast, more than enough time to have several helpings, numerous cups of coffee and an unrushed read of the available newspapers, the previous afternoon editions of the London papers being the latest available. Holmes, seeing his friend comfortably ensconced in a comfortable chair and deeply immersed in The Times, offered to go off alone to collect Lestrade and bring him back so that he could register and perhaps take a breakfast before proceeding to face the ghoul of Glastonbury, if such a person would so avail him or herself. Watson commented that the offer was a sensible one and accepted.

Inspector Lestrade was often at odds with Sherlock Holmes and never so much as when Holmes would overlook the strict legality of his methods. Here in Glastonbury, however, he, Watson and Lestrade were all outsiders, invited definitely, but outsiders nonetheless. The London train steamed in on-time and Inspector Lestrade stepped out to be greeted by Sherlock Holmes who took the policeman's bags and led him toward Rutledge's dog cart. The short journey back to the Pilgrims' Inn was uneventful and Holmes took the time to introduce Lestrade to Rutledge, a witness who had provided some very important information.

Holmes did point out the tor in the distance but the line of view was not good for much of the time. He promised to take both him and Watson on a guided tour at some point but added that such an outing might be some time off as investigations had entered a critical phase. Lestrade, never one for history lessons unless they involved criminals being brought to justice, made noises simulating interest but was obviously less than impressed with old buildings and even older mythical kings. He was keen, however, to hear full details of the investigations made to date and what inferences they had permitted to be made. Breakfast and coffee would have to come first, however, before the two investigators could increase their number and become a team of three.

The Pilgrims' Inn dining room was deserted except for Watson who had advised the cook that there would be a late breakfaster, a Scotland Yard detective who would be staying for several days and who appreciated country cooking. The cook stayed on and came out personally to greet her late client and took an order to rival that of the ever-ravenous John Watson. Waiting for his meal to be delivered, Lestrade received a very brief overview of the coming day's expected schedule before Holmes thought to pass on some helpful local advice.

"Oh, by the way, Lestrade," Holmes announced, "Sergeant Holloway says to remind you of where you are and that Glastonbury is not London. I think he means to inform you that both you and your London methods could be out of place here."

"That could well be true, Holmes, but you never know; perhaps my methods and I and my warrant card from Scotland Yard may prove to be of some use," replied Lestrade who had removed his revolver from his pocket and was going through the motions of checking that its cylinder was fully charged with cartridges.

Holmes looked at his official colleague and said, simply, "Quite!"

The Maps

The arrival of Inspector Lestrade, albeit in only a semi-official capacity as no case had actually been opened to which he might be assigned, had raised the status of the investigation to a new level. He had advised the Taunton detectives that he would be looking into a number of matters which had been brought to his attention by two private investigative colleagues engaged by the Borough Council and who had sought his advice. He had received no reply to his communication with Taunton and took this as tacit approval for him to proceed, though he well knew that his involvement would be resented if he tried to take control of proceedings and the local police personnel. He also knew that the Taunton detectives would more than likely take control as soon as any crime was proved and after significant headway had been made. This, however, would be nothing new to the Inspector who had long operated within the bureaucratic framework of the police Force and was used to jurisdictional situations and disputes. His own superiors were amenable to his involvement and Lestrade assumed that this had come about due to semi-political connections existing between senior police office holders and the Mayor of Glastonbury. In normal circumstances such an arrangement might be considered unusual unless there was definite evidence of a crime having been committed.

Lestrade's meeting with Holloway followed along similar lines to that which the Sergeant had conducted with Holmes. Glastonbury was not London but was 'his town' and he wanted no disturbance of anyone's peace, especially his own unless there was a very good reason. The sergeant had to rein in his insistence on being kept informed as Lestrade's rank did carry a degree of general authority in matters of criminal investigation and the Inspector was not going to be dictated to by a sergeant. Still, the meeting was amicable enough and a general cooperative understanding was reached after Holmes delivered a truncated version of the previous day's events to the Glastonbury man, several key points being deliberately omitted.

Next came a meeting with Mayor Bennet, a meeting as brief as it was useful but something which was considered prudent to keep the man on-side yet away from the active part of the investigations. Before their meeting, Lestrade had explained to his two unofficial colleagues just how the situation 'behind the scenes' had so easily enabled him to travel to Glastonbury unassigned to an actual case and without objection from the local Taunton headquarters. None of this was mentioned to Bennet and the man was permitted to hold to his presumption that he was in overall charge which, at a bureaucratic though not operational level, he actually was.

The two solicitors, Randall and Jamison, were part of the investigation team but not experienced investigators. Their presence had helped Holmes and Watson gain some degree of local acceptance but their involvement could prove a hindrance now that Lestrade had arrived and the London men were keen to keep them on-hand but not actively involved. Some little diplomacy might be necessary to avoid the appearance of them being discarded out of hand. A lunchtime meeting might be amenable to the two solicitors and provide an opportunity for them to meet Lestrade and perhaps agree to take a less active part in the proceedings; such an arrangement might well prove very agreeable and even preferable for two busy and largely office-bound professional men. A message was sent off and a prompt reply received in the affirmative. The five would meet at the Pilgrims' Inn for yet another lunchtime meeting after which the investigations would continue in earnest.

With a little over an hour remaining before the meeting, Homes wanted to introduce Lestrade to ex-Sergeant Bridges but reconsidered having sensed that Bridges might consider that he was being pushed to divulge matters on which he was only prepared to give vague clues for Holmes, together with Watson, to decipher and then to follow with a great deal of discretion. "Better to wait," Holmes thought, "until we know more of these Street goings-on. George has given me all he feels he can."

There was a definite sense of matters beginning to clarify, at least a little. For one thing, the deaths seemed to be definitely connected and this pointed to deliberate intent or to a series of very unlikely coincidences. For another, there seemed to be a not-always friendly rivalry between the local Glastonbury historical enthusiasts and those of a wider-spread Somerset society and that something had at least some of societies' members excited and possibly prepared to resort to extreme tactics. What might connect these situations was as yet unknown to Holmes but he felt that it had something to do with the Glastonbury Tor and an archaeological find in Street. More questions would have to be asked but, with the hesitance of many to be drawn beyond a certain point, the answer might come only after Holmes, Watson and Lestrade had become physically, and possibly dangerously, involved.

With Holmes unwilling to waste a good working hour and Lestrade being less than interested in a short historical tour of Glastonbury, Watson suggested returning to the inn where he might convince Holmes to discuss, in some depth, all or any of the hypotheses which were circulating in his brain. Perhaps where Holmes was tight-lipped with his close friend and colleague, he might just be forthcoming with Lestrade.

Three of the inn's easy chairs found themselves repositioned so that the trio could have a close conversation and not risk being overheard, and Holmes, despite his usual reticence in divulging his thoughts before they had gelled into well-considered notions, agreed to share just a little. Reaching into his inner coat pocket, the sleuth retrieved a folder containing a quite old and somewhat tattered map of Glastonbury and Street and another of the general district. These were maps he had prepared as a lad from numerous official maps to which he had access and which had lain in his trunk unseen and unused for decades.

"Watson, you're a military man," started Holmes, "and would no doubt have read the odd map when you weren't sawing off some arm or leg. And you, Lestrade, when the Police actually did know what was afoot, they would have had to know how to get to where-ever things were actually going on. So, my little map should be child's play to you both."

"Show us the maps, Holmes," growled Lestrade shaking his head while looking toward Watson and trying to restrain a grin, "I think that Watson and I might just manage to follow them."

"Well, we'll start with the larger-scale map." Holmes declared, pulling over a small side table and placing it in front of him with the regional map facing away, "What I want you to note is the position of Glastonbury and Street in the scheme of things and the shaded regions marking out high ground. Now, the Poldens are not as high as are the Mendips and Quantocks but they do stand higher than the surrounding Levels and the road running northward through Street dips down to what used to be an ancient causeway across the Brue before the original Pomparles Bridge was constructed. In those early days the Levels were a great deal more marshy than today and extensive bodies of water abounded. Is that clear?"

"Yes Holmes." replied Lestrade, "That is certainly plain enough; now keep going."

"You will also notice how Glastonbury sits high at the edge of the Levels save for a low neck of land extending to the east." he continued, "Well, in days long gone when Glastonbury was a good deal smaller and long before that when its name may well have been something else, the land on which it stood was spoken of as an island surrounded by a lake formed from the waters of the Brue. The lake, however, disappeared when the Abbot caused a drainage canal to be dug to free up much more pasture and cropping land. The Brue seems tame enough at present but its name is from the Welsh and means something like 'swift' and turbulent'."

"A history lesson, is it?" asked Lestrade, a little impatient for Holmes to get to the point.

"I believe that history, or a version of it, is the key to our murders." replied Holmes as though he was reprimanding a surly schoolboy, "But I need to explain just a little more."

Both Watson and Lestrade knew that Sherlock Holmes was rarely wasteful of words and also knew enough to realise that he needed to give his hypotheses some sort of context. Holmes kept on with, "That island upon which Glastonbury stands, and on which we are now perched, has a very strong claim to being the mythical Isle of Avalon, an absolute fact for many who live here and in the lands about. Avalon has had similar renderings in Welsh and French such as Abal and Affal and Avallach and refers to an 'island bearing fruit trees', any local fruit having been appels or eppels before that term became used for a specific fruit we came to call apples after the coming of the Normans."

"Well, it's no wonder that I'm feeling a little hungry," commented Watson, actually finding Holmes' discourse quite interesting, "the island is named for something edible."

Holmes ignored Watson's comment and continued before Lestrade had a chance to contribute another.

"Now, we are all aware of the legend of Arthur and his Knights, though a great deal of licence has been invoked in its telling, but the fellow probably existed in some local regal capacity at some time and we're told that he fell at Camlann and that his sword was given to the Lady of the Lake for safekeeping. Somerset abounds with ruins and relics and that sword, the mystical magical Excalibur, should it ever have existed, is still missing. My major current working hypothesis is that someone has dug up a sword hereabouts and groups have been competing with each other for its possession."

"Of course, I may be quite wrong," he added, "but my hypothesis could explain the extreme zeal we have sensed pervading the place."

"That doesn't explain the poisonings, Holmes." remarked Watson, "Would people kill each other over an old sword."

Lestrade gave a sudden "Hrmff" before declaring that, "I've seen people fight and kill over an old shilling, so an old sword such as Holmes describes and which could sell for many thousands of pounds would bring out the worst in people normally meek and mild. That is apart from the fight which would stem from its historical value to the nation, should it prove or even seem authentic."

A sudden drumming of the gong outside the dining room brought an abrupt halt to discussions on swords and ancient kings and Watson stood as if to declare the meeting over. Lestrade was not overly hungry and Holmes could see no reason to eat so soon after breakfast but the Doctor led the way and called for his companions to follow. They could continue their discussions over coffee, he suggested, though Holmes did insist that he alone be the one to decide on what matters to put before the solicitors.

A table for five having being occupied, the three Londoners sat about awaiting the arrival of Randall and Jamison who would surely arrive in the next few minutes. Holmes, taking advantage of the solicitors' absence, then told his two colleagues he suspected that a society existed in Glastonbury, perhaps being Somerset-wide, and that it may be organised along some quasi-religious line and could likely count persons of some significance among its members.

"I tell you this," he explained, "as I will be putting matters to Randall and Jamison which might sound strange, perhaps even bizarre, without you knowing my thoughts. I would ask you to go along with what I might say but not to interrupt or ask for further clarification. As far as the two solicitors are concerned, we are looking for a suspect acting alone."

Holmes got his message out just in time for the two extra lunch guests appeared at the dining room's entrance. Lestrade followed the lead of his two companions and got to his feet as Holmes beckoned the solicitors to join the group.

"Randall, Jamison," he announced, "I am glad you could spare the time to join us. I would like to introduce Inspector Lestrade of Scotland Yard, here to add an extra layer of authority to our investigations. Inspector, meet Alderman Randall and Alderman Jamison of the Glastonbury Municipal Borough Council, also solicitors practicing from offices nearby."

Lestrade stepped out from the table to greet the two men, the pair responding enthusiastically to his presence and offering whatever assistance they might provide in either of their professional or private capacities. The brief formalities completed, the five men sat and Watson raised his hand to summon the waiter.

The Bait

Meals were ordered and delivered but Holmes, ever the selectively tactful companion, commented teasingly and at Watson's expense on the doctor's ability to take sustenance whenever the opportunity availed itself. Watson responded with remarks on the eating habits of sparrows and of how the Pilgrims' Inn needed his support in this time of pending economic stagnation; thus, he claimed, he was being a benefactor to Glastonbury by dining generously.

Lestrade was long used to the sparring between Holmes and Watson, generally triggered by some inflammatory remark from the former, and Randall and Jamison had seen the process break a build-up of frustration and tension in their recent investigations.

"Mr. Holmes and Dr. Watson do like their little diversions," remarked Randall, "and I daresay it helps to give the mental strain from complex matters some degree of relief. We have spoken of the need for diversion when the thought process has met an impasse; Jamison and I often take to walking while Mr. Holmes prefers a bit of mental swordplay."

"Indeed he does," agreed Lestrade, "and that swordplay has often gone on until blood was close to being spilled; Holmes' blood, not Watson's."

Watson looked on grinning in silence and knowing full well that he was being baited by his two London colleagues in order to put the two Glastonbury men at their ease before they would be unknowingly and subtly interrogated.

Holmes then waited until the two solicitors had finished their meals and were substantially relaxed before beginning with, "We have revisited some of those spoken to earlier and have established that the four Glastonbury victims who succumbed were part of some archaeological society. They were involved in recovering ancient artefacts in the region and there had been some degree of friction between their society and another. Have either of you heard of anything of that sort happening?"

Randall seemed a little uncomfortable and looked at his colleague who then took the lead to reply, "There are dozens of little groups in our region and they do like to argue, Mr. Holmes. In fact, it is what makes Glastonbury what it is in this modern day and people with all sorts of beliefs are drawn here for the mysteries, the source of so much dissent. There is also the problem of ownership and I can tell you as a legal man who also sits on the Council that claims to whoever has priority over what has sometimes ended with men in helmets coming to break up the scrimmages of the overheated parties."

"And if John Staunton were to have made a significant discovery," pressed Holmes, "would he have faced such a barrage of vitriol from others who claimed priority over all such finds?"

"Perhaps," replied Jamison, "but had Mr. Staunton made a discovery of that sort?"

"My reply is the same as yours," Holmes countered, trying to ascertain if Jamison knew more, "for as yet we have had heard nothing definite but did sense a degree of deliberate evasion of that very question."

"I had heard nothing about a discovery made by this Mr. Staunton," declared Jamison who then turned to his colleague and asked, "Had you, Randall?"

Randall, now seeming to Holmes and Watson to have assumed the status of the more junior of the two solicitors in contrast to prior impressions, simply gave a, "No, I can't say that I had."

"But might there be more?" pushed Holmes, "Perhaps some sort of a guild of greater significance than that a local archaeological club. There is something here, something just out of sight but which we have felt looking on and observing all we do."

"Well, Mr. Holmes," Jamison replied with a little uncertainty detectable in his voice, "I don't really know how to respond to that question. I could ask a few of my colleagues and get back to you with their comments. Would that be of use?"

Holmes could tell that both men knew far more than they were prepared to divulge, perhaps from being unsure if they ought or perhaps from some sense of fear. Unable to decide which, Holmes replied, "I believe that it would, Mr. Jamison, but if that could be done quite soon it would be a decided advantage. The case is very close to becoming an official Scotland Yard investigation after which any possibility of discretion being exercised will be removed."

Holmes did not say what might be the repercussions but he could tell that both Glastonbury men had been rattled somewhat. Jamison looked at Randall and both stood and began making their excuses to leave while assuring the remaining trio that they would make the enquiries Holmes had referred to.

Each then turned to Inspector Lestrade and Randall repeated their greeting with, "It's been a pleasure to meet you Inspector; I'm sure that we shall be speaking again quite soon."

"Likewise for me, gentlemen." Lestrade replied, "I would note, though, were I you, that should the Yard become officially involved, my directions would overrule those of Holmes. Also, while Holmes is a gentleman, I am not and I do not have the luxury of being able to withdraw from any situation not to my liking. This warrant card of mine operates both ways and these copper's boots I'm wearing are made for stomping, and stomp, they will. So, when you speak to your friends, remind them of the reach of that card and these boots."

The solicitors made their way out of the Pilgrims' Inn unsure if they had just been threatened or given a somewhat more than subtle hint. Both, though, knew that Lestrade's words were sincere and that Scotland Yard would not stop until someone was facing the noose. They also knew, being members of the legal profession, that anyone who impeded an official investigation or even failed to fully cooperate could and likely would be charged as an accessory and could face a significant penalty.

Watson sat back in his chair and looked at his two colleagues, saying, "Well, that shook them up, Lestrade, and probably ruined their digestion. I fear they might have to resort to one of Fredericks' famous antacid preparations to get through the rest of the afternoon."

"And that would a problem, would it?" asked Lestrade, unaware of the situation with the difficult doctor who attended each of the four deaths.

"We have much more to tell you, Lestrade," Holmes informed the inspector, "and as we have just baited one of our traps, we shall have a little time to go over the case in more detail."

Returning to their previous location, each of the three men retook the chair he had occupied before lunch and Holmes went to some significant pains to give Lestrade as complete a picture of the situation as was possible. It was obvious that more information had to be collected but much of that would not be lying around waiting to be picked up. There were matters in Glastonbury of which few locals were prepared to speak and of which many may have been completely ignorant. George Bridges had given Holmes a strong hint but there were the matters which Harry Walters wanted to discuss away from his employer's and work-mates' eyes and ears. That discussion would have to wait until work had finished, though there were others who had yet to be questioned, one doctor in particular, also an apothecary and a herbalist.

"Three makes too big a group to go about questioning people, Holmes," remarked Watson, "Perhaps you and Lestrade should leave me here or give me something else to do."

Holmes smiled and replied, "What you say is true, my friend, but your medical knowledge is what we'll be needing when we call in on Portland and Fraser. One of them is a murderer, I fear, or in league with one. Perhaps you'll be able to tell which of them it is."

"And," he continued, "we shall have to speak again with a doctor or two. I should expect that they might be receiving replies from their distant colleagues who had enquired about their patients' symptoms. That, my friend, is your area of expertise and we can't have you sitting around reading newspapers all day; it's a waste of our resources and bad for your digestion."

With Holmes' pronouncement on Watson's indispensability, the time for talking had come to an end and the trio started toward the shared premises of Fraser and Portland, apothecary and herbalist. Lestrade, ever the detective and being far more observant in his own way than Holmes would ever have given him credit, looked about as he and his colleagues passed through the High Street, the collective hum of its various enterprises echoing in miniature that of the far noisier metropolis to the east. Glastonbury was certainly small when compared to London and within its precincts could offer fewer places to hide so that any suspects were concentrated into a smaller area; however, and as Lestrade had been pointedly advised, Glastonbury was not London and the rules which operated within its boundaries were different. Also to consider was the broad region beyond into which a felon might abscond, though the options for escape were as few as the roads leading away. Should the detective chase a Glastonbury denizen to a town as close as Street, he would find that the rules had changed again, though any and all such local rules might alter if the interests of Street were being deliberately compromised by someone from Glastonbury. To make matters more infuriating, the wily inspector might well find that a greater Somerset would do things in yet other ways and look after its own before pandering to the distant statutes of Westminster by which other outsiders had tried unsuccessfully to completely smother the age-old local methods of removing difficulties.

Lestrade's warrant card and copper's boots might not always be as intimidating as he presumed.

On entering the combined premises, the trio was welcomed by Horace Portland who, having recognised Holmes and Watson, came out from behind his counter to greet his inquisitorial visitors.

"Good afternoon, gentlemen." he stated confidently and in a rather gracious manner. "I do recognise Mr. Holmes and Dr. Watson and I would presume that this gentleman with you would be Inspector Lestrade of Scotland Yard."

"There's no need to look startled, inspector," he continued, "there are few secrets which long stay that way within Glastonbury. Eyes and ears everywhere, you know, and an abundance of wagging tongues."

"So I am led to believe," responded Lestrade displaying his warrant card and a little annoyed at the attempt to put him in his place as an outsider. "But I, too, am here to use my eyes and ears, passively for the time being, but I do believe that Mr. Holmes has a few questions to put to you and Mr. Fraser. Or is that Dr. Fraser?"

"Oh, no, no. It's definitely Mr.," replied Portland, now a little shaken with the question and his almost apologetic response. "Mr. Fraser is in his compounding laboratory."

"Perhaps, then," broke in an insistent Holmes, "you might be able to help us."

Portland nodded to indicate the affirmative and set about collecting stools for them to sit on and, having placed a "closed" sign on the now shut door, bade his visitors to ask away.

Holmes than put it to the herbalist, "You prepared an infusion for Mr. John Staunton some time back, did you not, the man who later died?"

Portland acknowledged with a hesitating nod that he had, and added, "But not from my preparation. He had reported good results from its use."

"And Dr. Fredericks was somewhat unimpressed with what he saw as your interference?" Holmes pressed, noting that the herbalist was showing signs of becoming agitated, perhaps just unsure of where the questions were heading, perhaps nervous about words which had passed between himself and Fredericks at the time.

"Mr. Staunton came to me, Mr. Holmes," Portland insisted. "I did not approach him, nor do I seek to poach any doctor's patients with false claims of magical cures. I have built up an extensive knowledge of nature's abundant living apothecary and use it to select herbs which help the body to help itself. If there is any magic in that, it is the magic of a Providence which has placed a bounty of good health within the reach of us all. I make my living by offering both that knowledge and my expertise in collecting and preparing what others cannot and my business compliments that of Mr. Fraser with whom I have a good working relationship."

"But, are not some of those agents of natural beneficence to humanity also poisonous in the extreme?" Holmes asked somewhat provocatively.

Portland looked directly at Holmes rather alarmed at what might have been construed as a veiled accusation and replied, "One may drown in an excess of water but would also die for want of a life-sustaining drink, Mr. Holmes; therefore one would approach a raging torrent differently than a beaker of water on a hot day. One has to know the material which one dispenses and how it works on the human body and how much is too much. My example is extreme, I grant you, but it serves to illustrate my point."

"Indeed," Holmes conceded, "but some have been pushed into raging torrents and we are here to determine if that was how Mr. Staunton met his end."

"Not by me, they haven't," Portland angrily replied. "I'm interested in health and extending healthy lives, not its removal. Now, if you have something to accuse me of then do so, for I have nothing to hide and have done nothing of which to be ashamed."

"You do use digitalis in your preparation, just a little, do you not?" asked Holmes, baiting the herbalist and ignoring his understandable outburst.

"Yes!" was the herbalist's curt reply.

The Keys

"But Horace Portland would never harm a living soul, Mr. Holmes," came a retort from the doorway to Fraser's laboratory. "My profession removes the immediate cause of an illness while Mr. Portland's keeps the body's systems in balance so that many of our common illnesses can't take hold. You cannot possibly believe that my good friend here would have anything to do with the death of Mr. Staunton or any of those others; it's goes against everything the man stands for."

"Ah, you must be Mr. Fraser," Holmes responded. "We haven't actually met unless you count our very brief encounter on the train. We are here to gather facts and the facts may well be unpleasant; this gentleman with Dr. Watson and myself is Inspector Lestrade from Scotland Yard, as you no doubt already know. We are keen to get matters sorted before the newspapers can do any more damage to Glastonbury's reputation and visitor numbers."

Harold Fraser stopped his rebuke toward Holmes and stood open-mouthed for a few seconds while looking at Portland for some sign of what to do next. Before either could respond, Holmes continued with his questions, though Fraser was now the subject of his attention.

"Did you, yourself, have dealings with Mr. Staunton, the deceased man?" continued Holmes. "Did you, for example, make up the antacid mixture for him on behalf of Dr. Fredericks?"

"Well, yes; I did, as it happens," replied a now somewhat nervous Fraser. "I am an apothecary and such mixtures are commonplace, though Mr. Staunton's as I recall had a small quantity of peppermint oil added for effect, though the standard mixture is not at all repellent to the taste."

"Interesting!" commented the sleuth applying his most suspicious sounding vocal tone. "And was Dr. Fredericks as annoyed with you as he seems to have been with Mr. Portland here?"

"Why should he be?" came back angrily from Fraser. "He prescribed a mixture for a patient, and I filled that prescription with exactly the right preparation. I made it up in my compounding laboratory just behind me. I keep meticulous records, you know. Just stay there while I get my compounding book."

Before Holmes could assure him that he had no reason to doubt his words, Fraser had disappeared back into his laboratory and returned a few seconds later with a thick, leather-bound foolscap-sized book filled with the details of every mixture he had ever produced in the last five years. He thrust the book onto the counter, flicking through the pages until he found the entry he sought and then insisted that all three London men individually confirm its veracity. He then produced a second smaller book, one listing his customers and indexed to the larger book, and repeated the process of confirmation. That done, he slammed both books shut and demanded an explanation.

"Your regional police have been unconvinced, to date," Holmes declared, "but Scotland Yard has despatched its finest and most capable investigator to confirm that there is a case of murder to be answered. I am convinced absolutely that such is the case and I must press everyone who had contact with the victims for what information they may be holding. In some cases, that information will be incidental to the matters, in other cases it may hold the key to identifying the murderer or, indeed, the murderers."

Neither of the two Glastonbury men could manage the feeblest of comments so Holmes continued with, "Now ... about Dr. Fredericks. I would appreciate it if you would both describe your relationships with the man; your personal and your professional relationships."

"Ah ... Dr. Fredericks," fumbled Fraser. "What about him?"

"Exactly my question," countered Holmes, "though specifically in relation to yourselves and generally in relation to anybody else whose dealings with the doctor might seem irregular."

"Did Dr. Fredericks," Holmes then asked quite pointedly, "approach either of you over anything concerning Mr. Staunton, other that writing a prescription for an antacid preparation? Mr. Portland, I know, has something to tell us about the doctor's dissatisfaction with Staunton's use of herbal products."

"That is correct, Mr. Holmes," admitted Portland, "and his manner was quite unnecessarily offensive but, as I don't rely on his referrals for any of my business or interfere in his, I told him not to interfere in mine. I believe that Mr. Staunton continued to purchase Mr. Fraser's preparation as well as mine even after he started to improve. Dr. Fredericks may not be the most polite of people or the most willing to admit being wrong but I can't see him being in any way involved in these deaths."

"Is that what you are saying, Mr. Holmes?" asked Fraser, worried that he might be in some way implicated. "Do you think that Dr. Fredericks is involved?"

"He is involved with all four local deaths," Holmes replied, "in that he determined the causes of death and signed the death certificates. He also had professional contact with at least one of those victims before his death and clearly had issues over challenges to his prescribed course of medication. Such involvement may prove to be completely innocent, but it is something which neither I nor Scotland Yard is prepared to overlook."

"Did Dr. Fredericks have access to these premises outside of working hours?" asked Lestrade, providing extra pressure on the apothecary and herbalist.

"Well," started Fraser, "he does have a key to the front door and to my laboratory with its stocks of medications; just for emergencies, mind you. He rarely avails himself of that access and has always left details and returned to sign my medicinals' register. He has no access at all to Mr. Portland's ingredients or preparations, all of which are locked away, as are mine."

"Are you certain of that?" Holmes pressed further. "And Mr. Portland, have you ever noticed anything awry with your products, anything recent?"

"Nothing missing, Mr. Holmes, but, now that you say it, a number of my stock preparations did seem disturbed a few months back, but only in their placement on my shelving; my locked shelving. I presumed that I had been rushed and had not been quite as tidy as I meant to be."

"May I examine those keys of yours, Mr. Portland?" Holmes asked, now virtually certain of Fredericks' involvement beyond the incidental.

Portland produced his keys which Holmes took and examined before passing them to Inspector Lestrade who declared the front door key and lock to be reasonably secure. The herbalist was then asked to lock his shelving, after which Sherlock Holmes produced a selection of commonly encountered key types from his pocket and proceeded to try each on Portland's locks. A muted click was heard as Holmes turned the fifth of his keys and the shelving door yielded without effort.

"Mr. Holmes!" Portland retorted, "I don't know what to say. I'd thought my keys were unique. The builders who did the carpentry work said they were. Where would someone get another?"

"Where, indeed, Mr. Portland?" Holmes replied. "The key is of a type found commonly enough for cupboard and wardrobe locks and a great deal of furniture seems to find itself bought and sold in this part of the world. Anyone who could get through the front door might easily obtain such a key and gain access to those shelves of yours and their contents."

Before either of the two Glastonbury men could respond, Holmes stood, thanked each for his cooperation, called his two colleagues and proceeded with them out through the front door.

"If your thoughts are the same as mine, Holmes," declared Lestrade as they proceed along the street, "then this Fredericks has just found himself high up on the 'decidedly suspicious' list."

"I do concur," agreed Holmes, "but what would have been his motive? It can't have been jealousy or petty revenge gone too far. Something else is behind this, something deliberate and very nasty. We need a few more nails before we start sealing coffins in this case, gentlemen."

"Harry Walters?" posed Watson.

"Indeed, Watson," replied Holmes, "he has something he earnestly wishes to tell us and I have questions I earnestly wish to put to him. Unfortunately, we must wait until evening to approach him at Mrs. Waldron's lodging house."

"Where to next?" asked Lestrade, now seeing the prospects of a juicy case of murder looming.

Holmes gave a long "Hmmm!" before declaring, "I think we might barge in on Dr. Baxter and ask if he knows any more than before. If he's busy, we might interrupt Dr. Baxter's peaceful existence. Lestrade, try to look sick."

Lestrade gave a forced cough and followed it with a contrived wheeze and asked where he might obtain medical attention locally, adding that Watson's London remedies wouldn't work in Glastonbury. Watson gave a sigh of mock despair and reminded the Scotland Yard man that they were there to investigate a case of murder possibly involving a Glastonbury doctor and that he should weigh the risks of consulting one very carefully.

Luckily for the trio, it had been a slow day illness-wise in Glastonbury and Dr. Baxter was discovered lurking behind a semi-circle of paperwork with a look of frustration on his face.

His nurse announced the three visitors and Baxter bade them to enter, suggesting that tea would be a welcome treat for all of them. With that, he collected an assortment of chairs from his waiting room and set them in his surgery and bade all to sit and await their refreshment.

Watson, having previously spoken with Dr. Baxter while accompanied by Brian Jamison, began by introducing his two colleagues, emphasising the recent arrival of the Scotland Yard inspector and the significance which his presence held for the investigations. He then handed the reins over to Holmes whose opening words were interrupted by the arrival of rattling tea cups and their ancillary culinary implements.

"Tea will be but a moment," announced the nurse who seemed to have taken command of numerous duties and functions supplementary to her employer's. Watson was unsure that she was a nurse but the lady did have the appearance of one and was duly introduced as Mrs. Baxter, the doctor's wife and, seemingly, his masterful Jack, or perhaps Jill, of all trades.

"Bring a cup for yourself, my dear," Baxter told her, "and join this assortment of detectives. You may well have information which might interest them."

"Mrs. Baxter takes an active part in the practice, then?" queried Watson, impressed by Mrs. Baxter's commanding presence, though she was only serving tea he reminded himself.

"Mrs, Baxter is another Dr. Baxter, Dr. Watson," replied Baxter, "and just arrived this day to play her part in our Glastonbury practice. In some parts, the rustle of her skirts would be enough to dampen the enthusiasm of some patients, but many here are looking forward to a gentler application of medicine than is otherwise available, myself excluded of course."

"How wonderful!" announced Watson who had stood and offered a congratulatory hand to a newly qualified colleague, "When time permits, you must tell us of your studies and ambitions."

"Certainly, Dr. Watson," she replied, "when time permits. But first I must attend to our teas. I'm afraid I daren't let Maurice brew it; he always manages to make it undrinkable."

The newly arrived Mrs., and now Dr., Baxter disappeared and could be heard in the rear kitchen as she removed a kettle from the stove and poured the boiling water into a teapot of substantial size. This she carried into the surgery to begin dispensing teas into cups and offering milk, lemon and sugar to what she saw as her guests, despite the visit being a professional one. All had refused her offer of more substantial solid refreshments, and the group then settled down as Holmes prepared to begin with his questions.

"We have become aware of a complicated assortment of connections between the victims and of some degree of friction between them and other, as yet unidentified, parties," announced Holmes. He then continued, "There is an archaeological aspect to all of this and I was hoping to gather any information which might link ancient objects and deliberate poisoning using, I believe, digitalis among other hazardous plant types. Have you received any reply from your distant colleagues about the natures of their patients' illnesses?"

It was a declaration as much as it was a question and the two Drs. Baxter looked at each other uncertain of who should answer. Mrs. Baxter said that, as she had just arrived, it would fall to her husband to answer but that she had been aware of active archaeological sites from a visit several months previously, though only through general gossip in the waiting room.

"Digitalis could well have been involved," announced Maurice Baxter, "but the symptoms do overlap with those of many other afflictions. At that time of year, we have respiratory ailments, you know, coughs and colds and infected throats and our apothecaries are at their busiest."

"And what of your herbalists?" insisted Holmes, "Do you also keep them busy?"

The two physicians looked at each other and both started to speak at once, each trying to say that they had no objection to the use of herbal remedies but had concerns that some might resort to seeking magical cures when they may actually be in need of urgent medical attention. Holmes then asked if he knew where the patients beyond Glastonbury had come from.

"I've had one reply, Mr. Holmes," Baxter stated, "and that told me the patient was from Bristol."

***

TO ARMS

The Knights

Bristol is not so very far from Glastonbury, not in distance, not since the coming of the railways, but it is of a different world, a world of commerce and shipping, of tides and departures, of faraway lands and exotic cargoes. Some historians tell us that it began as Brycgstow, a name speaking of goods being held safe and dry in readiness to be dispatched by sea or carted by road over its bridges and causeways to all parts of the country. Others say it derives from the Saxon rendering of the Welsh Caer Odor as Bricstow for the Fortress on the Gorge. Of the actual facts of its naming, no one can say with certainty but it has a commanding presence and through the centuries its people have been as hardy and as enterprising and as spiritual as any, but its mystic past is as nought against that of its enigmatic inland sister settlement.

Holmes would, however, in time find a connection between the two, and that connection would prove to be an ancient one.

Outward appearances would suggest that Bristol and Glastonbury were as different as two habitations could be, yet there did seem to be a curious concentration of Bristol dwellers having visited Glastonbury only to seek medical attention on their return home for maladies seemingly contracted elsewhere, presumably in the town by the tor. The numbers were not overly high but people had died who, according to local wisdom and insistent newspaper reports, should not have and the nervousness was proving contagious.

Bath, too, had been mentioned, though fleetingly, and Holmes was calling on old and hesitant memories to remind him of what it was he had heard said of the place so many years before. It was, he believed, nothing of a sinister nature, simply incidental and yet it had nagged at him since he had remembered mention of the "Knights of the Circle". It would come to him but he had done too good a job of storing those old memories away. A few days before and he would have considered those memories to be superfluous clutter interfering with the effective functioning of his super-efficient mind but now they were needed to bring substance to vague and hazy notions of presumed importance; he would have to remember where he hid them.

Bristol and Bath -- connected by the Avon. Bath and Glastonbury, both in Somerset and both of spiritual significance; the former to the ancients, the latter likewise but retaining those ancient links into the modern day. The memories he sought had something to do with Arthur, or the much repeated legends of a mythical king with attachments to the land which became Somerset, that he knew, but the significance eluded him. After all, these were memories from his childhood and childhood memories had a way of undergoing drastic change after the serious business of adult life had rendered them barely recognisable as long unused mental fragments.

Holmes, Watson and Lestrade had obtained all they could from the two Dr. Baxters and, as they made their way back toward the town's centre, both Watson and Lestrade noticed that Holmes had entered into that intensely introspective state from which there was no dragging him. It was a state brought about by a mind battling to hold disparate ideas together while groping for that glue which would bind them into a coherent hypothesis. Holmes could finally hear the hunt master sounding the call "to horse" and the quarry rustling in the underbrush fearful of being flushed from its hiding place and out into the open; the hunter was unsure of just what it was that he was hunting but it would soon reveal itself.

"Oh dear," said Watson to Lestrade as he observed the intensity of his friend's expression, "I do believe we are in for a revelation of some sort. There's no point going on to see Walters, least of all because he won't be home yet, but more for the fact that our silent friend here is thinking ... and you know what that means."

"Indeed I do, doctor," replied the Scotland Yard man, mindful of his futile attempts to do so in the past. "But it's a pity he doesn't have his pipe. Perhaps we ought to call into the inn and collect it and I can check for messages. Perhaps we can all check for messages."

"A quite timely idea, Lestrade," agreed the doctor, "seeing that we are but fifty yards from the inn's entrance. And while we're there, I'll see if we can't rustle up two cups of coffee, three if Holmes can return from wherever it is that he's been in that mind of his."

Receiving no argument to the contrary, Watson and Lestrade picked up the pace, each taking up positions either side of Holmes and each taking hold of one of the sleuth's elbows and dragging him along the street and then into the Pilgrims' Inn.

Watson sat his friend in one of the inn's easy chairs and went off in search of his friend's pipe, tobacco and matches while Lestrade checked the front desk for messages and summoned the coffees. The former items were quickly found and given to their owner who wasted no time in filling the pipe's bowl and igniting the tobacco while Lestrade returned with two telegrams, one for Holmes and one for himself. Holmes took his telegram and looked at it without opening its envelope while Lestrade opened his to read that a parcel had been despatched and that he should expect to be able to collect it from the railway station that evening, or the next morning at the latest; it was not to be trusted to the regular postal service.

Lestrade had an inkling of what the parcel might contain but he and Watson were alternating their looks between each other and the as yet unopened message for Holmes.

The rattle of a tray bearing a coffee pot and cups and sundry other items brought their impatient observances to a halt as Watson pulled across a small table and uttered the words, "Well, what's it going to be Holmes? Are you going to keep us in suspense or shall I pour the coffee and you can read your telegram to us?"

Watson had been loath to interrupt Holmes' train of thought but knew that his friend was expecting a reply from his brother, even though Holmes had not informed him of sending one. The fact that Lestrade's superiors had so easily acquiesced to his involvement, that the Taunton detectives had not objected and that Mayor Bennet was so confident of assistance, had spoken, in Holmes' assessment, of Freemasonry's long reaching links. Only someone of Mycroft Holmes' status and influence could confirm it and suggest ways to circumvent any unwarranted interference.

"Pour away, my friend." was the reply and Holmes proceeded to separate the envelope from its contents as clouds of smoke billowed forth from a pipe working away at its maximum.

"Good, good," Holmes stated, as much to himself as to his two anxious colleagues. "At least that is confirmed. We are the bait which may catch our elusive fish or we are to be the excuse for others having done nothing and failed. But we've all been that before, have we not, gentlemen?"

Holmes had received a seemingly benign reply from his brother in Whitehall but that reply was rich in simply coded information which would be meaningful between the Holmes' brothers but would elicit no suspicion from anyone else. The reply "FM confirmed with SY and JB likely partners at dance," was a message sent in plain sight of Freemasonry's involvement and that those at the Yard were giving sympathetic and brotherly assistance to Jonathon Bennet, the mayor. How Mycroft would ever know such things, Sherlock knew better than to ask.

Observing that the tobacco in Holmes' pipe had been reduced down to a blackened mass of ash and that the man was eagerly sipping his coffee, Lestrade posed the obvious question, "Well, Holmes, none of those elusive fish of yours are biting down our end of the boat, so what does that telegram tell you and what has that pipe of yours knocked loose in your brain? Watson and I would like to be kept informed, you know. We've been baiting hooks all day for not so much as a nibble from a goldfish."

"Things begin to clarify, my friends," the sleuth replied as he pondered on the second part of Mycroft's telegram before explaining the significance of the first to his colleagues.

"No surprises there, Holmes," declared Lestrade, no stranger to the intrigues of his official colleagues who shared special handshakes and went quiet when he entered a room, "The long arm of the law, indeed."

It was the second part of the message which had interested Holmes the most, the words "JB invited to other ball and commitments may clash" telling Holmes much more than those of the first part and giving him few options other than that of confronting him directly.

"Gentlemen." he said as he raised himself to his feet, "I would ask that you both go and enquire after whatever this Walters has to tell us. I have an urgent meeting to attend with the mayor and I just hope he will be there in his office to attend it himself. He will have something to tell me or we shall be on the first train back to London in the morning. Murder has been done but personal gain may not be the motive, though personal loss is behind the reason we were summoned, at least in part."

"Please, no questions; not yet," Holmes continued. "Something shall be forthcoming, or else we shall be going forthwith; it is that simple."

Both Watson and Lestrade had, from long and bitter experience, learned not to push Sherlock Holmes when he had no intention of being pushed; it was the ultimate in futility and only ended with their complete and utter frustration.

"We'll do as you suggest, my friend," agreed Watson with a frustrated Lestrade nodding his approval. "But please let us know what is happening, and soon. If there has been murder done, as you have so definitely declared, we do not wish it to be done to any of us as well."

Watson had uttered his words with both force and conviction but they were wasted as Holmes had taken to his heels and departed the Pilgrims' Inn a great deal faster that he had entered it. There was nothing to do but follow his lead and wait for him to return with startling news or directions to pack for an early morning departure.

Holmes was animated to a degree not witnessed by Watson and Lestrade for some time, not for some months since a case was brought to him by a desperate woman with a hidden, though unfortunate past and had ended with a blackmailer being bludgeoned to death and he, his house and all of his incriminating documents being incinerated. Holmes could easily have identified or even captured the agent of death and fire but his sympathies lay more with the victim of blackmail than with the blackmailer. As far as Holmes had been concerned, justice had been served and the public good had been improved. In this case, however, he felt that he was being used by those who may be guilty but who were most certainly operating with ulterior motives. Holmes may have been willing to turn a blind eye in some circumstances but Lestrade did not have the luxury of such an option.

Glastonbury's Town Hall was mere minutes from the Pilgrims' Inn and Holmes was nowhere near out of breath as he bounded up its steps and made his way past objecting junior officials before banging on the Mayoral chamber and then entering without waiting for the pompous invitation to "Enter!"

The mayor was in, as Holmes suspected he would be, and stood, shocked and almost tripping over his chair. Holmes quickly spoke up before Jonathon Bennet had a chance to speak.

"Mr. Mayor," began Holmes, totally neglecting the overtures of overblown hype which Jonathon Bennet expected from his grovelling petitioners, "I am here to ask you about the Knights of the Circle and the Way. Answer my questions truthfully, answer them now and answer them fully or our contract is void, and my colleagues and I shall be headed east in the morning. This is not a request; you may consider it an ultimatum."

The Ultimatum

Watson and Lestrade, still in the Pilgrims' Inn with their heads spinning in the wake of their friend's rapid departure, looked at each other for what seemed an age but in reality amounted to little more than five or ten seconds before Lestrade spoke.

"Well, it seems that Holmes has left us, Watson," declared the policeman, a wry smile forming on his lips. "So I suppose we should be off to find this Walters fellow and see what it is that he wants."

"There are two problems with that plan," replied the Doctor, a little annoyed at being, once more, left out of Holmes' confidence. "One being that Walters will not be home yet and the second being that he specifically sought out Holmes to share whatever it is that he knows. Let's just sit down and enjoy our coffees and wait until Holmes returns or the working day ends for Harry Walters."

"So," declared an agreeable Lestrade, "it's coffee and pipes for us both, then."

That said, the doctor and the policeman settled into their comfortable chairs to await the telling chime of the clock or the return of Holmes, whichever would come first. Mayor Bennet, meanwhile, was still dumbstruck by the sudden invasion of his own inner sanctum and the fiery delivery of Holmes' ultimatum, something he was completely unprepared for and no less for the manner in which it was delivered.

"Mr. Holmes!" shouted the mayor, "This is not the way we attend to business in Glastonbury. To what you are referring, I have not the least notion."

"I have information to the contrary, Mr. Bennet," Holmes replied, unwilling to cede the man the least bit of ground on which to advance or retreat. "Your brotherly network has cleared the way for myself, Watson and Lestrade to enter this quagmire of deception, that much is profoundly apparent, but you have other brothers, sisters too by all accounts, and it is to them of whom I refer."

233

The mayor was again struck dumb and Holmes jumped forward, continuing with, "Speak up, man; your options are few and your time is fast running out. I will not be used as some dupe for those who will not emerge from the shadows. Now, tell me of the Knights or the world shall hear of them from me!"

"Mr. Holmes," the mayor responded, his voice now conveying a tone of pleading verging on the panic-stricken, "you put me in a most difficult situation. I have taken an oath and am bound by it unto death. Such things cannot be revealed or ever discussed with those not privy to the secrets of sacred Somerset, not even with those to whom you first referred."

Sherlock Holmes kept his fierce gaze directed into the mayor's eyes and saw true fear in those windows to that cornered man's soul. Holmes knew, though, that desperation expressed was not for fear of what Holmes might do, rather of what some other person might do should Holmes carry out his threat. The mayor could tell that the London man held no fear for what he or any of these mysterious knights might threaten and that significant concessions would have to be made to this Sherlock Holmes, the very man whom he had assumed he could control.

Seeing the panic rising in the man's eyes, Holmes knew it was time to offer him a way out, a very narrow pathway down which he might escape total ruin and possible death. Holmes relaxed his ultimatum just the merest fraction and said, "I shall wait in this room for thirty minutes and not one second more. Speak to whomever you must but come back with the answer I need or I leave and your mysterious Knights are exposed for all to see. Now go!"

Bennet did not need to be told twice. He rushed from his rooms calling for numerous underlings while furiously writing note after note and sending each off to summon those who could be contacted. The Knights may have been centred on Glastonbury but it did not follow that all lived there or even nearby, but Holmes reasoned that if Bennet could get just two or three senior representatives to come within the time allocated to him, they might just agree to take him into their confidence. From his high vantage point in the mayor's rooms, Holmes could see the movement of pedestrians and carriages on Magdalene Street but not so those who might approach across the abbey complex from the east; this mattered little except that Holmes did not like unnecessary surprises, especially from those who might well wish him harm.

Holmes sat himself on a wide inner window sill behind the mayor's desk and from which he could observe both the street and the mayor's door, observing that he might chance an escape through the open upper floor window if suddenly assailed, though the risk would admittedly be significant. Alternatively and somewhat more persuasive against all but the most fanatical attacker was the revolver he had secreted within his coat. It was loaded and Holmes knew how to use it though he preferred the less lethal though temporarily more acutely painful procedure of cracking knuckles or knee-caps with a single stick to dissuade an opponent. Unfortunately, he had neglected to bring even a stout walking stick on this occasion.

Bennet did not return to his rooms, obviously preferring to confer with his knightly companions to explain all before approaching Holmes. He still wanted Holmes to solve the murders but did not want the true reasons for their occurrence to be revealed. A show of justice being served and a declaration of Glastonbury now being safe for pilgrims to return was all that he wanted. Unfortunately for him, he had indeed engaged the country's premier investigator but had known nothing of that investigator's intimate links with the town and region. Had he been a less dictatorial sort given to impulse he might have discussed his intentions and discovered the detective's regional connections.

The minutes went by but Holmes did not feel the tension, nor was he overly expectant of positive results. His mind was one which was able to redirect its attention to matters away from immediate concern and focus on alternative situations which may require the use of his special talents. He had put the matter of Glastonbury and knights to one side and was contemplating the likelihood of links between hereditary tendencies toward premature baldness and the preponderance of younger bald men arrested for embezzlement, something toward which Lestrade had directed his attention in the course of general conversation. This mitigated the tedium to an extent but it was merely a mind game to prevent the sleuth from making premature assumptions on what would occur at the end of Bennet's thirty minutes.

Waiting has a way of coming to an end and Holmes noticed a flurry of excitement on the street below and leaned over to see what and who the fracas involved. On the footpath outside he could see Bennet hastily marshalling three people inside, two men and one woman, though he thought he recognised one of the men as one of the underlings the mayor had recently despatched. The voices were muffled but it did seem that Holmes' ultimatum had borne some fruit despite the brevity of the period he had allowed for a positive response.

Holmes again looked down and saw one other, a younger man he recognised and now running across Magdalene Street, obviously in a hurry and presumably, Holmes thought, keen to beat the thirty-minute deadline. What he did not see was another man approaching at a significantly slower pace from the east through the abbey complex and past the reputed grave of Arthur and Guinevere.

"Five, in all, so far at least, including Bennet," Holmes thought to himself, oblivious to the belated sixth. "I do hope that will constitute a knightly quorum."

Keeping one eye on the door and his ears pricked for the sound of footsteps approaching the mayoral chamber, Holmes kept glancing outward but could see no others hurrying his way. He did not expect trouble but was prepared for it should it come his way. People had been killed and he knew better than to assume the best of intentions of anyone under stress. He had known of those who had trusted to the better nature of others only to fall dead with a knife embedded deep in a generous heart.

More minutes ticked by until, finally, the door opened wide just short of the deadline and Jonathon Bennet walked in, somewhat relieved, ahead of four others, three men and one woman. Holmes recognised only one, apart from the mayor, that being Wilson Pettigrew, one of the men he had seen but not spoken to on the train, one of the group of four seemingly headed by Renshaw and including Fraser and Portland. Pettigrew was the only one of the four railway travellers Holmes had not interviewed and was now keen to see where the man fit in. The woman and two other men were completely unknown to the sleuth.

There were an awkward few moments as all stood looking at each other, Holmes now certain that he was in no physical danger and Bennet sensing that Holmes' initial condition had been met and that the secret was safe for the moment. How things would go from here, he could not even guess; unlike his usual meetings, he had no prepared agenda to follow and no rules of procedure to refer to and no authority to rebuke those who veered from the same. Holmes had the upper hand and was not about to relinquish his advantage.

The five sat, the mayor retaking his seat of office behind his desk and seeming to regain a little of his prior overconfidence, while Sherlock Holmes sat alone facing the four visitors directly with the mayor off obliquely to his right.

"I don't really know how to begin," started the mayor, "so I will forego the formalities of introductions and ask that Mr. Holmes tell us just what it is that he knows and what he would have us tell him. Does that suit you, Holmes?"

Holmes nodded his assent but was interrupted almost before he could say a single word as the mayor's door yielded to gentle knocking and slowly opened. All in the room stood, Holmes out of respect and surprise and the rest out of a duty-inspired deference as someone of obvious importance to the Glastonbury people entered with an air of solemn importance and great presence.

"Master," Bennet pleaded, "please take my chair. In such circumstances, it is yours. We were afraid that you would not be able to attend on such short notice."

"I had been expecting such a call, ever since Mr. Holmes had arrived back in Glastonbury," was the Master's authoritative reply as he moved to take Bennet's chair while keeping an eye fixed on Holmes. "In so many ways he is a man of Glastonbury, of Somerset, and is related to one of us who departed this life many years back. I do believe he can be trusted. I also believe that his two companions might be taken into our confidence, to some extent at least. They are both men sworn to the Crown, they are both men of honour and men of action and might favour us with an oath of compliance, if not loyalty."

Holmes had sat silent and motionless through the Master's words, though he could not hide the hint of a smile which betrayed the satisfaction he felt with the way things had transpired. He stood up on the Master's bidding and approached the mayoral desk from behind which strode the Master. A warm handshake and the placing of the Master's left hand on Holmes' shoulder bespoke of something more than friendship; it was akin to a father greeting a son about to undergo an initiation of some significance.

"George Bridges, it's you!" declared Sherlock Holmes. "I might have known but I confess I didn't. Perhaps I'm not the detective people say I am."

The Way

Bath, a location visited since ancient times for its waters rising warm and infused with the spirit of the very Earth from which it came, had been well known to the ancient Britons and revered by the peoples who had raised the great stone monuments and travelled to Stonehenge to greet the life-renewing morning sun at the winter solstice. The Romans had taken to the place as much as any but had also, after their own time-honoured fashion, built enduring temples in stone over the holy springs so that their own gods could be honoured alongside the native deities and spirits, and so that the waters could be more easily entered by those who sought their powers of healing.

But, healing though those waters may have been, they had not been able to bring life back to the body of the fallen Arthur after it had been taken to the sacred springs by his knights on their way to the holy Isle of Avalon.

Bristol, up-river from Avonmouth and then a settlement near the gorge guarded by the Celtic fortress, the Caer Odor, was where the victorious army of Arthur had been encamped at the end of a savage campaign for the removal of the Saxon invader from the lands of a people now following the banner of the Pendragon and shouting for Saxon blood. Blood had definitely been delivered as Arthur had won twelve consecutive regional battles, the bards wildly exaggerating the man's personal prowess against fearful enemies, foes tangible, mythical and supernatural. He had then embarked for Gaul where other Germanic hordes had been taking advantage of a Roman hiatus and flooding into the territories of his distant kinsmen who, having provided aid against the Saxons and Jutes in Britannia, now called for payment in kind against the rampaging Alemanni and Franks in their own lands. As in Britannia, the resistance had been successful in holding back the human tide, for some significant time, but messengers brought news of Arthur's nephew Mordred's betrayal, the man usurping power and carrying off Arthur's queen Guinevere.

A king of those times had to personally meet every challenge or be discredited and Arthur knew that Mordred's act would signal a split in the loyalties of the Britons and invite a renewal of Saxon incursions. Time was of the essence and Arthur hurried back with a contingent of loyal warriors intent on gathering more loyal followers on his return and then meeting Mordred on the field of battle to redeem his honour, his kingdom and his queen. Arthur would have to avoid the Saxon strongholds to the south east of Britain and sail around the Cornish peninsula into the Bristol Channel to again enter the Avonmouth, there to stop and assess how things stood in

Bristol and beyond. He then had to regather what strength he could before Mordred had time to prepare for the return of the true king or to consolidate his hold further.

What more victories the king might have seen is mere conjecture as the battle of Camlann would prove to be the last for both men, Arthur and Mordred, the details on who fell first being lost in the telling of the stories but, fall, both men did, neither one ever to stand again, never to lead and never to rule. The loss of Arthur was beyond disastrous, beyond belief, so much so that a great many of his people refused to believe it and the cult of the sleeping King of the Britons arose and was carried across the land, that king being hurt but healed and waiting for the call to action to again go forth and defend his homeland.

No one truly knows the location of Camlann, nor do any know the size of the forces which faced each other. Some have said that two great armies converged, others that it was a challenge man to man between Arthur and Mordred, more of a duel, and that a retinue of knights stood by either man as seconds and witnesses. Arthur was, though seasoned by almost constant warfare, no longer the youthful warrior king, but Mordred was in his prime and eager to keep his new kingdom and his life, both of which he would forfeit should Arthur prevail. The shock of both leaders falling, presumably by each other's hand, was to prove so dispiriting that hostilities ceased immediately and the mortally wounded men were carried from the field by their loyal knights. The fate of Mordred's body has been argued ever since but Arthur, still living, was said to have been carried to the healing springs of Bath.

The Saxons would regather their strength and increase their numbers and gradually regain territory over the coming years as Arthur's hard-won gains were progressively lost. The spirit of Arthur, though, was infused in the landscape and even the Saxons felt it taking hold in themselves as Wessex emerged, only to become the battleground in a war against the new Danish invader. Did Alfred, king of the West Saxons and later dubbed 'the Great', feel that spirit of Arthur inside him as he did battle with and finally stemmed the Danish advance amid the Somerset marshes? Perhaps he did and perhaps there were those at the time who had honoured the ancient King of the Britons and swore to protect and maintain his legacy. Perhaps those who so swore begat an order of knights, sometimes combative, sometimes monastic, which would keep its silence and its secret through the coming centuries. Perhaps the order of the Knights of the Circle was not one of local men and women playing at harmless intrigue; it may well have been a line descended unbroken from those now-ancient days of turmoil, one which had survived the wars of conquest and religious dissent which had been so destructive. The youthful Sherlock Holmes had listened to the tales told of those days by the wagoneers and merchants he had befriended and had heard the slips of those often too-talkative tongues revealing snippets which, at the time, had meant nothing more to him than a good and intriguing story about a fanciful and probably fictitious subject, or so he had assumed.

Merlin, sometime priest, sometime astrologer, sometime magus and magician and provider of wise council to Arthur, knew that the situation was hopeless but accompanied the injured king and his knightly contingent to the waters of the Avon, there to see Arthur transferred to a light barge which would carry him to the sacred healing waters of Bath. To have been taken there by horse or war chariot would have meant certain death along the way with the jostling and bumps delivered by a road fallen into disrepair since the Roman exodus. When peace might have been restored, Arthur's experience with the legions would likely have seen much of

Rome's legacy repaired and maintained but, at the time, the Saxon and the Briton were still very far removed from seeking cooperative accommodations with each other.

Alas, Arthur would succumb almost in sight of the Roman edifice raised above the springs but his body was carried and immersed in those waters of life, though to no avail. Arthur's time had come and the spirit of the great king had left its mortal body to become one with the land. Even the entreaties of Merlin could not go against what the land, the Earth, had demanded and claimed. Arthur was born of the Earth and his spirit was now called back and no human had the power to prevent its return. All that humans could do was to ensure that the relics of his earthly existence were protected. His body would be interred and guarded, the story of his life would be retold, the places sacred to him would be maintained, his sword would be held safe and kept ready for him should his country command his return.

Arthur had returned to his homeland when called but had fallen doing his duty, as had so many of his followers before him, and he would now complete his journey with the aid of his faithful knights. That journey would be a sad one for the living but they, too, had their duties to perform and, perform them dutifully, they would. To reach their final destination they would first return to the army waiting for news at the Caer Odor near to the Bristol which would one day come to be and from there carry their King in procession to the wide waters and marshlands of the Brue estuary. There Arthur would be placed on a floral funeral barge for the final part of his "Way," his approach to the sacred Isle of Avalon where the Earth would envelope him.

Thus, the "Way to Avalon," Arthur's final journey, could be said to have begun in Gaul before wending its way in stages toward his earthly destiny and his subsequent entry into legend. The Way, though, had become something else over the ensuing centuries, something more; it had become a calling, a life's calling and purpose for the devotee who held the legend of the living king as something sacrosanct and had sworn an oath of duty to defend it against all comers. As with many devotees, though, a duty to defend could be interpreted as a licence to attack any and all who might simply seem to pose a threat to the secret or its holders. A devotee unfulfilled in other areas of life is not so many steps away from becoming the unthinking fanatic.

The Master, George Bridges, after being brought out into the open as the leader of the Knights of the Circle and now seemingly oblivious to those other knights looking on, peered into the eyes of Sherlock Holmes and made unspoken contact with the detective's very soul.

"We, here in this room, Sherlock Holmes," Bridges began, "are six of those chosen and sworn to keep the secret and uphold the honour of someone greater than ourselves, someone who lived and breathed and fought and ruled the lands about us in years now long passed into the mists of time but whose spirit is still with us. His bones, too, lie hereabouts, though the body is but a temporary house and is as nothing to the spirit it once contained.

"Much is known, much is unknown, and much is unknowable about those ancient days and the folk who lived through them." He continued after a brief pause, "But the greatest of our kings was one of them and we who have come after, have a duty to uphold his memory."

"I had recalled, incompletely, those memories I had held deep down from my earlier days in Somerset," Sherlock responded, "and among them was one about the 'Knights of the Circle' and something about 'The Way' and I knew that they had something to do with the legendary King Arthur. At the time, they were just stories told by the locals and, of course, everyone knows of Arthur and the Knights of the Round Table, but I had always assumed those stories were just that, tales told to tantalise the young listeners. I had also assumed that there had been some substance to the legends but here I am speaking with, I would presume, the living links in an order which claims to go in an unbroken chain back to those who carried Arthur to his final resting place."

"We claim nothing, Mr. Holmes," interrupted Mayor Bennet, quite speaking out of turn in the presence of the Master. "We are the links in that chain, even though those links are made from stock not exclusively descended from the ancient Briton. We here have Briton, Saxon, Norman and other blood coursing through us, and Arthur is the king whose spirit has captured us and claims our allegiance."

"Well said, Mr. Bennet," declared the Master. "Although done a little out of the designated order of procedures. Still, we can understand your eagerness to put our special visitor's little misunderstanding to rights and forgive your presumption."

"As for Sherlock Holmes not being the detective people thought him to be," continued George Bridges dropping somewhat his masterful tone of authority, "he did pry the greatest and most deeply hidden of all secrets out of those sworn to keep it, did he not?"

Sherlock Holmes looked into the face of his old friend, raised his eyebrows, smiled and gave a silent nod of appreciative acknowledgement.

The Master

George Bridges was Glastonbury born and bred and, in his mind, a citizen of a contracted and ancient Somerset before being that of an England or a greater Britain. He was sworn to the Crown and had been both loyal and dutiful in word and action but had taken on and maintained a higher order of obligation since the age of sixteen. At that age, he was able to join the knightly order as a novice and, with his day-to-day responsibilities to the Crown and its subjects, rose to the rank of sergeant at which he remained, unwilling to seek higher office in the police service nor to leave the land and the people who had even greater claims on him than did constabulary, Crown or country.

His was, in so many ways, the role of a king's steward whose duty it was to maintain order and remove any danger to the townsfolk of Glastonbury, and the same could have been said of his role within much of the extent of ancient Somerset as he assumed responsibility step by step in the order of the Knights of the Circle. His predecessors had seen numerous layers of civic and spiritual authority imposed on the country over the centuries but had always managed to avoid entanglements, the worst and most threatening of which came at the time of the dissolution of the monasteries and the years of bloodshed following the religious schism of the Tudor reigns. Many ancient shrines, relics and artefacts were destroyed in the deliberated frenzy directed against all things deemed to suggest idolatry and papal influence and the supposed graves of Arthur and Guinevere were not spared. As fortune would have it and as a result of diversionary precautions having been taken to provide a false place of interment for Arthur and his Queen, the remains of both remained unmolested. The identities of those two bodies which did suffer molestation and dispersal prior to their later reinterment may have been known but had been lost to the ravages of time and religious fanaticism.

Bridges, Sergeant Bridges, was in the prime of his power as a policeman when a youthful and precocious Sherlock Holmes had wandered into the Glastonbury Police Station and began asking questions. Some of the wilder Glastonbury lads were not averse to throwing stones onto the police station's roof from an area to its rear which offered cover and the means of a speedy escape. The sergeant would at times wait and deliberately just miss out on catching the juvenile perpetrators but knew it was just boys playing pranks upon a figure of authority, as long as no damage was actually done. In fact, he could recall doing exactly the same thing when he was a boy and had always seemed to escape the feigned wrath of authority. This young lad, new to town and full of questions, though, was different.

Sherlock's aunt, Janet Holmes, had been a long-term resident of Street and was something of a recluse, partly by choice and partly due to her natural reticence to socialise, also partly due to the fact that some considered her activities to fly close to the definition of witchcraft. She did, however, have some friends and one of them was George Bridges.

It was to Bridges that she had expressed her dismay, firstly at the news of her younger brother's death and that of his wife and then at the news, some years later, that the younger of her orphaned nephews was to spend his summer school holidays with her as no one else was prepared or able to take him. To an older woman set in her ways and with no experience of children, the arrival of Sherlock was anticipated with some significant degree of misgiving combined with a feeling of some dread, particularly as she had never met the lad but had heard tales of his most extraordinary character. George

Bridges, married but without any children of his own, expressed sympathy with his friend's plight and offered to do whatever he could to assist, though his wife was adamant that she was not interested in looking after this unwelcome juvenile visitor.

Aunt Jane did make her nephew as welcome as she knew how and provided him with all of his physical needs but was too old and set in her ways to take on the responsibilities of his upbringing or provision of guidance. Sergeant Bridges had said to get the lad to call in to the police station and that he would keep a weather eye on him around town and instruct his constables to do the same. Sherlock, though, proved to be no trouble beyond getting in the way and asking the most complex and awkward questions which those less patient with lads of a generally good but boisterous nature would otherwise be. The sergeant did not offer the youthful Sherlock Holmes pity but did take more than a normal amount of interest in his well-being and, in time, become something of a mentor to the lad.

To most of the town, the sergeant was an amenable type who brooked no nonsense from anyone and generally kept the lid on all of the pots of crime simmering throughout the town and its surrounds. He was, unbeknown to all but the initiated, a significant office holder in the secret and ancient order of the Knights of the Circle and knew a great deal more of the region's secrets than most could have imagined. His manner of operation was anticipatory and largely pre-emptive while his approach was quiet, deliberate and authoritative. He was the ideal police sergeant and would make the ideal Master of an order sworn to keep secrets, the ideal heir to the leadership of the loyal knights of the great and legendary King Arthur.

The original Arthurian Knights made up a military order, a cadre of very capable fighting men who would have ridiculed the modern romantic concept of an armoured gentlemen mounted on a magnificently appointed charger. Theirs was a world of turmoil and invasion and they were an elite group to whom Arthur would entrust his strategies and orders and know that they would be transmitted to the tribesmen gathered about him and be brought to bear upon a determined enemy. Arthur had known Roman military service and was wise in the arts of war, and his court, as much as it could be, was made up of lesser war-lords to whom gentlemanly behaviour was a totally foreign concept. They were, though, both loyal and obedient, and necessarily so. War, to Arthur, was bloody, brutal, practically incessant and a means of survival and left little time for the niceties of life, such as they might have been in those now-distant days of danger.

A woman in the military ranks was, though not unknown, a rarity. Her function was generally one of providing for a family and remaining subordinate to a husband who, in his turn, owed a duty to a tribal leader to fight when called upon and suffer the privations of distant warfare and a possibly drawn-out and painful death.

In the tribal system prevalent in the region in those times, some women did hold ceremonial office of significant authority and were called upon to give counsel in many of the practical matters of life. With the death of a warrior, however, that function became enhanced and was largely taken over by senior women skilled in the preparation of the body for interment and practiced in the rites due to the dead. The male and the female stood face to face with complimentary functions in society and in death were charged with making different appeals to the various spirits of the Earth.

As tribalism faded and the notion of the Saxon state slowly took hold, male and female roles became further differentiated in some functions and were sometimes merged in others. The Knights of the Circle had long lost the military function it once possessed and had become a company of vigilant watchers whose activities did not rely on physical strength and military preparedness. What was required was a character infused with reliability and dependability as well as the ability to keep a secret and not yield to the temptations of vanity.

Janet Holmes, new to the area and ignorant of anything but the vague stories of an ancient and legendary king, had taken an interest in her adopted home's history and natural gifts. She had inherited a propensity for insight, one shared by some of her relatives, a gift which enhanced her ability to recognise the many plant species abundant in Somerset and to gain a masterful knowledge of their herbal properties. It was a chance encounter with two Knights of the Circle at which she expressed the opinion that the story of Arthur did not make sense and that his remains might well be found somewhere other than in the grave within the old abbey grounds. Her masterful and insightfully logical reasons for giving that opinion rang bells of alarm in the minds of the two knights who wasted no time in relating the news to the Master, the one holding that position immediately prior to George Bridges' incumbency.

Standard procedure in such a situation did not involve any denial or overly intense interest but a stance of non-committal indifference followed by a sustained program of observation and playing down any mention of Arthur. This, coupled with an attention-diverting program of religious observances and conveniently discovered relics from the old abbey and other sites had been generally successful while recourse to personal discreditation was not unknown. If any such sources of inconvenient interest had persisted and had been forcefully removed or killed, there was no record to be found, but the watchers were knights with a military heritage and were bound by oath to maintain the secret.

In the case of Janet Holmes, however, she had shown no signs of wanting to express her opinions to the public and, as several positions in the order had become vacant, it was decided to seek her out for her willingness to follow the "Way" of Arthur. Her investiture marked the beginning of a friendship between George Bridges and the reclusive lady of Street, one which was to bear strange fruit in the years to come when Sherlock Holmes arrived with only the barest of notions of what he would find in Somerset.

Janet would be many years dead when George Bridges was raised to the office of Master of the Knights of the Circle but the memories of her friendship and of her remarkably enigmatic nephew had stayed with him and he took some pride in having known and in many ways helped stimulate the development of a lad who grew to become a remarkable man. He had heard of someone assisting the official agencies in London with difficult cases but had given the matter little thought in distant rural Glastonbury, though he had wondered about the mention of a Mr. Holmes in a few official reports.

With the death of Janet Holmes, George Bridges' connection with Sherlock Holmes had been broken but he was unsurprised when, later, news of that London detective known as Mr. Holmes who possessed extraordinary powers of insight and deduction began to be reported with sensational hyperbole in the newspapers. He would be there if that detective should ever need his advice or assistance but had no reason to approach him otherwise; the duties of his office would preclude such contact after retiring from the police force and taking on the role of Master after the death of his wife.

Here, though, was that same Sherlock Holmes now arrived in Glastonbury, full of memories, full of suspicions and full of questions, questions which required answers which many were loath to provide. He had also arrived with friends who, though not as gifted as the great sleuth in their powers of deduction, nonetheless complemented their friend and each other and formed an indomitable crime investigation team. The Master, though, would demand some type of oath from all three before anything more would or could be divulged.

The Oaths

A messenger was sent to summon Watson and Lestrade from the Pilgrims' Inn but found the pair had decamped for places unknown some time before. The inn's manager could not provide any information on their likely whereabouts but the messenger was again dispatched to Mrs. Waldron's lodging house after he had returned to the town hall. This time the messenger was successful in his quest and discovered the two men walking back along Street Road having found Harry Walters at home and happy enough to give his information to the sleuth's colleagues.

Walters' information was brief but would prove significant in light of the revelations being made to Sherlock Holmes and soon to be imparted to Watson and Lestrade as his trusted confidants. With his intimate friend Beryl Armitage taken under what he considered to be doubtful and deceitful circumstances, Harry did not feel well disposed toward Dr. Fredericks for the comments made about the manner of her death and had remembered something he thought ought to be conveyed to Sherlock Holmes. The matter concerned a meeting he had observed and the conversation he had partly overheard between three Glastonbury men. He had not given the matter much thought at the time but, following on from his discussions with the London detective, it now seemed significant.

Wilson Pettigrew was a purveyor of second-hand goods, according to his business card, and Walters had witnessed two other men approach him outside his Street Road premises. Harry had been sent to give the second-hand dealer some assistance in loading a number of heavy articles for transport to the railway station for despatch to London, such an action not being unusual as Harry's employer, Adam Renshaw, had a working arrangement of mutual assistance with Pettigrew as their businesses did overlap somewhat. Renshaw and Pettigrew had waited outside for some time talking, though about what Harry could not say, until Dr. Fredericks came along in his carriage. It was at this point that the three men went inside to Pettigrew's office and continued their conversation which, at times, became quite loud and animated. The meeting lasted, Harry estimated, for about thirty minutes with him being close enough to hear some of the shouts of annoyance, if not anger, made by Wilson Pettigrew to Dr. Fredericks.

"I can't tell you much of what was said when things were calm," explained Harry, "but when Mr. Pettigrew got excited he yelled out something like 'Why did so many have to die?'"

"I don't like that Dr. Fredericks much at all," continued Harry, "but I didn't think Mr. Pettigrew meant anything other than perhaps things might have been handled better for the victims before they died. Thinking back on it and with what you two gentlemen and Mr. Holmes have been investigating, I thought it worth bringing to your attention but somewhere away from my place of work where eyes and ears are always open."

"You did right to tell us, Mr. Walters," Watson had declared to him. "But was anything else said, anything unusual, out of the ordinary?"

"Well, yes, as a matter of fact there was, Dr. Watson," answered Harry as another point came back to him. "I thought it was just the usual boasting that some of those fellows get into but Mr. Renshaw broke in between the other two and demanded to know something about 'That item' and that the Isle of Avalon would sink under the riches it might bring."

With such new and suggestive information given to them, Watson and Lestrade had been on their way back to the Pilgrims' Inn hopeful of meeting up with Holmes when the mayor's messenger found them. They were informed that Holmes was in conference with the mayor and several other people and that their attendance at the town hall was requested, a request to which they readily acceded.

On entering the mayoral rooms, the doctor and the policeman saw Holmes talking to an older man with whom he seemed to be on very good terms. Watson recognised him as George Bridges and said as much to Lestrade before adding that he had been a police sergeant in Glastonbury during Holmes' early visits during school holidays. Lestrade also recognised Horace Portland from his earlier visit and nodded to the herbalist who responded minimally to the greeting. Both Watson and Lestrade particularly noticed the mayor sitting quietly to one side of his own desk seemingly waiting for events to begin.

"Before we get into anything else," Holmes announced to the gathering, "I should like to confer with my two colleagues.

After that we may proceed with the matters we had been discussing earlier."

Holmes signalled for Watson and Lestrade to follow him outside the mayor's rooms where the latter two might inform him of any discoveries or revelations. Much had been revealed by the knights but that was under some duress and Holmes was not entirely certain of who could be trusted implicitly. Outside the closed door and in hushed tones, Watson then relayed the information provided by Watkins to an ever-eager Holmes who responded enthusiastically to each and every point. At the end of Watson's report, Holmes could not restrain himself.

"This is good information, indeed, Watson," he declared with undisguised enthusiasm. "Very good information. Combined with what you may hear in the next few minutes, it may prove to be the key to the case."

Holmes insisted that his two colleagues say nothing of Walters' information and then led both back into mayor's room to confront a most unusual group of people. There George Bridges stood and spoke.

"Well, gentlemen," he started, "just how to begin? I have information of a quite unusual and sensitive nature to impart and I will need your solemn words to repeat nothing you may hear before proceeding. If you cannot give me an absolute undertaking to remain silent on these matters, I would ask that you leave us immediately."

Watson looked at Holmes quizzically and Lestrade's face assumed the stoic look of the serious policeman facing an unknown situation. It took a few moments but Lestrade was moved to say that he would abide by whatever Holmes might suggest, a statement echoed by Watson.

More chairs were collected and the meeting of the six knights recommenced with its expanded bevy of London visitors sitting to the right of the Master and opposite the five other knights. The significance of Bennet sitting with the Glastonbury people was not lost on Watson and Lestrade, nor was the fact that George Bridges took the mayor's chair behind his ornate desk.

"Let us begin slowly," started Bridges who was yet to reveal his position to Watson and Lestrade, "and if you can agree to restraining yourselves further, we may go on to even more serious matters."

Three Bibles were produced and one given to each of the London men who were then asked to stand with Bibles held in the left hand while the right was raised in solemn salute declaring that the person doing so was acting in a free, open and sincere manner. The three were asked individually to swear on Bible that nothing would be revealed, though there would be a far more serious oath to be taken later should any or all of them be willing.

George Bridges then recommenced his narrative, saying, "We are all, here, seated in the town of Glastonbury which is a location eagerly sought out by pilgrims the world over for its spiritual significance. Nearby you will have noticed the commanding Glastonbury Tor topped by the great Tower of St. Michael's Church, now destroyed, sadly. We are situated on high ground in Glastonbury and are all-but surrounded by the Somerset Levels, now greatly drained but which in days now long gone had been covered by substantial bodies of water from which had protruded islands, now merely hills, which were eminently defendable and provided sanctuary from the floodwaters which occasionally raced through the region."

Master Bridges paused at this point and looked directly and deliberately at the three oath-takers before continuing with, "You are all, no doubt, and I am certain of the fact with regard to Mr. Holmes, familiar with the stories told of the legendary King Arthur and of his death and interment on the Isle of Avalon."

Holmes nodded at this point while Watson and Lestrade were confused and both wondered if the man would start telling fairy tales and relating the sagas of the ancient and famous British kings. Watson believed in and celebrated the feats of Alfred the Great which he knew to have occurred in the region but was uncertain if this fabled Arthur had ever actually existed outside of the long-retold legends. What he was to hear next would challenge his incredulity on the matter and require a very widely opened mind despite Holmes having placed the notion before him in stages throughout their brief time in Glastonbury.

"King Arthur was as real as you or I or any of us," Bridges declared with unfeigned sincerity. "He may not have been called 'King', and 'Arthur' may just be the way which we in this present day would render his name but the man and his deeds were and are factual and there exists an order of stalwart people who stand ready to guard his final resting place. That order has descended from the warrior captains who had sworn to guard the man in life and in death; we call them the knights, though their having sat at a round table is a later invention of the story tellers. That duty of protection had carried on in an unbroken line to this very day and you see about you some of the latest members of an order called the Knights of the Circle. For those who may not be aware of the fact, the town of Glastonbury stands upon high ground formerly surrounded by water, except for a narrow neck of land at the east, and that high ground is the Isle of Avalon and the final resting place of

Arthur, once the defiant King of the Britons and now the spiritual king of us all."

"But why does he need guarding?" asked Lestrade, "Isn't his grave just a few steps beyond this very building, and that of his queen? And hasn't that grave remained unmolested for centuries?"

"That is what a lot of people would believe," advised Bridges, "but we here can say different, though we cannot reveal such things to any but sworn Knights, and you would be quite surprised to find who might be counted among their number."

"But there must be more to warrant such attention," said Watson trying hard to determine what the fuss was all about. "King Arthur may well have been a real person but who would want to disturb his grave in this day and age?"

"That grave is not the original for its occupants," explained Bridges. "It was defiled some two hundred years ago by our own countrymen and, had Arthur been resting there, his remains might not have been recovered. As it was, it was only due to the zeal of a few individuals that the man and the woman who was buried with him were reinterred, though that man definitely wasn't Arthur, nor was the woman his queen."

"More than that I cannot tell you," he continued. "To be able to do so would require that you join our order and take a deadly oath of allegiance and obedience. Our activities are not so much active as they are passive and observational; we stand guard at a distance and watch and act in ways which bring about the desired end without confronting potential enemies directly unless there is no other option."

Silence. No one spoke for several interminable seconds, though Watson and Lestrade both turned their eyes upon

Holmes looking for some sort of a signal, some response at least.

Having gotten the three London men's attention and hearing no objection to the notions he had just presented, Master Bridges decided to push the matter that little bit further with, "You have learned much here in the last few days and we have learned to trust you. Should any or all of you wish to be considered for our order, that consideration would come with advanced standing and my positive recommendation. Although I am Master of the order, entry is by majority vote and is for life, though I do have the power to overrule in the negative, and your duties would be in the most part passive though the occasional call to action has been sounded over the centuries."

Silence again; then Watson spoke up.

"And those calls to actions?" he asked, "On chargers with swords, shields and lances, were they; or something else?

***

MYSTIC ISLES

The Chamber

Britain has ruins and monuments enough to satisfy the archaeologist for several lifetimes, should that seeker after ancient artefacts be granted such an extended existence, and those who find the landscape in any way boring have not the imagination or human inquisitiveness to seek contact with all those ancient lives invested in its form. Somerset may not have had an exclusive claim to historical priority over the rest of Britain but its occupants exceeded the national average for inquisitiveness about things past. They considered themselves to be living the region's history, as indeed they were and would increasingly do so in the future.

The Glastonbury Archaeological Society was a collective of amateurs interspersed with the occasional scholastic specialist and had close links with the considerably larger Somerset Archaeological Society, each body having numerous members common to both. Their activities were generally social with talks being given by members having particular interests while the odd visiting professional was convinced to address the eager locals and bring the latest thinking from the universities into the meeting halls and minds of those whose interests were observational and investigative but not overly interrogative and scientific.

The Glastonbury victims, Beryl Armitage, John Staunton, Phyllis Staunton and Rupert Wilkins, had all been members of the Glastonbury body, their interests ranging from casual to obsessive. The latter description fitted well the involvement of John Staunton who tended to steer discussions toward his favourite topics and who could be quite overbearing at times, though he was a genuine type who was well-liked and highly regarded. The man was also a member of the Somerset society and provided a valuable liaison between it and the smaller Glastonbury group. He also preferred the greater professional nature of the larger society and encountered occasional problems of deference when matters of site and artefact priorities clashed. His death was mourned far beyond his home town of Glastonbury and the loss of his enthusiastic presence was felt throughout the district and even rated a small obituary and tribute in several university archaeological journals.

The investigations of both societies generally amounted to visits to sites of interest, making measurements and preparing sketches, though photography was playing an increasing part in the recording process as the craft rose in popularity. Professional archaeologists had advised of the accepted procedures for removing ground cover from sites, though the general recommendation was to wait until properly trained personnel could attend. The latter recommendation, however, was often ignored as the eager amateurs impatiently attacked the sites with shovels and trowels to satisfy their curiosity and sometimes to prove that they knew as much as their colleagues from the universities.

The investigations of a site on the outskirts of Street had occupied the interests of members of the Glastonbury society for some two years. It had long been known as the location of a former Roman structure, perhaps a garrison tower, perhaps a local temple, which was well-documented in the archives despite its above-ground stonework having yielded to the needs of other structures over the centuries. The year prior to the deaths, however, had seen a flurry of activity on the part of a small group after John Staunton had noticed what seemed to be the start of a stairway leading downward and presumably to some sort of a subterranean chamber sealed off from view and forgotten for well over a thousand years.

That news had excited the Glastonbury group but it had been decided to hold off reporting the find until the extent of the underground structure could be determined. Advising the Somerset people risked the matter being brought to the attention of the universities which would, without doubt, claim priority of access and then limit or refuse the same to the local amateurs who made the original discovery. Four people who trusted each other made numerous forays to the Street site over several months, the Bridge of Perils now taking on a new significance as the foursome became wary of prying eyes and pointed questions; the discovery, whatever it was, would belong to them and their society and would be shared only when that fact had been fully acknowledged. Much of the excavation would be made under cover of darkness with the aid of small lanterns rendered invisible beyond the immediate site of soil and rubble removal but it proved difficult to keep the matter a complete secret so another nearby site of little real interest was disturbed minimally to provide a diversion.

It had been the misfortune of John Staunton to be recognised by Dr. Fredericks, his friend and trusted physician, as the medical man was returning from a visit to a patient in Street. The doctor stopped and insisted on knowing what was afoot, he also being a member, though not a very active one, of the Glastonbury Archaeological Society. Being informed of the need for secrecy, the doctor had agreed to keep his silence but afterwards began to badger Staunton for details with some insistence. Mrs. Staunton had been aware of her husband's increased interest in something, presumably archaeological, but took little interest in such matters though she did object to Dr. Fredericks' late evening visit. She did not like the man and trusted him less even though her husband did hold him and his capabilities in some regard.

The site had not been visited very often, except by the occasional few sheep which were set loose to graze, and the somewhat superstitious locals tended to avoid it for fear of encountering supernatural manifestations. The angle of the stairway and the positioning of the wall it must meet told the group they would not have an excessive amount of excavation to perform but the spoil from the digging might attract some attention if spotted. Darkness and efficient and discrete removal of the spoil would be two key factors.

The wall seemed to be part of a larger structure, shallow but extending outward below ground seemingly to provide some sort of protective stone awning, perhaps rainwater-diverting, for the smaller structure below. Perhaps the entire assembly represented a chamber constructed beneath a church now long demolished or a long forgotten and unsuspected chamber over which a later building had been raised before being abandoned and stripped of stone down to its ancient and reused foundations. Regardless, access to the chamber would require digging under the extended awning, if that is what it was, to gain access to whatever was being protected but Staunton and his colleagues knew that the stairway had to lead to something special to rate such an extensive level of concealment and protection.

After weeks of effort in secrecy and dim flickering lamplight, John Staunton's shovel gave a distinct 'clunk' as it struck solid stone. It took the determined digger another hour to clear away sufficient consolidated soil and rubble to be able to describe a doorway in the wall, one filled with stone bricks and sealed with some sort of solid mortar. Time had moved on, as had the season, and, though the shortened days gave more opportunity for working unobserved, the falling temperature meant that hands would be frozen and bodies would chill and slow the work considerably. The mortar's removal would require the appropriate tools; they would return after dark on the following night.

Had the foursome not been exhausted by their exertions that night, not one of them would have been able to sleep due to the excitement of the find and anticipation of what else might be uncovered. The hours of the following day seemed to go by at an incredibly slow rate but the time came soon enough for the return to the stone wall and its sealed doorway. John Staunton had equipped himself with chisels of various sizes and a range of hammers. Bert Rutledge had provided transport to the site and, as usual, would return an agreed number of hours later to take the four back to Glastonbury. Bert knew something was up but was someone who did not involve himself in matters which did not concern him and, in any case, had agreed to keep silent on the subject.

Unfortunately, Dr. Fredericks was not someone who could stay silent for long on such matters and had been unable to restrain himself from hinting to several colleagues that something of some significance had been located by the Glastonbury group. A number of the local medical practitioners had active interests in the region's history and historical sites, though only two were members of the Glastonbury Archaeological Society, Fredericks being one and Harrison being the other. Dr. Harrison had been a quite active member of the society but chronic health problems had curtailed his outdoor endeavours although not his overall interest. He had given very knowledgeable and interesting talks on the region's history and mythology but had ceased all activities only a few months before selling his practice to Dr. Baxter. The retiring doctor had suffered some sort of breakdown, possibly nervous Watson had suggested from the little information he had of the man, and had retired and moved off to live in Bath with relatives. If Harrison could have added anything to the growing body of data, it was now doubtful that it would be accessible as he was reported to have been showing the distinct and worrying signs of advancing senility.

Assembled at the Street site with new tools and with great anticipation, the four groped their way in the darkness to the site. The lanterns were lit once more and a little more spoil was cleared from the base of the stairway so that John Staunton could begin with his chisels. He had been worried about the noise of the hammer strikes and took the precaution of fitting a leather hood over the chisel heads but found that he would do more scraping of mortar than hammering. Concentrating his efforts on a central part of the doorway, Staunton found than an hour's work had loosened four of the stones. He could barely contain his excitement and the chill of the night air could not dampen his enhanced level of enthusiasm, nor that of his companions.

A sustained effort saw the sealed doorway breached and, with a little further effort, the hole was widened sufficiently to permit John Staunton room to crawl through on his hands and knees. Before entering, he had trained his lantern to illuminate the interior and had determined that no hazards were obvious in the chamber, one which seemed to have no other exits or entries to other rooms. He could make out a dark blocky form in the centre but could not identify any detail with the dim light; a second lantern, an oil lamp of greater brilliance, would be necessary. Beryl Armitage and Phyllis Staunton had been some distance off disposing of excess soil and Rupert Wilkins had entered the stairway to attend to lighting a dark lantern's wick before passing it to John Staunton who then trained its narrow beam inward.

Wilkins asked what Staunton could see and received the reply of "Not much from this angle," before suggesting that he not enter the chamber until the others had returned. Staunton acceded to this but had only a few impatient minutes to wait before declaring to his three companions, "I'm going in." The chamber was not quite high enough for him to stand up fully but did have room sufficient for several others, room which was soon taken up by the remaining three.

The chamber was well built and securely vaulted but held no sarcophagus, no embalmed body, no skeletal remains of any sort but there was, mounted atop a platform of stone and supported by two smaller stone blocks separated by the length of a forearm, an object. It was much longer than wide and a flattened oval in profile and bound by something having the texture of rough cloth sealed with some bituminous material. The object was too small to be a body, unless it was that of a child, though its shape and dimensions suggested otherwise. It was some five feet in length and eight inches in breadth and six inches thick and its mounting featured none of the personal inscriptions universally found in elaborate burial chambers. Whatever it was, it had lain there undisturbed for some considerable time.

The Order

Watson's question about knights on chargers had caused the gathered knights to break into knowing smiles, the reaction indicating to the doctor that the very same question must have been asked before, probably on many occasions.

"That would be a little too showy for our order, Dr. Watson," broke in Jonathon Bennet, "but should the opportunity come for a bit of medieval jousting, I'm certain we could come up with a suitable horse for a volunteer."

"Thank you … Mr. Bennet," came from the Master, his voice feigning disapproval but with an obvious hint of mirth at the thought of witnessing Dr. Watson dressed and mounted as a ridiculous latter-day Sir Lancelot.

"No, Dr. Watson," continued the Master after turning to face the visitors, "very few of us would ever be called upon to do battle of any sort, though we do have a designated sergeant-at-arms who has call on a few armed knights should matters get out of hand. Most of our activities, as I have said, are passive and diversionary. Our order mostly keeps open eyes and ears and reports any and all hints of suggestions of breaches of security. We are the guardians and, mostly, we stand guard as the great King's sentries."

"I can tell you no more without the taking of oaths," he concluded.

"And if we take those oaths," Holmes asked of his old mentor, "what then?"

"Then you are Knights Bachelor in our order, Sherlock," replied the Master, reasonably certain that he could convince Holmes and Watson to swear fealty to the ancient Avalon society, though not much for Inspector Lestrade. "Knights in training, if you will. However, as you have proven yourselves to be honourable people, and as the matters you are investigating would warrant some rapidity in advancement, your promotion to full knighthood would be a formality which would be declared without delay. All that is necessary is that I, as Master, make that declaration in front of you and in the presence of witnesses from our order. Then you would be privy to our secrets and subject to your oath to remain silent on them.

"Should any difficulties arise in the future," he continued, "we have the right to call on what services you may be able to offer. There will be no pageantry, no theatrics, no heraldry, no 'sirs' or 'madams', no parades, no flag waving or medal pinning, just requests for whatever service you are able to render when the call might go out for assistance. You would never be placed in compromising situations in your day to day lives."

The offer seemed simple enough but the knights were serious about their calling. Holmes, Watson and Lestrade were invited to take their leaves and consider what had been said and what had been offered, an invitation which they accepted. The three men rose and started for the door when George Bridges spoke.

"Sherlock, my friend," the Master began, "as you know, I knew your aunt well; what you would not have known is that she too was one of our order, one of our knights."

Sherlock Holmes looked at his old Glastonbury acquaintance and smiled before saying, "I had considered that to be a distinct possibility after hearing of the knight's existence, though there was no evidence to confirm it, none beyond the way you had spoken of her and from a note to me which she had penned just days before her death. We should speak of this later, after my colleagues and I have conferred."

A knowing nod from George Bridges signalled that he understood Sherlock Holmes was interested and would be a valuable asset to the order. Watson and Lestrade had said nothing, perhaps from their being unwilling to join, perhaps from not knowing what to say.

"I don't know about this, Holmes," admitted Lestrade as the trio made its way to the Pilgrim's Inn. "There are only so many oaths a fellow can, or should, make in one lifetime, though I admit my interest has been captured by this case and I'm itching to find out what's going on."

"I believe the oath of the knights is not one which would compromise any others you may have taken," responded Holmes, "but there is no other way ahead in this case."

"Watson, here," he continued, "has taken a soldier's oath to serve the Crown and another, the Hippocratic Oath, to serve those in need of medical attention. We might be able to think of some extreme example where one compromises the other but each one, in truth, is Watson's declaration that he will follow and accede to a higher principle in his actions, to the very best of his ability. You too, Lestrade, have sworn to uphold the law and are rightly bound by the word you gave when you graduated in blue. Let us not make rash statements at this point; rather, we ought to sit down, smoke a pipe or two and consider our options."

"Why wait?" demanded Lestrade. "You're going to do it, so let's be about it; in for a penny, in for a pound, I'd say."

"The Three Musketeers," advised Watson, "would have said 'all for one and one for all', at least in French, and there are three of us and the name Lestrade does have French origins, and we're all armed. Do you have a third war cry or clever saying to add, Holmes? I mean, you started all of this."

"What about 'the game is afoot Watson'?" the sleuth replied, "You always have me saying it in those stories you write. Three Musketeers, indeed; I don't believe they knew how to fire a musket, but they were excellent swordsmen according to Dumas."

"So," commanded Holmes, "what is the consensus? Are we knights, all of us, or are we not?"

"We are!" replied Watson and Lestrade in perfect unison.

"So onward, Athos, Porthos and Aramis," came the call from Watson in his best literary voice. "Though we do seem to be down one d'Artagnan."

The assembled knights had just settled down to enjoy their brews of tea and coffee when the three London men reappeared. Bridges and Bennet rose and waited for someone to say something; everyone looked at everyone else and the Master finally took it upon himself to ask the question.

"So, do we have three new knights or don't we?" he asked. "If we do, then we ought to be about taking these oaths so that we can be about the business of drinking our teas in peace."

A nod from all three men signalled the affirmative and Jonathon Bennet went off to collect three Bibles for swearing upon, though these would come supplied with an extra feature.

Holmes, Watson and Lestrade were asked to stand while the other knights present took their places. Master Bridges stood facing the trio while Bennet went from one candidate to the other handing each a Bible to which was attached a miniature dagger, a symbol of the deadly nature of the oath about to be taken.

Master Bridges began with an account of the times when the Romans had come and stayed and then departed leaving many of the native Britons infused with the customs and military methodology by which Rome had enforced its law throughout much of the land. The coming of the Saxons had begun before the final Roman departure and the native Britons had looked among their number for a leader, one who could rid the land of its new tormentors. There had been one family, one headed by a fearsome warlord who fought under the symbol of the dragon's head, the Pendragon, and took that as his family name. His son Arthur had served in the legions in faraway Scythia, as had many sons of Britannia, and returned battle-hardened and skilled in the ways of organised warfare. That son had been invited by the disparate tribes to take up a sword specially cast and tempered for a king of the Britons. It was longer that the Roman gladius but far shorter than the broadsword later wielded by the Scots who were coming into the north lands occupied by the fearsome Picts. Arthur was the only one ever to push the Saxons back in a sustained campaign in which he had been successful, only to be betrayed by his nephew Mordred when off honouring a pledge to the Gallic tribes who had supported him, tribes themselves coming under attack from beyond the Rhine as the Romans withdrew.

By taking the oath of allegiance to Arthur, each man would swear to defend the king's earthly remains and maintain the honour of his spirit and keep the secrets of the order of the Knights of the Circle. The dagger each received was symbolic of Arthur's acceptance of that kingly sword, Excalibur, and of the willingness for its receiver to defend both the memory and legacy of Arthur unto death if ever called upon.

The speech was filled with much theatrical gesturing and rhetoric but the matters were delivered and taken very seriously by all present. With each candidate holding both dagger and Bible, they each gave the answer "Yes!" to all questions asked, thus swearing to be held by the provisions of the order. When finished, Master Bridges looked the eyes of each individually and stated, "You are now a Knight Bachelor in the order of the Knights of the Circle."

Repeated three times for the three men and the first part of the proceedings had ended. Bridges then opened a box handed to him by Bennet and took out three ribboned medallions around two inches in diameter and stamped on one side with a rendering of the Glastonbury Tor set above the Isle of Avalon and on the other with the Pendragon, the dragon's head under which Arthur had fought and died.

Bridges then reapproached each new knight bachelor and, placing the medal's ribbon over the head and down onto the neck of each, declared them to be full Knights of the Circle.

With the business of oath taking at an end and formal declarations of knighthood completed, the Master thanked all present and congratulated the new knights. The day had moved along and much had ensued and the London men were keen to get back to their investigations. Watson, though, was feeling a little anxious and declared to his friends, "I don't know about the rest of you, but this knight is famished."

The Object

Mrs. Staunton, widow of John and a woman uncertain of in whom she might place implicit trust and also somewhat apprehensive of suffering her husband's fate, had held back a vital piece of information. It was not so much what she could tell people, rather what she could show to those in whom she could have complete confidence. The visits of Sherlock Holmes had brought the lady to the point of holding such assurance; she had wanted to share her extra knowledge with the London detective but, even with such a famous and trustworthy person as he, she had still been hesitant.

John Staunton had been a stalwart member of the Glastonbury Archaeological Society and, unbeknown to most, also a senior Knight of the Circle. The discovery of an ancient artefact would have excited him as much as any member of the society and the excavation near Street had started as a significant site worth evaluating before announcing it to the world. As he dug his way down the ancient staircase, one he had actually discovered, he began to feel that this was something more than special, it was going to be unique and of incredible national, even international, significance. He had come upon an outcrop of stonework to which he applied his spade and followed its profile to trace out and then reveal a rectangle of stone; it was too small in extent but too solid in construction, he thought, to be a small building. On digging at one of the narrower ends, he found a longer structure, probably the foundation of a wall, but digging down at the other end revealed one step, and then another. Those steps had to lead somewhere.

Finding the object in the chamber had been one thing, deciding what best to do with it was something entirely different. Photography was impractical in such a confined and darkened place and the group decided to take meticulous measurements and make sketches from several angles and vantage points. The object itself was tested for weight and found to be easily lifted by one person and, its resting place having been discovered and opened, it was decided to remove it to a place of safety and security in case word inadvertently got out.

The group had looked to John Staunton for suggestions and were more than supportive when he offered the use of a secure, lockable shed at the rear of his house. The shed was full of a great many pieces of old furniture and numerous packing crates and old rural implements. If the object was placed in one of the old crates it could be covered and other material pushed around and over it so that finding without guidance would be difficult in the extreme; more to the point was the fact that no one would know or suspect it was there.

Mrs. Staunton knew that something had been hidden there but, with the death of her husband, had paid the matter no mind until Sherlock Holmes had turned up on her doorstep with the promise of justice. Still, she did not reveal that something had been hidden all those months before, something which had excited her husband incredibly and may even, she thought, have contributed in some way to his illness at the time.

Having taken their oaths and become full Knights of the Circle, the trio once again returned to its Pilgrims' Inn lodgings only to find that Mrs. Staunton had entrusted an important message for Holmes with the manager, a message requesting that he contact her as soon as possible. Holmes, revealing the message's contents to his two colleagues, excused himself and proceeded swiftly in the direction of the Staunton house, there to be welcomed by a woman frustrated and clearly annoyed.

"Mr. Holmes, come in, quickly," she announced, dragging the man inside by his arm with no hint of her usual reticence but with obvious overtones of fear. Holmes had just cleared the doorway when he heard the door slam shut behind him but Mrs. Staunton continued pulling him toward her sitting room, directed him to sit and then checked her curtains to ensure that any prying eyes were denied access. Holmes was half-sitting, half-standing when the woman, somewhat distressed, pulled up another chair and sat close as if to tell some important secret.

"It's that Dr. Fredericks, Mr. Holmes," she started, "he's been pestering me about John's activities in the weeks and months before his death. It's a great deal more attention than he ever paid poor John when he was alive. He insists that John and the group he was with had found something, something special. I told him he was mad and was not welcome here, but he started to get angry and threaten me if I didn't hand over whatever it was. I threatened to send for the police and slammed the door in his face but I don't think he will be put off for long."

Mrs. Staunton took a deep breath and held it for some seconds before expelling it forcefully and continuing with, "I trust you Mr. Holmes and I know that you have connections hereabouts you cannot speak of, but, and I don't want that Fredericks knowing, John did find something. I don't know what it is but I do know where it's hidden."

"Indeed," was all that Holmes could manage at that point, though the widow's fear of Fredericks now seemed far greater than had been her earlier loathing of the man. "This Fredericks," he continued, "becomes more bothersome with every mention of his name."

"This 'something'," he added, "is it nearby?"

"Yes," was the simple and instant reply.

"Then perhaps," Holmes suggested, "Dr. Watson, Inspector Lestrade and myself might take possession of it; with your permission, of course. That would protect whatever it is and remove the annoyingly persistent Dr. Fredericks from your doorstep. By the way, could you say how large or heavy the item is?"

"It's long and narrow," she replied, "less than a man's height, I would say, and was easily carried by one person. I didn't see it up close but I did see John carry it outside to the shed. You can take it with you, if you like; you'll just have to find it behind all that jumble."

"With your permission," Holmes responded, fearing that Fredericks might be lurking somewhere nearby with his unsavoury friends, "I'll return with my colleagues and we'll take the thing into safe-keeping, and issue a receipt for the same."

"No need for a receipt, Mr. Holmes," declared the widow, "the word of a knight ought to suffice."

"Yes," she continued to the incredulous Holmes, "I may not be very interested in the subject but my John's activities were no secret to me. I wasn't sure but your reaction tells me that my suspicions were well-founded. You are a Knight of the Circle, even though you cannot confirm this to me. Just continue with John's work and I will be both thankful and satisfied."

Holmes could not have moved faster, rushing back to the Pilgrims' Inn to summon Watson and Lestrade whom he had sent on to the home of Mrs. Staunton while he rushed to the town hall, hoping to find the knights still assembled. He was in luck as the group had decided to discuss a number of matters and were intrigued with what Holmes had to tell them. Eager to involve the knights, Holmes nevertheless wanted to catch up with his two London companions before they arrived to take possession of the item and excused himself, promising to return with something of great interest, though what that would be he had no clue.

Mrs. Staunton was waiting anxiously and opened her door to Watson and Lestrade just as Holmes caught up with them. Collecting the key to the shed, she led the trio outside, opened the door and pointed, saying, "It's in there, right in the middle, John said. It's in a long crate lying down and covered by a tarpaulin. Please take it and do with it what you will."

The crate was quickly located and the item carefully removed and carried back into the house. Mrs. Staunton quickly led the way to the front door which she opened to allow her guests to exit with the mystery object. Watson had the object held firmly in his arms while Lestrade walked ahead to watch for obstacles. Mrs Staunton gave Holmes her husband's notebook containing sketches and other site details from Street. The walk to the town hall was uneventful and within ten minutes the item was being placed on a long table in a room to the rear of the mayoral chambers.

"I suppose we should break the thing open," mused Lestrade. "It looks like a big ant's egg, but I suppose there'll be no giant insect inside."

"I hope not," said Bennet who had just sent off for a selection of saws and knives as well as a hammer, "but there's no time like the present to find out. Now, who's going to do the honours?"

The implements duly arrived and the door to the room was shut and locked. With all eager to see what was held within, the Master took charge and picked up the hammer, though he quickly replaced this when he saw Watson, army surgeon that he had been, pick up a saw.

The Master then deferred to Dr. Watson whose fingers were shaking a great deal less than his. The doctor took up the small saw and slowly and carefully began to score a shallow cut completely around the object, though not penetrating its interior, and returned precisely to the spot where he had started.

"It's not too late to stop," said the doctor. "We haven't breached the casing. If anyone thinks we should wait for the so-called professionals, now is the last chance to speak up."

"The professionals, be damned," yelled Master Bridges. "They'd take it from us and the credit with as well. Those parasites will have to wait in line; this could be the find of the century."

That said, and with all in the room holding their breaths, Watson continued cutting. He deepened the cut with several full passes around the object until he thought it had been penetrated at one small point. "It looks as though this outer casing is about a quarter of an inch thick. Someone should hold its end as I cut through the rest of it."

Bennet came around and took hold of the soon to be severed section of casing while Bridges applied sufficient pressure to the rest to steady it as Watson proceeded. The others in the room simply looked on in silence and with great anticipation. Ever so slowly, ever so carefully, Watson moved the little saw back and forth, gently applying pressure as the blade's teeth cut away at the brittle bitumen and bandaged fabric, age old but having kept the degenerative elements of centuries away from the contents. After interminable minutes, Watson felt the saw move freely and Bennet felt the end section come free as the teeth cut through the last connecting sliver of casing.

"Hold tight, Master," said Bennet as he pulled the severed casing end away and watched as several wads of fine woven material fall to the floor.

"It's hard to say what that is," admitted the mayor, bending down to examine its texture. "Whatever it is, it's very brittle and disintegrates to a powder as soon as I put any pressure on it with my fingers."

"No matter," replied the Master, "Let's just see what the stuff was protecting."

Watson had discarded his saw and indicated to Bridges that he would reach in and retrieve the rest of the object's contents. With the object repositioned on the table and Bridges holding it steady, Watson gripped what looked like some leathery material, hard but intact, wrapped as a bundle and extending far into the casing. Slowly pulling on the leather, and with Bennet standing by to offer assistance as required, Watson felt the bundle give way and continued pulling as Bridges withdrew the casing in the opposite direction until the leathery bundle sat on the table with bits of disintegrating cloth spreading about.

The woven material seemed to have been used to prevent the bundle from moving about and was easily dislodged, regardless of it disintegrating at the slightest touch. The leather was different; it contained whatever had been in need of hiding and had hardened over the centuries but not to the point of being brittle – great care would be required in its removal to protect its contents, provided that they, too, had not disintegrated.

Watson, ever the surgeon, used all of his patience and skills to test one corner and then another before simultaneously applying very slight pressure in one direction and deliberate subtle tension in another. The leather did give a little but Watson would not be rushed; as a newly sworn knight, his particular skills were being called upon and he was not about to give less than his full and complete attention to the job at hand. Minute by minute, inch by inch, the leather yielded a little more until, with the help of three more sets of hands, the bundle could finally be opened to reveal to item within.

All stood back, disbelieving and unable to speak; the rest of the group pushed forward to see the item but were as dumbstruck as the others when it came into view.

It was a sword; its hilt and its scabbard being a little the worse for the age of their material of construction but intact. The Master gripped the pommel at the hilt's end and gently exposed the upper part of the blade and was amazed at its condition. It was tarnished a little but exhibited no sign of rust, indicating that the casing had excluded water and air from the time it was sealed.

The sword was not made for ceremony; it was for use in battle and had likely cleaved enemy skulls and limbs and pushed past shields to penetrate the torsos of outwitted adversaries in a dozen or more battles, only then to have the blood congealing on it washed and wiped from its pommel, hilt and blade after it had been about its deadly business.

There was little suggestive of ornamentation on its form but upon both sides of its quillon block, right in the centre of its cross guard, the group could make out some sort of figure. Careful cleaning away of dusty bits of disintegrated leather and cloth packaging started to reveal the outline of an engraving, one familiar but unbelievable to the group looking on. Some sort of red filler material still remained in the grooves but the depiction was unmistakable; it was nothing less than a fiercely defiant dragon's head, the Pendragon symbol of Uther taken up by his son Arthur against the Saxon. All in the group wanted to shout the word but none dared say it. It took some little time but the Master finally found his voice and with it he uttered, in hushed tones …

"Excalibur!"

The Artefact

Arthur was dead; his dream was in tatters; his people had fallen in behind him and had pushed the invader back but had not inflicted a fatal blow, not in any way. The Saxons had come and would stay, always there but never quite able to subdue the spirit of Arthur's people. They had been pushed so far but would not be pushed further; only in the centuries to come would their king finally conquer the nation of Britain as his spirit assumed its destiny and infused itself into the hearts of all calling themselves British.

The Battle of Camlann began as an act of justice taken by a wronged king against a treasonous member of his own family, a nephew who might well have assumed power at a time when Arthur could no longer take the field due to age or injury. This was not to happen and Mordred's betrayal was made all the worse by his acting when the king was absent and repaying a debt of honour to his related Gaulish tribesmen; Mordred's usurpation of power, abduction of Arthur's queen and defiance of a sacred trust could only be remedied by the two men meeting face to face in a deadly personal combat.

The site of the Battle of Camlann has never been determined and in all likelihood never will as there was none of the usual deadly litter from the clash of massed ranks of warriors, Arthur's return being enough to recall those who had wavered back into his service. The battle was short-lived, just minutes of fearful slashing and battering by two men upon each other, one a wronged king seeking justice and the other an impatient and treacherous prince desperate to retain his ill-gotten fiefdom and willingness to accommodate the Saxon. Those present as witnesses told of how both men had fought with incredible fury until Mordred's sword finally found Arthur's abdomen at the same time Excalibur cut through the side of Mordred's neck. Both fell, Mordred dying almost immediately as blood surged from his neck wound and Arthur clutching a deep stab wound below his heart and losing consciousness within minutes.

Sir Bedivere had taken it upon himself to collect Excalibur from the field after Arthur had fallen. He had cleaned off the blood of Mordred from one of its edges and taken the scabbard from its sash-style baldric which had been removed and dropped to the ground before the two met in battle. As the injured Arthur was being conveyed to Bath and its healing springs, Bedivere, knowing that his king was indeed dying and would not recover despite the healing powers of the waters, had reverently prepared the weapon by cleaning it further and applying oils to retard its deterioration. The scabbard, likewise, he had cleaned and prepared for being reunited with Excalibur and for eventual interment with the fallen warrior king; the spirit of such a king, he knew, could never find rest without the symbol and instrument of his power and authority at his side.

The final, sad segment of the Way to Avalon was made by a small contingent of knights and a retinue of followers, including his distraught queen Guinevere. As the king's body was taken from the barge on the wide waters astride the Brue and up onto the sacred Isle of Avalon, Guinevere had called upon those accompanying Arthur to swear that his body would be protected from the ravishes of time and enemies and that his spirit would be revered throughout the ages. She would join him in both body and spirit when her own time came. The knights and the followers formed a circle around the body of Arthur raised on a wooden platform and so swore; the Knights of the Circle had come into being.

The Glastonbury Tor had seen numerous structures rise on its summit through thousands of years as different people discovered the power of its position and setting. Arthur had stood upon it and scanned the wide lands about for signs of encroaching enemies and reinforcing allies. The isle stood practically surrounded by dangerous waters, some deep, some marshy, a natural moat over which an enemy could not easily approach in stealth or in great force. There was, though, a narrow neck leading off to the east, dry land but eminently defendable by a small force against huge odds. Within the tor, however, two small crypts had been built by people long forgotten and Arthur had ordered these expanded and strengthened, their entrances disguised and readily blocked off should the isle ever be taken. They would be the last refuge of the king, one from which he would one day rise and retake his assailed lands. Over the coming centuries, the sites would find themselves built over and forgotten by all but those sworn to remember and stand guard.

Arthur was interred in the larger crypt and its entrance was then covered, hidden and guarded until the time when Guinevere would rejoin her husband in eternal rest. At that time the crypt's entrances would be sealed, all but one, that being a distant concealed doorway to a long tunnel leading inward from the side of the tor.

The wars between Briton and Saxon were not over and would continue, though the knights dare not reunite Arthur and Excalibur at that time lest his spirit should find its final rest and the land be lost forever. The sword would be entrusted to the Priestess of the Waters whom later chroniclers would contort and dub the Lady of the Lake, for safe-keeping. Excalibur would lay ready for Arthur to reclaim when he was eventually recalled; the king and his sword would lay in a direct line of sight of each other but stay separated, the man entombed within the great tor and his weapon sealed within the high ground across the Brue. The site of Arthur's tomb was to remain a closely guarded secret but the location of Excalibur had been lost, though it had long been sought after by the knights through the centuries.

Now, here was Excalibur, found, intact and potent. But what to do with it?

Should king and sword be reunited? Should the people of Britain be told? Would a reunification finally see the end of the Arthurian spirit or would the knowledge reignite the enmities of old and set the sons and daughters of Britannia against each other in bloody combat?

John Staunton had known that he and his group had found something momentous but the dilemma stemming from the sword's discovery would increasingly trouble the Master. The knights' oath was to guard Arthur, not to reunite him with Excalibur. He knew how easily people could be led into mindless argument and confrontation from the most trivial of provocations; this sword was the missing half of a formula for revolution, a bloody civil war in which no one would win but all would lose. His excitement over its discovery would be tempered considerably when he had time to consider the possible repercussions. There were also those in Glastonbury who knew that something of great value had been discovered, three people keen to take possession of it and offer it for sale to buyers who might be prepared to part with immense quantities of sterling to possess it. It was a prize worth killing for, some might contend, and the deadly artefact may have already have claimed several lives without ever having been drawn from its scabbard.

Dr. Fredericks knew there had been a find, though he was not privy to any of the details, especially of its incredible location. The man had his pretensions but was increasingly falling into unreasoning anger when challenged about his competence. That he had been a long-time member of the Glastonbury Archaeological Society did speak of his interest in matters of historical interest, of the importance of knowing who had gone before and why things were done the way they were. His major failing, apart from losing control of his emotions under stress, was that he needed to own things, things which no one else possessed.

Dr. Fredericks had, in his early years, been a cooperative colleague of Dr. Harrison, now departed from Glastonbury, both having had interests in the history of their region. While Harrison's interest tended more towards matters academic, though, Fredericks was drawn to the collection of trinkets, objects of definite interest but which could also be displayed to demonstrate his cultural inclinations to others. Harrison tended to be quiet and introspective while Fredericks was of a type which could be both self-important and boastful and this had tended to increasingly push the two men apart professionally and socially.

The accidental encounter between Fredericks and Staunton near the secret Street archaeological site, though fortuitous for the former but unfortunate for the latter, was of little significance to the doctor at the time but had lingered as a niggling irritation in the depths of his memory until something pushed it to the fore. Harrison's practice had been ailing for some time as the man's mental faculties began, little by little, to fail him. A member of the Glastonbury Archaeological Society, Harrison, unknown to Fredericks, had also been a Knight of the Circle for quite some considerable time and, as becoming of his nature, had been the epitome of secrecy in his professional life and in his adopted and sworn loyalty to that greater calling. Unfortunately, the man had increasingly seen enemies at every corner and became prone to making rash statements which included references to a long-ago mythical king and his modern guardians. It was such a statement which got Fredericks to thinking about his own seemingly innocuous encounter with John Staunton on the outskirts of Street.

A verbal attack by Harrison upon Fredericks when the former had been suffering an explosive episode of mental torment had escalated and ended with the latter having to physically restrain his unfortunate colleague with the aid of two passers-by. It was clear that Harrison could not continue administering to the public and moves were made for the sale of his practice and for his retirement and removal to where he could receive treatment. Relatives had arrived to assist Harrison in preparation for a move to Bath where the man might be assessed and transferred to either a convalescent sanatorium or, if necessary, to an asylum where he might be restrained. Fredericks was not unduly alarmed at his colleague's situation, they had never actually been friends, but was intrigued by Harrison's accusation that he and others, including John Staunton, had been hiding something, something of incredible significance which he said ought to be reunited with its original and rightful owner. It was only when Harrison had yelled out, "Excalibur shall strike you all down!" that he realised just what that 'something of incredible significance' might be. If such an ancient artefact had been uncovered, even something remotely resembling the real thing, or the imaginary, it would be worth possessing for its own sake or for the absolute fortune someone might pay to have it.

Sherlock Holmes and his two London colleagues had not been privy to the details surrounding Harrison's downfall and departure but a chance mention by Jonathon Bennet of that departure having left a gap in the knightly ranks had caused the new men to enquire about the circumstances in their capacities of investigative agents and official detective.

"Nobody took any notice of Harrison's ravings, Mr. Holmes," had declared Bennet, "for the man was clearly suffering from some serious breakdown in his mental capacity. He did, I am led to believe, make some mention of Arthur and Excalibur but this was explained away as some random manifestation of his lifelong interest in the subject. Now that we have all gazed upon that ancient item, it is clear that word of Staunton's discovery may well have gotten out. One of the four excavators may well have made mention of the matter to Harrison, perhaps during a medical consultation, and Harrison, we do know, in his ravings had mentioned it to Fredericks."

Holmes nodded his assent, now seeing the side of Bennet he knew must have existed for him to have retained municipal power for so long. Here was the man who had dropped his façade of pomposity and become the practical analyser of people's actions and motives; he had gone up significantly in Holmes' estimation.

"We must keep this to ourselves," Holmes warned the knightly mayor and the others, "there are several matters to consider. The artefact should be securely stored away, perhaps here in the town hall, as there is great danger inherent in the knowledge of its existence and whereabouts. Mr. Bennet and Mr. Bridges should attend to that matter and Watson, Lestrade and I should retire to our pipes and think about murders and murderers."

Strong inklings of guilt and logical suspicion of methodology would not suffice in this case. Holmes knew what he would most likely have to do but needed to ponder the matter before embarking on a dangerous ploy. There was nothing he could prove absolutely about the murders of the four Glastonbury people or the poisoning of the others from Bath and Bristol but, if it could be arranged in the proper manner and with reliable witnesses, his own murder might effectively bring the murderer to justice.

The Trap

Another factor had just entered the puzzle into which the three London men found themselves embedded, a puzzle whose degree of difficulty was high enough to begin with but had proved to be more of a highly complex enigma as Somerset's mysterious and mythical past piled increasing layers of uncertainty onto a case of deliberate and multiple murder. To add to the investigators' confusion, they had found themselves members of an ancient order of knights which at first sounded like people playing historical games but turned out to be very serious, quite ancient and possibly having deadly consequences should any of the players treat it in any way flippantly.

The extra factor came in the person of Dr. Harrison, recently departed from Glastonbury for Bath but also a brother Knight of the Circle, one who had invoked Excalibur in threatening terms towards Dr. Fredericks but who had been dismissed as being mentally incompetent and very confused at the time by all who knew him and his situation.

Some weeks after blundering upon John Staunton near the secret Street archaeological site, Dr. Fredericks had met with Dr. Harrison on a completely unrelated matter but, though wholly unaware of his medical colleague being a Knight of the Circle or that such a knight or order even existed, brought the matter up in conversation. Fredericks had assumed that Harrison, being interested and very knowledgeable in all things archaeological where Somerset was concerned, would have some knowledge of what Staunton had been up to. The more he had thought about it, the more he had become convinced that something of significance was being investigated and perhaps some building, grave or artefact of immense importance had been discovered. He had been inclined to the last of the three possibilities as the first two would be virtually impossible to keep secret indefinitely and would have been announced to enable the kudos of the find to be claimed by the discoverer.

Presuming that he knew far more than he was telling, Harrison had demanded that Fredericks and Staunton and the others hand over what was not rightfully theirs. Fredericks could make no sense of Harrison's rants but, when threatened with being struck down by nothing less than the mythical Excalibur, realised that his guess had been correct, though he could not believe that the item would actually be the sword of Arthur but something which he might, one way or another, possess and then perhaps secretly sell. He also realised, though it did take some time to sink in, that Harrison had mentioned not only Staunton but "the others." It did not take him long to discover their identities as Harrison, being well acquainted with the Society's more active amateur archaeologists, was unable to restrain from mentioning their names. Within four weeks of that meeting, all four of the Street site excavators were dead.

Holmes had suspected Fredericks' involvement in the deaths but had no definite proof, nor had he known if the man would have acted alone. Harry Walters' witnessing of the discussion between the doctor, Renshaw and Pettigrew and the reported mention of "people having to die" was suggestive in the extreme on both points of conjecture, those of the doctor's complicity and having co-conspirators, but could be explained away as innocent discussions by local people about dreadful events in their locality. The truth was in there somewhere, hidden away lest it be discovered and forced out into the open to be seen for all of its malice and ugliness. It would have to be coaxed from hiding and lured into a trap from which it could not escape but needed a suitable bait. Truth knew that if it stayed put, it would never be discovered for what it was but might well reveal itself if provoked to the point of distraction by the man who had annoyed almost everyone he had met at some time or other, that man, that bait, that agent provocateur being Sherlock Holmes himself.

As with so many cases with which Sherlock Holmes had become involved, the more he looked into this case, the more intricate the arrangement of its fine details became. The passing of time, however, and the productive use of it in mulling over all of the facts, questioning and testing each one's veracity in relation to all of the others, had told him that a deliberate crime had been committed. Most deliberate criminal acts stemmed, as he well knew from his vast experience and insight into the criminal mind, from either passion or greed or both. There were medical doctors involved in this case, and Sherlock had often commented on the fact that a doctor gone bad is the worst of all criminals for the knowledge a doctor held of the human body and of the many ways its proper functioning could be brought undone. Sherlock Holmes, though, in his turn, had just such knowledge of the criminal mind and knew that its own arrogance was its Achilles' heel. The great sleuth would use that arrogance and the criminal would eagerly step into a trap which would snap shut heavily on that ever-vulnerable heel and seal its owner's fate.

The first part of the trap involved a visit by Holmes to Wilson Pettigrew with questions about Dr. Fredericks' and his possible part in the four Glastonbury deaths considering the unsatisfactory official causes of death which he had assigned to each of the victims. Holmes was keen to unsettle the doctor and assumed that Pettigrew would communicate with him without delay. Adam Renshaw would also be visited and asked what he might know or suspect of Pettigrew's involvement in the movement and sale of stolen items from local houses or about the break-ins at both the Glastonbury and Somerset Archaeological Societies premises. Holmes had only suspicion to work on regarding the two local businessmen but was keen to get them both and Dr. Fredericks suspicious and distrustful of each other and force a confrontation in which one or other of the trio might inform on either of the other two. It was well within the bounds of probability that the two businessmen had nothing to do with the deaths but did suspect that Fredericks did or had knowledge of the murderer's identity. Their business practices would undoubtedly have been sharp and sailing close to the wind where strict legality was concerned, though neither man seemed a fool or an out and out criminal to the sleuth but their discomfort at the thought of them being suspected of complicity in a capital crime might just force a reaction.

Holmes had also visited Mrs. Staunton with a suggested response should Fredericks approach her again regarding the item which had been hidden in her back shed. She should not admit to knowledge of anything but simply say that he, Sherlock Holmes, had taken over all of her husband's effects and was about to remove several items to London for assessment and safe-keeping.

Meanwhile, a reaction of sorts had been provoked but Renshaw thought twice about contacting the second-hand goods dealer. He was suspicious of Holmes and had an inkling that he was being goaded into something and did not want to rush off precipitously lest that demonstrate that he did actually have something to hide, something less than strictly legal which he and Pettigrew had been involved in. He put the matter to one side for the moment and quite deliberately got on with a number of tasks which involved him being in front of his premises and well in the public eye. Pettigrew, though, decided to seek out the doctor and ask him how their names had become associated and just what had Sherlock Holmes been referring to. The doctor's response was explosive and left Pettigrew stunned and unsure of what to do next, also uncertain of his position with respect to any illegal activities in which Fredericks had been involved.

The doctor, however, did not stop to think. He went off at a run to confront Mrs. Staunton and demand to know the whereabouts of the item which her late husband had uncovered. The widow's response was determined, despite the furious and threatening nature of Fredericks' demands; she stood her ground and defied him to his face.

"My husband's effects have been entrusted to a most trustworthy agent and are soon to be on their way to London," she declared in a challenging tone. "I never liked you, Dr. Fredericks, and I know of no reason to change my low opinion of you after the way you have spoken to me this day. Now, you will leave me alone or you shall answer to the law which will most-definitely be on my side. You are trespassing and making threats and that makes you guilty of a criminal act; two criminal acts, actually."

Fredericks took this to mean that Sherlock Holmes, possibly accompanied by Dr. Watson and Inspector Lestrade and a number of Glastonbury men, would be taking the item to London where it would be removed forever from his reach. He knew that the three London men would likely be lunching at the Pilgrims' Inn and, so, made his preparations for a decisive encounter. It would be the move of abject desperation and foolishness but Dr. Fredericks was well beyond reason at this point, his obsession for possessing something of great and unique significance and value having taken him over completely. Harrison's mind had failed clinically, but that of Fredericks was operating with a single obsessive objective and all control had been surrender. He had gone mad, but dangerously so. He had entered Sherlock's trap but his rage would make him an extremely difficult quarry to subdue.

Holmes had no real idea what form Fredericks' reaction might take but he did suspect that it could have deadly consequences, especially for him. If he had to make an educated guess, however, the weight of probabilities would be suggestive of poisoning by natural substances administered in an unknown way. Perhaps it would occur by ingestion, perhaps by injection, it was just impossible to prepare for all contingencies but Holmes knew that his life could and probably would depend on him and his companions staying vigilant.

Fredericks had not taken the rejection and taunts of Mrs Staunton well. He had retreated to his practice, one now suffering due to his repeated non-attendances and increasingly objectionable manner with his patients, to plan his response. His knowledge of poisons was profound and, despite his objections to the use of natural herbal products as medicinal agents, he had built up a wide knowledge of how nature could attack humanity and how humans would react to nature's many plant-based defences.

He did not have to think long or look far; the answer to his torment was to be found growing decoratively at the front of his premises. Its large, lobed and rounded leaves provided a green background on which its purple bell-like flowers could stand out to attract the complimentary comments of the passer-by. Few in Glastonbury would have known or even suspected its true nature though visitors from the rural surrounds might have recognised the killer lurking in the doctor's garden but would likely have paid it no mind.

Dr. Fredericks knew what he had and what to do with it as his gloved hands picked handfuls of the newest and most succulent leaves and quickly thrust them into a leather satchel. The poison within would stay viable and deadly for days and the slightest touch by a person's bare skin would result in a reaction though a determined rubbing on an exposed site could cause massive cardiac trauma and very likely result in the ultimate death of the recipient.

The time for lunching came soon enough and Fredericks made his way to the Pilgrims' Inn and the unsuspecting Sherlock Holmes and his meddling companions. The doctor's plan was not well thought out, just barely considered as an act of desperation with revenge standing by as a back-up ploy. As usual, Sherlock was watching the others partake of their meals with considerable relish while he sat back barely nibbling on a bread crust and sipping on his coffee. Beside him was a rounded parcel some five feet in length and about eight inches in width, wrapped in several sheets of coarse brown paper and secured firmly with a taut and sturdy hempen twine. It may have looked like the original item which John Staunton and the others had retrieved, but it was bait for a very nasty and cunning fish, a fish about to bite down hard on something it could not resist.

Fredericks did not stop to think, he simply and brazenly walked into the inn, located the trio at its table, strode quickly to the motionless Sherlock Holmes and, reaching into his satchel, retrieved a great handful and rubbed it vigorously over the cheek and neck of his intended victim. Grabbing hold of the paper-bound bait, the assailant yelled, "Now die, you meddling fool." before running out of the inn toward his home at considerable pace.

Sherlock Holmes, having stood up at the attack made upon him, began to stagger, his balance and consciousness appearing to fail as the poison entered his system. The detective fell heavily to the ground as Watson rushed to his friend's side.

"He's murdered me, Watson," Holmes managed between gasps. "That Fredericks is guilty of two crimes now, but perhaps only two."

***

JOUSTING KNIGHTS

The Huddle

Dr. Fredericks had been desperate; he had given in to his delusions and to greed and had been found out, though what he did not realise was that not a single shred of definitive physical evidence connected him to any of the crimes. In his mind, though, he had to get rid of the greatest danger to himself, that danger being the mind of Sherlock Holmes which was step-by-step advancing toward an undeniable truth.

A broad knowledge of the potencies of the district's poisonous plants would have made the doctor more of a suspect had that knowledge been apparent to the investigators earlier, but the attack on Holmes had not been in the form expected in that the poison was applied directly from the plant onto his skin, the plant's defence against attack on itself by browsing animals wanting to eat it being used against Holmes. The sleuth could look back to the times he pondered on the use of plant defences as proxies in human assaults on each other but he would first have to recover from a personal instance of such an assault upon himself.

As Sherlock Holmes lay virtually motionless on the floor of the Pilgrims' Inn dining room, save for short spasms of slight twitching of his arms and legs, Lestrade and Watson got to their feet and rushed to their friend's side to render what aid they could. Watson yelled to the inn's manager, who had come running on hearing the shouts of Fredericks, telling him to rush upstairs to his room and collect his medical bag. The manager went off at speed to comply with Watson's military-like order while the medical man looked to the care of his fallen comrade.

"Top pocket, Watson," Holmes managed between spasms. "The antidote. Quickly."

Watson, uncertain of what Holmes had said, asked his friend to repeat his words but was pushed aside by Lestrade.

"He wants the antidote, Dr Watson," yelled the police inspector grabbing at Holmes' coat and feeling for a container of some sort.

"Here, give him this; by mouth I assume," insisted Lestrade, who had retrieved a small vial containing a syrupy liquid, something obviously prepared by the sleuth himself for just such an emergency, and handed it to Watson who removed its stopper and, cradling Sherlock Holmes' head in one arm, proceeded to pour its contents into the quivering mouth of his poisoned friend, taking care that each few drops of antidote were swallowed before the next few were administered.

Holmes' spasms began to lessen and his breathing became more regular until he could be propped up against the dining room wall with the aid of a few seat cushions.

"A close one, that, Watson," he managed after a few minutes. "Remind me never to rub that stuff on myself in future, my friend. And thank you also, Lestrade. I'm afraid I'm likely to be around to annoy your colleagues down at Scotland Yard for a few years yet."

"Fredericks is gone," he continued, "but he won't get far. He's acting out of desperation and I do believe that he's gone mad, or very close to it. We ought to get Sergeant Holloway after him, though, before he can do anyone else any harm. Tell him and his constables to mind what they do, though. We don't want Fredericks wiping those leaves of his over our local policemen and doing them mischief."

Seeing that his friend was recovering well and that Watson now had matters in hand, Lestrade went running off toward the police station to get the search for Fredericks started. Action had to be taken swiftly as the Glastonbury doctor was obviously out of control and a danger to those who might inadvertently confront him in his current erratic mental state. Lestrade was prepared to shoot the man should he threaten anyone with those leaves of his which had done so such mischief to his friend, a friend who had survived an attack by being prepared, though how Holmes knew what to expect was beyond Lestrade at that point.

The Pilgrims' Inn had rarely, if ever, experienced such a disruption to its orderly functioning and serene atmosphere and the uproar would have caused mass panic had the earlier reports of murderous poisonings not kept the town free of the usual influx of pilgrims at that time of year. A small group of concerned lunch-goers abandoned their meals and gathered about the stricken form of Sherlock Holmes but showed relief as the man was seen to quickly recover his faculties as the antidote went about its internal work. It would be a full twenty-four hours before Holmes would throw off the effects of the attack, but that did not stop him from trying to get to his feet to follow Lestrade in his hunt for the lethal doctor.

Restraining Sherlock Holmes at this point was not overly difficult as his body, though having the deadly action of the original poison countered, was working ever so hard to purge itself of a concoction of chemical agents it clearly did not appreciate being forced upon it. The manager and two others assisted Holmes to an easy chair in the vestibule while others followed, eager to help or just with that curiosity common to humanity when one of its fellows becomes injured in some way. The sleuth was recovering well but was still physically weak though his mental faculties seemed, if anything, enhanced by the experience, and his thoughts were finding their way to a tongue seemingly unable to resist expressing them. Much of what he said made no sense to Watson, let alone the people huddled around to give what assistance they may. On realising that Watson was a medical man and had matters under control, the onlookers one by one left the huddle and returned to their meals or vacated the inn to get on with their daily business.

"What on Earth was in that antidote, Holmes?" demanded Watson who was checking his friend's pulse which, though fast, had now steadied. "Whatever it was, it certainly countered the effects of that shrubbery, or whatever it was, which Fredericks rubbed on you."

"Just a little something I prepared following the notes my Aunt left me," replied Holmes, now feeling decidedly better, though still given to the occasional mild spasm in his limbs.

"That shrubbery, as you call it," he continued, "was just a little of what Somerset can offer the unwary wanderer. It's not uncommon in these parts, though it is often encountered elsewhere and under many names."

"Names like what?" asked a curious Watson, now extremely relieved that his friend seemed to be returning to a semblance of normality.

"First things first, Watson." replied the sleuth. "What's being done about Dr. Fredericks? Has a search for him begun? If he leaves the vicinity of the town he could be very hard to find; he knows the ways and wilds of Somerset like the back of his own hand. We must be after him."

"That's all in hand," Watson reassured his anxious friend. "Lestrade's on the job and has gone off at a run to find

Sergeant Holloway and get him and his constables tracking the man down. I mean, a doctor and all; he's a disgrace to his profession and unworthy of the title he holds and the trust placed in him by the community."

"But," he continued, a note of careful insistence apparent in his voice, "what was that stuff he rubbed on your skin? It was deadly and you were lucky that Lestrade's ears are better than mine. He heard what you said and found that vial you had hidden away. Why on Earth did you not tell us of your suspicions and preparations? That's just typical of you, Sherlock Holmes, and one day it will be your undoing as it almost was today."

"Yes. Yes," Holmes begrudgingly admitted. "But if I had told you of my suspicions and of my preparations, you would have been on alert and that might have dissuaded Fredericks from making his attack, and we would not have a solid case against him. Now, even if we can't prove his guilt in the other matters, we have him for his attempt upon myself and that will see him away for the rest of his life."

"But you haven't explained just how you knew what sort of attack you might suffer," repeated Watson. "Just how was it that you did know?"

Sherlock Holmes managed a knowing grin and said to his medical friend, "Now Watson, you do know my methods and you have had a greater chance to observe Fredericks' premises than have I. So, what was it that you noticed on approaching those same premises which might explain my preparations? Could it have been something growing?"

"Well," mused Watson, "he did have a neat garden with splashes of colour throughout. It wasn't large, mind you, not as I recall. Did something growing in that garden provide Fredericks with his deadly green weapon?"

"Excellent. You saw," exclaimed the sleuth, "but unfortunately you did not observe whereas I saw, observed and took action, though I do admit that I did start somewhat ahead of you with my knowledge of poisons and my aunt's detailed instructions."

Sherlock Holmes then paused to make himself a little more comfortable before continuing, the effects of both poison and antidote being, at times, at little uncomfortable physically and causing fleeting bouts of mild nausea. As relief came to his beleaguered body, he leant forward to continue with his somewhat patronising explanation, saying, "You may have noticed, with those colourful splashes you mentioned, that there were, interspersed among them, blue flowers somewhat bell-shaped and reminiscent of a medieval monk's head-dress, though somewhat more colourful than would have ever been permitted by any order of those times, or of ours for that matter."

"Well, now that you say it," Watson hesitatingly agreed, "I do recall something of that nature; and quite attractive they were."

"The flower, yes, to us and especially to the bee," continued Holmes, "and I certainly know something of bees my friend, for the plant gets something in exchange for the nectar it provides that little flying agent of pollination. But, should a bee, if it could, or a hare or cow decide to munch on its leaves, it would immediately feel the effects of the poison within and, should it recover, know never to repeat its attacks on the plant's foliage on pain of death."

"So, that plant is … what, Holmes?" asked Watson, eager for his friend to get to the point.

"Well, some would call it Monkshood," replied Holmes, "for reasons obvious if not so appropriate, but I have known it as Wolfsbane, the bane or killer of wolves, presumably because they would chew on its leaves in the same manner that a dog might eat blades of grass. It has been called Haresbane and Badgersbane and a lot of other creatures' bane I'm sure and it can be deadly to humans by the mere touch of the leaves with the bare skin, which is why Fredericks was so energetic with it on my face and neck."

"Well," commented Watson, interested but disapproving of the risk taken by his friend, "if it had worked as intended, it might well have been renamed Sherlockbane given the interest your death by such means might have elicited. And the antidote … where did that come from?"

"Why, from my Aunt Jane's note books, Watson," came Holmes' ready reply. "Though I did have to trust that she had recorded the ingredients and quantities correctly, otherwise Fredericks would be facing the rope or the insane asylum for life."

"You take too many unnecessary risks, my friend, far too many," Watson admonished.

"Life itself is a risk," countered Holmes, "and who on this Earth can be assured of tomorrow? It is the risk which makes the mundane just that little more bearable."

"Holmes," Watson suddenly queried, remembering his friend's words when it seemed they would be his last, "what did you mean when you said that Fredericks was perhaps guilty of only two crimes? What were you telling us?"

The Search

"Two crimes, only," repeated Holmes, "I did say that, didn't I? Well I must admit that Lestrade and his colleagues might count things a little differently than I, but there is the attack on myself, merely a case of attempted murder now that I've recovered, and there is the deliberate murder of John Staunton by poisoning, either with wolfsbane or with digitalis going by the reported symptoms, though my money would now certainly be on the former."

"But enough of this for now, Watson," Holmes continued, eager to get into the hunt, "just help me to my feet and we can be off after Fredericks."

"You can stay exactly where you are, Sherlock Holmes," reprimanded Watson, "Lestrade and Holloway will have that matter well in hand and will soon have the fellow complaining from the inside of a gaol cell. Believe me, Holmes, if you even so much as try to stand in your condition, let alone go off chasing poisoners, I shall call the manager and have you physically restrained. Tomorrow morning will be far more than soon enough for you to attempt a little physical exertion. Good God man, you almost died."

Sherlock Holmes had to accede and any further insistence he might make would be doubly futile as his medical friend's threat to have him restrained was sincere and as the sleuth did not yet have the strength to stand, let alone to go off chasing criminals. Lestrade, meanwhile, had found Sergeant Holloway at his desk, busily recording details and filing away documents, the man dropping all such matters on seeing the look on the London detective's face.

"What is it, Lestrade?" he demanded, well knowing that something urgent had brought the man running and, on being informed of the details of Fredericks' attack on Holmes, Holloway called the only constable he had handy and ordered him off to find the other who was out on a foot patrol around the main business centre while the third was at home asleep after a night's duty.

"Be quick about it, constable," he bellowed as the young policeman grabbed his helmet and went off at a run while taking his police whistle from his top pocket, ready to alert the other constable on patrol when he reached the vicinity of High Street. Watson tending to Holmes in the Pilgrims' Inn could tell something was afoot when he heard the shrill note of one policeman signalling to all within earshot to render assistance without delay and then the shouts between the uniformed pair as the man sought came within sight of the seeker.

"We're to get to Dr. Fredericks' premises immediately and wait," the first constable yelled; the second nodding to signal that he understood as both went off at speed, hands on helmets, to await further instructions.

"The sarge says not to go in," added the first, "and to hit the doc on the head with a truncheon if he comes at us with anything that looks like a plant and not to let him get close. Don't know what's going on but the sarge sounded very serious so we'll just do what he says. I don't like Doc Fredericks much, anyway, so we won't have to hold back."

"What's it all about?" demanded the second constable. "You must have some idea."

"I don't know, I said," came the insistent reply. "But that Inspector Lestrade from Scotland Yard was jumping up and down at the sarge and yelling something about the doc and someone being poisoned. That's all I heard before the sarge started yelling at me. Let's just get to the doc's place and do what we're told and wait."

The two constables continued on their way, all the while dodging pedestrians and carriages as they ran along and across High Street. Holloway had likewise grabbed his helmet, walked out on to Benedict Street and commandeered the first carriage which came along and ordered its driver to take both him and Lestrade to Fredericks without delay. The driver knew better than to argue and, so, turned his carriage about, took his unexpected passengers on board and set off in the direction ordered.

Arriving outside the premises of Dr. Fredericks, the two constables stood guard, not quite knowing what to do but knowing that it should not go against the orders of their sergeant. They did not have long to wait, however, and they could soon see the commandeered carriage coming swiftly along with the sergeant and inspector on board, both men preparing to jump to the roadway as soon as they were close enough.

"No movement as far as we can see, Sarge." offered one of the constables.

"That's Sergeant to you, constable," corrected Holloway, "especially when we're in the public eye. Now, let's see you banging on that door while I check out the rear of the place for back doors and hidey-holes. If he comes at you, hit him before he can get too close; he's as much as admitted his guilt in some of these murders and if he feels cornered he might well strike without warning."

The three uniformed men had drawn their truncheons but Lestrade, having witnessed the effects of the plant leaves on

Holmes, was determined that the doctor would never get anywhere near close enough to do any mischief upon himself. He had drawn his revolver and stood ready to shoot to kill if things went awry.

"Dr. Fredericks, it's the police here," yelled the more senior of the constables. "Now, open this door and come out and show us your open hands as you do. We don't want to come storming in and have things get nasty. Come on, sir, it's the best way, the only way."

Nothing. Not a sound came forth from within so Sergeant Holloway repeated the message at the rear of the premises but with the same result.

"Well," yelled Holloway, "he's either in there or not but he's not answering his door so we'll have to go in a drag him out."

"Before you go and do that and risk lives," suggested Lestrade to the sergeant who had returned to the front, "why not send one of your constables on this carriage to see if Holmes has got any more of that antidote. And he might ask Dr. Watson to come along as well, if he thinks he can leave Holmes for a while."

"Good thinking, Lestrade." came from Holloway signalling to his senior constable. "We'll do just that before going in."

A wait of ten minutes saw the return of the constable with John Watson in tow, the doctor indicating that he did have a small amount of antidote remaining in the vial, probably sufficient, he considered, to revive one more victim of an attack such as that to which Holmes had been subjected. He also produced his army revolver and indicated his willingness to use it should circumstances demand such an action.

"Hopefully, it won't come to that," the sergeant advised, "but you are, of course, entitled to defend yourself and any member of the public under threat. We'd be better served, however, if you could stand by with that antidote and administer it if necessary. If two of us go down, though, look to my constables before you look to me; and that's an order, doctor."

"Understood," was Watson's one-word reply.

Sergeant Holloway then advanced toward Fredericks' front door and indicated for the senior constable to follow him. Once more, the front door was bashed and a futile call was made for Dr. Fredericks to come out. Holloway tried the door; it was unlocked and yielded as the doorknob was turned and gentle inward pressure was applied. He called out again but, again, received no reply. The sergeant held his truncheon out in front and at mid-chest level ready to strike the solar-plexus or the throat should Fredericks attack. The senior constable followed, back toward the hallway wall while continually keeping watch for attacks from behind. The hallway opened up into a waiting room around which chairs had been arranged for patients; on the floor, however, the still-twitching form of Fredericks was discovered, still alive but obviously unwilling to be taken in that state. Holloway told the constable to stand back while he carefully prodded the now-discovered fugitive with his truncheon in case a ruse was in play. There was no response and the constable was sent to summon Watson and the antidote.

"Do what you can, Dr. Watson," directed Holloway. "Though your skilled hand might have arrived a little too late, I fear."

"I fear you are correct, sergeant," agreed Watson. "But I'll see what I can do if you'll immobilise that hand of his holding that wolfsbane. I'd hate to have him come to and kill me while I'm trying to save his life."

"Certainly doctor," came from Holloway as he pressed down a heavy boot on the man's wrist.

"Too late; he's gone." came from Watson, checking for traces of a pulse. "Probably for the best, though. He had little of any promise ahead of him to look forward to; the rope, perhaps, or a lunatic asylum more likely. I know I'd rather be dead than suffer the latter."

"Indeed," concurred Holloway. "Might I ask you to officially pronounce death and record the probable cause, Doctor Watson. Your name carries weight in these parts and the coroner will be pleased. I don't expect that a post-mortem examination will be required, though the Taunton detectives might insist on one if they condescend to exert themselves for unimportant Glastonbury."

Watson made a few notes to use later at the police station where the appropriate forms were to be found; he noted the time, the exact address and room, the victim's discoverer, the appearance of the dead man and the fact that his mouth was full of partially chewed plant leaves with the appearance of wolfsbane. He especially noted that Fredericks had expired as he was attempting to apply an antidote to the poisonous plant. He carefully took a sample of the chewed leaves, another of those in the dead man's hand and a third from plants growing in the doctor's front garden, plants showing signs of having leaves recently removed, and placed these in paper bags found in the dead man's surgery.

That done, Watson began his walk back to check on Holmes and inform him of Fredericks' demise by his own hand. Lestrade quickly spoke to Holloway and promised a written report of the proceedings and then rushed to catch up with Watson. The carriage driver was asked, not instructed, if he might take a constable back to the police station so that he could arrange for the police wagon to be prepared for the collection and removal of the deceased. Responding to the request, the driver set off with his charge while the Sergeant and remaining constable stood guard.

Sherlock Holmes took the news with little outward show of emotion but admitted that he was disappointed to be denied the opportunity to interrogate the doctor, though he had to also admit that the exercise would likely have been a futile one.

Word had gotten out of the attack on Holmes and the Pilgrims' Inn vestibule began to fill with an assortment of well-wishers, including Mayor Bennet, the solicitors Randall and Jamison and, quite naturally, George Bridges. Others came also, but decided against crowding the man on hearing that he was in good health and spirits and would make a full and rapid recovery. In time, all left, each having been assured that matters were well in hand and George Bridges promised to communicate the details of the day's events with the local knights, including the trap Holmes had set using himself as bait.

Now, with the London trio alone in the inn's vestibule and readying themselves to help Holmes upstairs to his room, the great sleuth looked up at both Lestrade and Watson while stating emphatically, "This doesn't end yet, my friends, there is still more we must do."

The Assessment

Watson and Lestrade eyed each other on hearing those words concerning unfinished business from Sherlock Holmes, each man knowing that the sleuth spoke the truth but also quite aware that they were not privy to their friend's thinking.

309

Fredericks was dead and that had been an indirect result of Holmes shaking a buzzing hornet's nest of conspiracy and providing a hollow prize for the doctor to win. The parcel grabbed by Fredericks during his attack on Holmes had been a dummy, something prepared to look as though it were genuine and about to be taken to London. It had, in fact, contained nothing more than a rusty garden spade, one which might be said to have dug the doctor's own grave for him. When Fredericks viewed the rusty garden implement instead of beholding the magnificence of King Arthur's revered Excalibur, he knew with his last sane thoughts that he had been duped and that he had overplayed the last hand he would ever be dealt. For him, there was only one option left and that was to take his own life and deny his tormentors the satisfaction of seeing him squirm in the dock.

The London pair helped Holmes up the stairs and saw him settled into his room at which time Watson demanded from his friend, colleague and, now, fellow knight, "Now, just what crimes did Fredericks commit and what ones did he not? Come on, Holmes, Fredericks could have missed you and gotten either one of us instead with that poison plant of his. You owe it to your friends who stand by you to tell them just what it is that's going on in that brain of yours."

Holmes smiled as he sat back on his bed and rested his head and shoulders on several stacked pillows, aware that he was expected to keep faith with those with whom he had shared many past dangers and needed information which only he seemed to possess.

"Well, it's like this," Holmes began. "One crime was against me and that would have been enough to put the doctor out of circulation. Attempted murder done in full view of a Scotland Yard inspector would have done it for him, I believe you would agree. I have no fully reliable evidence for his guilt in the murder of John Staunton but his access to an extremely poisonous plant and to the means of delivering it in secret via one of Horace Portland's herbal concoctions specially prepared for the victim is suggestive in the extreme. When these facts are coupled with that of his being seen handling that same preparation after Staunton's death and that it had disappeared right afterwards, the case for his guilt builds, as it continues to do when we hear from Mrs. Staunton that the doctor was extremely angry at his patient, her husband, having resorted to what the doctor called quack remedies."

"And the other deaths," probed Watson, "what of those? Would the facts not support the notion that he was guilty of those as well?

"There is no evidence that they ever consulted Fredericks professionally," replied Holmes. "But someone else may have been implicated in those deaths and perhaps the spate of poisonings, though to get a conviction would be unlikely and an admission virtually impossible. The man is no longer compos mentis and neither is he in any position to reoffend."

"Harrison!" exclaimed Lestrade. "You suspect Harrison. But he is a knight, so Bridges tells us. Why would he want to draw attention to Glastonbury in such a way and why would he want to kill anyone? I don't follow your reasoning."

"Reason does not enter into the matter. He is, or was, a knight on a quest," Holmes began explaining to his friends. "And his was a mind steeped in the traditions and beliefs of his, our, knightly order as well as a man incredibly involved physically and intellectually in the region's historical curiosities and archaeological investigations. He, too, had access to and knowledge of the availability and potency of numerous poisonous plants growing in the region and his medical knowledge made him as much a danger as Fredericks became, though the latter did act originally with his mental faculties intact. No, I just cannot remove his name from my possible suspect list but, without any actual evidence, neither can I advance the man's guilt status beyond that."

"I'm going to have to come up with a plausible report for my superiors at the Yard," mused Lestrade. "I don't like holding back information but what would the commissioner make of me telling him that I failed to disclose everything in order to protect the fact that the mythical sword Excalibur had just been dragged from the grip of the Lady of the Lake but a secret order of ancient knights didn't want to reunite it with King Arthur in his secret tomb under the Glastonbury Tor in case it sparked revolution throughout the realm? He'd have me walking the beat in the middle of Dartmoor within a week, or confined to Bedlam."

"Not to mention what we knights might do to you," Watson commented with the hint of a serious smirk visible on his lips. "Remember those little daggers; the Circle is a military order in essence, my friend, and we don't want it called to action."

"No, indeed," agreed Holmes. "Now, if you two would leave me to rest a little, you can be off organising a meeting of the knights and then another with the town council. If we are going to come up with a story for official public release, we want to be in full agreement as to what facts to include and what to withhold. I'm also certain that Bennet's special handshake will ensure that your superiors won't question the details of your official report."

"No doubt," affirmed Lestrade, who then added, "You get some rest, friend, while Watson and I get about distorting the truth. If we distort it enough, perhaps Watson could write a

312

story about it, including how you almost got yourself killed. I'd buy a copy, just for that."

"Be off, the both of you, and let me get some rest," ordered Holmes seeing Watson's feigned annoyance behind a determined countenance.

And, off, both men were; off to seek out George Bridges and then Jonathon Bennet. The knights might meet that evening at the Pilgrims' Inn to save Holmes the effort of moving premises while a special mid-morning council meeting convened at chambers after Holmes had recovered his strength overnight might begin to set a plan for rescuing Glastonbury's reputation in action. Sergeant Holloway was the wildcard in the current game, though, for it was uncertain just how much the man knew and how much might be entrusted to him concerning the details of about to be massaged official reports.

It was well past mid-afternoon when Watson and Lestrade appeared on the doorstep of George Bridges and possibly too late to convene a special meeting of the Knights of the Circle if a significant number were to attend. Bridges, one time police sergeant in Glastonbury, was no newcomer to doctored reports, especially ones which might otherwise embarrass those in high office or show up certain persons' shortcomings. He had been one to keep his local patch in order and free of destructive influences and had little interest in patches beyond his own. He told the two London men that they should expect an assembly of knights at eight o'clock that evening at which time a decision would be made about what ought to be reported and what ought not.

That agreed, the two men explained that they were then off to confer with Bennet in his capacity as mayor and the nominal employer of Holmes and Watson in their capacities of special investigators; they also explained that they hoped Bennet might call a special meeting of aldermen for the following morning at which time an official statement could be prepared for public release. Bridges could see no reason to object, especially as Bennet would also be present at the meeting between the knights, and set off with the London pair, though on a series of quite different errands.

Time still permitted a visit to Mrs. Staunton to give her first-hand news of the day's incredible events. The two London men were uncertain of just how to break the news and not let her think that some degree of guilt might find its way to her, given that she had provided material evidence of a motive for murder on the part of Fredericks, guilt which neither Watson nor Lestrade had any intention of letting fall the way of the widow. Their mission was unnecessary in regards of the news of Fredericks' death but they were able to give her details witnessed first-hand by them both and to assure her that Holmes was in no danger and had taken an antidote within seconds of being poisoned.

That duty done, Watson and Lestrade decided that there was little more they could do but go back to the Pilgrims' Inn and prepare their preliminary reports, though Watson's would simply contain the basic medical facts and require only minor amendments depending on the upcoming meetings which would decide just how far the truth had to be stretched, and in which directions. First, though, a look in at Holmes to see how he was faring would be necessary to allow both men to relax sufficiently to be about their official tasks, however preliminary. Of course, these tasks would need to be attended to without delay as the dinner hour was approaching and the men, hopefully including Sherlock Holmes, were afterwards to be called as knights sworn to keep secrets and they would need to be alert.

Holmes was alert, neither sitting nor standing nor laying down but propped up much as he had been when they had last seen him. Both poison and antidote were still in his system, though one had been very effective in its nullifying work on the other, but residual quantities remained as did the products of nullification. He had thought that a pipe might help but was uncertain of the action of nicotine on either of the two recently ingested agents. Wisely, he had decided that compromising his recovery would result in a tirade of well-deserved verbal indignation on the part of his medical friend, as well as serious threats to have him hospitalised.

Dinner that evening was a quiet affair, Holmes dining alone in his room as per his wish and Watson and Lestrade occupying their own quarter of the dining room and being spoiled for choice as regards waiters. Holmes ate sparingly as usual and the meals of the doctor and the inspector were uninspiring, as much for the fare on offer that evening as for their incidental involvement in the death of another human being, regardless of the dead man's general unpleasantness and criminal guilt.

By eight o'clock, the inn's dining room had been vacated by all guests save for Watson and Lestrade and, as George Bridges and Jonathon Bennet entered, the two London men rose, excused themselves and went off to collect their recovering friend. Several others joined the group, others the London trio would mostly recognise except for two who had not been present at the earlier meeting of the knights.

Some had taken seats, some were speaking in pairs and trios, but all stood and went silent as Holmes made his way down the stairs and into the dining room unassisted but wisely positioned between Watson and Lestrade. None of the knights spoke as their order's protocols insisted that the Master had the right of first words at any Circle meeting. George Bridges then took a masterly stance away from the now-coalescing groups and indicating by an index finger pointed to the chairs then raised to the lips that all should be seated and silent. Sherlock Holmes, though, was offered a chair at front and centre of the gathering in view of his current infirmity and for the vital part he played in the extraordinary events.

"Gentlemen and, of course, lady," he began, "it is with a great deal of relief that I am able to pay tribute to the person and not the memory of a recent addition to our ranks for his decisive though, dare I say, somewhat reckless willingness to place himself at risk for the greater good. Mr. Sherlock Holmes acted for Glastonbury, certainly, but our fair town's interests had overlapped our own by a considerable degree, and he started a process by which a threat to our ancient secrets was nullified in an unfortunate manner, though justice may be said to have been delivered indirectly."

"Our meeting here this night will be brief but decisive," he continued, "and I shall now call upon Inspector Lestrade, a knight of our order, and of Scotland Yard in a manner of speaking, to give us the facts of the matters at hand which will serve the needs of justice and also maintain out order's ability to function in secret as it has done for so many centuries. His police detective's view of the world and mode of expression will prove to be an asset of incalculable value in this regard."

The Reports

Lestrade stood and gave a short but detailed account of the discovery of Excalibur and of the desire of Fredericks to obtain it for reasons uncertain but having to do with either personal pride, arrogance and possessiveness or for great monetary gain. He also described how Fredericks, in all probability, had poisoned Staunton but also how Holmes believed that some of the other poisonings in and beyond Glastonbury may have been the work of Dr. Harrison, a fellow knight, under the deluded belief that they posed threats against the order and its secrets. It was Harrison, it had emerged, that had inadvertently placed the notion of Excalibur's discovery into the mind of Fredericks.

"This, of course," Lestrade then assured the gathered knights, "will not be the report I shall be making to the Yard. That report will simply declare that Fredericks poisoned several people to get at a number of valuable archaeological artefacts while in a state of mental imbalance, the proof of this being the attack upon Sherlock Holmes which I personally witnessed. Harrison will not be mentioned in any way even though it does seem a little unfair to dump his guilt, if in fact he has any, onto Fredericks, though it's likely the latter man deserves the bulk of it, or all. Other poisonings beyond Glastonbury will be judged to have had no direct connection to the local ones and will be put down to an unusual preponderance of poisonous plant growth due to the unusually high temperature, rainfall and humidity of last summer in the Levels and the fact that pilgrims are adventurous sorts who venture further afield than the rest of the population. If such a story is acceptable to those here and to those of the council with whom we shall be speaking tomorrow, I believe that we can put the public's mind to rest on the matter and Glastonbury can be about its business of transferring funds from pilgrims' pockets into those of the locals."

Watson was amazed, as was Holmes, though not so the other knights who had not had sufficient time to get to know the man and his tendency to speak in short sharp sentences which were business-like and very much to the point. Here was

Lestrade articulate and showing some degree of sympathy toward a criminal while seeming to be willing, even eager, to compromise the strict tenets of his profession and work in with a secret group for the greater good. Even his wry sense of humour came to the fore as he took command and virtually instructed the group on how it ought to proceed to placate those in power and convince the otherwise hesitant visitors to Glastonbury that all was well. It was, he said, a deranged medical doctor who despatched four of his patients and then himself, while an over-exuberant Nature had been responsible for everything else and it was now safe to return. Basically, he told them that a scapegoat had been found and that everything deemed unpleasant could be dumped at its feet.

George Bridges looked toward Jonathon Bennet who took that as his cue to stand and assure Lestrade and all others present that he was certain there would be no dissent on the matters from any of his aldermen and that a special ten o'clock meeting of the Council had been convened for the following morning. That said, and as no dissention or questions were forthcoming from those present at the current meeting, the Master stood and declared proceedings at an end while thanking Lestrade for his words of guidance. Bennet lagged behind the group exodus from the inn and spoke to the London trio, expressing his appreciation and explaining his strategy for the coming morning.

"Gentlemen," he declared, reasserting his mayoral dignity, "tomorrow's council meeting will not require Inspector Lestrade to speak unless he desires to do so. I shall call upon Mr. Holmes to repeat the details of the official report which the good inspector will be preparing, of course without any reference to ancient kings and swords and circles of knights. A small number of journalists has been notified and will likely be attending and will, no doubt, be pressing for answers to ridiculous questions as well as the ones we anticipate. If things look like they are getting out of hand, I shall call a halt to the proceedings on the pretext that Mr. Holmes is still suffering the effects of being near-fatally poisoned and is under doctor's orders to return to his lodgings immediately following the meeting. I think that the reputation of Mr. Holmes and the authority of Scotland Yard should satisfy most of the journalists but we shan't try to stop their conjecture lest it appear that we are trying to control the reporting of the news, even though we are."

"So, we're giving the journalists something to chew on to keep them quiet," mused Watson. "I can see how Sherlock Holmes picked up some of his skills as a lad in Glastonbury. Perhaps I should bring my medical bag along to give credence to the notion that Holmes here might collapse at any time."

"An excellent idea, Dr. Watson," replied Bennet, eager to be in at least nominal control. "Those newspaper scribblers have played merry hell with our town recently and now we can repay them in kind. We can't overplay our hand, though; those journalists will always have the last word if they smell the slightest odour of a cunning rat."

"I think he means you, Holmes," commented Lestrade nudging Watson's arm while a broad smile spread across his face.

"Quite," Holmes had to agree.

Bennet then stood and admitted that he was exhausted after such a day, despite him having taken no physical part in the final acts of desperation by Fredericks. He could see light at the end of the tunnel and it felt as though a great weight was being lifted from his shoulders and that Glastonbury would be able to begin to rebuild its way back to normality, perhaps better, as the publicity generated might produce a positive result over and above the simple recovery desired.

"Until tomorrow, gentlemen," he said by way of a parting gesture, after which he followed the line of retreat from the inn just taken by his fellow knights. In the morning, he would assume full control of the town's affairs and appear robed and bemedalled in chambers at the head of his phalanx of aldermen, all ready to meet the world in a show of formal appreciation of the fact that it was he who had summoned the great Sherlock Holmes to rid Glastonbury of its troubles.

A call for pipes and whiskeys was wasted on Holmes; not only was he still recovering from the effects of both poison and antidote, his mind was filled with thoughts which he did not wish to be put into the proper order. Atypically, he was enjoying the mental parade of long repressed memories from those youthful days and weeks spent roaming the local countryside and absorbing the character of the Levels and of the towns and monuments they encompassed. A convalescence, as short as it was destined to be, might be wasted if he did not take the opportunity to indulge himself just a little and relive the fondness he felt for an experience cut short by his aunt's death all those years ago.

He refused the helping hands of Watson and Lestrade as he climbed the stairs and made his way along the hallway to his room and retired for the night. His two companions could see that he was recovering well and that a good night's rest would see him restored, perhaps not fully but to a level which would see those incredible faculties of his functioning like those of the automaton he often seemed. His heartbeat had been practically restored after having been drastically lowered in the wolfsbane attack and the antidote had pushed it in the other direction; if stimulus were avoided, the balance would be restored. A large whiskey, a pipe, perhaps two, however, would allow Watson and Lestrade to mull over the day's events and consider the possibilities which the morning might bring before following their friend's lead and retiring themselves.

Morning saw the trio up early and ready for the day's activities, though these were still some hours off. Lestrade had said his piece the day before and now it would be the turn of Holmes to respond to the prompting of Bennet, but not for some time yet. There was nothing for it, Watson declared, but to take the opportunity to indulge in a hearty and filling breakfast.

"It'll do you good, Holmes." he declared to his friend, now recovered to a remarkable degree. "Your system has suffered an attack and has been fighting against an intruder and has used up a great many of its reserves. As a medical man, and your friend, I insist that you join Lestrade and me and fill up the inner man so that the outer one can function to his capacity."

Holmes nodded a begrudging agreement and did eat more than would normally be expected.

"That poison did you a world of good, Holmes," remarked Lestrade. "I must remember to feed you some more just so I can see you eat."

"Food is poison to the man who values clear thinking," replied Holmes. "But I can't disappoint Watson; I must give into his vast and insistent medical knowledge sometimes."

The trio went over the official story numerous times and tried to anticipate the types of questions the journalists might put to them. It had been Lestrade's experience that the seekers after the next and juiciest story had the incredible knack of seeing the tiniest flaws in the most plausible and well thought-out official account. The only safe strategy was to keep things simple and to admit to numerous uncertainties along particular lines and not to be dismissive of suggestions, rather take the journalists' critical questions and appear thankful for their keeping the public appraised of the existence of unknown dangers. The press had its part to play in society but could not be allowed to run things. Bennet would introduce Holmes, Holmes would manage to get the words out, Lestrade would concur on behalf of the official agencies, Watson would ask Holmes if he were able to continue, Holmes would nod bravely and Bennet would ask for final questions. Then, after two questions had been ineffectually answered, the mayor would call a halt to the proceedings and thank all for their attendance and for the consideration shown to Mr. Holmes in his current weakened state.

At about fifteen minutes before the designated hour the trio climbed the stairs to the mayoral chamber. There they witnessed a jumbled collection of aldermen being brought under control by Jonathon Bennet who was determined to show that order had been restored to Glastonbury and that he, sitting beneath a portrait of Queen Victoria and resplendent in his robes and glittering adornments, was the keystone holding the structure together and without which everything would collapse into chaos. His considerable organisational abilities having been exercised, it was now time for the mayor to bask pompously and prominently in the light about to be shone upon his town, though Holmes would never again make the mistake of taking the man at face value as he had done in their initial confronting encounter.

Greetings were exchanged and special forward-facing chairs were positioned in front of and below the level of the mayor's glittering elevated throne and the aldermen's benches for the London trio. It was somewhat belittling for the three men and all for show, they knew, but it would soon be over. Other dignitaries, invited and self-appointed, arrived as did four journalists, two of whom had been specifically notified and another two who had gotten wind of a story about to break, in the parlance of their profession. Seating for the journalists had been arranged so that all would sit together in the front row of the visiting public. To anyone looking in it would seem as though a show trial were about to begin, a notion not so far from the truth as Dr. Fredericks had already been found guilty of everything and it merely remained to have that guilt formally declared along with the fact that the sentence had been carried out by his own hand. Given the nature of the special meeting, there were no late-comers, no stragglers, and as the hour of ten chimed on the town hall clock, Mayor Bennet stood and the clerk's ceremonial formalities declared to all that the proceedings had begun.

Mayor Bennet began by telling the assembly that his decision to bring in the nation's premier investigator had borne fruit and that, despite some degree of violent tragedy, the town of Glastonbury and the surrounding region had been freed of the difficulties with which it had been beset for a period of several months. That decision which he took, he explained, had the effect of demonstrating to the official agencies that a senior presence should be invoked and this had appeared in the person of Inspector Lestrade of Scotland Yard who would deliver the main findings of his official police report. Mr. Sherlock Holmes, he added, would not be giving a formal account of his own findings due to a serious attack made upon him the previous day, an attack from which he was still recovering but, despite recommendations to the contrary by his medical colleague, Dr. John Watson, had insisted on attending.

The meeting was something of an anticlimax as Lestrade's dull policeman's monotone repeated much of what everyone already knew or had assumed and finished with the declaration that Dr. Fredericks had been responsible for the Glastonbury deaths at a time when his mental faculties had failed him and he had given way to delusional thinking. No evidence had been found of the involvement of others in any related criminal activities and that he was certain that the coronial enquiry would concur with his findings. Before opening the meeting to general questions, the mayor thanked the London visitors for their diligence and complimented the press on the fact that its reporting had brought the matters to a head and enabled official action to be initiated.

The press, represented by four journalists whose burning fuses had been somewhat dampened, asked a great many questions. Some were unanswerable but not evaded; they were responded to directly or in terms of phrases such as "many uncertainties remain" and "that is yet to be determined" and "that unfortunately died with Dr. Fredericks" and other such judiciously prepared attention deflecting quotes. Sherlock Holmes had a number of questions put to him and he responded in his usual cryptic manner until the mayor saw his opportunity to call proceedings to an end as the great sleuth was becoming fatigued and needed to return to his sick bed.

There was little if anything left for the press to bite into and the matter went the way of so many news stories which had begun as exciting exposés full of intrigue and misdoings by officialdom only to fade as the public's interest waned for lack of further sensation. The mayor was happy, the journalists were content, Master Bridges retained his secrets, Scotland Yard had its man, Sherlock Holmes had his victory. Alas, John Watson was denied the opportunity to present the gory details in his own inimitable style as he was technically complicit in a cover-up of illegal activities; the doctor, however, contented himself in the knowledge that he had been made a Knight of the Circle, though nobody could be told of that either.

The Blush

Sherlock Holmes was bored. For the sake of appearances, if not his health, he had remained in the Pilgrims' Inn since the special council meeting had concluded the day before and he longed to be out and about his old haunts. He had fasted and abstained from tobacco for the rest of that day but resorted to a small evening meal followed by a pipe which was followed by another.

"A man cannot think with all of this clean country air around him," he declared, and he puffed away while igniting the contents of the bowl for a second time. "I do believe, Watson, that a little smoke in the lungs and nicotine in the veins is just what I need to get my mental faculties going again."

"Or another case," responded his medical friend knowing the man only too well.

"Well, Glastonbury will be quiet in that department for some time to come," Holmes declared while feigning desperation. "But there is the matter of our circular compatriots to look into, just you and I now that Lestrade has made his farewells and departed for the criminal cauldron of metropolitan London. What say you, friend, to an amble around Glastonbury after breakfast and the possibility of lunch with George Bridges?"

"Well, I don't like to eat alone, or amble about by myself for that matter," replied the doctor. "I do want to hear more from

Bridges about our order; I must confess that I'm not sure who's a knight and who's not."

"But I also want to call in on the Drs. Baxter and hear of Mrs., or rather the more recently qualified Dr., Baxter and her specialities and interests," he continued. "I hope that Glastonbury will welcome her methods and not revert to some of the quackery that passed for medical care in some parts of town."

Breakfast was unexceptional for Watson and uninspiring for Holmes but was soon done with and the pair stepped out across High Street to examine the ruins of the old abbey and the site where Arthur was believed, by a public willing to believe so, to be entombed with his Queen and awaiting a call to arms. Knowing what they knew, it was a little disappointing to read the inscriptions but the historical significance of the site, even without the alleged Arthur actually being present, was not lost on either of them.

A walk to and around the tor was next and Holmes felt no sense of residual weakness from his recent poisonous attack and was keen to reach the top and view St. Michael's remnant Tower up close for the first time in decades. He also wanted to show off "his towns" to his friend and point out the salient features of both Glastonbury and Street which had presented themselves to him as a young lad full of wonder and questions.

"Could we not hire a couple of sturdy mules?" Watson joked to his companion. "It does look like a considerable climb."

"Watson, I'm surprised at you," came back the good-humoured retort. "That someone as thoroughly British as yourself would balk at the chance to walk on what is truly hallowed ground below which lies the first who might call himself King of all the Britons, is truly unbelievable. No, we shall walk and, in doing so, feel the very centre of our ancient nation beneath our feet as we climb to those heights from which Arthur once gazed and declared all that he saw to be his and himself to belong to it."

"Those who would seek a history deeper than that," he continued, "are those who would never be satisfied with nature's beauty and bounty and have no right to call themselves truly British."

"That's a bit poetic Holmes," declared Watson, "especially for an unemotional sod such as yourself. I do believe a little Wordsworth or Coleridge is about to burst forth from those enigmatic lips of yours, but it's a little out of season for daffodils."

"Quite so," Holmes agreed, "but a few lines from Daffydd Nanmor or Guto'r Glyn might gladden the hearts of Arthur and Guinevere should they be listening. We should never forget just who the original Britons were and of what they sang, my friend, nor of the passion with which they sang it."

"I'm ashamed to say that I'm unfamiliar with their works, Holmes," admitted Watson, "but that is something I shall rectify at my earliest opportunity, though my Welsh is abysmal and I shall have to seek out a translation, even though that is certain to have lost much of the magic generated when that language is spoken beyond the Bristol Channel. Formerly, I had paid the tongue little heed but now have a desire to hear the echoes of Arthur's actual words from his living descendants. Perhaps we might delay our return to London for a few days, or longer. I'm certain there must be a Welsh policeman currently in desperate need of your special gifts, Holmes."

"I daresay," replied Holmes, "but our bland London accents make us strangers here and more so in those magical hills filled with melodic voices, my friend. But I have found the Welsh to very hospitable people when paid the proper respect and a short tour would be most enjoyable."

The banter between the two friends made the climb as nothing and they soon found themselves looking outward while tracing the courses of roads and river below them. This was much as Holmes had done all those years before and, no doubt, had Arthur, though the roads would have been far fewer and the waters more extensive in his day.

"Magical," declared Watson. "I can see why you are drawn back here, Holmes."

Holmes did not reply; there was no need for Watson had summed the vista up in one word.

Neither man could say how long he stood there. Each had been taking in the countryside spread out below them and marvelling at the remnant tower and trying to imagine the ruined church in its prime and the motivation of those who had built it and worshiped within. Time moved on, as it had done for all those who went before, and the pair made its way downward, determined to return with Bridges to be told of more secrets than the most ardent pilgrim could ever imagine.

George Bridges had been aware of the movement of his two new knights and anticipated their arrival and their desire for questions, more than he was prepared to answer all at once.

Holmes and Watson found the Master's front door wide open, beckoning them to enter as friends and companions and fellow knights. A lunch had been prepared and a table set and, before either of the visitors could speak up, their host appeared with a welcome as warm as any they had ever felt and offered them the hospitality of his home.

"You have seen and experienced much in these past few days," he started as the meal progressed, "but much more has happened than you might think."

"If I may," Watson politely interrupted, "Holmes and myself are keen to learn more of the Order and of the sites of particular relevance to it around Glastonbury."

"Yes, yes; all in good time, Friends." stalled the Master, "And in that good time you shall be entrusted with a great many secrets, but not all at once, not today."

"I can tell you, however," he continued, "that a decision has been made about Excalibur now that its hidden location has been determined. After all the furore and excitement has abated, Excalibur will be resealed as it was found and then reinterred in that hidden location. Then the land beneath which it had lain for all those centuries will be acquired by a trust set up by Randall and Jamison on behalf of a series of companies incorporated in Bath and called the Somerset Circle which would see a substantial building erected over that vaulted chamber containing the sword of Arthur. The knights will now have two prime sites to guard until such time as Arthur is no longer needed or the land disappears beneath the oceans; the days of our Order and our secrets are set to continue for some time, you would agree."

"I feel as though I had compromised those secrets somewhat by turning up here and asking questions," Holmes admitted, almost ashamedly.

"A secret, Sherlock, one worthy of the name, is one worthy of being kept," replied Bridges, "and I had told you nothing, which is what I was sworn to tell you. Anything you now know is largely the result of your own efforts, something you had discovered using your own means or were well on the way to finding out."

"You know," he continued in a somewhat reflective tone, "we knights know the truth about Arthur's resting place but we are content for others to look to that tomb up by the abbey. Some might also say that his spirit dwells upon this Isle of Avalon while others would insist it is infused in the character of our countrymen. But, if I had to get all poetic about it, I'd say that a need for the spirit of our fabled king to awaken definitely arose, and we were not disappointed with his response. Regardless of any need for Excalibur, friend, these eyes have witnessed, in these last few days and assisted by the undaunted daring of John Watson and Inspector Lestrade, the living spirit of our ancient king go forth into battle in the character, person and actions of Sherlock Holmes."

"George, you say too much," objected Sherlock.

Watson, ever his friend, looked on grinning like the Cheshire Cat, also of legendary though sometimes ignominious fame, and said, "Why, Sherlock Holmes, I do believe you're blushing!"

....

Also from Allan Mitchell

Sherlock Holmes novellas in verse

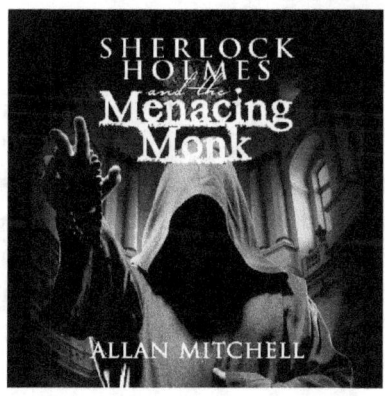

All four novellas
have been
released also in
audio format
with narration
by Steve White

Sherlock Holmes and The Menacing Moors
Sherlock Holmes and The Menacing Metropolis
Sherlock Holmes and The Menacing Melbournian
Sherlock Holmes and The Menacing Monk

"The story is really good and the Herculean effort it must have been to write it all in verse—well, my hat is off to you, Mr. Allan Mitchell! I wouldn't dream of seeing such work get less than five plus stars from me..." **The Raven**

Also from Allan Mitchell

Sherlock Holmes and the Ley Line Murders is an adventure set around Salisbury Plain, specifically Stonehenge and numerous other ancient monuments which make the locality so intriguing. The dismembered bodies of four men have been found along the ancient ley lines stretching out from Stonehenge and the Press has got everyone panicky with reports of ancient ritualistic sacrifices, everyone except Sherlock Holmes. Holmes goes into fact-finding mode and visits the British Museum's library where an old book points the way to the ancient beliefs and to someone who would be able to provide insight and assistance.

Also from MX Publishing

MX Publishing is the world's largest specialist Sherlock Holmes publisher, with over a hundred titles and fifty authors creating the latest in Sherlock Holmes fiction and non-fiction.

From traditional short stories and novels to travel guides and quiz books, MX Publishing cater for all Holmes fans.

The collection includes leading titles such as _Benedict Cumberbatch In Transition_ and _The Norwood Author_ which won the 2011 Howlett Award (Sherlock Holmes Book of the Year).

MX Publishing also has one of the largest communities of Holmes fans on Facebook with regular contributions from dozens of authors.

www.facebook.com/BooksSherlockHolmes

www.mxpublishing.com

Also from MX Publishing

Our bestselling books are our short story collections;

'Lost Stories of Sherlock Holmes' , 'The Outstanding Mysteries of Sherlock Holmes', The Papers of Sherlock Holmes Volume 1 and 2, 'Untold Adventures of Sherlock Holmes' (and the sequel 'Studies in Legacy) and 'Sherlock Holmes in Pursuit', 'The Cotswold Werewolf and Other Stories of Sherlock Holmes' – and many more......

www.mxpublishing.com

Also from MX Publishing

"Phil Growick's, 'The Secret Journal of Dr Watson', is an adventure which takes place in the latter part of Holmes and Watson's lives. They are entrusted by HM Government (although not officially) and the King no less to undertake a rescue mission to save the Romanovs, Russia's Royal family from a grisly end at the hand of the Bolsheviks. There is a wealth of detail in the story but not so much as would detract us from the enjoyment of the story. Espionage, counter-espionage, the ace of spies himself, double-agents, double-crossers...all these flit across the pages in a realistic and exciting way. All the characters are extremely well-drawn and Mr. Growick, most importantly, does not falter with a very good ear for Holmesian dialogue indeed. Highly recommended. A five-star effort."
The Baker Street Society

www.mxpublishing.com

Also from MX Publishing

The Missing Authors Series

Sherlock Holmes and The Adventure of The Grinning Cat
Sherlock Holmes and The Nautilus Adventure
Sherlock Holmes and The Round Table Adventure

"Joseph Svec, III is brilliant in entwining two endearing and enduring classics of literature, blending the factual with the fantastical; the playful with the pensive; and the mischievous with the mysterious. We shall, all of us young and old, benefit with a cup of tea, a tranquil afternoon, and a copy of Sherlock Holmes, The Adventure of the Grinning Cat."
Amador County Holmes Hounds Sherlockian Society

Also from MX Publishing

The American Literati Series

The Final Page of Baker Street
The Baron of Brede Place
Seventeen Minutes To Baker Street

"The really amazing thing about this book is the author's ability to call up the 'essence' of both the Baker Street 'digs' of Holmes and Watson as well as that of the 'mean streets' of Marlowe's Los Angeles. Although none of the action takes place in either place, Holmes and Watson share a sense of camaraderie and self-confidence in facing threats and problems that also pervades many of the later tales in the Canon. Following their conversations and banter is a return to Edwardian England and its certainties and hope for the future. This is definitely the world before The Great War."
Philip K Jones

www.mxpublishing.com

337

Also from MX Publishing

The Detective and The Woman Series

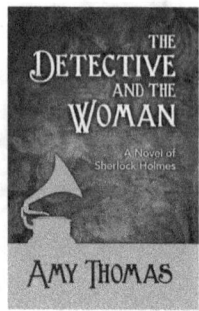  

The Detective and The Woman
The Detective, The Woman and The Winking Tree
The Detective, The Woman and The Silent Hive

"The book is entertaining, puzzling and a lot of fun. I believe the author has hit on the only type of long-term relationship possible for Sherlock Holmes and Irene Adler. The details of the narrative only add force to the romantic defects we expect in both of them and their growth and development are truly marvelous to watch. This is not a love story. Instead, it is a coming-of-age tale starring two of our favorite characters."
Philip K Jones

www.mxpublishing.com

338

Also from MX Publishing

The Sherlock Holmes and Enoch Hale Series

The Amateur Executioner
The Poisoned Penman
The Egyptian Curse

"The Amateur Executioner: Enoch Hale Meets Sherlock Holmes", the first collaboration between Dan Andriacco and Kieran McMullen, concerns the possibility of a Fenian attack in London. Hale, a native Bostonian, is a reporter for London's Central News Syndicate - where, in 1920, Horace Harker is still a familiar figure, though far from revered. "The Amateur Executioner" takes us into an ambiguous and murky world where right and wrong aren't always distinguishable. I look forward to reading more about Enoch Hale."
Sherlock Holmes Society of London

www.mxpublishing.com

Also from MX Publishing

THE VATICAN CAMEOS
A SHERLOCK HOLMES ADVENTURE

"An extravagantly imagined and beautifully written Holmes story" – NY Times Bestselling Author LEE CHILD

RICHARD T. RYAN

When the papal apartments are burgled in 1901, Sherlock Holmes is summoned to Rome by Pope Leo XII. After learning from the pontiff that several priceless cameos that could prove compromising to the church, and perhaps determine the future of the newly unified Italy, have been stolen, Holmes is asked to recover them. In a parallel story, Michelangelo, the toast of Rome in 1501 after the unveiling of his Pieta, is commissioned by Pope Alexander VI, the last of the Borgia pontiffs, with creating the cameos that will bedevil Holmes and the papacy four centuries later. For fans of Conan Doyle's immortal detective, the game is always afoot. However, the great detective has never encountered an adversary quite like the one with whom he crosses swords in "The Vatican Cameos.."

"An extravagantly imagined and beautifully written Holmes story"
(**Lee Child**, NY Times Bestselling author, Jack Reacher series)

Also from MX Publishing

The Conan Doyle Notes (The Hunt For Jack The Ripper) "Holmesians have long speculated on the fact that the Ripper murders aren't mentioned in the canon, though the obvious reason is undoubtedly the correct one: even if Conan Doyle had suspected the killer's identity he'd never have considered mentioning it in the context of a fictional entertainment. Ms Madsen's novel equates his silence with that of the dog in the night-time, assuming that Conan Doyle did know who the Ripper was but chose not to say – which, of course, implies that good old stand-by, the government cover-up. It seems unlikely to me that the Ripper was anyone famous or distinguished, but fiction is not fact, and "The Conan Doyle Notes" is a gripping tale, with an intelligent, courageous and very likable protagonist in DD McGil."
The Sherlock Holmes Society of London